# The KNOTTY PRINCES Club

# *The* KNOTTY PRINCES CLUB

## SAINT VISTA PACK REGIMES: GILDED SANDS PACK, BOOK 2

*by*

## GINNA MORAN

SUNNY PALMS PRESS

ISBN 978-1-951314-78-1 (soft cover)
ISBN 978-1-951314-79-8 (hardcover)



Cover design by Silver Starlight Designs
Cover images copyright Depositphotos

For Inquiries Contact:
Sunny Palms Press
9663 Santa Monica Blvd Suite 1158
Beverly Hills, CA 90210, USA
www.sunnypalmspress.com
www.GinnaMoran.com

*To Ashley Koederitz,*
*Thank you so much for your invaluable contribution towards*
*The Fox Project! This knotty story is for you! XOXO!*

# Chapter One

## *Kinsey*

### Stolen

"We should put her in the fucking trunk. I can't stand how strong she smells like those bastards." A car door slams, and I blink my eyes open again, trying to find the will to fight against the sedation.

"I'm not risking losing sight of her." The world shifts as the man sets me on the front seat of a vehicle heavily scented like cigarettes and citrus.

"Who fucking cares, Brock. She's used. You got to get it out of your head that she will be anything other than fucking trouble. The princess, on the other hand...she's perfect." The second man speaks about Holly.

"I care. Now just get in and shut up, Vance. Don't test me today. You've fucked up enough already. We're lucky that the fucking wannabe king is a cowardly bastard." The man, Brock, slides behind the steering wheel while the other guy gets in the back. I wish my body would cooperate so I could see exactly where we are on the property, but I'm also afraid to move. All I know is I need to act fast. If they get out of these walls, I'm not so sure that I'll ever see my guys again. These men aren't just some club owners. They're powerful. They're the leaders of Platinum Shores and also a reigning pack within the Pack Regimes. They rank the same as the princes of Gilded Sands.

Vance grumbles from the backseat and slaps his hand against my headrest, sending my soul out of my body for a second. At least, that's what it feels like. It's enough to help me focus. I peek through my heavy eyelids, staring at the winding driveway. It's a quick shot to the gate, exiting the palace grounds.

The vehicle lurches forward, sending me into the dashboard. I don't move, acting as if I still haven't gained awareness. A hand grabs my shoulder and yanks me back to the seat. Brock restrains me with his arm instead of putting the seatbelt on me. His skin is so close that I can nearly taste the citrus. I count the seconds, knowing I have to do something. I have to fight. I have to distract him. We can't leave. But I'm also afraid that if we crash the car, I'll go flying. I could get severely injured or worse. And Holly? I need to think of her as well.

"Help me with the seatbelt." Brock growls the words, stomping the throttle, pushing us faster.

The cool strap slides around me, and I summon my bravery. I can't let it click into place. I can't let it trap me.

Shooting upright, I sink my teeth into Vance's arm at the same time as I swing my fist down between Brock's legs, punching him in the cock. I thrash and manage to slap Vance behind me. He hollers, yanking away. The car swerves, and Brock swears. Shit. He doesn't slow. I need to keep fighting.

Pushing through the fog of whatever drugs I was given, I scratch and scream, hitting everything I can. I don't stop. I won't stop until they force me to.

The car slows, coming to a halt. I snap my eyes open to get a good look at Brock. And then I see the knife on his belt. He doesn't even have a chance to block me before I lock my fingers to the hilt, pull it out, and stab him in the thigh.

He shouts and smacks me, jerking his hand to grab me. I twist in the seat and kick him in the face. I manage to get him in the neck, stealing his breath as I smash my foot against his Adam's apple. I blindly find the handle and thrust open the door, managing to get more space between us. Vance hops from the backseat, exiting the vehicle to chase me. I roll a couple times, scrambling to get to my feet.

"Get back here, bitch. Don't make me hurt you. We had a deal with Winston. You belong to Platinum Shores. If you don't uphold the deal, we'll take down this fucking territory." Vance rushes toward me, not giving me the chance to decide if I'm going to surrender to him or not.

"Hurry the fuck up and grab her. I need you to drive." Brock growls with his command, his hand bloody from where he puts pressure on the stab wound with the knife still lodged in. I wish I would've gotten him a little higher. Ensured he wouldn't be procreating anytime soon. But alas, the universe has always been against me.

I duck and meet Vance's charge. But instead of trying to plow him down, I drop to the cement, tripping him. He slides across the driveway, hollering as he suffers road rash. I hop to my feet, my head spinning. I push through the dizziness and turn around. The palace isn't that far away, but I'm sure Vance can outrun me. And then there's Holly. I spot her blond hair blowing from the open back door.

I dash toward the car, my mind set before I can even think anything through. Brock holds his arms open, attempting to snatch me. I swing my fist and punch at the knife, dislodging it. I pray he bleeds out. I beg the universe to destroy him. He howls and drops to his knees, clutching his leg. I jump into the driver's seat and put the car in gear, stomping the throttle. It's been forever since I've driven, but my panic turns my movements automatic. I don't even bother closing the doors as I peel forward, sending white smoke and the scent of burning rubber through the air.

I hit the brakes, sending Holly rolling to the floor. It's enough to pull her from her unconscious state, the drugs not lasting long. Maybe because we didn't eat very much. Maybe because we are damn lucky. Regardless, if I can get her mobile, we can get to the panic room. There, no one can get us. I know the back way. We can just go through the door, and it'll lock behind us.

"Holly, can you hear me? I need you to brace yourself. We've been drugged and kidnapped. Please try to get it together. They're after us still." I jam the gear into reverse and look over my shoulder, stomping the gas pedal again, aiming to run over the fucking bastards before they can get us again. It's the best weapon I have at my disposal, and I will not let them take me away. I've been through too much to have to deal with this again. The king will not have won. He's going to regret ever betraying us like this...if he's even alive.

With the thought of King Winston comes the memory of the gunshot. Fuck. What if these bastards went after my guys?

Shit. Terror courses through me.

A shout echoes through the air, and I scream as Brock tries to grab the door. I jerk the wheel, knocking into him enough to get him to let go. I glance in the rearview mirror and tense at the sight of Vance aiming a gun. Something pings off the metal, and I hunch down, tears blurring my eyes.

This can't be happening. This has to be a nightmare. Why is it that we keep facing one threat after another? We can't just have our peace to take care of each other.

"Kinsey?" Holly's soft voice tugs me from my panic. "Check the glove compartment. People like this always keep spare weapons."

She's right. There's no way these two alphas would come into another territory and face the leaders of one of the Pack Regimes without enough arsenal to ensure they could get out alive if things went down.

I smack my hand to the dashboard until the glove compartment pops open. I spot the handle of a small gun and pull it out. I don't know much about shooting, so I carefully hand it to Holly. She's been trained by her brothers. I just hope she's clearheaded enough to use it.

Vance continues to shoot at us. I realize he's not trying to kill us. He's trying to force the car to stop by either popping a tire or just breaking it. My nerves twist my stomach, and I clutch the steering wheel, my knuckles turning white. Grinding my teeth, I keep low, maneuvering the vehicle back and forth in a zigzag pattern, shaking us. I can't make it easy on him. He doesn't seem like the type to give up either.

Silence fills the air as he stops shooting. It makes things worse for my anxiety. I stretch my neck to peer over my shoulder, catching sight of him. He's out of bullets, but he pulls out another weapon from a holster under his jacket.

"Holly, can you shoot? Open the window and scare him. Get him to take cover so we can get out and run." The palace looms closer. I know if we stop, Vance will catch up to us. He'll chase us inside. We can only get so far. A pack like Platinum Shores might not be alone. They could have members waiting outside. I don't know how much more I can handle. The drugs wear off, but I feel like shit with the ups and downs of my adrenaline. I could crash the car. Make a lethal mistake. I just need to get out and run to safety. I need my pack.

"I don't know if I can take the shot. My vision is blurry." Holly groans, sitting up and coming into view in my mirror. Her painfully slow movements try to steal my hope. If she can't scare Vance, we'll never make it.

"Just shoot. Pull the trigger and shoot." I slow the vehicle to maneuver the road, flicking my attention out the back every few seconds. The driveway curves around the side of the build-ing, heading toward the back. That's where we have to enter to get to the corridors leading to the panic room.

I hit the switch to open all the windows, and a gust of air blows my hair from my face. Another gunshot rings through the air, shattering the side mirror. I scream and jerk the wheel, running over a couple of yard lights.

"Holly, now! Now!" I shout, coming up to the door, still seeing Vance chasing us. The fucker can run fast as hell, but it's not like I could speed with the short distance.

Holly hangs out the window and pulls the trigger, the action enough to get Vance to drop and scramble toward a decorative wall separating the path from a garden. We have maybe two hundred feet. Two hundred feet before he can run and overpower us.

Jerking to a stop, I park the car, hopping out. I rush to grab Holly from the backseat and swing my arm around her, dragging her with me. She stumbles, her legs shaking and weak, her head still spinning, but my adrenaline helps me see clearly. My body knows that if I don't hustle, they will catch us. There's nothing like a game of cat and mouse to get me to flee. I'm not the type to fight when I can just run.

"The best access door is just over there. There's a latch that'll let us downstairs into the basement corridor." Holly waves her hand toward an immaculately landscaped area with hanging ivy and hydrangeas blooming in beautiful purple and blue colors. I would've never found the hatch had she not pointed it out, the secret door resembling a yard statue. Except it isn't made of heavy marble or stone. It's some sort of lighter material. Most likely hollow metal.

I mess with the statue, managing to pull it up to reveal a second door with a security lock. Holly enters the code, but it only turns red instead of opening.

"Maybe I typed it wrong. Try 5-7-8-2-0-1-1-3-4." Holly chants the code as if she has spent her entire life memorizing it. Maybe she has.

I type in exactly what she says, moving quickly but accurately, my hands steady. Again, the light flashes red. We're denied access and can't get in.

"They might've put the palace on lockdown. If that's the case, no one can get in." Holly chokes up with the words, her fear hitting her hard in this moment. "Fuck. Fuck. Fuck. They're going to get us. They're going to fucking get us. I'd rather die."

I grab her arm and force her to her feet, spinning to look at the property. We could try running toward the line of trees leading to an orchard, or we could just go to the backdoor and hope someone sees us.

"Don't think I won't shoot you, Kinsey. I wanted to keep you alive, but you're not worth it. We only need one omega." Brock's voice booms in my ears, his words stabbing into me, stealing my breath. It triggers my fear instincts, and I whip around to face him.

Holly grabs me, shielding me protectively. "Stay back. I'll shoot you." Holly's hands tremble as she aims the gun at Brock.

"It's over, princess. You're coming with us." This comes from behind me, and Holly pushes me back, using the wall to block us, giving us a view of Vance as he comes around the other side.

"Shoot him," I whisper, clinging to Holly's sides. "Shoot him."

Vance chuckles, shaking his head. "She's not gonna do it."

It's enough to get Holly to swivel, aim the gun, and pull the trigger. The bullet grazes Vance's shoulder, startling him. He hollers and runs forward, charging us. Brock does the same, now determined to trap and disarm us. I'm a dead woman. I know it. They've already declared that I'm not worth the trouble when they have Holly.

Holly shoots at Vance again, this time getting him in the gut. He trips and falls, face-planting on the ground. Holly doesn't have a chance to turn to Brock. His hand locks around her wrist, squeezing tightly. She screams as she drops the gun, and he shoves her hard into me. Pain explodes in my head as I clunk it against the wall, the force enough to send stars peppering through my vision. I fall forward, throwing my weight at Holly, hoping that I can just hold onto her enough that Brock can't do anything.

He drags the two of us, but Holly joins my deadweight, and he has no choice but to let us go.

He growls and pins Holly on top of me with his boot, bowing to press the barrel of his gun to my forehead. Sobs rack my chest, and I stare at him, refusing to close my eyes. He will see what a monster he is. I want him to live with looking into my eyes as he pulls the trigger.

A gunshot resonates through the air, ringing in my ears. I startle as blood and flesh splatter over me, the side of Brock's head disintegrating under a bullet. The light vanishes from his eyes, and he falls forward, crushing us beneath him. Holly shrieks and shoves against him, his heavy weight suffocating us, squishing us to the ground.

"Fuck! Fuck!" Wilder's voice twists around me, squeezing me as tightly as the weight of both Holly and Brock. But it doesn't steal my breath. It fills me with the strength I had forgotten I had. Wrapping my arms around Holly and Brock's body, I shove as hard as I can, rolling Brock's body off us.

"Holly, it's over." My hoarse voice burns my throat with my words. I squeeze her from behind, holding her tightly, trying my best to keep her together as she loses her shit and falls apart.

"Kinsey, Holly. Fuck. Are you hurt? Did he injure you?" Wilder grabs Holly off me, and she clings to his side, sobbing into his throat. With his other arm, he manages to scoop me up and balances me on his other side. His muscular arms flex as he holds our weight, letting us hug him as the adrenaline wears off. "Arsenio, help me. Desmond, make sure those fuckers are dead."

I open and close my mouth in shock. "Enzo?" All I can think about is not hearing Wilder say his name. My chest tightens. What if something happened to him? What if Brock or Vance shot him like they shot the king?

"He's inside. He's fine. I'll take you to him." Wilder hands Holly to Arsenio, readjusting me in his arms so that I hug him with my entire body.

"The king? He drugged us. This is his doing." My teeth chatter as my body turns cold despite the warm air outside. I can't focus. My mind just whirls through the events over and over again. The breakfast and feeling sick. Realizing that we had been drugged. Knowing how the king betrayed us and offered us as restitution to the Platinum Shores Pack. How they nearly kidnapped us. How I stabbed Brock and how Holly shot Vance. It's too much. Everything is too much.

"I suspected as much, Kinsey. Don't worry. We're going to handle him." Wilder strides forward, taking me inside through a glass door that leads to a sitting area.

Handle him? He's been shot. That would mean...

"He's alive?" Rage burns through me. That man shouldn't be alive. He should be dead. He should have to deal with the consequences of his actions. Brock turning against him and shooting him was supposed to be karma. It was supposed to prove that what he had done was wrong.

But I guess he wouldn't know any of that unless he did live through this. It doesn't change how I feel, though.

"Barely. We have the medical staff working on him. Enzo is overseeing it." Wilder grasps the back of my neck, easing me away from him to look at me. His blue eyes sheen over with something darker, sadder. He looked like this when I watched Gillian, my former dealer, die on the streets in the Gutter District.

"After everything, you're trying to save him?" Disappointment sizzles through me, overtaking my anger. My mind can't grasp why he allows it. He, out of everyone, should want the king dead.

His face pinches into a series of hard lines. "Kinsey, I know he deserves to die. I know—"

"If you know, then why are you saving him? Why are you allowing him to live? He drugged us. He gave us to the Platinum Shores Pack as restitution against you. He knows that we betrayed him. Yet here you are, trying to save him. What are you thinking, Wilder?" My voice rises in pitch, my voice squeaking the words.

"Take a breath. I can explain." Wilder locks his gaze on mine, slowing down.

"He needs to die. There's no other option." I dig my fingers into his shoulders. "He needs to die."

Wilder's features sharpen even more. A dozen emotions cross his face before they vanish completely, his ability to disguise what he's thinking like a wall building between us in this moment.

I can feel his denial deep in my soul. He knows that the king should die, but he's not going to see to it.

"Kinsey, I'm sorry." He tightens his mouth. Wilder inhales a few deep breaths, his body shaking in a way I've never felt before. His jaw shifts as he swallows hard. "We can't kill him."

I lose my shit, my sobs shuddering through me. It's as if his words trigger a bomb inside, shattering my being. Letting King Winston live isn't justice. It's punishment to me. I have to continue knowing that this piece of shit of a human being lives on. That he could retaliate and hurt me again.

My heart breaks, the pain intense enough to feel as if I'll die. "Wilder, please. Please don't save him. If you save him—"

"Kinsey, we can't," Wilder says, cutting me off, leaving no room for me to argue. "Arsenio, I need you to take her. I'll take Holly." Wilder holds me out to his brother, ending our conversation.

Words never felt so final. I guess he is our leader and what he says goes, even if I want something else. Even I deserve something else. He does too, yet he's denying us all justice and peace. At what cost? I'm afraid of the price.

"Come here, sugar. I need to feel you for myself. Let me take care of you." Arsenio kisses my temple, holding me tight. "We'll get through this. You need a moment to breathe and settle down. You're in shock."

I close my eyes and don't respond to him.

My body shuts down, and I close off completely.

A part of me shatters.

I'm afraid I will never fix that piece of me again.

# Chapter Two

## Kinsey

## Business

"Explain to me why? You obviously agree with Wilder. Is it because he's your father?" I squeeze my eyes shut, trying to keep my voice from rising with my anger. "I can understand if it's because of that, but—"

Arsenio cuts me off with a kiss, his rude interruption infuriating yet exactly what I need to calm down. "It's purely business, sugar. I know you want him dead—we all want him dead—but you know that he needs to renounce his reign and pass it on to us for a quiet, easy transition of power. Saint Vista is full of packs that'll put up a fight for the sole reason that they can. We need to ensure he names one of us as our new pack leader. If he's dead, he can't do that."

I know this. They've told me this a dozen times. But still, the stubborn part of me can't accept it. I know that my pack is powerful enough to face outside threats. Look at today. This was a setup from their own fucking father, and we still managed to succeed.

"So, what does this mean if he lives? Can you even trust that he will follow through with your demands? He doesn't trust you already." I know I should just believe in Arsenio and the others. They know what they're doing but having them answer my questions helps relax my screaming nerves. I can't function on blind faith. As much as I want to. As much as I know I should. My past won't allow me to.

"He won't have a choice. If he wants to live now, he will have to agree. What he's done, betraying us, won't be tolerated. We've already started the process. It's not uncommon for a pack to do so when their leader is injured. This attack actually helped push things into our favor. King Winston can't claim insubordination. But we can claim that he is too weak to keep going in his position." Arsenio sets me on my feet just outside a room in the palace I've never been to. No, not a room, something else. A hospital? I guess you could call it that, but it's more like a medical center. "Now, sugar. I want to prepare you for what you're about to see. We have an entire medical staff, and they're currently stabilizing King Winston. Enzo is with them, and he's a bit…bloody. Don't freak out."

"Can you just bring him to me? I don't want to see your staff work on that bastard. Please, Arsenio. I know and understand your reasons, but if you make me go in there, I will try to kill him. He was going to ruin everything. Protecting you is my biggest priority." I scrub my hands across my cheeks, rubbing away the stickiness of my tears.

His sharp features soften as he releases a quiet laugh. "Protecting you is our biggest priority, you mean. Don't think otherwise. We're your alphas, and it's our duty to see to it that you're safe, happy, healthy, and completely satisfied."

His comment helps ease the tightness in my chest. But it doesn't change the fact that I will do whatever it takes to protect them, even if it means killing their father. Could there be repercussions? Absolutely. Do I care? Fuck no. The only thing I have left to lose is them, and King Winston is our biggest threat. If it comes down to him or us, I'll choose us. I'll be the omega my princes need. This wouldn't be the first time fear gave me unimaginable bravery. I've never been brave because I was fearless. I was brave because I had to be.

"Then just get Enzo, please." I bounce on my feet, rubbing my hands together. "I'll wait here."

"Are you sure?" Arsenio tightens his jaw as if he doesn't want to leave me alone. But it's only a dozen or so feet to the room I can hear commotion trickling from.

I nod and nudge him with my knuckles. "Like I said, I can't be anywhere near the king. Just hurry back to me." Waving my hand, I get him to give in to my demand. He might not listen if I'm not persistent. Everyone's too high-strung and emotionally drained.

Arsenio heaves a deep breath and rolls his shoulders, forcing his feet to carry him to the room with the king. Several voices buzz out, and Arsenio stands in the doorway, looking over everything. I can't see much from my position, but I can see people in scrubs and medical gear. Bright light shines from the room, the sterile scent enough to mess with my head.

Enzo comes into view, blood staining the front of his shirt. Shadows darken under his beautiful sapphire eyes, probably remnants of the drugs forced into us.

Striding to me, Enzo engulfs me in a hug and kisses me sensually, lifting me off my feet and spinning me around and away from the room. He combs his fingers through my hair and leans down, capturing my gaze.

"I heard you fought like hell, baby. I hope you know how proud I am of you. It took everything in me to fucking stay with that devil instead of following my brothers to you." Enzo purses his lips, his eyes roving down my face as he takes a small step away, searching over every inch of me.

"I stabbed one of them. Holly shot the other. There was no way we were going to let them take us from you. Your father tried to give us to them as restitution for your actions against Platinum Shores." My voice trembles with the admission. "They didn't even really want me anymore because we've bonded, but they were taking me just because they wanted to spite you. They really had their sights set on Holly. She protected me. She shielded me when they threatened to murder me."

My breathing quickens with my words, and a part of me relives the moment all over again, sending my mind spinning and my body shaking. I wobble on my feet, my knees going weak. I can still feel the metal of the gun against my forehead. The fear. How heavy a body felt dropping on top of us.

"The king did what? Fuck. I'm going to kill him. He's a dead man. This changes everything. My brothers are dipshits. I can't believe them." He didn't know. It's clear by his morphing concern boiling into anger. Wilder must've kept his suspicions to himself because he knew Enzo would react this way

Spinning on his heels, Enzo abandons me, rushing back toward the medical room. He reaches for his gun. I should've realized that he might not have known everything, and his brothers might've been waiting to tell him, because he is always the first to act. And it gets to me in a good way. This is what I wanted. Wilder and Arsenio think about what is best for our future, but Enzo thinks about what is best for me in this moment, which is revenge.

"Stop everything!" Enzo shouts, waving his gun as he closes in on the medical room.

Arsenio cuts him off, shoving him out of the way and sending him sprawling across the floor. "Ignore him. He's in distress. Lock the door and don't open it for him."

Enzo hops to his feet and bares his teeth. He charges toward Arsenio. His anger permeates in hot waves. I can nearly feel it caress my skin, warming me up. "You traitor!"

Arsenio punches Enzo, knocking him into the wall and to the ground. "Calm the hell down, brother. We have a plan." Grabbing Enzo by the back of his shirt, he hauls him from the ground, dragging him away.

"Fuck the plan. He nearly got our girl taken! Nearly killed!" Enzo strikes Arsenio in the knee, sending him to the floor.

Tackling him, Enzo shoves his hand to his throat. Arsenio gasps with a growl, swinging his arms, trying to push Enzo off. The two of them throw punches, wrestling to overpower each other. My chest clenches at the pain they inflict as they attempt to subdue each other. They shouldn't be fighting. Not now. Not ever. Everyone's emotions run too hot. Including mine. It helps clear my desire for revenge. I won't accept it at this cost.

"Stop it! Stop it, now!" I scream, rushing them. Tears burn my eyes. It hurts me on a deep level to see them turn against each other. I understand where they both come from, but it shouldn't be like this. Not over me.

They roll over and over across the floor, trying to pin each other, not letting me yank them apart. I bounce on my feet, looking for an opening. There is only one way to get them to stop as they ignore me, too caught up in the fight.

Taking a breath, I psych myself up. I just hope my plan works.

"Don't hurt me!" I shout in warning. It distracts them enough to slow them down. Jumping forward, I flop on top of Arsenio's back. "Stop!" I shove my hand between them, my wrist grazing Enzo's nose. My scent freezes them in place.

Enzo snatches my arms, dragging me up Arsenio's back until I straddle his neck. Securing my knees firmly against his shoulders, Arsenio manages to swing his body up until I'm riding on his shoulders, the quick movement making me tighten my thighs. Enzo pushes up to his feet, swiveling to glance at the closed door where the medical staff works on his father. Leaning forward, I throw Arsenio off balance as I lock my fingers to Enzo's hair, yanking his head.

"If you two don't stop, you're going to be in trouble. I have been through so much already today. I don't want to see you fighting. I desperately want the king to pay but not at the expense of you beating each other up." I stretch forward until Enzo takes me from Arsenio's shoulders. The two of them sandwich me between them, smothering me with their muscular bodies. It's enough to suppress my trembles, and I rest my head on Enzo's shoulder, breathing in his skin while I kiss the crook of his neck. I hate today. I hate that their father betrayed them, and I had to fight alphas. I hate that as an omega, I'm so easily discarded for being used and bonded. I hate that Holly, as a princess and omega, faces a shit show just because of her order.

But mostly, I hate that I have to deal with not being able to live my life and love my guys while they do the same. I would think because of their position and power on the Pack Regimes of Saint Vista that things will be easy, but I'm pretty sure things are harder.

"Baby, it breaks my heart that we underestimated King Winston. He should've never been able to get to our staff like this. I've failed you. I want to make it up to you. The only way I know how is through his murder." Enzo strokes his hand along my back, keeping an inch of space between his brother and me. The subtle gesture doesn't go unnoticed, and Arsenio slides his hand around my shoulder and rests his arm against my clavicle, forcing space between Enzo and me.

"You don't think I want that, brother? I wanted to pull the trigger myself. But you know how things are. If we murder him, we'll be stripped from our position. Other packs will see that weakness in Gilded Sands. Other territories will also try to come in. We have gone over this, hundreds of times. It sucks. It really fucking sucks. But you have to trust that we're making the right decision. We just need King Winston stable enough to get him to sign everything over to us. We need him to renounce his reign and claim us as the next kings." Arsenio rests his chin on my shoulder, trying to peek at Enzo as he avoids his gaze. I know he feels guilty for going against their plan and his brothers, but I also know that he would do things over again.

"He's stable enough right now. This is our opportunity. Call Wilder and Desmond. Make sure they bring Holly. We need them here. King Winston needs to put Holly's life in our hands as well." Enzo straightens his back, easing me away just enough to grab my chin to look at me.

We stare at each other in silence, his eyes roving over my face, turning down to stare at my lips. I ease closer and kiss him, unable to resist his pouty mouth. I'm just so relieved that I was able to talk some sense into him, to give Arsenio a chance to explain everything.

"I'm not sure I should leave you and Kinsey alone. So, you need to get Wilder and Desmond. Okay? I'll stay here with King Winston." Arsenio steps away, leaving a cool space on my back. I want nothing more than to beg him to come closer again.

I whimper, the sound pathetic and automatic, my very being craving what my mind denies. "I want to go with you. I know you want to keep me from the king, but I want to face him now. I want him to know how messed up it was of him to do this. I want him to know that he was the one in the wrong. Let me do this. Please. I think I'm ready."

Arsenio doesn't speak, and I can sense his gaze locking on Enzo even though I don't face him. The two of them have a silent conversation, probably wishing that they could have a second alone to discuss things, but neither of them will leave me.

"Please," I repeat, twisting my torso to do my best to look at Arsenio.

He stares at the ground, wringing his hands together. "Are you sure, sugar? You said you were going to kill him if you saw him."

I shake my head, sweeping my hair back and forth. "I thought that's what I wanted, but I know you'll take care of me and handle it. I trust you guys as my alphas."

Enzo holds me out, his body rigid. "The only way I'll go get the others is if you give our girl what she needs right now."

Arsenio hesitates, scratching his arms. "I just don't know if this is a good idea. She's been through a lot, brother. As soon as the adrenaline wears off—"

"We will deal with it. There's going to be a lot of fucking aftercare today." Enzo hands me over to Arsenio. "Just give her this. Give it to her, and I'll return as fast as I can to handle the aftermath."

Arsenio swallows, the noise audible as his Adam's apple bounces. "Fuck. If this is what you really want, Kinsey, then fine. But at the first sign of panic or distress, I'm taking you out of there. Do you understand? I'm not playing with your mental health after everything."

I press my lips together, trying to keep my body in control. "Yes. I'm sorry that I'm putting you in this position, but please. It's the only thing that's going to help me move past this. I never got the chance to face my uncle after what he did to me and my parents. I'm haunted by that. I don't want to be haunted by this too."

Arsenio adjusts me in his arms, ensuring that I wrap my legs around him to hug him close. Enzo doesn't say anything as he moves away from us, running to find Wilder, Desmond, and Holly. I hide my face against Arsenio's shoulder, breathing in and out slowly, getting my racing heart to finally settle. I've always been afraid of monsters. I've been afraid of brutal alphas and all leaders on the Pack Regimes of Saint Vista. But right now? I'm so angry that fear doesn't touch me anymore.

I will not give King Winston that sort of satisfaction. I'm stronger than that. I've already been broken and shattered on many levels but I have rebuilt myself stronger than ever. Arsenio is now a steel wall around my concrete body, protecting me in a way that I have needed, and my parents had always wanted.

Knocking on the door, Arsenio calls out to the staff that it's him. I squeeze my eyes shut, listening to the commotion as one of the nurses opens the door. Machines hum and the staff chatters with each other, ignoring the beeps of all of the medical equipment.

"Is he stable enough to talk to?" Arsenio asks, shifting me onto his hip so that I can get a better view of the room.

My blood cools seeing King Winston sprawled on a table, his body exposed apart from a sheet covering his genitals. There's blood everywhere, covering everyone, and it looks like the king has been shot more than once in the chest.

"He is. We're cleaning out the wounds. I do suggest that we sedate him soon." A man in full medical gear with a face shield and mask stands beside the bed. "It'll be better than the local anesthesia and restraints. We'll no longer have to monitor his consciousness and worry about if he will wake up."

"My son..." King Winston's voice draws my attention. "Get away. I declare you—"

Arsenio rushes forward. "Everyone out. Now!" Pointing at the door, Arsenio motions to the staff. "I will take it from here."

The surgeon doesn't move. "I suggest—"

Arsenio pulls out his gun. "Out!"

He fires it at the wall, startling everyone. They flee the room in fear, not wanting to find out if Arsenio is as brutal as his father. Slamming the door, Arsenio glowers, stiffening with his rage. If I didn't grab his chin, forcing him to look at me, I'm sure he'd snap and finish what Enzo wanted to start.

"Let me talk to him," I say, leaning in close, breathing against his mouth.

He slowly nods his head as he sets me on my feet. "I won't allow him to talk back." He shuffles forward, standing over King Winston. Slapping his hand over his mouth, he ensures he won't speak. "Listen carefully, Winston. If you try to disown and banish me again, especially with witnesses, you'll regret it more than you regret ever having me."

The king remains silent, his eyes narrow and his forehead wrinkled.

"Go on, Kinsey. Speak your mind." Arsenio holds my gaze.

I lick my lips, curling my fingers in, digging my nails into my palms. I open my mouth, finding my nerve, but a machine blares. King Winston's eyes roll to the back of his head.

His vitals flatline.

# Chapter Three

## *Kinsey*

## New Reign

Arsenio drags me away, cornering me as the medical team floods into the room once more. I peek over his shoulder, spotting Wilder rushing our way. Desmond, Enzo, and Holly follow behind, not chasing after him. My stare locks on Holly's, and she pushes past Desmond to come to my side. I wiggle until Arsenio puts me on my feet, and Holly wraps her arms around me in the tightest hug. She's just as shook up as I am about everything. I'm sure she wants to see the king dead too.

"Get him stabilized so we can have him declare an heir to the throne immediately," Wilder commands, standing at the end of the bed as he watches the team work on his father.

"Yes, Your Majesty. We'll do what we can." The surgeon does something I can't see, and the machines kick off before they start beeping again. "He's lost a lot of blood. We are doing what we can, but unless one of you donates, he might not make it."

"Fuck no. I'm not doing anything for him after he set this shit up." Enzo crosses his arms over his chest, glowering at Wilder.

"It has to be you. You're the only match, brother." Wilder locks his hand around Enzo's elbow, tugging him closer. "Don't fight us over this. We will hold you down."

Oh shit.

"Son?" King Winston's soft voice murmurs through the air, drawing my attention away from the impending fight between Enzo and Wilder. "My heir. I need you."

Enzo balls his hands, his muscles rippling and cording on his arms. "You were trying to renounce me as your son and heir to the throne. You gave the love of my life to an enemy pack because you're bitter and petty. A fucking coward. You should've thought about that, Dad. I'm not doing fucking anything for you."

"Son? Please. Don't let me die. Our legacy will end." King Winston's head lolls, his eyes rolling.

"Make your decision, prince. We're out of time." The surgeon stares at Enzo.

"You hear that, father? If you want help, you must declare one of us as Gilded Sands' new king. Your staff here will bear witness, and you will sign the testament." Wilder pulls out his phone. He waves it at King Winston while Desmond steps forward, pulling out a folded piece of paper from his jacket.

"I'll do anything." The king opens and closes his mouth, his voice weak and his eyes struggling to remain open. "We have faced many challenges as a family, but this was my greatest mistake. I declare you, Prince Wilder, as my next in line and Gilded Sands' new king."

"You must declare Kinsey as our omega, too." Wilder sets a pen in King Winston's hand, curling his fingers around it.

"I declare Kinsey as your omega." King Winston scribbles slowly across the paper as Wilder records everything as the medical staff bears witness. "I officially agree to retire and renounce my power of the throne and myself as leader of the Gilded Sands Pack."

Wilder snatches the pen away and turns to Enzo. "It's done. Do what you have to and don't argue. This is what we have been waiting for, brother. Don't let me down. Don't let our pack down because of your anger."

I slowly step forward, sliding my fingers through Enzo's to squeeze his hand. He looks at me for the first time since he re-entered the room, and I reach up and caress my fingers across his cheek and down his neck, rubbing his skin slowly, gently, just leaving my scent behind to help calm him down.

"I will stand beside you through everything. This is what we need, Enzo. Your father will have the life he deserves. I promise." I squeeze his hand again, watching as he finally relents and allows the medical staff to do as they need to perform a blood transfusion on the king.

Everything happens in a blur as Enzo shuts down, keeping his eyes closed and ignoring everything that happens. He wants to kill his father, not save him, and the scent of his anger runs hot and spicy the longer we sit here.

"We will sedate him now, King Wilder." The surgeon clears his throat and motions to Wilder's father. "It would be best if he had time to rest. I suggest only one of you stays so he remains calm."

Enzo scoops me up, not waiting to hear his brother's response. "Good luck with that. I'm taking our girl out of here."

"Take Holly too. Don't leave the premises. We have to make the formal arrangements for Wilder's coronation and his declaration of our shared ruling." Desmond touches my cheek, strolling with us for just another moment longer. "I'm sure word will get out soon enough, and we need to be ready."

"Yeah, okay. What the fuck ever. I don't care anymore." Enzo swivels and holds his hand up to Holly.

"You should, brother. This is everything we wanted and needed for our pack. We can't fuck this up." Wilder remains by King Winston's side... I guess he's not really King Winston anymore. He doesn't deserve such a title any longer.

"We already have. Our father should be dead. You know he's going to go back on his word." Enzo rubs his lips together. "So be prepared when he does. He's a dead man. That's a promise."

I peek over my shoulder at Wilder, Desmond, and Arsenio. Enzo is right about that. I'll never feel safe as long as that man lives. We might not be able to do it now, but his reign is over. He will die, even if it has to be by my hands.

I will never allow another alpha to ruin my life again.

Now that's my promise to my pack. To me.

This territory is ours.

"As king, I need to return the bodies to the Platinum Shores Pack. It's in our best interest to send them a warning." Wilder stands in the doorway to Enzo's suite, not entering like he normally does.

"I want to come with you." Enzo shifts to the edge of the bed. Turning to me, he gives me a long look, his eyes pleading with me not to argue. I know he needs to do something, anything, to get his mind off things. And as long as Wilder is with him, I know the two of them will be safe together.

"I think that would be a good idea." I lick my lips and scoot next to him, getting to my feet. I take his hands in mine, pulling him to my chest. Enzo widens his legs until I can stand between them, and I kiss him, giving him the affection he craves.

"I was hoping the two of you would agree. I want Desmond to stay here with Holly, and Arsenio is anxious for some of Kinsey's affection." Wilder finally enters the suite, crossing the room to us. He drapes his arms over my shoulders, hugging me from behind. Pressing a kiss to my throat, he works his way up to my ear. His soft breath tickles my hair, and I shiver. "It'll give you a chance to be ready for me when I return, my brat. I'm going to need far more attention than any of my brothers after everything today. If that's okay..."

I tilt my head, letting him explore my neck more, his lips feather light as he trails to the sensitive spot where my throat and shoulder meet. "Whatever you need, Wilder. We need to celebrate."

He groans deep in his throat, easing away from me to spin me around. Enzo silently gets to his feet, giving us some space as he goes to prepare. I'm sure he'll stock up on every weapon he can get his hands on. I'm sure he will also wear some bulletproof attire. They're going to need it. I just hope there isn't a huge confrontation.

I stare into Wilder's light blue eyes, reaching up to stroke my hand across his cheek, wanting nothing more than for him to be able to breathe in my scent the entire time he's away. "Be safe. I expect you both to return to me uninjured. If you come back with even a bruise or a scratch, you're going to be in so much trouble. Do you understand?" I remain tightlipped and stern while Wilder cracks a smile.

He dips his chin in agreement. "Understood, my little brat, who thinks she's my alpha."

I can't stop the smile from crossing my lips. "We can always do a little roleplay."

Wilder releases a playful growl and snatches my hands, turning me around. He bends me over the bed and spanks my ass. "You will have to overpower me first."

I stretch my neck to peek at him. "You know your brothers will help."

Hooking his fingers to the back of my pants, he yanks them down, exposing my ass. Once again, he spanks me, the sting radiating through my body and zapping me right in my clit. I release a soft breath and freeze, savoring the sensation.

Wilder growls again, leaning closer until his weight presses on me. "You're lucky I don't have time to fuck you right now, brat."

My heart pounds as my body buzzes, pleading for him to get me off. "You do if you don't knot with me."

"Give her what she wants, brother. That's an order. I'll get the car ready, but don't think I'm not going to watch my security feed later." Enzo strolls to the bed and smacks my ass before he leans down and kisses the hot spot he leaves behind. "Love you, baby. I'll bring you home a trophy or something."

I pant and squirm as Wilder continues to pin me in place, deciding if he wants to give in or not. The door clicks closed as Enzo leaves, and I reach behind me and grab onto Wilder's shirt, arching my back in the process.

"You heard your brother. Fuck me. It's all I want right now. Please. I need you." My voice turns breathy as I listen to Wilder unbuckle his pants. He releases my hands and massages his fingers into my hips, working his way down until he spreads open my ass cheeks to get a better view.

"You're so sexy. Let me feel how wet you are." Wilder teases me with his tip, sliding inside of me, sending my whole body buzzing. "Fuck, you've drenched me already. It's going to feel so good."

I hum my agreement, resting my cheek on the mattress as Wilder gets closer, dipping his finger inside me, slickening his hand as he prepares my ass with a finger, making me moan and squirm. My body relaxes under his attention, and I wiggle more, the anticipation making me arch up with the need. His lust sets me off even more, my slick ensuring my pleasure, no matter how he fucks me. I'm made for this. Made to be fucked every which way. I crave it.

"This is torture," I breathe. "Fuck me already, Wilder. Do it. I want to hear you moan my name. Let me feel how hard you are. Make me ache in a good way that lingers for days every time I think about this."

Wilder spreads me again, aligning his body to mine. He moans in pleasure as he slides into my ass, the slickness of my body welcoming him with ease. I gasp at the pressure and moan, my nipples pebbling and my clit begging for attention. I reach my hand down and play with myself as Wilder rocks his body in and out of me, just testing me, savoring me, letting me get used to the girth of his cock. He locks fingers around my wrist, yanking my hand away from my body only to pin it at my head. He maneuvers his hand under me and takes over, wanting to give me the pleasure himself.

I moan as goosebumps prickle over my skin. Wilder picks up speed, thrusting quicker as his hand remains steady, rubbing circles over my clit until I reach my peak.

I press my face to the mattress, muffling my moans, and Wilder uses his other hand to grab my hair, pulling my head back so he can hear my voice.

"How does it feel, Kinsey? Do you like when I fuck your ass?" His voice turns deep, his words turning me on. I know how much he likes me to vocalize everything.

So, I give him what he wants.

"Mmmhmm. Do it faster. I want to think about it for days. Show me you're my alpha. I want to feel you come." I dig my fingers into the mattress as he growls and holds me in place, thrusting harder, my slick wetting me even more. As an omega, I can give him what he craves in any way he pleases.

"You're so tight. I wish I could fuck you how I really want. Just the thought of you taking my knot over and over again drives me crazy." Wilder leans down and stretches my neck back to kiss my jaw.

I moan and dig my toes into the floor, holding my body in place more. "That's why you need to hurry back. I want you. I need you, my king. My leader. My alpha. I can't wait for the ecstasy you bring me."

Sliding out of me, Wilder flips me onto my back, grabbing my knees and bending them to get a view of my body. "I want to watch your face. I need to see how much you enjoy me. I want you to see how much I love you. I want to make you come over and over again before I finish."

Wilder aligns his body to mine once more, and I bend up enough to watch him enter me. I moan with a whimper, his words getting to me in a good way. He strums his finger over my clit, picking up speed again as his hips bump against me. Our eyes meet, and we watch each other, his pouty mouth open with his heavy breathing, the scent of his desire seducing me. I could stay with him forever. I wish he didn't have to leave. I want our celebration to start now. I can already fantasize about our future and how I'm officially their omega, declared by their father. The throne is ours. They're going to change Gilded Sands for the better, and I can't wait to be by their side and bear their children, growing our pack and our power.

I'll help them strive for the best and ensure a better future for not only omegas in our territory but also for betas. And who knows? Maybe we can start a revolution and bring equality across Saint Vista. Maybe even some of the other regions like Calico Proper, now that we have proven to the Platinum Shores Pack that we're not to be messed with.

Wilder moans, his body pulsing as he prepares to come. I arch my back, stroking my fingers over my nipples through my shirt until I reach for the hem and lift it up, exposing my breast to him. The sight alone gets him off, and he grunts with his orgasm. He thrusts deep, his body tensing, his finger continuing to work over my clit until I come again, my orgasm matching his. I scream out with my pleasure, reaching for him, pulling him on top of me so I can feel the weight of his body. So, I can taste his skin and bury my face in his throat to leave a mark on his neck with my teeth. I won't let him leave otherwise. I need the world to know that I'm his queen. I'm his omega. His mate.

"Fuck, Kinsey. I love you. I love you so damn much. It pains me to even consider leaving, but it is my duty. All this bullshit will come to an end soon. And when it does, I'm going to never let you leave the bed. We're going to survive on pleasure and bliss." Wilder crashes his lips to mine as if he can't get enough, and I glide my tongue across his, moaning as he slides from my body.

"Then hurry back. I want that. So desperately. More than you know." Wilder lifts me up and carries me to the bathroom, taking me into the shower even though this is Enzo's suite. Usually, he'd never fuck me in one of his brothers' rooms without them around, but with Enzo's permission, he takes advantage of it. I'll make sure to leave my scent over his, smearing away his subtle claim of dominance. I'll make sure to change the sheets as well.

A knock sounds on the bathroom door. "All right, asshole. I know you're done. Let's get this over with."

Enzo enters the bathroom and gives us a once-over. Arsenio stands behind him, drinking me in, the lust clear on his face. The two of them don't give us space, and Enzo grabs a towel and holds it open for Wilder to let me in. Arsenio takes over to dry me off, and I kiss the two of them. I wanted nothing more than for all of us to be together.

"Come on, sugar. Let's go back to my suite. We have to pick out some formal wear. Go over the menu. Do a couple other bullshit things." Arsenio takes the shirt off his back and pulls it over me as if he can't resist. I don't argue, and neither do his brothers.

"This is real, isn't it?" My heart picks up pace at the thought. I'm afraid, and not of being declared as their omega or the fact that they have officially taken power from their father. What scares me is that the world might not see me worthy of being queen. Of being their equal.

Arsenio nods. "It's going to be amazing. I promise. I can't wait to show you to the world."

"I just hope the world is ready." I hug him close, peeking over his shoulder as his brothers leave.

"The world doesn't have to be. Only us," he says, kissing my forehead. "And I'm more ready than I've ever been."

If only I was as confident as he was. I'd give anything to match his certainty. Life never treated me well for long, though. Good things have never lasted.

Right now, things feel surreal. Temporary. I'm terrified it'll all fall apart. And then what?

I shove the thought away. I can't think like that. We've been through so much already. It's time we rise.

# Chapter Four

## *Wilder*

## Warning Present

*Desmeister: Allies confirm it's all clear.*
*Me: How long?*
*Desmeister: Ten.*
*Me: Only need five.*

I tuck my phone away and glance up to stare at the border wall of Calico Proper, leading into Platinum Shores. Enzo drives up an incline until we get a view of the stunning blue ocean expanding into the horizon. I hate to admit it, but Platinum Shores has a beautiful territory, one I wouldn't mind seizing as ours. All it would take is annihilating the leader at this point. As the leader of Gilded Sands, I can now formally declare war and demand the Pack Regimes recognize our power and need for an expansion, considering the shady workings of Platinum Shores, buying and trafficking from Saint Vista. No region wants to lose omegas, especially to another, which is their greatest mistake. They don't care if they are packless. The Pack Regimes of Saint Vista will place them. And with my brothers and me now in charge of Gilded Sands, we can guarantee they'll get loving packs. After seeing the reality of bad negotiations with Holly and Kinsey, there is no fucking way I'll knowingly allow this shit to go on.

"I think we need to be direct and hang them upright on their doorstep." The twisted bastard. He gets it from me. "Make a point." Enzo switches lanes, turning to get into the short border crossing entrance.

As alphas and part of the Pack Regimes of Saint Vista, we don't have to declare our reason for entering another region, only stating where we're heading. We'll be tagged with a tracker, but it's easily removed. All packs do it.

"As much as I want to agree, we need to act the part of victims, considering they came into our territory. Arsenio already registered the incident. We'll hand the bodies over to their security. But don't worry, brother. I've strategized a little present once they've been delivered." I remain expressionless, keeping my gaze on the border patrol as they wave us forward.

He shifts in my peripheral vision, the weight of his thoughts almost palpable. I glance at him from the corner of my eye.

Enzo stares at the side of my face, his features scrunching with curiosity. His intensity feels as if he's nearly able to listen in on my thoughts. "What aren't you telling me?"

A grin stretches across my face. He might be diabolical in his rash planning but I'm a master of strategy and diabolical. At least, that's what Arsenio called me. "I had our mortician insert a special little plug."

Tipping his head back, Enzo roars a laugh. He smacks his hands on the steering wheel and dances in his seat. I knew he'd appreciate it. "You didn't."

"Sick fucks deserved it. They were lucky to be dead because if they weren't...fuck." I tap my fingers on the dashboard, not finishing my disturbing thoughts out loud. I shake my head, collecting myself before I get angry. "Regardless, we'll make a point. You'll be able to see their faces when they realize how screwed they are." I clear my throat, suppressing my need to react.

He punches my leg. "You psychotic son of a bastard. That's not even something I'd come up with."

My brows pinch together. "We must teach them early on. Touch Kinsey and die. Mess with Holly and pay. Try to screw us and be fucking annihilated."

"Fuck yeah. Burn their shit down." Enzo glowers at the windshield. Slowing the car at the booth, he rolls down the window.

I lean forward and look at the officer. "The hearse is ours too. We have a delivery to Platinum Shores."

The patrolman glances at the hearse and nods, slapping the tracker sticker to the windshield. I reach out and peel it off, bringing it inside. Enzo stomps the throttle, peeling forward, leaving the booth in a cloud of smoke. The hearse follows behind us, not stopping. The relaxed laws for leaders of the Pack Regimes, regardless of region, make this easier.

Tapping his finger to the dashboard screen, Enzo turns on our visuals, viewing the hidden cameras installed around the car, giving us a view of the streets around us. We don't usually drive what I'd describe as an incognito tank, but we have to be prepared since we're entering a territory unannounced.

*Desmeister: Platinum Shores got word you're coming.*
*Me: Good.*
*Desmeister: Stay safe, brothers.*
*Me: Sending the declaration to the Pack Regimes now.*

I click out of the text message and open the files with the signed documents of the transfer of power and all assets from our father to me, along with the evidence of the Platinum

Shores crime—not regarding Holly and Kinsey but toward our father. We'd be in a more difficult position had the assholes not tried to murder King Winston.

I'm sure their leader would kill the two pack members if they weren't already dead.

"Turn right at the next street." I sit up straighter in my seat, my muscles bunching with my nerves. I know we have this handled, but it doesn't get any less nerve-wracking. I have more than myself and my brothers to think about. Kinsey needs us to return without incident...or at least in one piece.

"Tell Jude to hustle. He's letting too much space fall between us." Enzo slows down, preparing to turn right.

A siren blares in the distance, and before I can see the police vehicle, I know it's heading in our direction. I'm sure the Platinum Shores leader will try detaining us for some bullshit reason until they can come up with something to file against our notion for war.

"Pull over," I snap, sending a message to my cousin Jude. I promised my aunt that I'd ensure his safety on the trip. He's just turned of age to join our security personnel and be declared a beta for the Gilded Sands Pack, something my father had been putting off, knowing that Jude would be more loyal to me over him.

*Me: J, get out. Leave the hearse. I'll cover you.*

Flinging the door open, I aim my gun, peering around as the sirens grow louder. I spot a man in a uniform sneaking from the alley just behind Jude. Without hesitation, I pull the trigger, shooting a warning shot.

Growling, I yell, "Stand down, or I won't miss next time. We're here as a courtesy to return the fallen members of the—"

The man aims, and a gunshot rings through the air. Jude ducks instinctively as the man stumbles and falls face-first to the ground. Enzo grumbles under his breath and smacks the roof of the car.

If it wasn't for him, Jude would've been hurt. I shouldn't have given the douchebag a warning.

Rushing forward, I yank Jude with me, covering him as a patrol car screeches around the corner, its red and blue lights flashing with its blaring sirens. I shove Jude into the backseat and hop in, slamming my palm on the dashboard.

"Drive, fucker!" I yell, tensing as Enzo fires his gun once more.

Plopping behind the wheel, Enzo stomps the throttle, screeching forward. I shoot out the window, firing at the tires, ensuring no one follows us. I toss the tracking sticker to the street, watching it flutter to the sewer. Annoyance crashes through me that I didn't get to see the anger on the faces of the Platinum Shores Pack's security personnel, but this isn't over.

It will be soon.

I can already feel my power grow.

Platinum Shores will be ours.

"I'm sorry, Angelo. There is too much proof against you. Your accusations remain unfounded. We find it in your best interest to shed whatever grudge you hold against the Gilded Sands Pack and move on before it's too late. Any further attacks will not be tolerated. We stand with King Wilder." A leader from the Valley View Pack Regimes clicks off his camera with his final word. No region meeting has ever been so satisfying.

"Be grateful Saint Vista doesn't demand restitution. I'd vote that the Calico Proper Pack Regimes give them your territory." Another leader growls with his words and hangs up the video call.

"Actually, I'm rather fond of that idea." One of the leaders from Calico Proper remains expressionless. "King Wilder, you have my approval to take what you see fit."

Angelo, the leader of Platinum Shores, smacks his hands on his desk. "Like fucking hell—"

"Meeting adjourned," another leader says, cutting him off.

One by one, the video calls disconnect until I stare at Angelo, refusing to disconnect first. I'd love to hear his threats and all the ways he plans to destroy my kingdom. Narrowing his eyes, he glowers at me in silence. Enzo shifts closer, backing me up even though miles of distance stand between us and the douche. He would throw the first punch if we were having a meeting in person.

"You heard your region head. He stands beside me in taking your kingdom. I should do it. I mean, I really should fucking do it, but I'll give you a day to pay for all damages and to resign as the leader of your territory. You may offer it to another alpha in your pack or one of your allies." I tap my fingers to the desk, watching his anger morph into fury. Most Alphas would rather die than submit to another, which makes this even more satisfying. I already had my father beg for his life, and I plan for Angelo to do the same.

"You're a dead man, Wilder." Angelo sits up straighter.

"Tell that to your pack. Your falling members are proof otherwise. How are they, anyway? You should be grateful that I returned them." I don't see the bodies, but I know they would be nearby. At the least, they'd be in the same building until they're properly put to rest.

Angelo bares his teeth. "You fucker!"

Latching his fingers to my shoulder, Enzo bends over me, glaring at the camera. "I'm tired of waiting, brother. It's time we do it. Now."

A smile crosses my face. "As you wish, Enzo. Pull up our spy feed. I want to record this from another angle just for Kinsey.

She will sleep better knowing we have taken care of Angelo completely."

Realization smooths Angelo's features, his sharp anger morphing into shock and then fear. Enzo clicks on the feed, cutting off Angelo while shifting the view to his office. I was right about the bodies being close. They remain on view for his pack members to visit. And he chose the wrong place to have his meeting.

"Wait. We can—" The camera shakes as a loud boom sounds through the speaker a second before a bright light devours Angelo.

The bombs we planted inside his pack members detonate, and the camera cuts off completely. They'll have at least destroyed his palace, and unfortunately, his pack now will suffer for his actions.

Enzo sighs a breath beside me. "I want Platinum Shores. Their authority was so fucked up. It'll be a lot of work, but I want to change things there. I want to prove ourselves immediately. We can announce it at the coronation. I will take the king persona."

I roll back in my chair, swiveling to face him as he kneels beside me. We both know that Arsenio would be the next one to take a territory. But right now, I don't want to argue with him. I know he's really pissed off about our father and our decision to keep him alive.

I'm angry with myself, but I know it needed to be done. And we can't just annihilate him yet. It would bring suspicion to us, especially now that we have attacked Platinum Shores.

"How about you sleep on it, little brother? It's a lot of work, and Kinsey might not want to go there all the time after everything. We should talk to everyone else first." I remain expressionless, bracing myself for him to react. Surprisingly, he doesn't blow up at me and instead only pats my cheek, trying to fuck with me by leaving his scent behind.

"Goddamn it. There's no way I want to ever be away from Kinsey. I was too caught up with my anger to think about it. I know she's not going to want to leave our home here." Enzo uses my desk to pull himself to his feet. "I want to make the announcement. Are you cool with that?"

I stretch my arms over my head and nod. "Absolutely. I have a couple things I must do before we have the ball to announce our reign."

The last thing I want is for Enzo to follow me to the medical center, where our father remains under the watch of one doctor, our aunt and cousin. He could use a break anyway. I know he feels like shit knowing that because of his order, he can't exactly do what the rest of us can regarding the Pack Regimes.

Enzo's eyes darken, and he doesn't move right away. "If it includes killing our father—"

"You'd be the first one in line. Promise." I scratch my fingers through his hair, ruffling the strands. He's not the only one who can scent shit around here, and he'll regret messing with me when all Kinsey can smell is my fragrance over his.

He swats me. "Thanks, big brother. I know how much you have struggled with being first in line. I hope you know that allowing me the pleasure will be even sweeter, because my betrayal runs deeper. He never expected this from me. I can't wait to fucking see him be put to rest."

Damn. Enzo has a darker side than I realized. I knew he was good about closing himself off when it came to doing what we had to do to control our enemies, but this is a bit more unexpected. It has to do with Kinsey and the fact that we all know her heat is coming. It makes us all a bit more aggressive. But it will be worse for him. He's far more possessive because of where he lands in our pack. He feels he must prove himself because he's younger.

I just hope he doesn't mess things up.

"I'll tell Kinsey that you asked me to fuck her on your behalf. She'll be so exhausted that you'll just get to cuddle the hell out of her. It'll serve you right for screwing her on my bed." Enzo grins with his words, probably thinking of a million ways to get back at me.

"Whatever makes you feel better. Now hustle your ass. I want everything handled by tonight." I shove him playfully, making him swing at me. I duck, and he misses only to have me shove him again.

Instead of trying to retaliate, Enzo laughs and jogs away, beating me to the door. I act as if I'm going to sit at my desk to handle mundane paperwork until I hear him head upstairs.

I should feel bad about keeping this visit to our father a secret, but I want to save my brothers the pain of having to face him over and over again. He was supposed to love us. He was supposed to help us grow and turn us into respectable men instead of trying to break us at his will to turn us just like him. And for that, I want him to know he will pay. He will suffer until his last breath.

Pulling out my phone, I tap on Arsenio's name and shoot him a text.

*Me: I'm heading to the medical center now. Why don't you meet up with Enzo and Desmond and take Kinsey out for a bit?*

*Arsenio: You sure? I can stay and help you.*

*Me: I'm good, brother. I want you to take the day off. Enjoy our success. You know I'm too high-strung for that shit.*

*Arsenio: We're going to have to work on that.*

*Me: Tomorrow. Take our girl shopping. Let her get everything she wants.*

*Arsenio: Got it. Don't stress out. We have your back.*

*Me: I know.*

I tuck my phone away and bring up all the paperwork that transfers power from my father to me. The Pack Regimes of Saint Vista approved the transition, and it's official. I'm now the leader of Gilded Sands.

Platinum Shores will be next.

I quickly send Calico Proper an email with my claim to the territory and abandon my computer, hoping I don't have to deal with any more of this bullshit for a few days. It's expected for our pack to close down our territory while we get everything together.

I stare around my office, realizing that I'm procrastinating. It's unlike me to not stay on top of things, but I also can't stand the thought of facing Winston again. But I don't want Arsenio to know. I need to be strong for all of us. He doesn't need that sort of burden.

Gathering my nerves, I stride from the study and head downstairs to where we've set up a medical wing to prevent having to transport our father and risk him coming up with some sort of plan to retaliate. He'll be cut off from all communications and a prisoner in our palace until the announcement. We'll ensure he knows what it's like to be less than. I want him to regret all his life choices. To regret ever thinking that Holly, and Kinsey, for that matter, are just possessions to be sold or traded.

My anger clouds my vision, and I stop outside of the door, wondering how I even made it here. It's as if my body acted instinctually, bringing me to where I needed to go while allowing me to lose myself in my thoughts.

Soft voices trickle through the door. I hesitate for only a moment before turning the knob and cracking the door open. Aunt Melina and Jude look up at me. Aunt Melina stands by the head of Winston's bed, leaning over and petting his hair. Jude stands in the corner, looking at his phone. He offers me a waning smile, his eyes duller than I'm used to. It probably has to do with the attack. He's going to grow up real fast the next few months while we adjust.

"Why don't you two take a break?" I leave the door open behind me, nodding my head and its direction.

Jude glances at Aunt Melina. "That's a good idea, Mama. How about we get something to eat?"

Aunt Melina doesn't respond right away, looking into Winston's eyes for a long moment. He doesn't acknowledge my existence, but I know he's aware. He's purposely ignoring me.

Jude gives up on trying to get his mom to go and closes the space to me. Leaning in, he whispers, "I didn't have the heart to tell her the truth."

I sigh and pat him on the back. "I'll have a talk with her later."

Jude leaves without another word, respecting me as his new leader. He trusts that I'll handle the situation. While Aunt Melina is his mother, it's my duty to inform our entire pack of the circumstances.

I shuffle forward, keeping my head held high. My father tries to intimidate me, even lying down, his sudden scowl stabbing into me as if his eyes can shoot knives.

I drape my arm over Aunt Melina's shoulders. "I know you're worried about Winston, but he's going to be fine. Why don't you go pick out a dress for the coronation ceremony? I would love it if you stood in place of my mother."

Tears fill Aunt Melina's eyes. "What? Are you sure, Wilder?"

I lean down and rest my head against her temple. "Absolutely. My omega might need some direction as well."

A guttural groan sounds from my father, drawing my attention to him. I whip my gaze in his direction, meeting his glower with my own.

Aunt Melina misses or purposely ignores our silent confrontation, because she leans forward and touches Winston's cheek. In any other moment, the action would be one of compassion. But right now, Winston considers it an act of power because of his current status.

He snatches her wrist and squeezes them tightly. "I command you to call my army. My treacherous sons have been cut off from our pack. They're taking advantage of my current state. If you don't, you will face the consequences."

Aunt Melina screams out, trying to yank her hand away. Winston tightens his hold, and I'm afraid he'll break her wrist.

I pull out my knife and point it at him. "Release her. You're in distress and confused, father."

"Blasphemy!" He ignores my blade and twists.

So, I swipe my dagger along his arm, cutting him enough to get him to release my aunt.

Anger rushes over me, and I grab the front of Winston's hospital gown and yank him, growling in his face, baring my teeth. He jerks his head forward, smashing his forehead to mine. Stars pepper my vision, but I don't let go. I lose myself to my rage, placing my fingers around his throat. I squeeze as hard as I can, wanting nothing more than to show him who the true alpha is. I desperately need to force him into submission.

"Wilder, stop! You're killing him!" Aunt Melina grabs my arms, trying to overpower me.

I ignore her and don't stop.

I need to do more than put my father in his place.

I need to kill him.

I will kill him.

I stare into his eyes as his face turns red and his body slumps back. I've never wanted so badly in my life to watch someone die.

Who knew this would be so satisfying?

Revenge is sweet, but justice is sweeter.

King Winston will never hold power again.

58

# Chapter Five

## *Desmond*

## Alpha Control

I swear I can't leave my brothers alone for even a fucking couple of minutes before they let their oncoming rut get to them. I don't even think they realize it yet. Kinsey grows closer and closer to her heat, and it really messes with my brothers.

I'm glad that I didn't go with the others on their trip to the city, because Wilder will kill our father if I don't stop him.

A part of me wants to let him.

Actually, all of me wants to just cheer him on.

"Wilder, stop! Stop!" Glass shatters, and my aunt screams.

Jude rushes down the hallway leading from the kitchen, seeking out the glass shattering sounds and his mother's screams. My stomach twists. Wilder would never hurt our aunt, but the blood-curdling pitch of her voice tightens my chest. Jude beats me to the door and throws it open. Blood is spattered across the floor and wall, marring the pristine white of the medical room. Aunt Melina cowers in the corner, behind the hospital bed, covering her eyes with her hands. Wilder shifts on the floor with a groan. Pieces of a vase scattered around him, the gash on his head pouring blood down his neck. Shit. Shit. Shit. What the fuck?

"Goddamn it! What happened?" I ask, nearly slipping on the bloody floor.

"Your brother was trying to kill me!" King Winston clutches a blade, throwing it at Wilder hard enough to sink it into his arm.

I lunge forward, tackling Wilder. "Check the fucker for any other weapons!" I shout to Jude. The bastard took Wilder's knife. He's obviously feeling fucking better.

Wilder thrashes beneath me, fighting against my hold. Jude joins me, and together we drag him out of the room to put space between him and our father. Aunt Melina follows us, shutting the door and resting her back to it. Two of my teenage cousins peek from the staircase landing, concern lining their faces.

I manage to pin Wilder with my hand to his throat. "You're scaring the kids. Knock this shit off now."

Wilder stops struggling and glares at me. Just when I think he's about to submit, he breaks his hold and punches me in the face, knocking me off him. He flips onto me and shoves his palms to my chest.

"Don't you ever fucking try to dominate me in front of our pack again." Wilder leans in, his eyes dark with his anger. "I'm your alpha."

His words shock a wave of anger inside me. I knew it. I fucking knew it. My brothers told me time and time again that I'm their equal, but this proves that I'm not. I will always be a beta and beneath them in their eyes.

"Screw you, Wilder!" I sucker punch him in the throat, knocking him off me. I grind my teeth and push to my feet. "We were supposed to be in this together. We were equals. But obviously, you can't stand the idea of someone else taking control when you are clearly incapable of it. If I didn't know any better, I'd think that Father was commanding you. Now go fuck yourself."

I flick my gaze to Aunt Melina and Jude, but I don't say anything to them. Aunt Melina doesn't look injured, only scared. And despite our father's attack, he's not going anywhere. He can barely get out of bed. He just needs to be alone.

"Desmond, wait. Wait, I'm sorry." Wilder struggles to get to his feet, his voice hoarse and his eyes shifting as if he might be dizzy. And maybe he is after getting clocked over the head with a vase.

I know if I stay, I'll continue to push him. I'm just so over today. I need time alone. I want him to really think about everything he did and said. I'm not going to just forgive him and shrug it off this time. I have too much to lose. I'll not allow the others to dominate Kinsey because they feel they are more deserving because they can knot with her. I can give her everything she needs too.

"Desmond! Come on, man. Let's talk." Wilder groans but doesn't chase me. I don't think he can.

I don't look at him. I don't respond.

I walk away.

"You look absolutely stunning in that dress, pretty girl." I stroll a few feet to Kinsey and slide my arms around her waist. "I'm almost afraid to let the world see you. They'll all get weak in the knees."

Kinsey shifts and turns around, cupping my face with her hands. "It'll just make it easier for them to bow before you, my soon-to-be king. They'll know I'm yours."

I get hard at just the thought. Kinsey knows something went down between Wilder and me, but neither of us wanted her to know to what extent. I'm still not ready to talk to him. I just want to bask in the love of the most perfect omega I've ever laid eyes on. The most perfect woman I have been blessed to be loved by.

"Damn straight. No one will tell us otherwise. I don't care if I can't bond with you like my brothers. You're still mine." I don't intend to say the words out loud, but my mouth betrays me. I just can't help it. My emotions are all over the place. I'm usually better at concealing them, but Wilder really got to me.

"Oh, Desmond. You fulfill me in ways they can't. You know that, right? You're exactly who I need you to be. Just because you aren't an alpha doesn't mean anything. And to be honest, I might enjoy being knotted by them, but I fucking love that we don't. It's more freeing. We can do whatever the hell we want. And when my heat comes..." Kinsey presses her lips together, a strange look crossing her face. Her sweet scent permeates the air with her emotions, and for the first time, I realize that she's nervous about the idea. Giggling, she kisses me again, distracting herself and trying to brush off her comment. "Never mind."

I ease away and tilt my head to the side, capturing her gaze. "Come on, Kinsey. What's up? I can tell something suddenly bothers you."

She closes her eyes, breaking my gaze as she tries to hide whatever is going through her mind. I don't want to push her, but if there's something I can do or say that will bring back the heat of her passion and snuff out her concerns, then I would do anything.

"It's nothing. Just nerves. It's been a very long time since I've had to physically go through a heat. I've only had to once before, and...you know." She lifts and drops her shoulders.

My heart sinks into my stomach, knowing exactly what she's talking about. Because Kinsey was to bond with another pack. She was tortured during her heat, and her uncle ruined what was supposed to be an amazing moment in her life.

I scoop her up and hug her close to me, kissing her jaw and down her throat, snuggling my face to the crook of her neck until she laughs.

"I wish I knew exactly what to say to you to help, but I can't even fathom being in your position. I hope you know that we'll take care of you. You'll never go through anything so horrendous ever again. I'll slaughter anyone who tries." It's in a moment like this that I wish I was an alpha. She would react to my pheromones, knowing the truth to my words. I need to make sure my brothers know her feelings. They're obsessed with the idea. They want nothing more than to knock her up and grow our pack.

They need to know that it's more than that.

"I know." Kinsey squeezes me tighter, engulfing me with her entire body. "Like I said, it's just my nerves. It doesn't help that I don't know exactly when to expect it. The suppressant pills really fucked with my body. It could be longer and more intense. I'm afraid how it's going to mess with your brothers as well."

"They're already showing signs of rutting. Wilder—" I snap my mouth shut, not wanting to get into it. I don't want to start anything, because I know that Kinsey will confront him. He's already stressed out enough. I don't want to ruin anything between them because of my feelings. Kinsey needs a strong alpha like Wilder, even if it means him controlling everything. "Wilder is getting aggressive toward others. It's something he's going to have to work on."

Kinsey's brows pinch together, and she studies me, a dozen questions crossing her beautiful face. We talk about anything and everything, but I don't want to ruin this moment. I want to enjoy getting a first look at what she's going to look like for her announcement as the omega bride of our pack.

Taking a step back, I lace my fingers through hers and spin her around, watching as the flowy hem of her dress sweeps the floor. "But let's not talk about him anymore. I just can't get enough of you. This dress is incredible. It makes me want to rip it off as if you're a gorgeous present I can unwrap."

Kinsey's face flushes, her cheeks reddening with her appreciation. I spin her again, twirling her toward me until I dip her backward. She shrieks with my dance moves, and I grin, bringing her back up only to place my hand on her lower back to pull her in close, holding her hand up while our bodies sway together. She lets me lead, following my steps effortlessly without looking down, her eyes staying trained on mine. I don't think I've ever danced with someone that felt like the perfect mirror image of my body. Our pelvises rest together, and I spin her around again, wishing I didn't have to stop to turn on music. Because that would be what makes this moment absolutely perfect.

"I had no idea you were such an incredible dancer, Desmond. What else are you keeping from me?" Kinsey rests her hand on my shoulder, slowly mapping her way to my pec.

"Nothing in particular. I just don't want to give away everything at once. Seeing the look on your face in this moment... I had no idea I could continue to fall so madly in love with you. I hope you know that. You're the one person I want my life to revolve around. You're everything I need to feel as if I'm worthy and complete." I slow down, swaying to the imaginary beat in my head. "But I also love that I don't have to be all-powerful for you to love me."

Kinsey smirks, her full lips so kissable. "You know, you make me feel powerful. I love that you give me my way too."

"Because you deserve to feel powerful. I know my brothers struggle because they don't want you to have to be powerful. They don't see things the way we do. If you want to dominate me, I'll let you. It's rather thrilling." My cock hardens at the thought, and I lean in and press my mouth to hers, my desire getting the best of me as I imagine everything she'd do if she were my alpha. Who would have thought I'd be so turned on by it?

Kinsey shivers, drawing her fingers lower and lower down my torso until she grazes my hard-on, sending pleasure crashing over me. "Desmond... You love the idea, don't you?"

I hum under my breath. "Absolutely. My pleasure is yours."

We stare at each other for a long moment, just studying our expressions as Kinsey's hearty fragrance permeates the air. I want to know what little dirty thoughts cross her mind and if we're really on the same page. I lick my lips and lean in, pressing my mouth to her ear, inhaling a breath of her skin.

"If you guys are naked, you better make some room for me." Enzo thrusts the door open without knocking, barging into the shared space that we have given to Kinsey, so she feels as if she has things of her own and not only things she has to share with us.

"No such luck, man. You were a few seconds too early." I spin Kinsey around, playing keep away with my brother, using my body to shield her. "But I can change that. Me first, though."

"Don't even start." Holly pops in from the hallway, a smile lighting her face. "I've made appointments for Kinsey and me.

Our hair, nails, makeup, a massage—everything. She's going to be mine until the coronation. Got it?"

Enzo narrows his eyes, play-growling. "Look at you, Ms. Alpha. If I didn't know any better, I'd think you'd been lying about your order."

I groan and shake my head. "Let's fucking hope not. I can't be the only one who isn't an alpha." I laugh it off, trying to keep myself composed even though Holly and Enzo both give me a look, their obvious concern as palpable as Kinsey's.

"It isn't as awesome as you imagine. But I get it, brother. You get to avoid all this pre-coronation crap by watching over our pack. I'll be knocking some sense into Wilder. He made me a promise and nearly broke it with his bullshit attempt at murdering Father." Enzo tightens his jaw, lowering his voice.

I shove him, pushing him toward the door. "Exactly. Get to work, little brother. This will be my only chance to have something you don't."

He raises his hands as he exits Kinsey's room, and I slam the door in his face, making him laugh. I know he could overpower me and challenge me, but thankfully he doesn't. I don't know if I could take it right now. I know it's juvenile of me, but goddamn it. Why is it bothering me so much?

I sense both Holly and Kinsey staring at the back of my head. I scratch my fingers across my neck and turn slightly to face them.

Kinsey closes the space first and engulfs me in a hug before Holly joins her, sandwiching me between them.

"This has to be so fucking hard on you, Des. Everything has been a lot lately. I wish that none of this order bullshit mattered for us. I'll never understand the difficulty of being anything other than an omega." Holly squeezes my shoulders.

"She's right, Desmond. That's why we have to take advantage right now. And don't worry. They're not going to control everything. We're doing it as a pack, remember? Even me."

"As long as they keep their word." I keep my voice low, not wanting to upset Kinsey. I know it's all in my head. I know it's because of the circumstances and all the bullshit. But I can't help it. Kinsey makes it so easy to talk. So does Holly. We've always had a very communicative relationship being the outcasts of our immediate family since neither of us manifested into the alpha order.

"They will," Kinsey insists, snuggling close to me again. "Me and you can team up and show them just how dominating we can really be otherwise."

"You guys can also just fuck all over the palace and make it known. Sneak into their spaces. Remind them." Holly giggles at the thought. "But after I leave. Which is another thing I wanted to talk to you about. I want to ask you for a favor, Desmond. I need you to mediate the conversation. With the threat of our father over and me not having to stress out about someone picking me out a pack, I'd really like to experience what it's like to live on my own."

I blink my eyes in surprise, shifting to drape my arm over Kinsey's shoulders while I face Holly. "You want to move out?"

She nods her head, her face expressionless. "I want to live as a beta for a while. Under the radar and out of the Pack Regimes' sights. You guys can make that happen now. I was talking to the Silverstein Pack, and they have an apartment not far from them that I can take. I'll still be close, but I can have something of my own for a while."

"I think that's a fantastic idea," Kinsey says, rubbing her hand over my side.

A part of me wants nothing more than to deny my little sister and protect her from the world. But another part of me knows that she deserves a life of her own. She deserves to find her own path.

I reach out and scrub my hand over her pale blond hair. "I'll do whatever you need, Holly. I just can't believe you're growing up."

She reaches up and pats my cheek. "I've been grown-up for a while, Des. I just need to figure out everything else now."

I hug her and Kinsey against me, feeling the lightness of Holly's happiness, but I don't automatically turn her down. But I get it. I feel it deep in my bones. It's in this moment that I realize maybe I also need a little bit of space from my brothers.

I really need to think about things and my place within our pack.

"I think we all feel the same, Holly. Things are about to change, and for the first time, we don't have to answer to King Winston." I guide them both toward the door.

"I just can't wait until we don't have to deal with him at all." Holly glances at me, a sorrow in her eyes that I'm not sure will ever disappear.

"Soon. I promise." A promise me and my brothers will keep. This territory in the world is ours.

# Chapter Six

## *Kinsey*

## The Coronation

Everything in Saint Vista always happens so fast. When a leader renounces reign or is killed, a replacement must step up quickly. Not only because it'll weaken the territory and leave our people open for attacks, but it could also cause unrest within the reigning pack.

I stand on the balcony, staring over the grand ballroom of the Gilded Sands Fortress. My guys will use Winston's place for all of their formal appearances, ensuring that no one outside of our pack enters our palace.

I thought our home was massive, but it can't even compare to Winston's. The ballroom is several thousand square feet alone, with a wooden dance floor, a stage for a band on one side and a platform with a podium on the other. Long tables with floor-length tablecloths, huge bouquets of mixed flowers like chrysanthemums, roses, and different white florals decorate them as centerpieces along with mirrored glass and twinkling string lights.

It's almost magical. Elegant and formal. Fitting for royalty. And as I stand in my flowing, lace and crystal bead-studded gown in the same shade as Enzo's sapphire eyes, I feel as if I'm queen already. While I'll be announced as their omega, I won't actually be able to receive a formal title from the Pack Regimes until I give them an heir.

My heart races at the thought. This is happening. This is really happening. I get to bond with the men of my dreams. My perfect alphas and beta. My knights in bulletproof armor.

But why do I grow more nervous by the second? I both love and freak out at the idea of my impending heat. My body has begun to change already, and things grow more fragrant. Desire constantly clings to me, and it takes everything in me not to plead for sex. For pleasure and bliss.

Desmond slides his arm around my waist, pulling me in close. We stay out of reach from the top packs from Saint Vista and the bordering regions. They'll never get close to me. My guys want to make an example of how an omega should be cherished and loved. Protected and treated as the most special beings in the world. This is our chance to make a difference. I wish my parents were here to see this. I wish no one, including my former intended pack, had ever been sacrificed for me to get to this point in my life.

Soft music trickles through the air, and I step closer to the railing and clutch it, watching as Wilder steps from the crowd and onto the podium, his tuxedo hugging his body in just the right way, defining his muscular biceps. He looks incredibly sexy with his hair styled and his eyes shining with his own excitement. I can only imagine how incredible this feels for him, finally reaping the benefits of all of his and his brothers' hard work.

Arsenio and Enzo remain guarded, each of them standing watch on both sides of the stage. Everyone in the crowd hovers around and bows slightly, acknowledging his presence as a new leader within the Saint Vista Pack Regimes.

"It is a great honor to stand here today, accepting the crown and the authoritative position of Gilded Sands." Wilder straightens his shoulders. "Even though the circumstances were not ideal, my pack has felt ready to grow and adjust for a bright future. If you are standing here before me, please know that we highly respect you on many levels, from leadership to allies. Those of you among us are some of our most trusted, and we're ready to announce the change in our hierarchy. I might be taking the crown today, but from this moment forward, I will be sharing it with my brothers. We find great benefit in coming together with our different ideals, desires, and expectations for our people. We want to progress our territory and move away from the outdated, oppressive ruling, which my father laid forth. It is with great pleasure that I also announce Saint Vista's very first leading beta. We have decided that the man worthy of taking control of our brand-new territory and the Platinum Shores Pack should belong to Desmond of Gilded Sands." Wilder turns his attention to the balcony, and Desmond freezes beside me, his muscles stiffening.

I had no idea Wilder and his brothers had planned this. And from the look on Desmond's face, he had no idea either.

The crowd murmurs before clapping, remaining respectful though it looks as if some of the alphas might disagree with Wilder's announcement.

I squeeze Desmond's hand and smile, giving him a little shake to help put some sense back into him. A dozen emotions cross his features before he composes himself and offers Wilder a slow nod. From our spot, only his brothers can see us, but now we must join them on the stage.

"Please rise as my brother takes the new crown of our growing kingdom." Wilder motions to his cousin, who brings out several ornate crowns and a tiara.

Desmond guides me toward the velvet curtain of the balcony and the expansive staircase. I stop him before we can come into view and turn to face him. I cup his cheeks with my hands and stretch up, kissing him softly.

"This is incredible. I'm so happy," I say.

Desmond doesn't respond, but he does kiss me back. I want so desperately for him to tell me what's on his mind. To help me decipher his scent, covered by a masculine cologne.

We reach the top of the grand staircase, every other step blooming with bouquets of white and lavender flowers along the railing, and Desmond pauses. He adjusts his tuxedo jacket, taking a moment to drink everything in.

"Is this real?" he murmurs, clearing his throat. "This can't be, can it?"

I love that Desmond's brothers wanted to surprise him with such a monumental gift, especially because he's always struggling with his order, and this means that they truly believe he is worthy of being a leader. On the other hand, I can tell that Desmond has been thrown off. He's conflicted over something and making such an announcement in front of all of our people and allies might not have been the best idea.

I squeeze his hand. "It's definitely real. Now take a deep breath and show everyone how amazing you are. My handsome, powerful, smart, and incredibly sexy king. I believe in you. I can't wait to celebrate in private. Just you and me."

He puffs out a breath and guides me down the stairs, studying me to ensure I don't trip on my high heels peeking out from my ballgown. Heat crawls up my chest and neck, and I turn my eyes toward the floor, afraid that I might accidentally catch the gaze of someone in the crowd.

The crowd remains standing, shiny dress shoes and a couple pairs of glittering heels the only thing I can see from my down-turned attention. Soft applause continues until we reach the podium, and Wilder's strong vetiver and forest scent engulfs my senses, calming my racing heart.

Extending his arm, Wilder coaxes me to leave Desmond's side. I stroll forward tentatively, a part of me wanting to remain firmly by Desmond's side while another part of me wants to fall into Wilder. But I can't deny our king. He's the leader of the Gilded Sands Pack until he signs the formal announcement. If I deny Wilder, it would be seen as rejection. Desmond kisses my temple, showing me that he understands. I can read them unlike anyone else can, knowing what to do by their scent alone.

I curtsey and allow Wilder to spin me into his arms, where he dips me backward, kissing me passionately, nearly erotically, in front of everyone. This is his proof of claim on me. This is proof that I am officially the Gilded Sands' omega.

He snuggles his face to the crook of my neck as he brings me back up, enveloping me in a hug. It's as if he will only allow the crowd to glimpse quick peeks of me by blocking their view with his muscular body. And I don't mind it. I don't want their focus.

Desmond clears his throat, adjusting the microphone. "It's always like you to shift attention away from yourself, brother."

Wilder chuckles, the gravelly sensation rumbling against my cheek. "And it is always like you to steal it. So, this works out, doesn't it?"

Desmond smiles, his handsome face lighting up. "It's quite the honor to be named as the king and leader of Platinum Shores." His voice rises as it bellows through the speakers, his confidence radiating from him. "But you won't get rid of me quite so easily. Our alliance will merge these two kingdoms into the force our people need. That is my promise. I will rule with the guidance and power of my entire pack."

Soft applause hums through the air, the murmurs growing louder. The crowd doesn't know how to truly react apart from being cordial. We won't hear anything until after the ball. At this point, I think we'll take what we can get. Right now, I want to celebrate. My pack deserves this—a night of fun without the looming threat of their father or rivals hanging over them.

"And speaking of my pack, I'd like to welcome my brothers and trusted advisors to the stage along with His Majesty and former King, Winston, to announce our engagement to our omega and future queen." Desmond nods in my direction. "Our beautiful, perfect Kinsey of Gilded Sands." It doesn't go unnoticed that he declares me a part of the territory instead of giving recognition to my birth pack and territory.

Wilder doesn't give me a chance to think about it before he lifts me off my feet and carries me to the podium. Enzo and Desmond meet me with a kiss from each of them, and the applause from the crowd heightens in volume.

"Keep your gaze on me, Kinsey," Wilder whispers, touching my cheek. "I don't want you giving the fucker even a second glance, okay? This is all for show. To prove the king is alive and able to pass on his reign."

I swallow, my nerves twisting my stomach. I never planned to see King Winston again. He should be locked in the dungeon where he belongs and not out and about, within reach of several of his allies.

With my thoughts, I break my gaze away from Wilder and peek around him, spotting King Winston in a wheelchair with Arsenio pushing him. Hunched forward and pale-faced, he looks like he's on his deathbed. It somehow makes me feel a bit better. I hope he regrets all his life choices. Knowing him, he probably only regrets failing. The fucker.

Wilder laces his fingers through my hair, gripping close to my scalp to turn my head back to him. The subtle gesture sends a shiver through me, his pheromones getting to me in the best way. It triggers my omega nature, and instead of fighting against it, I give in.

"I told you not to look at him, my brat. You're lucky I can't spank you for disobeying." His voice rumbles with his deep voice, and he leans in and crashes his mouth to mine, lifting me up and carrying me toward the edge of the stage.

"I think this is enough of a show. Let's fucking party and celebrate our new reign. Expect invitations to our ceremony to bond with Kinsey. She deserves the world and not some half-assed declaration here!" Enzo's voice roars through the speakers, booming through the room.

I break away from Wilder and watch as he strides toward Arsenio and grabs the wheelchair. Our eyes meet, and he winks at me, pushing Winston out of the spotlight.

Wilder tries to steal my attention again, but I can't keep my eyes off the king. Enzo leans into him and whispers something. The king whips his head up and grabs onto Enzo's waist. He grabs a gun so fast that Enzo doesn't have a chance to take it back. But he doesn't even try.

The gunfire pops through the air, ringing in my ears, and the crowd scatters as Winston aims the gun again at Enzo. His shaking hand makes it impossible to get a good shot, and Enzo dodges around him.

"You're dead! You're all dead!" Winston pulls the trigger again, sending a bullet in the direction of the crowd. People scream, and Wilder spins around protectively, using his body as a shield.

I cling to him, my heart racing. I don't understand. I know that my guys are now on high alert. The king should've never gotten Enzo's gun. It's almost as if he allowed it.

"I'm going to beat the shit out of him," Wilder mutters, his fingers digging into my ass. "He's in so much trouble."

I was right. This wasn't accidental.

I wiggle in Wilder's arms, peeking over his shoulder as Enzo grabs onto the back of Winston's wheelchair and yanks it over, sending him sprawling to the floor. The gun falls from his hand and clatters on the floor.

Snatching it up, Enzo snarls. "Traitor!" Enzo yells, aiming his gun at Winston. "You're guilty of treason, trying to murder our best ally. I order the death sentence. Do you agree, brothers?"

I open and close my mouth, shock cooling my blood.

"As the leaders of our pack and within our territory in Saint Vista, we call upon our closest allies to take a vote." Arsenio adjusts his jacket and strides closer to Enzo.

"I vote yes. He's no longer fit for any further decision-making. He has brought nothing but turmoil to our territory. His actions speak volumes today. It is in his duty to pass on the reign of power to those capable when he is not." This comes from Beckett, the alpha and leader of the Silverstein Pack. I hadn't even realized he was here. "Who is with me?"

The crowd roars with their agreement, and I realize how hated Winston truly is. All of this was just for show. And Enzo took advantage to get his revenge. To get revenge for all of us and to make a point.

"Close your eyes, Kinsey. This wasn't supposed to happen with you here. Close your eyes." Wilder shifts one of his hands to cover my ear, but I can't look away.

I need to see this. I need to see the outcome.

"You heard them, you fucking bastard. You're sentenced to death by my hand. May you burn in Hell." Enzo doesn't hesitate as he pulls the trigger and shoots his father in the head.

I startle and jerk in Wilder's arms, but I still watch. I need to make sure the king is truly dead and out of my life. This solidifies everything. My pack mates are officially the rulers of this territory.

Gilded Sands and Platinum Shores are ours.

I can finally breathe easily. We can move on with our lives and have the future we want.

Silence fills the ballroom. Enzo swivels toward the crowd and gives a sharp nod.

Instead of turning into a somber occasion, everyone cheers. This is a celebration, after all. We're celebrating a new order. A new kingdom.

Who knew that death could bring such happiness?

Such a relief.

"Kinsey, are you okay?" Wilder asks, adjusting me in his arms until he can look in my eyes.

I slowly nod my head as everything fully sinks in. "I'm better than okay. I'm perfect. Please carry me to your brothers. I want this moment to be all of ours."

Wilder relaxes, his muscles loosening. "You truly are the strongest woman I know. I'm sorry that the world had to be so shitty to bring us to this point."

"I would do it all again as long as it ended with you, Wilder. You and your brothers. I will survive everything just for our future. I want you to know that. You're my king and my alpha. You're mine, now and forever." I kiss him softly as the world stirs around us.

Wilder smiles against my mouth. "And you are ours. Always."

# Chapter Seven
## *Kinsey*

## Change the World

"Are you sure you don't want to see him for yourself, lil sis?" Arsenio stands in the doorway to Holly's room, where we lay together, watching TV. We didn't stay long at the Gilded Sands Fortress, leaving Wilder and the others behind. According to Arsenio, coronation celebrations sometimes last a couple of days. Once my adrenaline wore off, I was ready to go home. I've been hanging out with Holly ever since, giving Arsenio a chance to do whatever his brothers needed from here.

"The formal announcement was enough. I never want to give him another ounce of my brain space. Good riddance.

I'm just glad he's never going to try to hurt me again." Holly rests her head on my shoulder, keeping her eyes trained on her fingers, twisted and linked together.

"Good fucking riddance," I add, squeezing her.

"We'll punish and slaughter anyone who ever tries to hurt you two. Enzo sentencing Winston to death helped to kick off our rise in power on a note no one will challenge. For once, Enzo's rash behavior benefited us. I know Wilder is nervous about everything, but I believe it's for the best." Arsenio steps forward and meanders toward me as if he resists running to scoop me up. It's hard for all of us to be apart, even when I'm just spending time with Holly. I blame my upcoming heat, but it could be everything else as well. Right now, space is Arsenio's enemy, and it's the one thing we struggle to defeat because something always comes up. Life problems.

"So, what now? Are things going to change a lot? I know we need to start planning for your bonding ceremony with Kinsey, and I'm sure you guys will be making babies soon. I need to prepare myself as well." Holly squeezes my knee, summoning strength from my closeness. We've talked about this before, but she is only now slowly bringing it up to her brothers. She's ready to start a life of her own outside of their shadow and away from everything that comes with the Gilded Sands Pack's name.

"We'll need to work out the logistics of our new reign and announce the formation of our council, but apart from that... You two should get to enjoy everything our kingdom has to offer. No more hiding. We want you to be able to go out and not have to worry about someone retaliating or fucking with you. While it's a bit difficult, considering our status, we'll make it work." Arsenio perches on the edge of the bed, resting his body against mine as he reaches out and places his hand on top of Holly's. "Once we get everything in order, then we'll have a pack meeting. Wilder's declaration of Desmond being the leader of Platinum Shores kind of threw things off a bit."

His voice deepens with his comment, and I stare at the side of his face. Arsenio doesn't meet my gaze. It's now that I realize that he might be upset about Wilder's decision. As second oldest, he should've been up for the position of leading that territory and expanding their pack's power.

"Wait, Wilder did what? Oh shit. Are you okay, Arsenio?" Holly recognizes what I do and sits up straighter. I was so happy for Desmond that I didn't really think about what it meant for him or Enzo. Putting a beta in power without an alpha leader is unheard of.

Arsenio shrugs. "I'll get over it. I know why he did it, but he should've talked to us first."

"Why did he? I want to know that too." I lick my lips and tap my fingers to his cheek, getting him to look at me.

"You'll have to ask him, sugar. I don't really want to think about it right now. I just want to have some fun with you." Arsenio strokes his fingers across my arm, pushing my hair over my shoulder.

"There's no fun in our rooms. If you want us to have a great time, why don't you take us out? You know, I'm running low on suppressant pills. I don't want to stop taking them even though Dad is gone. I just want to act like a beta for a bit longer. At least, until you guys give in and let me go on a couple of dates. You know how much I like the Silverstein Pack." Holly bounces on her bed, her crush on the pack intensifying her scent. It's not as strong because I know she has recently taken a suppressant pill, but it's still noticeable to me. Everything is stronger right now. I wonder if maybe I should take one too.

Why would I think that? It's the nerves. It's been so long since my last heat. And that one was a fucking nightmare.

"So that's what the sudden need for freedom is about, huh? You know Wilder is going to be tough to persuade. But I want you to know, Holls, you have my blessing. If this is what you want, I think that the Silverstein Pack will treat you well. And they know we'll kill them if they don't." Arsenio remains even with his expression, proving that he's not even joking.

"I'm going to pretend that I didn't hear you threaten my possible future pack and relish in the fact that you'll get Wilder to see things my way. I love you, big brother. You've done so much for me, and I think it's time that you get to finally do stuff for yourself. For Kinsey. I don't want you constantly having to worry about me anymore. I know you don't think it, but I'm an adult. I'm ready to grow my own pack." Holly stretches her arms and hugs Arsenio, squishing me between them.

I laugh and squeal, feeling her excitement as if it's my own. I'm so happy for her. After everything we have both been through, we deserve better. We deserve to have the life we want with the men we love. Men that will treat us with care and respect.

It almost feels as if this is all a dream.

But thankfully, I won't be waking up.

Arsenio groans and pulls himself away. "Goddamn. I'll let Wilder know that we're going out for a bit. Call the Silverstein Pack. Let them know we're inviting them out for dinner and drinks."

Holly claps her hands and scrambles to get off the bed, rushing to grab her phone from her desk. "You are the best!"

Holly strolls toward her bathroom, lowering her voice for some privacy. I scoot across the bed and into Arsenio's lap, draping my arms around his neck, facing him. "You really are the best. Do you think the others will be okay if we go out without them? I don't want to cause any more issues if you guys have some disagreements. Maybe we can meet before-hand and discuss—"

Grasping my chin, Arsenio cuts off my words with a soft kiss, not letting me finish speaking my thoughts aloud. As much as I want to know what's on his mind, his interruption leaves me breathless, and I decide to drop it. "Or not. I guess it can wait for later. The Silversteins will be with us anyway."

Arsenio grins against my mouth. "That's right. It's my time with you, sugar. I plan to enjoy every second of it."

His words bring a smile to my face, and I kiss him again, feasting on the taste and sensation of his mouth against mine. I know that each of my guys needs time alone with me, and I've vowed to always give them what they need, even if it's something like this.

I press my palm to his chest, easing him away. His body throbs beneath me, and I slide my fingers down and caress his hard cock. "If you don't resist me now, I'll let you have your way with me, and it wouldn't be right to do such acts in Holly's bed."

"I draw the line there. I love you guys, and I want you to both have incredible sex all the time for eternity, but not in front of me or in my space. Ugh." Holly places her hands on her hips, her eyebrows raised as if she's ready to pounce on us to tear us apart.

"I suppose I deserve you being a cock-block, considering that I have always been a cock-fortress for you, keeping every damn person away." Arsenio stands, lifting me up with him. He spins me around and plops me on my feet. "Now for you, sugar. Let's get you changed. I want you in a dress for me." Humming, he leans in and adds, "Something easily accessible for me."

I smirk, my body prickling with oncoming desire. "Whatever you want."

"That's exactly what I want to hear." Arsenio turns me away and spanks my ass, getting me to shuffle toward Holly. He points at her. "You need to wear jeans, lil sis. Don't argue with me."

Holly glares at him and shakes her head. "I knew there was going to be a stipulation."

I grab her hands and tug her toward her wardrobe. "Don't worry. He didn't say anything about your shirt. I'll help you pick out something." I crane my neck and stick my tongue out at Arsenio. "Pick us up in thirty."

Arsenio doesn't argue and pulls out his phone. "Take a suppressant pill, Holly."

"Got it," Holly says.

I flick my fingers at him. "Just handle what you have to, so we can have some fun. We'll take care of ourselves right now. We got this. Now shoo."

Shaking his head with a smile, Arsenio leaves the room. Holly and I turn to each other and screech, jumping up and down as if we just found out we won the lottery or some shit. And maybe we have. We get a day out. We don't even have to really hide.

Who knew that normal would feel so extraordinary?

Arsenio is right. This is what we need. I plan to savor every second of it.

I shouldn't be nervous, but I am. It'll take me a long while to get used to the idea that I'm no longer in hiding or passing as a beta. I hope it gets easier, at least.

"What's wrong?" Holly asks quietly, leaning between the front seats as Arsenio strolls around the hood of his sedan to open the doors for us.

I shrug. "I kind of wish I had taken a suppressant pill too. I'm not sure I'm ready for this."

Holly hands me her purse and whispers, "Front pocket."

I startle at Arsenio swinging the door open and clutch onto Holly's bag. I laugh and smile at him without saying anything, allowing him to help me from the car. I adjust the little black dress Holly picked out for me, the bodice dipping into a deep V-cut, showing off my cleavage and lack of a bra. Arsenio will go nuts when he realizes I skipped the panties too.

Extending his hand to Holly, Arsenio helps her out, and I take the chance to pop one of the suppressant pills into my mouth, swallowing it dry. I clear my throat, regretting it immediately. Why did I just do that? Why did I have the sudden need to hide it, too?

"Thanks for the suppressant pill, Holly," I blurt, the unbidden guilt tightening my chest. I've been forced to hide the last few years that my fear triggered the reaction now. The last thing I want is to hide from Arsenio. If only I thought about it before actually doing it.

Scrunching his brows, Arsenio gives me a long look that speaks volumes. Confusion laces the fragrance of his dewy apple scent, warming it a bit. Is it anger? No. But I can't decipher exactly what he's feeling through his pheromones, considering how quickly the suppressant pills take effect, messing with me already.

"You took a pill, Kinsey?" Arsenio rubs his lips together, reaching up to touch my cheek. "What for?"

A dozen responses flit through my mind. What can I say? I'm not only nervous, but I've been thinking about other things more and more, especially when I start to feel out of control again, like with my rampant sexual desire. I know it's going to just get more intense until I'll need the relief only my alphas can provide. I try to suppress the memory of my last heat, but it comes back in full force, consuming me.

My wrists hurt for weeks from the restraints. I thought I'd die on the bedroom floor along with the men who were supposed to claim me as their omega. If I hadn't fought as hard as I did—

"Kinsey?" Arsenio shakes my shoulder, yanking me from my thoughts.

Whoa. I'm losing it. I hadn't realized I just checked out of reality to lose myself in my dark memories.

I puff out of breath between my lips and blink my eyes, trying to get myself together again. "I'm sorry. I took it because I'm nervous about everything...but mostly about being an omega." It might be ridiculous to reject my order, especially because that's the part of me that is adored and cherished by my guys, but I can't help it. I'm a bit fucked up. I thought I was more resilient than this.

"Arsenio, why don't you drop it for now? Just let us have our fun. It's okay for us to ignore our trauma and focus on other things if we want. You can't possibly think you can fix us with a short discussion about it with some heartfelt affirmations." Holly slides her arms around me from behind, hugging me. "Kinsey is strong enough. She has been passing as a beta for years and dealing with this. You don't need to coddle her."

A mixture of emotions crosses Arsenio's face, and the warm cinnamon spice of his flaring anger heats up his scent. He cracks his knuckles, composing himself instead of snapping.

I think if he were any of his brothers, he might have yelled at Holly. But right now, I'm glad he doesn't. Because Holly's right. I don't want to think about why I'm this way and how I just did something stupid without thinking or without considering how he'd feel about it.

"The fucking suppressant pill will wear off. Let her have that right now. It's not selfish for her to want to be in control of her own fucking body." Holly takes a step back and crosses her arms.

If Beckett didn't call her name, Arsenio might've actually exploded on her this time. I know he doesn't think I'm selfish. I'm the only one who does right now. Because I am. I did this for me.

I step forward and give Arsenio a small push back. "It's okay. I'm fine. I wasn't thinking when I popped it. I won't do it again."

Arsenio snatches me up, crashing his mouth to mine as if it's the only thing he can do to keep himself in control. From his nearly overwhelming scent, breaking through the rising suppression of hormones, I know he might be going into a rut soon because of me. If I'm not consistent with taking the pills or not, it might fuck with him and the others.

I rub my fingers over his neck and to his back, exploring his muscles and letting him kiss me deeper until he has to pull away to gasp for breath.

"I don't think you're selfish, Kinsey. I want you to know that. I just was thrown off. I hadn't realized you still felt the need to control your order with drugs. I won't lie. It bothers me." Arsenio eases away from my mouth, rubbing his fingers across my cheeks, scenting me. "I should've recognized it, and I didn't. That's what bothers me. You're nervous about going into heat because of what happened to you, and I realize now that it was my failure to assume I could make you just forget everything."

My eyes burn with tears. I hate that he feels like he's letting me down. It's not the case. "Arsenio, you do help me. It's not your fault that I'm fucked up. You do everything you can, and I really don't want you to blame yourself. I'm terrified of going into heat, but I know that it'll be better this time. I want it for you. I want to bond that way so badly. I...I don't know how to explain it. Can we just go inside? We're high on our emotions, and I think we could both use a drink and a good time."

Swallowing, Arsenio kisses me once more. "Whatever you want, sugar. We're going to work on this later. Whenever you're truly ready. We'll put a plan in place. You can control everything. We can even go into lockdown."

I smile and nuzzle my nose to his. "That might be a little extreme."

"Nothing is too much for my queen." Arsenio sets me on my feet and slides his fingers through mine. "You should expect only the best from now on."

My heart flutters, and my tense muscles finally relax. I embrace the moment and step in close to Arsenio, letting him wrap his arm around me protectively.

"You should have those kinds of standards too. I want you to have nothing but the best." I stroll with him, heading toward the grand building of a swanky restaurant with an exclusive club on top.

"I already do. I have everything I could ever want right here with you, Kinsey." Arsenio reaches into his pocket and pulls out a velvet box. "I was going to wait until we got inside, but I can't wait a second longer. I want you to know my promise is forever. You're my everything."

My eyes widen at the marquise-cut emerald stone, glittering with diamonds surrounding it. "Oh, Arsenio. It's beautiful. I love it."

Arsenio stands in front of me and slides it on my finger. "You're mine, Kinsey. My omega. My mate. And my queen. I know you've already agreed, but this is me formally asking for your hand in marriage. I want you to have the final say. Will you be my wife?"

A smile crosses my face, and I bob my head. Calling someone their wife far exceeds the union set before an omega. Because this is more than a pack planning out a future of power and an alliance by using omegas as property to be sold and traded. This is something that runs deeper. This is based on love. Pure love.

"Yes! Oh, God, yes." I jump back into his arms and kiss him.

This is a moment that I want to relive over and over again forever.

It's such a private and personal moment—but I want to shout out to the world.

And I plan to.

This is just the start of changing everything.

Our love will change the world.

# Chapter Eight

## *Kinsey*

## Dealer

Arsenio holds me on his lap, resting his hands on my stomach. His warm breath tickles my ear, and the two of us watch as Holly dances with Beckett's younger brother and the only member of his circle within his pack who is blood-related. Jordan was the first beta Holly had talked to when we first met the Silverstein Pack at the diner near Enzo's condo.

"I hope you realize that my little sister likes Jordan too." Arsenio rests his head on my shoulder as he speaks to Beckett across from us in the booth.

"What about me? Has she said anything?" One of the other betas, Wesley, speaks up from beside Beckett. From what Holly has mentioned, he's Beckett's best friend. They grew up together, and when Beckett took the Silverstein Pack's leader position as the strongest alpha after his father passed away, he made an alliance with Wesley and his fraternal twin Isaiah.

Watching the Silverstein Pack interact with Holly makes me more invested in her need to own her life. She deserves it after everything she's gone through. I never knew I'd love someone like a sister, and I'll put her brothers in their places if they try to deny her the ability to claim her own pack.

"No, man. Sorry." Arsenio shifts me slightly, his body hard under my ass, my closeness setting him off constantly.

Wesley frowns before he composes himself.

I place my hands on the table. "That's only because she would never talk to her brothers about you. But she tells me everything." I smile with my words, flicking my attention to Holly. She waves at me with a laugh as Jordan spins her around.

Wesley lightens up, his stern face softening. "Really?"

"Let's just say that I would love to tell you, but this guy right here doesn't want to ever hear about anything that's on Holly's mind." I wink at the broody beta and rest my head back on Arsenio.

Beckett howls a laugh and punches Wesley. "Told you." Turning to Arsenio, he meets his gaze. "I have no problem with

Holly liking my pack mates. I thought you knew that I wasn't like all the other fuckers of the Pack Regimes."

Arsenio shrugs, his protectiveness of Holly peeking through with every comment and gesture he does. He won't let his guard down despite their alliance because Holly means a lot to us and our pack. "Just making sure."

Arsenio's phone chimes, giving Beckett, Isaiah, and Wesley a chance to excuse themselves to join Holly and Jordan. I watch them all surround her, circling her in a wall of muscle she clearly enjoys, her smile widening as she twirls, sending her pale blond hair sweeping with her movements.

Arsenio groans and slides me off him and onto the seat. He pulls out his phone and glances at the screen. "It's Enzo."

I peek at the screen as he reads.

*Baby Brother: Wilder got in touch with the dealer again. He's sending someone your way with what Holly needs. Only she can complete the transaction. Donahue wants to establish a relationship since they're going to her and not us. It's the only way this will work. We've arranged an agreement that lets him continue to travel to Platinum Shores as long as he doesn't bring that shit into Gilded Sands.*

"He's fucking crazy," Arsenio says, tensing.

I snatch the phone from him before he can tell Enzo as much.

*Me: Kinsey will escort her since she knows how to handle the situation.*

I type as if I'm Arsenio.

*Baby Brother: Like hell you will, baby.*

Of course, he knows it's me. Arsenio would never just agree to send me with Holly to meet with a drug dealer.

*Me: So you're telling me that you want me to just standby and not help my sister since Arsenio can't? I don't think so. That's how this arrangement is going to work. I'll be fine. I took a suppressant pill like she did. We won't be setting off any dumbass alphas.*
*Baby Brother: You're in so much trouble.*

Snatching the phone from my hand, Arsenio steals it away to dial, and puts it up to his ear. He slides away from me, mumbling under his breath, trying to keep his conversation with Enzo a secret. I hear the words kill, Wilder, and dangerous but not much else. Arsenio hangs up the phone and turns his attention to me.

I hold my palm up to him, stopping him before he can even say anything. "The only way I'm not doing this is if you go all alpha on me and make me submit to you right here and now. This is something I've done dozens of times. I'm not backing down this time, Arsenio."

He flares his nostrils, resembling Wilder in this moment. If I didn't know any better, I'd think he was about to call me a brat. I know he's thinking it.

"I know you want to protect me, but you need to trust me to handle this. The dealer won't hurt an omega. They won't touch us because they know whose pack we belong to. They mostly don't want the confrontation with an alpha, especially when it comes to suppressant pills." I grasp Arsenio's hand, squeezing his fingers. "Now, do you know where they want to meet? It's an unspoken rule that we must be early. They'll want to scope things out to make sure this isn't a set up by the authority."

Arsenio growls, the rumble of his annoyance vibrating through me. "We are the authority."

I lift and drop my shoulders. "You can be nearby. Just keep out of sight. I'll handle this."

"You shouldn't have to handle anything." Arsenio's scent grows even warmer.

I'm sure it's taking everything in him not to completely deny me. I don't usually push back this hard, but I want to prove not only to him but also to myself that I'm strong enough. I don't know exactly what comes over me. I'm sure it has to do with the suppressants and the fact that my emotions are wild and that he's going to go into rut with my heat. All I know is that my mind is set. Should I feel bad that I have put him in this position? Maybe. Wilder would never allow me to get away with us. I think we both know it. Arsenio is determined to stay calm and collected. He always has been.

His phone chimes again with another message. I look at him expectantly, waiting for him to show me what Enzo said. I'm sure he's just as upset. This is something that Desmond should've handled with me, but it wasn't in the fates. I wouldn't give up this moment with Arsenio either. A little drug deal isn't going to ruin it. If anything, it'll solidify my desire to remain strong even in these uncertain circumstances.

Holding up his phone, he glances at the screen. "The dealer is five minutes away. They want you in the back alley. I don't like it. I think we should just wait for some other time. This is too abrupt. I haven't had a chance to study the area to guarantee your safety."

"They do it like this on purpose. You just have to trust that I can handle myself. I know how to act in front of other alphas. So does Holly. We'll be together." I stretch up and kiss him softly, feeling the tightness of his mouth as he resists giving into me. So, I don't stop until he can't. He groans against my mouth and brushes his lips to mine, igniting desire inside me. "If you can just give me this, I'll give you whatever you want later. I do want this night to be yours."

His groan turns into a purr, and he reaches between my legs and touches me gently, gliding his finger over the seam of my body, realizing I'm not wearing any panties. "God damn, sugar. You're going to set me off. It's taking everything in me not to pull you back onto my lap to fuck you right here."

I bite my lip and slide out of the booth, pulling away from his touch. "Like I said, let me handle this, and you can have whatever you want."

Arsenio doesn't remain in the booth, quickly following me to get to his feet. He's not going to let me get too far out of his reach. There's no way he's going to sit placidly by as I leave the building.

He grabs my waist and pulls me in close, guiding me through the crowd and toward Holly, surrounded by the Silverstein Pack, looking happier than I've ever seen her. I wish I didn't have to interrupt this moment.

Pulling away from Arsenio, I spin in front of him, sending my dress flowing. It's enough to catch Holly's attention, and she squeals and raises her arms, curling her fingers to get us to come closer to them. The Silversteins break apart, allowing me into their circle, with Arsenio joining them on the edge. I take Holly's hand and spin her, dancing with her for a minute.

I gather my nerve to tell her what's about to go down and lean into her ear. "Your brother set up a drug deal for the suppressant pills. You and I are meeting the dealer outside right now."

Holly slows down and pulls away, meeting my eyes. "Now, now?"

"They'll only deal with us." I rub my lips together, studying her face for a reaction.

She doesn't give much of one and just nods her head. "I guess I should get used to taking care of myself, huh?"

"With the way the Silversteins look at you, I'm going to guess it won't be for long. It'll be a good thing, though." I keep my words low and flick my gaze to Beckett, staring past me at Arsenio. "Now, come on. We have to go through the back."

Holly turns to the guys. "We'll be right back." I assume they know about the suppressant pills, but I don't know how aware they are of Holly's plan to continue taking them. I'm not going to get in the middle of that, because I have my own shit to deal with regarding the pills.

Arsenio grabs me by the shoulder, stopping me from moving away with Holly. He reaches into his jacket and pulls out a pocketknife, the small blade discrete in his hand. "I want you to be on guard. Don't hesitate to stab the asshole if they try anything. All you have to do is push right here, and the blade will flip out." Arsenio shows me, and I try it a couple times, feeling the Silversteins' gazes watching the two of us.

"What about me, big brother?" Holly wiggles her fingers. "I need some cash, right?"

Arsenio groans and digs into his pocket. "I fucking hate this," he mutters under his breath, handing Holly a wad of money. "I'm not going to give you a weapon because I know you can throw a decent punch. I'll be nearby. Remember to keep your space. Keep your discussion at a minimum. And just be fast. There's no need for small talk or any sort of conversation. Get as much as they have available."

Wow. I don't know why I'm so surprised. I've struggled so hard to make it month to month with the pills, and Holly can buy everything available. I wonder how my life would've turned out if I had that sort of luxury. Not that it matters. I wouldn't change anything up to this point.

"Got it. Now don't worry. Buying pills isn't even that bad. It's not like you don't have influence now. I'm sure other packs do the same." Holly offers a smile, keeping her voice light.

Except it's not true. Using this medication to illegally pass as a beta is a serious crime. It's enough that the Pack Regimes could intervene. I've heard stories. The Pack Regimes need omegas. They wouldn't allow us to just ignore our order. They believe our duty is to serve pack leaders and to breed. At least, it's that way for most. The ones in power.

"You know I'll always worry about you, Holls. You're my baby sister forever." Arsenio squeezes her shoulder and then turns to me. "Be quick. I don't want this to take away from our night together."

I kiss him just long enough to test my own restraint and hook my arm through Holly's. Arsenio blocks the Silversteins, preventing them from automatically trailing behind us. I hear him and Beckett murmur, and I peek over my shoulder and offer a smile. It's forced and hard to maintain, but I want to remind myself how brave I used to be. With my guys' protection now, I can feel how I've really taken to my place as an omega, relying on them. I know it's okay, but sometimes it's good to just do something for myself while helping Holly learn to also take care of herself without her brothers.

Leaning in close to me, Holly nudges me toward the hallway in the back of the club. From her assertion, I think she's been here before and knows her way around. I know Arsenio wouldn't have taken us somewhere he had no idea about. My pack knows not only the region of Saint Vista, but they have also studied all of the neighboring areas as well. It's part of being part of the Pack Regimes.

"I can't believe we're doing this," Holly whispers. "Is it weird that I am kind of excited?"

I laugh, her comment helping to ease the sudden fear inside me. "To me, yeah. But I get it for you. You're a little trouble-maker. Danger doesn't faze you as much."

"You'll get that way. My brothers will make you feel invincible." Holly bumps her hip to mine and guides me toward the stairwell leading down to the back alley.

"Just remember feeling and being invincible are two different things. When you're on your own, fear is your friend. It'll keep you cautious and make things a bit easier. I was being a bit reckless when I was discovered. I was overwhelmed with my annoyance over a bad deal. I said things I should've kept to myself, and that pissed someone off. Your brothers were actually there, then. They stood up for me." It almost feels like forever ago that I found myself being blackmailed into working for Madame Tamsin. I'm just so grateful I don't—

I freeze in my tracks, pulling Holly to a stop just before the exit. The familiar scent of bitter coffee overwhelms me, my memory triggering me in a way I hadn't expected. I can't believe I can still recall exactly how Madame Tamsin smelled, especially when she was in a bad mood.

"Kinsey? What's wrong?" Holly gives me a little shake, pushing me out of my thoughts.

I shiver and shake my head. "It's nothing. I thought I smelled a familiar alpha. My old handler." Gathering my nerves, I push my hands against the door to the back alley. "It's nothing. I'll be okay. Let's just get this over with."

I step forward into the alley only to have a strong wave of coffee and something spicier like clove assault my senses. I don't even have a chance to fully grasp what's happening before a strong hand locks on my wrist and yanks my arm over my head. Madame Tamsin laces her fingers around my throat and shoves me against the wall, growling under her breath.

"Kin—" Holly's voice cuts off as Madame Tamsin drops me and snatches her, slamming her into the wall beside me.

Something dark rushes over me, and I click the button on the small pocketknife, sending the blade flipping out. I throw myself forward and jab the knife into Madame Tamsin's smooth calf. She hollers in surprise, her leg giving out on her. Yanking my arm, Holly drags me to my feet. It's as if I can't control my anger. Instead of running, I launch at Madame Tamsin and collide into her, straddling her as I use all my strength to pin her down. Holly doesn't try to pull me off. Instead, she grabs the knife and aims it at Madame Tamsin's throat, forcing her to freeze in place.

"What the fuck? What the actual fuck! Who do you think you are? This is the omega of the Gilded Sands Pack. They'll take your head for this. Where are you from? Tell me who your pack is." Holly shakes with her anger, nicking Madame Tamsin's throat.

I lean in, getting in Madame Tamsin's face. "This is the alpha bitch that sold me to fucking Platinum Shores."

"Release me, omegas. Now. You will be obedient girls, or I'll put you in your places. This is your one warning." Madame Tamsin bares her teeth, scowling and grumbling, her muscles tense. "Hurt me, and you'll never get your fucking drugs."

Holly hesitates, but I don't. Swinging my fist, I punch Madame Tamsin in the nose. Everything happens so fast that I can't brace for her strength. She knees me in the back, knocking me forward over her head and into Holly. The world blurs, and yells echo through the air.

"Kinsey!" Holly screams. "Don't touch her!"

Madame Tamsin towers over me, wobbling on her feet. Jerking her leg, she kicks me in the chest, stealing my breath. I open and close my mouth, desperately trying to suck in air that doesn't come.

I black out.

# Chapter Nine



## World in Ruins

I hear Holly scream from the partially opened door. Fuck. It's been five minutes. Five fucking minutes. How the fuck has something happened already? It should've been easy. It was basically supposed to be an exchange of money for pills, and the two of them should've been back. I regret letting them go out at all. No damn pill is worth either of them getting hurt. I don't give a fuck if Holly wants to try to pass as a beta. Right now? I don't want her to leave the palace at all. I need to keep her safe with Kinsey. The world is just too damn dangerous. They both had already taken a pill and still, someone went after them.

Unholstering my gun, I kick open the door and automatically shoot at the wall, the sound of my gun startling the female alpha as she kicks Kinsey's lifeless body.

My heart explodes with panic, and I aim my gun at the alpha.

The sound of the safety clicking off another gun snaps in my ear. "I'd reconsider shooting my dealer. She had every right to fight back, considering she was attacked first. Tend to your omega and let me handle my wayward employee."

The alpha's comment knocks some sense back into me, and I lower my gun. I scowl at the man, threatening him with my gaze, praying silently that he doesn't do anything stupid. Beckett and his pack, now looming by the building, helps my nerves. I rush toward Kinsey and Holly, pulling Kinsey from the ground.

"Kinsey, sugar. Wake up. Hey, I'm here. Please open your eyes." I hold Kinsey on my lap, stroking my fingers over her temples.

Her lids flutter, her eyes rolling. She doesn't speak. A soft whimper escapes her pouty mouth and nearly guts me. I want to kill that bitch. I want to kill the man who intervened.

"I only disabled your omega. She'll be fine in a minute." The bitch keeps her space as she tries to defend herself with a flimsy excuse. "She stabbed me."

"Because you fucking sold her to Platinum Shores!" Holly points her finger. Beckett quietly closes the space to her, ensuring she doesn't try to lunge.

"Control her. She has no right to speak to me like that." It's Tamsin. I don't know why it didn't click. She looks different. Thinner. Weaker. And somehow, she has found herself as a dealer. What the fuck is going on?

"In my territory she does. Do not undermine the authority of the Gilded Sands Pack. She is my sister and the princess of our territory. Kinsey will soon be queen. I should arrest you both. This gives me the right to punish you." I get to my feet and adjust Kinsey in my arms. Turning to Beckett, I nod to him. "Restrain them. All deals are off."

Beckett's pack acts for him, grabbing both Tamsin and the man who I realize is Mr. Donahue. I've never met him in person, and I've only heard about him through my brothers.

Mr. Donahue growls. "Now, now. This is not necessary. It was all a misunderstanding. I had assumed that these omegas were just betas. That's how well the drugs work. I'm sure Tamsin didn't recall your omega from her staff. She sees a lot. She only pays attention to those she favors. You cannot blame her for acting in self-defense when someone just launches and attacks. Let's be civilized. We all have our priorities, and we know yours is getting your hands on some more suppressant pills. I just want to do business and leave. No need to sully our budding alliance."

Funny how he backtracks once he's out of a position of power, unable to threaten us with a weapon.

"That's still unacceptable. Kinsey's hurt." I flare my nostrils and bare my teeth at Tamsin.

She rolls her eyes. "The little bitch is faking it. She knows her way around alphas, and she's playing you. I've taught her well."

Kinsey tenses in my arms, finally aroused awake by the situation. She doesn't talk, though. She'll let me handle it.

"I don't give a fuck. I want you on your knees and begging for forgiveness. That's the only way this is going to work out. You're also banned from my territory. You're not welcome here even as a dealer." I jerk my gaze to Donahue. "We'll be working with you directly."

Donahue nods. "Absolutely. I only brought Tamsin because omegas tend to be less threatened by females. You know this."

From what Kinsey tells me, that's actually quite the opposite. She finds female alphas to be more cruel. Less perceptive and violent. Males tend to just want sex and attention.

"You might want to reconsider. That doesn't matter now. Get the bitch to apologize and send her on her way. You're welcome to join me to discuss things further. I do not agree with your practices, so before we completely agree to allow you

to use our territory as a passageway, I want to set some rules."
I point at Tamsin. "Bow down now."

She crosses her arms and takes another step back, bumping into Jordan. "You'll not humiliate me like this."

Jordan kicks the back of her knee, forcing her legs out from under her. I want to give the man a fist bump for his actions. That was brave of him, considering he's a beta. "He said bow."

Tamsin shakes with her anger, her bitter scent wafting through the air. "I would rather die than apologize."

"Tamsin, just apologize. You've already caused enough problems for the Gutter District. As your authoritative pack, do as I say, or I'll rip you from the power of the Vixen Lounge." Donahue steps on her hand, crushing her fingers under his weight.

She hollers, her voice deepening, "Fucking fine! Sorry."

A part of me wants to knock her off her feet and demand she tries again, but I don't want to put Kinsey through this a moment longer. She shouldn't have had to face this woman ever again. I know she would prefer if Tamsin was just gone.

I stroll closer and tighten my grip on Kinsey while I reach down and grasp Tamsin by her chin, rubbing my fingers over her cheek so she remembers. "Never come back to this territory. I will kill you if you do. Things are changing, so you better fucking learn to adapt, or you will get your wish."

I jerk her by the neck, sending her sprawling across the ground. I don't wait for her to get up and leave and instead motion to Beckett to bring Holly. Donahue follows silently. His obedience proves his intelligence. He's a smart man. He's not going to challenge a more powerful alpha, especially outside of his territory. That's probably what makes his business so successful. He knows how to strategize and negotiate power compared to just taking it by force.

"Once again, I apologize for the behavior of Tamsin. She's learning her new position and paying off her debt to me." Donahue keeps behind me, letting me lead the way.

"As long as we have an agreement that she will never step foot in my territory, we will be fine." I wave to the booth where we were sitting. "Have a drink and relax for a moment. I need to care for my omega and make sure she's okay."

I don't wait for a response and carry Kinsey to the bathrooms. I block the door by pushing the lounge chair in front of it. At least this is one of the nicer bathrooms because of the exclusivity of the club. It is set up with a sitting area and sink separate from the toilets.

I gently sit Kinsey down and touch her chin, getting her to look at me. "I need you to say something, sugar. Where do you hurt?"

Kinsey stretches her arms for me to step between her legs. I hug her close and kiss her neck, snuggling against her. She shakes but doesn't cry. It's more of the adrenaline wearing off her.

"What hurts?" I ask again, wishing I could just inspect every inch of her.

She clears her throat. "My ribs are sore, but I'm going to be okay. It's more...fuck. I never thought I would see her again. I'm sorry. I didn't mean to attack like that. I don't know what came over me."

"Don't you dare apologize. This is not your fault. You have done nothing wrong. It was my mistake. I should've denied Enzo and just went with you. I had no idea Donahue was going to be here as well. I was just expecting some lowlife or something." I hug her again, just wanting to breathe in her scent.

"Mr. Donahue doesn't trust his inventory with the weak." Kinsey tilts her head, silently begging me for a kiss.

"Oh, but he does. I bet he'll rethink his trust in Tamsin. I'd say that you proved she was weak, but you're my badass. She never stood a chance against you." I mold my lips to hers, kissing her cautiously, a part of me afraid of hurting her since I can't believe that she's a hundred percent unharmed until I see her naked body for myself.

"I tried my best. You should've seen her face." Kinsey eases only a millimeter from my mouth. "I just wish I had more skills. You need to teach me how to properly defend myself."

It goes against my instincts to agree with her, despite knowing she's right. It was different with Holly. She's my little sister, and I always knew she'd leave the pack one day. With Kinsey, she shouldn't need to know how to defend herself. Except it's wrong of me to have that much self-assurance. The best way for me to protect her is to teach her how to take care of herself.

"Or at least the proper places to stab. Maybe how to hit without feeling like I might've sprained a finger. Definitely how to block myself from being kicked senseless." Her voice softens, cracking with what surely is the memory of her encounter with Tamsin.

I encase my hand around hers, pulling her fingers to my mouth, kissing them tenderly. "We'll use my brothers to practice. Remind them who's truly in charge."

She giggles. "Is that so?"

"Mmmhmm." Sliding my free hand over her collarbone, I ease the fabric of her dress away, exposing her cleavage. I kiss the flush crossing her chest, my desire consuming me. I force myself to straighten my back. "Let's handle this bullshit and head home, okay? I want nothing more than to take care of you any way you might need."

Kinsey stops me from standing, grabbing the front of my shirt to pull me closer. "You can do that here...I mean, make me feel better. Make me forget."

Her hand glides down my stomach and to my pants, rubbing over the hard length of my cock, pressing against the fabric. I moan at the sensation, my breathing quickening as she slides the zipper down.

"I can't ever deny you." I crash my mouth to hers, sliding my tongue between her lips, tasting the sweetness of her affection.

"But you're going to have to. Just for a bit." Kinsey strokes me for a moment longer, getting me riled up.

"We'll see about that, tease." I slide my hands along the hem of her dress and to her thigh, wishing I could smell her desire in the way I prefer.

Gasping, Kinsey clings onto me as I slip my finger between her legs, her slick hot and wet, begging for my knot. She spreads her legs wider, rocking her hips, riding my hand in a way that drives me wild. Kinsey blindly grabs at me, unzipping my pants and pulling my cock free. Her fingers join mine inside her until she glides her palm over my hard-on, stroking up and down.

I moan in pleasure, my balls tight and throbbing. It would be so easy to shift her on top of me, but I resist. I hold back just a little. The last thing I need is to knot with her outside of the safety of our palace, and right now, only her pussy will do.

Flipping her onto her back, I rub my thumb over her clit as I add another finger inside her, loving how she squirms with her need for me. Her back arches and she tightens her hand around my cock, gliding her fingers up and down more desperately, trying to make me come first. It will satiate me for a while, but nothing can compare to what it's like to claim her, not releasing her until we both get our fill. It makes me anxious, almost ornery, and I grunt with my oncoming orgasm. Kinsey covers my tip with her hand, filling her palm with my seed, using it to slicken my body even more. The lust continuing to pour through me shakes my body. Kinsey screams out with her pleasure, and I kiss the noise away, silencing her as she reaches her peak. What I wouldn't give to thrust inside her, ravishing her over and over.

"I think I'm ready to get out of here. I don't want to waste more of our night talking to Mr. Donahue." Kinsey waits for me to compose myself to carry her to the sink, helping her clean up. It's enough of a distraction to calm my balls, helping me focus. I can't let my desire go more to my head than it already has. I know we've already taken long enough to test the drug lord.

"We'll be fast. I'll make sure my brothers know and can take over—" The muffled pops of gunfire sound through the door, grabbing my attention.

"Oh, God. Holly's out there," Kinsey says, hopping from the counter.

I swear under my breath, unholstering my gun. I thought this bullshit was over. No fucking alpha should be brave enough to fire a gun inside a public club. "Stay here. Hide."

I don't give Kinsey the chance to argue and charge toward the bathroom door, shoving the lounge out of the way. Flinging the door open, I aim and prepare to shoot. No bastard is getting away with this within my territory.

Holly's high-pitched laughter cuts over the music, and she squeals with the applause. I freeze in confusion, sweeping my gaze around the club. A crowd of people stands in a semi-circle with Holly in the center, readying to fire a gun at where Donahue positions bottles on the back of the booth.

Fucking hell. Holly was never one for subtlety. She's showing off her skills on purpose. I can tell with the way she looks at the Silverstein Pack.

Wilder would lock her ass up again if he saw her.

"Brother! Where's Kinsey? You guys good?" Holly calls, drawing the crowd's attention to me.

I tighten my jaw and motion for Holly to come closer. "That's enough fooling around, lil sis. Mr. Donahue and I have some negotiations to handle."

I catch sight of Kinsey hovering in the hallway, peeking out. She must've heard Holly and came out, ignoring my command to hide. I extend my arm out, motioning her to come to my side.

Holly pops out her bottom lip. "That's no fun."

Of fucking course it's not fun. Life isn't fun. I refrain from telling Holly as much and slide my arm around Kinsey's waist, pressing my lips to the top of her head. "After. I promise."

Donahue chuckles and rubs his hands together. "He's right. After everything is in order, we'll have something to celebrate. An alliance."

I straighten my shoulders. "We'll see, Donahue. Make your pitch."

He motions toward the booth. "You'll see I'm right, King Arsenio." Using a title that hasn't been made official shows just how charming this alpha tries to be, but I can see through him. I know his type.

"The world will be ours," he adds.

He says it in a way that makes Kinsey stiffen. I give her a look and squeeze her hand. The world will never belong to a man like Mr. Donahue. Like I said, I know his type. He would watch the world burn. We need better alliances than that. We need packs that will help us start the fires and put them out. We need packs ready to rebuild.

As for Donahue...I plan to see him perish with alphas like Tamsin.

The world is ours, not theirs. I'll leave them in ruins.

# Chapter Ten



## Celebration of Death

How the fuck did I end up in this position? Oh, right. Because I took the liberty of ending our father's life in front of all the strongest packs in our territory. Now it's my duty to arrange his celebration of life...or better yet, his celebration of death. No one is upset by this loss.

"I should just fucking throw you in the dumpster out back and be done with it. We don't need to keep the tradition. You fucked things up. You destroyed this family just like you destroyed Mom. You deserve this!" I slam my fist onto the top of the gleaming casket, closed to hide the fact that I can't stand looking at his face, even in death.

My phone beeps, drawing my attention.

*Arsehole: We got three months' worth of pills and a direct connection to the drug lord. On our way back now.*

I flick my attention to the time on my phone. I hadn't realized Arsenio had kept Kinsey and Holly out all night and half the morning. I've been in here the whole time, choosing invitations and announcements. Going through photos and documents along with the trust outside of what our immediate pack gets. My aunt is guaranteed sanctuary at the Gilded Sands Fortress along with any other children from her bloodline. It was the one thing my father had kept his word for regarding my mom's wishes. She always wanted to make sure her sister was safe.

*Me: What else have you been doing while I've been busting my ass?*

*Arsehole: Dealing with a run-in with Tamsin. Kinsey was in an altercation, but she's fine.*

I growl and throw my phone, watching it hit the chair in the study. Kinsey was in a fight under his watch? He's in so much damn trouble. If he thinks I was busting my ass here, he better brace himself. I'm going to whoop him like our dad used to do to us when we were teens.

My phone dings several more times as I compose myself, doing my best not to shove my father's casket off its rollers and onto the floor. It would serve him right. I don't even want him in here, but it is what it is. The study is open for those closest to him to view and visit until the celebration tomorrow.

Snatching my phone up, I glance at the screen.

*Arsehole: Enzo, don't be mad at Arsenio. You should've seen me. I stabbed her.*
*Arsehole: She had to beg for my forgiveness.*
*Arsehole: Mr. Donahue sees her for the pathetic alpha she is.*
*Arsehole: Holly was so brave too. You'd be proud.*

I can only imagine what kind of trouble the two of them got into together. They like to test the boundaries. Kinsey would've never let Holly participate in a drug deal alone. I know her well enough to know that she would've protected her.

*Me: I'm so proud of you, baby, but I also want to bend you over my knee and smack that ass of yours. You could've gotten seriously hurt. If anything ever happened to you, I would never survive it.*

*Arsehole: Don't talk like that. I'm a little badass. I'll only get stronger. You're going to ensure it.*

A smile crosses my face, and I squeeze my phone as if I can squeeze Kinsey in a hug. I hadn't realized how much I really missed her and how much I hate being apart even if it was just for the night.

*Me: Damn straight, I will. Now hurry your ass home. I've been forced to plan this funeral bullshit on my own, and I could really use your smile.*
*Arsehole: Oh, Enzo. I'd have helped had I known.*
*Me: I wouldn't have let you. This isn't your burden. I would never allow you to help me carry this shit. You can just make me feel better after. I can't wait for our night.*
*Arsehole: The wait will be worth it.*
*Me: I know.*

I tuck my phone away and stroll toward the study door, making my way to the library where Desmond and Wilder hunch forward in their chairs, staring at the papers spread out across the coffee table.

I swallow my jealousy, knowing that Wilder is discussing plans for Platinum Shores with Desmond. He knew I wanted that territory. It would've been tough to constantly have to move back and forth to see Kinsey, but I'd have done it. It's just that I've always been last as the youngest. I know Desmond can handle it, but...I'm an asshole.

I knock my knuckles on the doorframe, grabbing their attention. "Did you guys know Arsenio kept Kinsey and Holly out all night? They're on their way back now."

Wilder flicks his attention to me and nods. "Did you ignore the group text?"

I scrunch my nose and pull up my phone, noticing unread text messages from five different packs, along with the group chat I have with my brothers and Holly. I probably just saw Wilder's name flash across my screen and ignored him, knowing he'd come to me if he really needed something.

I scratch my neck. "I've been busy. It seems like I missed a lot of bullshit."

"It's better that way, Enzo. You have a lot to deal with. I know this can't be easy on you." Desmond gets to his feet and saunters to my side, draping his arm over my shoulders. "We all know he was a dick, but you were his favorite, and he wasn't—"

"I hope he rots in hell," I say, growling as I step away from his attempt to console me as if I'm grieving instead of pissed the fuck off that our father ever put us in this position to begin with. "I'd much rather just dump him somewhere."

Wilder sighs and straightens his back. "We'd all like that, but this is protocol. We have to show respect in front of the other leaders of the Pack Regimes. They can't know the changes we are planning. Naming Desmond as the leader was tricky enough."

I remain expressionless. I have to remind myself that Desmond is worthy of being the face of a new territory connected with ours. Our ability to work together and see each other as equal is what will help progress our desires. Not many other packs work like a democracy. Many of them have their leader who makes all the decisions on everyone's behalf. Mostly, they make their choices based on what suits them best without consideration for anyone else.

"Fine. We'll go through with the ceremonial pyre and be done with it." I hang my head, staring at the floor. The last funeral I attended was Holly's, and before that, my mom's. But this is unlike theirs. For one, Holly's was for show. I was too young to even really process my mother's.

Because I pulled the trigger on my father, I'll be the one standing before our people. I need to ensure that they truly know my act was justified. I cannot have anyone question it.

"And then after, we need to focus our full attention on Kinsey. She's on the brink of going into heat, and she's terrified. Arsenio told me that she popped one of the suppressant pills, so it wasn't like her pheromones set off the fight. She's torn between wanting to give us the world but also facing memories from her past. We need to ensure that she feels safe, secure, and prepared. I don't want her to regret anything." Desmond nudges me, getting me to look at him. "This is important for you three as alphas."

It takes a second for his words to click but hearing him mention that Kinsey panicked, even being with Arsenio, enough to pop a pill hurts me in a way that I didn't expect. I don't care if she wants to take suppressant pills. I would suck up my feelings to give her the chance to choose what is right for her, but I don't want it to be because she's afraid. I don't want it to be because she had been traumatized during her last heat. I need to support her in any way I can as her alpha.

"Fuck. I hadn't realized." Wilder clenches his fingers, cording the veins in his muscular arms. "I had assumed she was okay. She told me she wanted to bond and breed. But if she doesn't..."

"We'll figure it out when that moment comes. I'll take her away if I have to. Or you guys can go stay in Platinum Shores. Either way, we need to be here in whatever way Kinsey needs," Desmond says, patting Wilder on the back.

I hate that he's right. But in this moment, I need to offer up and do everything I can to see that all our needs are fulfilled. I don't want Kinsey to doubt anything. She is our queen, and I'm ready to grow our pack. It's all I desire. Taking care of her and our family and raising our babies like the treasures I know they'll be.

"Absolutely," I say, giving Wilder a glance. I can't tell what's going on in his mind from his lack of expression, but his scent declares that he's as mixed up in his emotions as me.

We've always expected to mate immediately with our chosen omega. It was never a question as we've been preparing for it all our lives. So, this is different.

As long as we keep our feelings in check, though, we'll be okay. Kinsey is ours forever. This doesn't change anything.

A knock on the door draws our attention, and I twist and spot Arsenio and Kinsey standing together.

"We figured we'd let you know we were back. None of you checked your phones." Arsenio twists his mouth to the side.

One look at Kinsey shows that she caught some of our conversation. We were probably talking too loudly, not concerned about the staff hearing us.

"Baby," I say, striving toward her and Arsenio. "Are you okay? Do you need me to love up on you?"

Kinsey smirks, but her face doesn't light up like it usually does. "I do, but I heard you guys talking about my heat. You should know that I'm okay. I'm not going to take any more suppressants. It was...I wasn't thinking when I did it. I didn't mean to disappoint you."

My heart skips a beat, my thoughts faltering as my mind goes blank.

"You could never disappoint us, Kinsey. We understand to the best of our ability what you're going through and how you feel. You don't have to feel obligated to do anything for us, but we should talk about it. You shouldn't feel as if you have to hide anything. You don't have to be brave either. We're a pack, and we're here for you. You're our queen." Wilder closes the space and touches Kinsey's cheek. "And now that we'll be putting our father to rest, we can truly focus on us. The Pack Regimes expect us to take some time to ourselves to adjust, especially with the breeding season coming. They won't even have time to concern themselves with our affairs."

Breeding season. I used to be so fucking annoyed about it, because basically, all the territory shuts down. Alphas tend to have to stay home just in case. The only one who's ever really gotten to experience what the world is like when alphas and omega are within their walls is Desmond. Betas look forward to it. It's the only time that they have control.

I wonder if it's going to drive him nuts.

We'll have to talk about that too.

Arsenio kisses her throat. "And with Holly moving out, we don't have to worry about—"

"What the fuck do you mean Holly is moving out?" Wilder tenses with his words, taking a step back from us. Holy fuck. The spiciness of his shock and annoyance sets me off, and I flare my nostrils and fist my hands, preparing to tackle him if I need to.

"You didn't prepare him?" Arsenio asks Desmond, the two of them sharing a long look.

"Holly was supposed to tell him." Desmond holds his hands up. "Don't get pissed off at us. You knew it was coming, Wilder. She's an adult, and I can't blame her for wanting to get the fuck out before the breeding season. She's been a prisoner and needs her freedom now that she doesn't have to worry. We'll have everything worked out."

Wilder growls. "It's not safe yet. I can't protect—"

Kinsey reaches out and presses her hand over Wilder's mouth. "You have given her the best gift by teaching her how to protect herself. Trust her. This is what she wants, and she deserves to decide. You promised me this would happen when you took control. You would make changes so that omegas would get rights and not be treated like property or things just to breed. Giving her this will prove it. Please, Wilder. Holly isn't the only one who needs this. You do too. It's okay to let her be independent."

Damn. I wish she'd talk to me that way. Maybe I need to be a little bit bratty. She reversed the roles, and I'm here for it. I mean, I enjoy seeing Wilder get put in his place. It'll help him stop acting like an alpha fool. We all know that we're a bit testy right now. We'll go into rut the same time Kinsey goes into heat. None of us needs that sort of assholeness. Also, it'll really prove what kind of control we truly have.

"You're such a brat-girl. If my brothers weren't here, I'd punish you for that mouth of yours. You're the only one who can get away with talking to me like that. I hope you know it." Wilder scrubs his cheeks.

Kinsey beams a smile, her face lighting up like the sun, dragging me closer in a gravitational pull I can't resist. "I know."

I shudder at her comment, the sexy breathiness of her voice tickling me right in the balls. And now I'm horny as hell.

I need it to be my time with her, so I can initiate one hell of a naughty time. Arsenio won't, and no one will argue about it. Because we have the fucking funeral. Goddamn. I want nothing more than to get it over with.

Wilder kisses Kinsey, and I step back, giving them space before their lust sets me off even more. I glance at Desmond, who looks ready to pull the two of them apart, risking the safety of his limbs. He'll be extra cautious now. With the way Kinsey's been taking suppressant pills, we won't be able to truly know exactly when her heat will start. All we can tell is that it could be any day. Any moment, really. And from what I've read, her heat will be twice as intense and possibly way longer. We just need to be prepared.

Arsenio clears his throat. "All right, brothers. We need to get shit finalized. Do you need anything from me, Enzo?"

I press my lips into a line. A dozen answers swirl through my head. What I really want is for someone else to do this shit. I don't regret my actions, but these consequences are worse than I expected.

"I should be good. The staff knows to relocate his body to the family plot for the ceremony. I've requested only our pack and the leaders of his allies to come. No one else really cares, anyway." Which is true. When I was going over the list of people to invite, I could easily cut out half of them. We don't need entire packs here. They'll come back for our union to Kinsey. That will be enough.

"You've been planning this all by yourself, Enzo?" Kinsey's soft voice catches my attention. "How are you holding up? I feel bad that I haven't asked. I've been too concerned with myself."

A smile stretches across my lips, and I lift and drop my shoulders. "That's how it should be. I'm good. I promise. I just have to check on the catering real quick, and then everything's good to go. We don't even have to attend. Just shaking a couple hands will be good enough."

Arsenio sets her on her feet, and I can tell with one look that he knows Kinsey's going to ask to help me. "Why don't you go with him and make sure the dessert is to your liking, sugar? I need to go over everything with Wilder and Desmond about Donahue."

I'm going to owe him one. Fuck yeah, to having an amazing brother.

Reaching out, I offer my fist to him, bumping my knuckles to his. "That sounds like an excellent idea. I saw a couple pieces of cake with your name on it. Help sweeten you up after some of the bullshit."

Kinsey wiggles her fingers at me, finally begging me to lift her up into my arms. I'd carry her everywhere if I could. I love when she's extra affectionate, wanting to bury her face in the crook of my neck to tease my skin with her lips and tongue and teeth.

"Oh, and little brother? Remember what we discussed? Now, it's your turn. I'll give you extra time." Arsenio motions to his finger, and I cock my head, realizing that he went through with the formal proposal. It was something that we were each going to do spontaneously because that's the best way to show Kinsey just how much we love her.

I feel in my pocket, touching the ring I picked out that fits with Arsenio, Wilder, and Desmond's. "I owe you one, Arsenio."

He shakes his head. "Nah. You handled so much already. I'll get going." He kisses Kinsey on the cheek. "Have a good time, sugar. Try not to fill up on cake. I want to share some with you later."

Kinsey smiles and motions for Desmond and Wilder to close the space. The four of us hug her between us, smothering her with our love and affection. She groans, her scent growing as the drugs battle to keep her in control.

If Jude didn't knock on the doorframe, drawing our attention, I'm pretty fucking certain we'd all take turns banging our girl until she orgasms at least twice as many times as us.

"Sorry to interrupt you guys, but you have an early visitor. It's not for the funeral. He says he's from out of the region."

"It's probably one of the packs from Platinum Shores. I'm not sure that the Pack Regimes put out a notice yet. I think they're waiting until after the funeral." Wilder cracks his knuckles, bouncing on his feet.

"Good luck with that. We'll see you later, brothers." I carry Kinsey away from them and past Jude, heading toward the grand staircase leading down to the kitchen.

I catch sight of a familiar man in the grand foyer, staring at the elevator, waiting expectantly for Jude to bring one of us to him. From my position, he won't be able to see me. I rack my brain, trying to think of how I know him. I've seen him before, but I don't think I've ever spoken with him.

My body cools when I realize who he is.

It's Kinsey's uncle. Holy fucking shit. I'm going to kill the bastard. Spinning on my feet, I rush back toward the library, listening to my brothers' voices. I can't let Kinsey know. If she realizes her uncle is here, she's going to lose her shit.

"Sorry, baby. I forgot I have to do something first." I stop in the doorway to the library and smack my hand on the frame. "Hey, brothers. I forgot about some paperwork. I need you to help me fill it out real quick before I take Kinsey." Turning to Desmond, I say, "Can you take her? I'll text you."

Everyone knows something's wrong without me having to say it, and Desmond quickly takes Kinsey from my arms, kissing her sensually, so she doesn't ask what's going on.

I don't give her a chance either.

Grabbing onto Wilder's arm, I drag him with me, getting Arsenio to follow. It takes everything in me not to pull my gun from his holster and shoot the man without him even knowing. He deserves death. He deserves every ounce of pain I can dish.

Another man stepping up beside him stops me from doing so. He's the head of Saint Vista's Pack Regimes.

Fuck me.

"That's Kinsey's uncle. He must've gotten word of her whereabouts after your coronation." I roll my shoulders, my nerves getting the best of me.

Arsenio and Wilder both swear.

"We have to do something. We must act now," I demand, steeling myself for the possibility of starting another war.

"We just need to get him out of here before Kinsey finds out." Arsenio straightens his jacket.

"Finds out what?" Kinsey strides toward us with Desmond scrambling behind her, yanking his shirt back down. She must've tricked him, knowing that we were hiding something, and caught him off guard.

Wilder charges her, but she dodges around him, only to trip and fall on her hands and knees next to the banister. She freezes, her gaze directed below at the foyer. I was right. It is the fucking monster alpha from her past.

"No," she whispers. "No. No. No. "

"Desmond, take her to your room. Now," Wilder orders.

He quickly scoops her up and spins. My heart clenches, listening to her soft cry.

Her uncle is a dead man.

I will make him pay.

# Chapter Eleven

## *Kinsey*

## Power Switch

"They're going to kill him, right? He's not making it out of here alive?" My hands tremble as I pace back and forth with Desmond strolling beside me. I couldn't sit still with how fast my heart races, but I also know he doesn't want us to leave the room.

Desmond cuts in front of me, meeting my gaze. "Take a big breath with me. In and out."

I try to do what he says, but my breathing remains uneven as I gasp, feeling as if I can't breathe well. Cupping my cheeks, Desmond gets into my face and kisses me, slowing down my gasping. I shiver, my body cool despite the warm temperature of the room. I'm on the verge of another panic attack. I feel as if I might die at any second if I don't know what's going on. Uncle Rommel is crazy to show his face here. He knows how he destroyed my life, and it's as if he wants to do so again. I can't have anything good if he can't. The selfish bastard.

"In and out. Come on, pretty girl. Give me one big breath. If you can do that for me, I'll do something for you. Anything you want." Desmond inhales a long breath, not releasing it until I finally manage to open my mouth and suck in air. I rest my forehead to his and close my eyes, breathing in his scent. How he manages to remain calm is beyond my comprehension. I'm sure his brothers are flipping out as much as I am. It's probably a good thing that I'm alone with Desmond. Our pheromones will fuck with each other right now.

"That's my good girl. Nice and easy. Just let me distract you. What is it you want now? You gave me what I wanted. It's your turn." Desmond doesn't put any space between us and instead kisses my jaw and works his way to my neck. "All you have to do is name it. A bubble bath? A massage? Me on my knees?"

His warm breath tickles my skin, and I dig my fingers into his shoulders, letting him mess with my body, awakening my lust along with something different. I love the sound of him giving me anything I want.

"I just want to feel in control." I swallow hard and stand on my tiptoes, caressing my lips to his forehead.

"I think we can manage that. Tell me what to do. If you want control, dominate me. Claim me as yours. It's all I've been thinking about since our last moment together." Desmond continues to work his way to my clavicle, biting at my shirt with his teeth to move it out of the way before he nuzzles his face between my breasts and licks my skin.

I latch onto his soft hair, guiding him lower, excitement warming between my legs. He gets on his knees and bows for me, letting me tower over him. I look down into his beautiful golden-brown eyes and stroke my fingers over his cheek, leaving my scent behind.

"I don't know if my idea of dominating you is the same as yours." I lick my lips, my heart racing as my chest rises and lowers with each of my quickening breaths, this time driven by desire and not fear. "Do you want me to act as your alpha, Desmond?" All I can think about is how alphas like to overpower betas if they ever decide to do anything with them, but it's not common. They would prefer to be with an omega.

Desmond studies my face, looking into my eyes for a long moment, his Adam's apple moving as he swallows. "Yes. Act as my alpha, but I want you to have complete power over me. Think of me as your omega, Kinsey. Let me show you exactly what it's like for you to have the control you want. Be in charge of my pleasure. Take control of your own. I have a couple things I took from your collection."

The idea sets me off, and I bite my lip between my teeth, imagining what it would be like if I were born into the alpha order. It's exhilarating even thinking that Desmond is going to allow me such a gift, trusting me enough with his body, heart, and soul. And I trust him just the same. If this is what he wants, then I will give it to him.

"I find it exhausting having to keep up with my brothers. Sometimes, I just want to be taken care of." Desmond remains on his knees, his hands resting on my waist. "Will you take care of me?"

"Just show me where everything is. I want you to undress and get on the bed. You're going to watch me prepare." I hold my hand out and help him to his feet, bouncing slightly with my excitement.

This act of intimacy that Desmond craves is something I've never really thought about, but the more I do, the hotter I feel. I want to really know what it's like to switch. Because usually, he's the one in control, his mindset like a competition against his alpha brothers.

Desmond laces his fingers through mine and guides me toward his sleeping area, a trunk resting against the wall. He opens the lid and shows me exactly what he meant when he said he borrowed a couple things from my collection, and I stare at the different dildos and butt plugs along with special panties that allow me to act as if I have a cock of my own. An alpha female doesn't need such things as she can morph her own body when she knots with an omega, but this is different. Enzo picked out these things playfully, teasing that he wanted to be prepared for any possibility. I wonder if a part of him knew. I also wonder if maybe a part of him wants to know the same way Desmond does. What it's like to have an omega claim you.

"Do as you wish, Kinsey. Let's figure out what we enjoy together. If you change your mind, just tell me. You don't need any special words. We'll talk through this all together. I just want you to know that you're safe, and I love you. We will always take care of each other." Desmond grabs a couple things from the trunk and sets them on top, moving away to give me a chance to look over everything.

Strolling back to the bed, he slowly undresses, taking his time to give me a show that sends my body buzzing. His muscles flex and shift as he steps out of his pants and boxer briefs, showing off his hard cock, twitching with his excitement.

He's so incredibly sexy, his scent warming me as I move closer, wanting to take a moment to appreciate him baring his body and soul to me. His desires. And I want nothing more than to do as he wants.

"Look how hard you are for me, Des. You want me to fuck you, don't you?" I lace my fingers around his girth, stroking him softly.

He purrs deep in his throat, loving my new assertiveness. "So much."

"Do you want to know how much I want to fuck you? Touch me and find out." I guide his hand down my torso to the hem of my dress. I shift my legs and show him exactly where I want him to explore. He lets me direct his hand, and I slip both our fingers inside me, feeling the slippery wetness of my slick.

He moans as I gasp softly, only letting him tease me for a minute, just getting my hand damp enough to tease him right back.

"You are so fucking wet." He leans in and nips at my throat. "I can't wait to taste you."

I grin with a small laugh. "Me first. I need to make sure you're nice and ready. I want to explore your body. Is that okay?"

He groans and nods, rubbing his hands across my shoulders as I lower myself before him to my knees, not allowing him to sit on the bed just yet. I lick my lips and kiss his tip, flicking my tongue along the bottom of his shaft slowly, sensually, just working my way to his balls as I reach between his legs and glide my slick finger around his rim, feeling him clenching and unclenching as I gently finger him at the same time that I take his cock in my mouth.

"Oh, fuck. Fuck. That feels incredible. Just like that." Desmond links his fingers through my hair.

I rub him gently, stroking his p-spot as I guide him in and out of my mouth, working him up just until I can feel his body ripple with his movements, his breathing quickening.

I ease away and slow down, tipping my head to look up at him. "I don't want you to come just yet. You're at my mercy. You will only do so when I'm ready."

He play-growls at me, my words prodding at him. And I love it. I love being in control. It's usually my pleasure in his hands, but this is different. I get to own both of ours.

I straighten my legs and stand tall, strolling around him to smack his ass once. "I can't wait to claim you how you want. You're going to be so sexy on your back." I hum with my words, stroking my hand across his broad shoulders as I complete my circle around him and take a step back.

"On my back, huh?" he asks, his voice deepening with his consuming lust.

I nod my head and grab the hem of my dress, tugging it off to show that I wear nothing beneath. "How else can you watch me fuck you?"

His eyes darken, his breath ragged. "You sexy woman. Damn. I can't wait."

"Too bad. Now sit back. I'm going to need your help." I nudge him back until he sits on the edge of the bed beside the collection of toys he pulled out of the trunk.

I glide my fingers over the dildos, picking one up that's about the same size as Desmond. He watches me with hot intensity, shifting on the bed in anticipation. Stroking his cock, he tries to pleasure himself, only to have me snatch his wrist and pull his hand away.

"What did I say? You're going to come when I'm ready for you to come." I grab his finger and suck it into my mouth, teasing him in a way that makes his muscles flex in anticipation.

"This is harder than I thought, but I'll do the best I can to control myself, Kinsey. I ache for you. You have no idea how badly I want more. I need more." Desmond pulls me closer by my hips and loops his arm around my leg, lifting it up for him to bury his face between my thighs.

I moan so fucking loud I'm sure the gods can hear, and I don't move, just enjoying the sensation, letting him get his need for control out of his system. His tongue laps at my body, flicking evenly and in perfect rhythm with my panting breaths that I come to my peak and scratch my nails into his shoulders as my orgasm steals my breath. I steady myself on him until I catch my breath and slide my leg off his shoulder. He grins at me, his mouth glistening with my slick, and I grab his shirt and wipe it off, softly patting his cheek.

"Do that again, and it will be longer until you come. Now help me put this on." I dangle out the strappy panties, and he takes them from me, holding them so I can step in easily.

He helps adjust them, making sure they fit properly, before turning me around and kissing me on my ass, gliding his tongue against my seam to make me shiver. "Is this the one you want to fuck me with?" he asks, lifting up the lifelike silicone dildo with veins and all. It even matches my skin tone, helping me imagine that it really is mine.

"What do you think? Do you think you can handle my cock?" I grin with my words, my voice lightening with my playfulness.

He chuckles and strokes his fingers over the soft material, holding it up to himself to compare. "If I can't, then I have some serious problems, considering that I know exactly what you can take."

I lean in and kiss the tip of his nose. "It's not a competition. I'm not your brother's. I'm your alpha right now. Your pleasure is my priority. You'll speak up, right? You're not going to just sit back and take it because you think that's what you have to do."

His smile fades with the new seriousness that crosses his face. "You know how much I love you, right? You would make a perfect alpha. I trust you. I know I don't have to be strong in front of you, Kinsey."

"You are strong regardless." I climb onto his lap, straddling him while we kiss and taste each other's lips, losing ourselves to the passion.

Desmond cups my breasts, rolling my hard nipples, and I gasp and push him back, my body wanting to give him more. I crave to see him beneath me, getting pleasure in a way only I can give him. He locks his gaze on me, trailing down to the strap-on. I squeeze lube onto it and stroke it playfully, imagining what it would be like to truly be an alpha. The control and power I feel in this moment hits me with wave after wave of electricity.

Desmond rests on his back, using pillows to prop himself up enough to see exactly what I do. I squeeze the bottle of lube over his puckering ass, his cock flexing in anticipation. I glide my finger around the rim and stare at his face as I slip it inside, taking a moment to stroke his hard-on with my free hand, ensuring him all the pleasure in the world I can offer.

He pants and moans, holding his knees for me, spreading his legs wide. His torso curls as he rocks his hips, trying to fuck my hand. Stretching, he grabs a vibrator for me. I scoot closer until I'm in his reach, letting him rub the toy over me, the vibrations stealing my breath. I've never felt so close to Desmond, and I imagine what our future together will be like—how adventurous and freeing we are with each other. He truly gives me something no alpha can, and I love him for it.

"I'm ready, pretty girl. Make me come. Please. Make me come." Desmond sets down the vibrator and locks his fingers to the dildo, pulling me to him. "Fuck me how you want. How I need."

I bend forward, crashing my mouth to his, kissing him passionately as I stroke his cock, pleasuring him as I align the strap-on to his body. Breaking away, he nips my neck, biting me hard enough to leave a mark. I grab him by the chin and suck his lip between my teeth, kissing him until he gasps.

"Tell me one more time how you want me," I whisper, my heart fluttering.

His undeniable trust leaves me on the edge of ecstasy, despite me giving him the pleasure he asks for. His mouth pouts with his heavy breathing, his handsome face scrunching with his desire. His cock pulses in my hand, and I rub my fingers down to squeeze his balls, rolling my palm over them.

"Fuck me, Kinsey. Fuck me hard. Make me see stars as I come." Desmond groans, easing up his hips as I test his reaction, slowly pushing the dildo inside him.

"You look so hot taking it," I say, feeling a strange emotion cross over me. It's more than lust and love. It's respect. It's raw, unbidden power given to me in the form of trust and vulnerability. My heart soars with the rocking of my hips, hearing him call my name, his face scrunched in pleasure as I jerk him off while fucking him just right.

"Faster," he murmurs, grabbing my free hand to rub against his cheek. "Make me come."

I pant with my movements, thrusting faster, clutching one of his knees while I work my hand up and down his shaft over and over. Desmond arches his back with his yell of pleasure, and he comes so hard that it splashes across my chest and stomach, the heat of his cum turning me on even more.

"I love you, Kinsey. I love you so damn much it hurts." Desmond grabs his blanket and cleans me off, only to yank me toward him, flipping me onto my back. "It's my turn to take care of you."

I grip the blankets, easing my body up so he can unbuckle the strap-on. My wetness drips over my thighs, my body ready and quivering in anticipation. Scooting lower, Desmond kisses down my leg, licking and sucking my skin. He bites the soft flesh of my thigh, and I whimper with need, craving the ecstasy he will bring me.

"God, you're so incredibly wet. I yearn to drown in your pleasure." Drawing his tongue over the apex of my legs, he uses his two fingers to spread me open.

He sucks my clit into his mouth, the pressure and bliss rolling through me with another uncontrollable breathy moan from my lips. I arch and squirm, desperate for relief. Planting a hand to my hip, Desmond pins me to the bed, not letting me move until my vision crowds with shadows as my body explodes with an orgasm so intense I can feel my release.

"So sexy," he murmurs, easing his face away. "Delectable."

I swallow and rub my lips together, grabbing for him to lie on top of me. "I need the weight of your body on mine. I feel as if I'll float away otherwise."

Desmond strokes his cock, his desire hardening him again, and he rolls me over, pressing his chest into my back, slipping between my legs from behind. I scream out with his deep thrust, the sensation almost as if he sinks into my soul, and I bite his pillow. Desmond sucks on my shoulder and neck, leaving one mark after another. Our bodies stay in perfect rhythm as he fucks me senseless. The only thing I can focus on is my building orgasm and the heat of his body pinning me down just how I want and need.

My muscles spasm and my toes curl, the intensity of my orgasm incredible. I scream into the pillow, riding the wave of my lust with Desmond until he finishes with a few deep thrusts, pressing into me. His warm breath tickles my ear, and he rolls off, pulling me onto my side to cuddle me from behind. We remain on the bed together, treasuring the moment and each other's company for who knows how long.

"You're everything I could ever want, Kinsey. I promise to give you whatever your heart desires. Let me bathe you and feed you. Then we'll cuddle some more." Desmond lifts me up with him, carrying me to the bathroom. "You're mine. Ours. I'll never take you for granted. I'll protect you with my life and more."

I smile and kiss him, my throat raspy from my moans. "You're so good to me. I'm not letting my uncle destroy my life again. I won't." I don't know why I say it. Mentioning the bastard that hurt me, so deeply that scars cut across my soul, could mess up the moment. It could ruin it altogether.

"Neither will we. I promise you that. We will take care of him." Desmond's jaw clenches with his words. "But try not to think about it now. We'll get justice for your family. For everyone he's ever hurt. He's not making it out of Gilded Sands alive."

He's right. Because there is no way I'll stand by and let that happen. I'm not the scared omega I used to be. The damage he caused only made me rebuild myself stronger than ever. He will fall by our hands.

I refuse to live in a world where evil prevails.

My past can't hurt me any longer.

I've already buried the trauma I went through. Now I'll bury my uncle.

I will reign as the Queen of Gilded Sands.

He'll see.

When he begs for mercy, I'll deny him. He'll watch himself burn.

# Chapter Twelve

## *Kinsey*

## Lose it All

"You have my deepest condolences, your majesties." A man in a fine suit stands before Wilder, Desmond, Arsenio, and Enzo. "I hope you accept the Jasper Crest Pack's support in this transition. His betrayal was a great shame."

Wilder offers a slight bow. "Thank you. We'll rise stronger because of this. Please, take your time and join us on the hour for the celebration feast."

Holly tightens her arm through mine, pulling me flush against her side. She blows her pale blond hair from her face and brushes her lips against my earlobe. "It's satisfying seeing so few people show up. My funeral had hundreds of people."

I raise my eyebrows, peeking at her in my peripheral vision. "That's the strangest thing I've ever heard."

"Try living through it." Holly covers her mouth, stifling her laugh.

Wilder swivels and looks at the two of us. We're both dressed in black with veils obscuring our faces. No one pays attention to us, which I appreciate. I can't seem to shake the fear that my uncle ignited in me with his arrival. I don't know how my guys managed to not blow up the palace with him in it, but my uncle planned his arrival strategically. One of the most powerful alphas escorted him here and back to his hotel, stopping anyone from acting rash.

But it's not over.

"Why don't you two go take your seats? No one will bother you. The Silversteins will be your guards tonight while we socialize and accept the pack offerings." Wilder curls his fingers at me, motioning me to stroll closer. "You have to be bored."

"Extremely." Holly tugs me forward, remaining by my side. "You're going to give me first dibs on the gifts, right?"

Enzo chuckles, breaking the tense silence engulfing us. "Lower your expectations, little sis. They're bringing things they think the bastard would've liked."

Holly huffs a breath. "Still."

Arsenio sighs and shakes his head, pressing his hand to her back, nudging the two of us forward between them. "You got it, Holls. We have everything we could ever want right here." Hooking his finger to my veil, he shifts it away from my face to kiss me. "Isn't that right, brothers?"

Enzo play-growls. "Well—"

Wilder elbows him in the gut. "Just go get settled. It's better if you walk without us. There is enough attention as it is. I'm not ready to show either of you off. We're under enough scrutiny, and it's better to just remain discreet."

"Always the fun stealer," Holly mutters, purposely patting Wilder on his cheek.

He uses his sleeve to wipe off Holly's scent the best he can, and I laugh and rub my fingers over the spot next. He snatches me and cups my face, ensuring there's no way I'll ever escape his scent mark.

"Careful, brother. You're going to get her all worked up. You'll be begging her to drag your ass out of here by the balls when she's through. That's a guarantee." Enzo smacks Wilder on the back.

"I don't beg," Wilder mutters, flicking Enzo. "Now hustle your bratty ass inside before I spank you all the way to the door. It's taking everything in me not to throw you on my shoulder and carry you away, forcing my brothers to deal with this."

Damn.

"Now that you mention it…" I lick my bottom lip.

"Go. Go. Go." Desmond intervenes, getting Holly to pull me along while Arsenio blocks both Wilder and Enzo from following me.

I raise my veil and grin at the two of them, my heart lightening with each of my steps. I shouldn't feel so happy at a funeral.

I shouldn't want to climb on King Winston's casket to dance the night away. But fuck it, I want to so badly. This is the only way that man can ever be put to rest.

Murmurs sound through the air. The staff set up a dozen tables on the grand terrace off the back of the fortress. A part of me hates that we had to come here instead, but another part of me loves seeing the place my pack grew up. If they didn't have such hard feelings, we'd move in. Instead, we've declared this open for all members of the Gilded Sands Pack. King Winston would've hated it, which makes it that much better.

"Look, there they are." Holly practically drags me in the direction of where Beckett, Jordan, Isaiah, and Wesley now stand from their seats at a rectangular table just off to the side of where my guys will sit, facing those here to show their respect.

Her scent sweetens as we stride closer, her excitement palpable enough to trigger my own. It's the strangest thing, but that's what happens when omegas become close. We can empathize with each other's feelings the way we do with our alphas, especially this time of year.

"Holly, Kinsey. You have the Silverstein Pack's condolences." Beckett bows deeply, making a show for the few guests watching us.

Holly groans under her breath, grabbing onto the front of Beckett's suit. "Don't you start. I'd prefer it if you wished me congratulations."

Jordan chuckles and pulls out a chair for her while Isaiah tugs one out for me. "A huge congrats, then, princess. Let me grab some champagne, and we'll toast." Jordan turns his attention to me. "What would you like, your highness?"

It's so strange to have someone who isn't my pack or the staff offer to serve me, but I do my best to accept graciously. "Champagne sounds good. Thanks."

"Three whiskeys for us, Jordy," Wesley says. "That's a good boy."

I gnaw on my lip, trying to remain composed. Holly loses it and laughs, her voice echoing through the air. Beckett holds his finger to her lips through the veil, trying to quiet her down. I know she doesn't give a fuck, though. Her father deserves absolutely no respect.

I slide into my chair at the end of the table and peer around the softly lit terrace, the twinkling lights creating a magical atmosphere I wish I could enjoy on any other day.

Holly whispers quietly, the rest of the Silverstein Pack giving her their sole attention. I try to give them privacy and focus my attention on the guests, inspecting each of them, trying to recall the names of some of the familiar faces.

Melina, my guys' aunt, strolls in, wearing a black gown and veil, only to take a seat at the table with her son. Jude catches me watching and waves. I nod my head, feeling suddenly awkward by the circumstances. I shouldn't be here. This despicable man doesn't deserve a funeral celebration fitting of a king. He deserves to be ignored and forgotten.

If Jordan didn't pop into my view, offering me a slender glass of champagne, I might've hopped up and left. I gingerly take the alcohol, grasping the stem, and Beckett offers a toast in the name of Gilded Sands.

Several people around us clink their glasses, and I hold mine up to Holly before downing it completely. Should I have drained it like a fish in need of water? No. But I need something to help dull the anxiety and to take the edge off things.

"Damn, Kinsey. Already making me go back to the bar." Jordan chuckles, stealing my empty glass.

I bob my head. "Maybe just bring two next time."

"Shit, don't do it. Wilder will kick your ass if you get her sloshed." Isaiah rests his elbows on the table, hunching forward to look at me.

"I'd never let him," Holly muses, twirling her glass. "So, bring me two as well."

Jordan claps his hands and then rubs them together. "Fuck, yeah, princess. As you wish."

Holly grins and wags her finger at Beckett and Isaiah, both trying to snatch her glass to slow her down. They succeed only to have Wesley hand her his, and she gulps it down, holding her finger out.

Heat pools in my stomach, the intoxication hitting me quickly with my empty stomach. I clutch the table as the room spins just a bit. A man calls everyone's attention, announcing the arrival of King Wilder and the royal princes of the Gilded Sands Pack, and I force myself to my feet even though my guys would never expect me to stand on their behalf.

Wilder shuffles ahead of his brothers, shaking a couple people's hands as he passes by and heads toward the main table. He turns slightly and says, "Thank you all for joining us to honor King Winston. Please make yourself at home. My brothers and I would like to keep this a small, intimate affair before the ceremonial pyre. Please enjoy this feast on behalf of our Royal Court. Your presence is much appreciated in these times." Wilder takes his seat at the head of the table, and Enzo, Desmond, and Arsenio stroll through the crowd and thank everyone for coming once more. Enzo stops at our table and sets a phone in front of me, the glittering case sparkling in the light. It's not his or his brothers' phones. I don't recognize this one.

"I figured it was time you had your own, baby." Enzo caresses my chin and bends down, pressing his lips to the top of my head. "Just give me a couple minutes, and I'll come and feed you. Don't you dare put your own fork to your mouth."

I giggle, his comment far funnier than it should be. I can't help it. "Then you better be quick. The second someone sets a plate in front of me, I plan to shovel it in. I'm starving. I might have also already downed a glass of champagne."

"Damn it. You make stepping away incredibly hard. I no longer need just a couple minutes. Give me thirty seconds. I'll be back." Enzo strides toward Wilder. A man reaches out and grabs onto his sleeve, stopping him in his tracks.

Smiling, Enzo turns to the man and gives him a bear hug, rocking him back and forth. He must be a cousin or an uncle, someone close to Enzo, for him to give that kind of affection. It's also enough to distract him from rushing back to me.

"That's uncle Lenny, our mom's brother and the alpha of her pack." Holly slides onto Beckett's lap to get closer to me. "He hasn't been welcome here since Mom died, apparently. I've only met him a couple times when my brothers snuck out to meet."

A blip of sadness tightens my chest. How terrible it was for Winston to cut them off from the family. Their mom's pack probably saw him for what he was and blamed him. I only knew him for a little while, and I do.

"Bottom's up, your highness." Jordan sets two long-stemmed champagne glasses in front of me, and I automatically take one and clink it to his tumbler.

"Thank you. I seriously needed this." I smile and take a sip, the bubbles tickling my top lip.

Holly raises her glass and clinks hers to mine. "Seriously. Just keep them coming for now, Jordy. When I finish this, maybe we can dance. No one will see over by the gazebo, not like they would care."

Jordan's handsome face lights up. "Sounds like a plan, princess."

The phone Enzo handed me lights up on the table, and I pick it up and look at the glowing screen. I nearly drop the thing at the sight of the background image of Enzo completely naked, standing in front of his mirror. Blush warms my cheeks, and I cup the phone, making sure that Holly doesn't accidentally see it and scar herself forever.

*Sexy beast: I didn't mean to abandon you. Give me just a couple of minutes.*

I peek over at him, still standing in front of his uncle. Arsenio hangs out beside him, and Desmond sits beside Wilder, allowing a pack to offer them an elegant, silver paper-wrapped gift. The custom is nearly universal, at least in this area. I never did get to open any of the gifts given to me after my family's death because my uncle took them.

I shove the thought away and focus my attention back on the phone.

*Me: I don't know if I can wait. Would this bring you back to me sooner?*

I glance at the Silversteins engrossed in conversation with Holly and quickly snap a picture of me bending forward, showing off my cleavage. I rub my lips together as I send it, hoping that only Enzo sees it.

*Sexy Beast: Mmm. More. Let me see your panties, baby. I want to imagine taking them off.*

I twist in my seat and glance in his direction. He wags his eyebrows at me with a mischievous grin, his handsome features darkening with his oncoming lust.

He's testing me.

I'll take his bait.

Is it wrong that I'm doing this at his father's funeral? I guess it depends on who you ask. I'm just trying to help get his mind off things. At least that's what I keep telling myself.

Shifting in my seat, I scoot closer to the table and lift the tablecloth slightly so I can hike up my dress enough to position my phone inconspicuously. I glance at Holly and the Silversteins again, making sure that no one sees me, and then I carefully and quietly snap a picture. I hit send and grab the glass of champagne, gulping it down again. The liquid courage tickles my throat, and I rest my head on my hands, using my arms to keep myself propped up. I clutch my phone, staring at the screen. It chimes in my hand.

*Sexy Beast: Fuck me. Goddamn. Give me one minute, and I'll sneak under that damn table and reward you for that. Fucking hot. Send it to Wilder. He needs to lighten up.*
*Me: Look at you, being such a good brother.*
*Sexy Beast: I'm the best.*

I laugh and shake my head, turning to grin at him. Wilder remains seated at the table, his head resting on his fist. Enzo was right. He looks miserable. I can't exactly blame him. He has a lot of responsibility and stress going on.

I bring up his contact, smirking at the fact that Enzo put him in as dickhead, the same name that he has on his phone. Tapping the screen, I send him the same picture, showing off my lack of panties.

I stare at Wilder, watching as he frowns, pulling his phone from his pocket. He taps the screen, his brooding, handsome face morphing into surprise. Flicking his gaze to me, we hold each other's stare. His brilliant blue eyes weigh heavy with his rising desire.

*Me: Do you like it?*

I turn my back on him, staring at my screen.

*Dickhead: You're in so much trouble, my brat. Teasing me when I can't come over to fuck you. I'm going to spank that tight ass of yours later. Maybe even that pussy of yours too. You just wait.*

*Me: You're all talk. All you're going to do is kiss me everywhere. I'm so wet thinking about it.*

*Dickhead: Just wait until I pin you down. I'm going to tease you until you can't take it anymore. You won't be able to touch me at all.*

*Me: I always knew you were a glutton for self-punishment.*

*Dickhead: I just have excellent control. You'll whimper and beg for my cock.*

*Me: That's what you think.*

*Dickhead: I don't think. I know. I can smell you all the way from here.*

*Me: You'll be the one begging me to take your knot. You'll see.*

Wilder doesn't respond right away, and I twist and watch him get up and walk away, heading toward the stairs leading to the grand garden below.

A minute passes, and I frown. I take another sip of my third glass of champagne, waiting anxiously until my phone lights up again with a picture. My body clenches at the sight of Wilder's cock, his fingers laced around the shaft. I never knew how much I would enjoy a dick pic from him.

*Dickhead: Come to the gazebo.*

I shift in my seat, my clit throbbing in anticipation. Was it a mistake to tease him? Maybe. But I don't give a shit. If he wants me to meet him, then I'll meet him.

*Me: Are you sure? What do you plan to do? I might need a little convincing.*

*Dickhead: I'm going to start off with that spank I promised if you don't get your ass here in the next sixty seconds. And then I'm going to hike up your dress, bend you over on the railing, and fuck you so hard that you'll feel as if you're touching the stars above.*

I squirm in my seat, chugging the last bit of my champagne. The hazy world moves around me, the intoxication hitting me harder now that I try to stand up. I take a breath and force myself to my feet, wobbling slightly on my heels.

*Dickhead: Get it together, brat. My brothers are watching you and think you need an escort. I want you alone.*

I flutter my lashes and throw my attention to the table where Arsenio, Desmond, and now Enzo sit and greet another man standing in front of them, offering them a velvet box.

*Me: I'll do my best. Don't worry. If one of them has to carry me there, you can share me.*
*Dickhead: Not now. They can watch. You're mine.*

I release a breath and straighten my back, handing my bag to Holly. She grins at me, giggling maniacally, happier than I have seen her in a long time. I guess funerals don't have to be sad, after all.

My phone chimes.

*Sexy Beast: You look like you need a hand, baby. Wilder said I can't help you unless you ask.*
*Me: He said you can't participate. You'd only get to watch.*

*Sexy Beast: That's the last time I'll ever try to cheer his ass up. Get ready for a long night. I'm claiming you next.*

Smirking, I wag my finger at him as I take a small step forward in the direction of the stairs leading to the garden. The thirty feet suddenly looks like a mile, and I try my best to not wobble. I regret picking out the stilettos. I didn't think I would be walking anywhere.

I use whatever I can to hold onto, steadying myself with the backs of empty chairs until I reach the wall that overlooks the property. The quiet terrace suddenly erupts with soft music, and I catch sight of a dozen servers coming out with silver platters covered with dinner plates.

Wilder chose the perfect time to need attention, because the guests will now be distracted with consuming their fill of the finest foods our pack has to offer.

Reaching the top of the stairs, I peer down the stone steps before me. Twenty stairs look like a hundred from this point of view, and I slowly make my way down, my stilettos shaking as I clutch the railing, my vision blurry from my intoxication. I regret the third glass of champagne. The second one too. I don't know what I was thinking, but I'm not sure I'm going to make it all the way to the gazebo.

I stop a couple steps before the pathway that leads to the garden. "Wilder?" I call, hoping I project my voice like I think I am. "I need your help. I'm too drunk."

"Here, miss. Let me help you." The familiar voice stabs me in the heart as a figure appears from the right side of the staircase.

I focus my gaze, seeing my uncle for the first time up close in years. The edges of my vision shadow, and I try to take a step back, hitting my heel on the step. I lose my balance and fall forward, only to have him catch me. His scent triggers my panic, and I scream, flailing my body in an attempt to escape.

This can't be happening.

This can't be fucking happening.

"Let me go!" I yell, swinging my hand but missing him.

Commotion breaks out from above, and I catch sight of Arsenio, Enzo, and Desmond all rushing down the stairs.

"Get your hands off my omega or lose them," Wilder says, his voice deep and growly with his anger. "This is a private affair, and you're not welcome here."

I gasp a dozen breaths, reaching out for Wilder as my uncle loosens his hold on me. Arsenio reaches him first and locks his arm around his neck, dragging him back. Spectators line the balcony, curious about what's going on. All I can think about is the smoky smell of cigarettes and musk now clinging to me, my uncle purposefully leaving his scent on me.

"Kill him. You have to kill him. He's a monster. He killed my parents. He killed the men who were supposed to be my pack." My voice shakes with my words. "He tortured me."

"I'd suggest you reconsider, King Wilder. We both know that she still belongs to me, and I must agree to give her to you. She is not the unclaimed omega like the Pack Regimes assumed. If you kill me, you'll have to hand her over to the pack I had previously chosen." Uncle Rommel remains placid in Arsenio's chokehold, not fighting him, proving that he's not a threat and giving him no reason to kill him immediately with all the witnesses. He knew exactly what he was doing, showing up uninvited to Winston's funeral.

"Watch your mouth before I cut out your tongue. You're testing the wrong pack." Arsenio shakes my uncle, tightening his hold.

"The negotiations were to take place tomorrow. You're trespassing here tonight, and that gives us reason to arrest you and punish you as we see fit as the authority of Gilded Sands." Wilder pulls out a blade and aims it at my uncle.

"I'm family. I have the right to be here." Uncle Rommel focuses his gaze on me, trying to lock me in his stare.

I turn my head away and hide against Wilder's neck. He's doing this on purpose. He's tormenting me because he didn't get what he wanted before. He's pissed that I didn't just bow complacently and accept my fate. I'm my mother's daughter, after all. She denied him, choosing only to be with my dad. She didn't fall into the role of the perfect omega, and neither will I.

"You lost that right the moment you betrayed your pack. Kinsey belongs to us now. We have already made it formal. No member of the Pack Regimes will go against us for a lowlife like you. You have no ties here." Enzo gets in front of Uncle Rommel, blocking his view of me. "Now, we'll escort you out. If you fight, we'll drag you and show just what happens when you test the new kings."

"Careful, Mr. Enzo. I know all about you and your pack and the activities you allow your omegas to participate in. I know what kind of connections and deals you make behind the back of the Pack Regimes. It would be a shame if word got out that you were allowing omegas in your territory to pass as betas." A wicked grin crosses Uncle Rommel's face as he challenges Enzo.

Desmond grabs the back of his brother's shirt, yanking Enzo a couple of feet away before he charges. He's baiting him on purpose. He wants us to make a scene.

"Just get him out of here. He's trying to get to us, and we can't let him." My voice comes out stronger than I think possible, and I wiggle in Wilder's arms until he sets me on my feet. He holds me by my waist, resting his chest on my back, and

I pull him forward with me, now sober and more confident with their protection.

Seeing my uncle again was my worst fear, but I feel impenetrable and invincible in this moment. Holly was right. My alphas make me stronger.

"Look at my niece. You've come a long way since I've last seen you, Kinsey. I always knew you were worth more than what your parents thought. Look at you, seducing leaders from the Pack Regimes." Uncle Rommel doesn't break his eyes away from mine, setting me off. "I've done you a great favor, you know. You should thank me."

Rage lashes through me, darkening my vision. I'm going to kill him myself. "Thank you? You think I should thank you? You're fucking sick! You're a monster. Fuck you!" I throw myself forward, wanting nothing more than to scratch his eyes out. To twist his dick so hard that it tears off. I want him to pay. He's manipulating my pack, and I won't stand for it.

Hands lock around my waist, yanking me back, and Enzo tosses me on his shoulder. I kick and scream, smacking his back and demanding that he put me down. He doesn't.

Wilder calls the security team to escort Uncle Rommel out, not doing anything that I desperately want them to do. I want them to hold him down while I ravage him, making him feel the pain he inflicted on me. I can't believe this. They promised to always protect me. And not only physically.

"You can't let him leave here alive!" I squirm and fight, forcing Enzo to pull me into his arms. "You have to do this. You're my alpha. You can't give him this power. If you give him this power, he'll just keep taking more until he kills you all, just like he killed the last pack I was supposed to be in. You have to do this, Enzo."

My eyes water with my unshed tears, and I blink them away. I can't let them fall. I won't let them fall. Uncle Rommel has had enough of my tears. He's not taking any more from me.

"Kinsey, please. Please stop fighting me." Enzo keeps his voice low as he carries me around the stone terrace, choosing to walk through the garden instead of carrying me through the crowd gathering to watch the drama.

"Then fight for me. He can't get away. He won't stop until he's dead, or I am." My voice cracks with my words. "You have to believe me."

"Of course, I fucking believe you and trust you. We just can't do as you ask right now. There are far too many witnesses. I will not do something to jeopardize my life with you for revenge and anger. I will not act rashly and risk him winning. That's what he wants. That's why he's trying to provoke us. I need you to believe me and trust me now. We will end him. You will get your justice. We just have to do it appropriately. We're too new. I cannot risk our futures." Enzo tenses with his words, his voice soft and pleading.

My head spins with remnants of the alcohol, and I give up and hang in his arms, unsure of how to respond. I know I'm being irrational. I know I need to do things a certain way. But my anger continues to consume me. And it projects not only at Uncle Rommel, but I'm suddenly so mad at Enzo. At Wilder, Arsenio, and Desmond. This isn't how I imagined things to be. I need the ruthless men I met the day they accidentally kidnapped me.

"You're risking everything by giving him more time, Enzo." I'm not even sure he hears me because he doesn't respond. He continues to carry me around the huge fortress.

I close my eyes, trying to settle my anger. But I can't. I can't do anything except shut down. This way, the world can't hurt me. Nothing can disappoint me. It'll be only me and my thoughts.

"Kinsey, did you hear me? I'm taking you home." Enzo strokes his fingers over my arm.

I don't respond to him.

I can't think about any of this when it feels as if I'm about to lose it all.

I was naïve to think I'd get a life of normalcy.

I was stupid to even think I'd get a life at all.

My heart aches. It's hard to breathe. At any second, my world might shatter.

And this time, I won't be able to pick up the pieces.

# Chapter Thirteen

## *Kinsey*

## Breaking Point

Am I being unfair, locking Enzo out of my room? I honestly don't know. My emotions get the best of me, my uncle's words tumbling through my head over and over again. I just need space. I need a moment to think and process. This was supposed to be a celebration, putting King Winston to rest along with his awful reign.

But I'm grieving. Not for the monster but for me.

With my uncle's arrival, I can't stop the flood of memories tightening my chest, making it difficult to breathe. I can hear his laughter as if he stands outside the door now, listening as my heartache threatens to end me. He took pleasure in my torment.

"Get out of my head!" I screech, smacking my temples, hoping that with the pain will come peace and clarity.

The door bangs open, smacking against the wall. A lock can't keep out any of my alphas if they truly want in. Enzo snatches my wrists and tugs my hands away, restraining me to him. I struggle in his hold, stepping on his feet, trying to break away. I just want the memories to stop. I want the world to freeze and give me a second to catch my gasping breath.

"Kinsey, stop. Please. Please, baby. You're scaring me." Enzo guides me backward until the backs of my knees hit my bed, sending me falling onto the fluffy duvet. He climbs on top of me, squeezing my hips between his thighs as he bows forward. "I got you. I'm here, and I'm not going anywhere. You have to stop hurting yourself. Please."

"He's going to kill me," I cry, refusing to submit to his pleas. "He'll kill you. He'll take you from me. He's coming. I know he is. He'll break in just like before."

"Shhh, shhh. We have doubled security. The palace is on lockdown until further notice." Enzo rubs his cheek against mine, trying to smooth away the trembles chattering my teeth without letting me go.

My mind whirls, refusing to believe I'm safe. The pounding in my ears thrums in the same quick rhythm as my heart. My instincts drive me crazy. I know better than to think my uncle will just go away. He's back with a vengeance, pissed off that I slipped through his fingers and bested him while doing so. I'm sure the moment he gets his hands on me, he'll hurt me twice as much. He'll break me until only dust remains, leaving no pieces behind for me to put back together.

"Listen to my voice, baby. Focus on my words. You're mine. My omega. My mate. My everything. That man will perish before he gets within a foot of you. He can't hurt you now. He can't. We won't let him. You won't let him. You're my badass, baby. I'll make sure you can kill a man with your bare hands to guarantee it." Enzo snuggles his face into my throat, feeling my body relax beneath his. "Do you understand? We're going to start practicing right here and now."

"Right n-now?" I stutter, my voice whining.

"Absolutely. Do whatever you think is right to get me off you, and we'll go from there." Enzo eases away, rubbing his thumb across my cheek, combing the hair from my face.

"I'm not kneeing you in the dick." My breathing slows the longer he stares into my eyes, searching my face with his sapphire depths.

"Well, how about we pretend you did? That's an excellent start, baby. Good thinking. Say you hurt my junk, then what?" Enzo rolls off me, faking a groan.

I scramble from the bed, putting space between us. "I run." Spinning toward the window, I freeze in my tracks, catching sight of the silhouette outside my window.

I wail in fear, stumbling back, trying to put space between me and Uncle Rommel. "It's him! I told you! Fuck! Enzo, help! Help!"

The world blurs as Enzo scoops me off my feet, planting his palm to my back, smoothing his fingers up and down my spine. He bounces slightly, crossing the room. I scratch my fingers into his shoulders, burying my face into the crook of his neck. "What are you doing? Stop! Call security! He's here."

Shadows edge my vision, my stomach twisting. Enzo sets me on the edge of the bed and gets between my legs, wrapping his arms around my waist.

"Kinsey, please. I'm so sorry. I'm so, so sorry. I should've killed him right then and there. If I had, you wouldn't be so afraid that you're hallucinating. No one is outside your window. It's impossible. We're three stories up, and your room doesn't have a balcony. I can show you." Enzo tries to ease away from me to get to his feet, but I cling to him, refusing to let him go.

I blink a few times, staring at the sheer curtains where I swore I saw a figure, but Enzo is right. I don't have a balcony. No one can be outside. It's all in my head. "Fuck. I'm going crazy. What is wrong with me?"

"Nothing is wrong with you. You're traumatized, and I've failed you. I shouldn't have forced you to leave the funeral. I should've done as you asked and killed that fucker. I'm so sorry." Enzo rests his forehead to my stomach, his voice lowering. "I don't deserve to have a woman like you. I know better. I shouldn't have put the damn law before us. Your feelings aren't worth the cost."

I sniffle, my breath hitching. His words break me as much as I feel them break him, and it makes everything that much worse. How dare my uncle make my alpha feel unworthy. How dare that bastard make him question his ability to care for me. My emotions got the best of me, and I've always been a little broken, but seeing Enzo on his knees before me like this? I'm devastated and angry.

"Enzo..." I gasp a soft breath, trying to get myself in control. "Don't say those things. It's not true. You can't blame yourself for my undoing. You just can't."

"I have to hold myself accountable. As your alpha, it's my duty to protect you in both mind and body. I've failed, and I want you to recognize it, so I can grow from it and ensure it never fucking happens again. That's the type of man I need to be for you. Always striving for better. Never just settling in old habits. So, please, Kinsey. Let me beg for forgiveness. Let me grovel and kiss your feet." Enzo eases away from me, remaining on his knees, his eyes glossy but his face stern. His cheeks redden with his swelling emotions.

"Of course, I forgive you. This is not your fault. I refuse to declare it as so." I grab his cheeks, tugging him closer. When he refuses to get to his feet, I slide from the bed and kneel with him, draping my arms over his shoulders. "You're exactly the man I need. Strong. Reliable. Fucking sexy as hell. You're open and honest and don't let me get away with shit. And mostly, you're here. You're here, and you'll never leave me."

"Never," he agrees, bowing in to caress his lips to mine. "And I'll prove it. I was going to give this to you earlier, but things came up, and then it didn't seem right. But it feels absolutely important for me to do so, right here and now. I know it's nothing fancy. I know I don't have hundreds of roses decorating a room or candles lighting every surface. I know I'm not lying naked on your bed with dozens of cupcakes waiting for you to devour, but I love you, and I can't wait another moment longer."

Reaching his hand into his pocket, Enzo pulls out a small dark blue velvet box. My breath catches at the sight of the glittering ring on a bed of satin. The platinum band matches the one Arsenio gave me, but this one has an opal stone a bit off-center with a dozen diamonds lining the band. And I realize that it is meant to connect with Arsenio's, coming together as a set. It's absolutely stunning. My heart rises with joy, my emotions turning from chaotic and mind jumbling to pure happiness, love, and appreciation. This was the last thing I had expected tonight, but I'm so grateful for it.

"I want to ask for your hand in a formal union. I know that I have claimed you as mine already, but I want to shout it to the world that you mean more to me than being my omega. You are my other half. My best friend. And hopefully, if you agree, my wife. I see that you've already accepted Arsenio's proposal, but I hope you have space for another." He chuckles with his words, knowing damn well that my mind is already set.

"Of course, I do, Enzo. And yes. Absolutely yes. I will be your wife. But I do have a stipulation..." I press my lips together, hiding my expression.

Enzo raises an eyebrow at me. "You want me naked with cupcakes on me, acting as your sexy beast of a table, don't you?"

I tip my head back and laugh, loving how he knew exactly what was on my mind before I even had to say it. "Maybe just the frosting. I'll lick every inch of you."

He play-growls and scoops me up, lifting me to my feet with him. He tosses me on the bed and grabs the hem of my dress, hiking it up until he shows off my lack of panties. "But I get to lick you first. I've had a fucking boner since the moment you showed me your pussy, baby. Do you know how difficult it was for me to refrain from sucking you right in front of everyone? I almost crawled under that table to see your hot body for myself."

"Maybe next time. The idea kind of excites me. Just imagine you making me come without anyone knowing." I lock my fingers through his hair, yanking him up further until his lips meet mine.

"Everyone will know. I promise you that. They'll know, and they'll be fucking jealous that your pussy is mine. Your heart is mine. And then my brothers would fucking probably line up behind me." He chuckles at the thought, sliding his hand down my torso until he reaches between my legs, gliding his finger over my clit until he dips it inside me.

I moan and squirm, letting his potent lust consume me, stealing away and burying everything bad that happened tonight in the back of my mind. Enzo makes it so easy to forget that the world spins outside of us. I'll let him continue to distract me. It's the only way I know how to protect myself. With him, I don't feel like I'm losing my mind. With him, I can easily shove my memories away.

"I'm sorry I couldn't give you what you needed tonight, but I'll give you everything you could ever want right now. I love you, baby. I don't want to remember this night as the celebration of my father's death. I want to remember it as the night the woman of my dreams agreed to marry me." Enzo kisses me again, breaking away to suck my throat until he nips the crook of my neck. His finger continues to work me over, slipping in and out of me as he strums my clit, the sensation like utter bliss.

I lift my hips, giving him space to pull off my dress, and he kneels between my legs, drinking me in is if I'm the most magical sight he's ever seen. I feel so incredibly sexy and desired in this moment. Undeniably loved.

Enzo fingers me until my body spasms, and I grab onto the duvet, clutching it as I arch my back. He purrs at my orgasm, watching me squirm in front of him, my body flying on the wave of pleasure he provides.

Locking his hands to my knees, he spreads me wider before him, propping my legs on his shoulders. He licks my leg to my thigh and bites me hard enough to leave a mark that'll take days to disappear. I gasp in his scent, the warm woods of vetiver and the coolness of mint opening me up to his desire.

He buries his face between my legs, gliding his tongue over the seam of my body until he sucks my clit into his mouth. He's not going to stop until I orgasm again. My pleasure lies in his hands, and he'll take care of me. I reach down and comb my fingers through his hair, panting and wriggling as the sensation intensifies. He wets his hand with my slick and then slides a finger into my ass, adding pressure as he fills me up in a way that leaves my body singing.

"You taste so good. If I could bottle up your love and savor the elixir, I would. Your scent calls to me. Your body needs me. And I need you. I can't wait until we can officially mate how I desire. I'll be the best alpha. I'll be everything you could ever want." Enzo murmurs and bites my other thigh, sending me over the edge with another orgasm. I squirt with my release, screaming out as ecstasy shadows my vision. The passion and heat of this moment warms me from the inside out, and I grab Enzo by the shoulders, guiding him up until our bodies align.

Sinking inside me, Enzo thrusts, his body pounding against mine, stealing my breath away. I bite him on his shoulder, tasting the bitter tang of his blood as I claim him with my mark. I scratch my fingers over his back, locking my legs around his waist, falling into sync with each of his deep thrusts.

"You feel so fucking good. So tight. I can't wait to fill you with my seed to watch you drip. It's the sexiest sight in the entire world." Enzo rests his hands by my shoulders and rocks his body in smooth motions until his cock swells, locking us in place, his orgasm setting me off with my own. We moan in unison, my body heating up even more as he does exactly as he wants, coming inside me and reminding me exactly what he desires when I go into heat.

And now that I think about it, excitement courses over me. My mind whirls with pleasure and love and lust and everything beautiful and magical in this world. We will build a family together. Only the most precious and valuable thing could ever come from such a bond. It'll make us stronger. We'll fight harder to maintain the life we have now.

Thinking about it swells my soul with desire. I shouldn't be afraid. This is better than any life I could've ever imagined. Our children will grow with the ideals they need to ensure the future of our pack thrives. They won't be born out of necessity. They'll be born from the strongest bond that could ever happen in this life. The bond of love.

My eyes roll as the orgasm continues, lasting as long as Enzo's knot, and I shake and quiver beneath him, gasping for air. He kisses me with enough passion to curl my toes. I dig my fingers into him, listening to him purr at the sensation of my nails breaking his skin.

The pressure releases after what feels like an eternity of bliss, and I bite Enzo one more time, wanting nothing more than for him to remember this moment. He will never think about anything else that happened today, and neither will I. Because this is the day that I accepted his proposal and realized just how much I want children with him. Just how much I look forward to him taking care of me as I deserve during my heat.

I used to question my worth, but with Enzo and his brothers, I no longer do so. Because I am worthy. They would never let me forget it.

"I could knot with you again and again if you allowed it. You're all I need to survive. I want to live between your sexy thighs and survive on your kisses alone." Enzo cups my cheeks as he eases out of me, keeping me in place long enough to let my heart settle down.

I kiss him once more, playing with the two rings on my finger, and he pushes up to drink in the sight of me beneath him, dripping with his seed, my body warm and blushing from our act of pleasure.

"So incredibly hot. Let me savor this moment a little longer, and then I'll draw you a bath." Enzo's eyes sparkle in the light, the sapphire depths like gemstones.

He traces his fingers along my body, memorizing every groove and curve until he imprints this moment in his mind forever. Scooping me up, Enzo carries me to the bathroom, cleaning me up and letting me soak in the tub as he cleans up the bed and grabs a few things from the kitchen. I step out before he returns and stand in the doorway, watching him cook for me at the small stove of my kitchenette.

How did I ever get so lucky?

"Baby, you were supposed to wait for me." Enzo smiles at me from over his shoulder. "Come lay down. Let me feed you in bed and give you the massage I promised."

I do as he asks, returning to the fresh sheets and fluffy pillows, but our scents still linger in the air. Enzo dims the lights, and I stare at the window, watching the dark night light up with the orange glow of a fire.

"It's finally over, baby. That fire signifies the end of my father's reign. Our power will be reborn from those ashes, and we'll thrive. I promise you that. This is our forever, and no one will get in our way." Enzo kisses my temple, staring at the glow outside the window.

"Absolutely no one," I agree.

For the first time, I don't have any doubts.

This is a promise I will keep.

# Chapter Fourteen

## *Wilder*

## Devilish Deal

Flames imprint on my mind as I stare at the fire consuming my father's body. I threw a couple pictures into the funeral pyre, letting them eat away at some of the memories I want to disappear with him.

I hate that I couldn't follow Kinsey. I couldn't just postpone the funeral. It is my duty as king to work through every piece of shit thrown at me, including the fucked up man I will hang by the cock before splitting his throat.

"It's over, brother. We'll get through this next obstacle. He can be bought. I know he can. That's what he's wanted this whole time." Desmond drapes his arm around my shoulder leaning in close, hugging me in a way he hasn't done in a while. I wasn't sure he would ever forgive me for letting my emotions get the best of me when I tried to dominate him, but I'm glad he at least tolerates me now. I still feel guilty for how things went down. I know that Arsenio and Enzo are also confused and annoyed that I didn't consult with them when I declared Desmond as the king of Platinum Shores. It was my way of trying to make it up to him.

"If we give in to his demands, he'll keep coming back for more. I know his type. He's like our father. He's like many of the low lives we've dealt with. He's just going to want more and more. I need to meet with the leaders of the Pack Regimes in the morning to discuss this whole situation. If they let him come in and try to upend our lives and stop the coronation of Kinsey as queen, they're going to open a shit show of problems. It'll give other packs the right to demand shit if they didn't agree with their leaders' decision in their omega's arrangements." I fist my hands, flexing my muscles as the fire blurs with my vision.

"You're absolutely right about that, and they'll be on our sides. We'll handle this appropriately. As soon as we get their approval, he's a dead man." Arsenio mutters the words from my other side, his usual laid-back demeanor now tense and stern. He walked Rommel out with our security team and made sure that he left. If it were Desmond or me, there would've been bloodshed. Hearing Kinsey's anguish and pain over the confrontation leaves a hole in my chest.

"May he rest in peace," a voice says, drawing me from my thoughts. Saint Vista's most prominent mortician closes the viewing window on the portable crematorium, releasing us from having to stand here all night. It was my request. When a family member or a pack mate falls, some packs will stand until the body turns completely into ash, no matter how long it takes.

"Let's get the guests out." Desmond squeezes my shoulder and guides me to turn around. "This isn't a party anyone wants to stay at."

He's right about that. Those obligated to show up will leave immediately when they're excused, and that is basically every-one on the terrace.

I straighten my shoulders and look at the small crowd gath-ered behind us. They shift on their feet, as anxious as I expect-ed, and I bow my head to show respect.

"May he rest in the eternity he deserves," I say, lifting my head back up and tightening my jaw. "Thank you for showing your support during this time. Our next gathering will be one of great happiness. It's an honor to lead you as our territory's king, and I hope it'll be many, many decades before we must gather like this again. I'll do everything in my power to ensure it. Here is to the strength of our pack and the loyalty of our territory." I raise my hand and nod my head. "That is my promise to you as your leader within the Pack Regimes."

No one applauds, and murmurs fill the air as they quietly say their goodbyes to each other and excuse themselves. I stand in my spot with my brothers until only Holly, the Silversteins, my aunt and cousin, and the staff remains on the terrace.

"Do you want me to meet up with the rest of our security staff, King Wilder?" Jude asks, rocking on his heels. He wanted to leave with them to ensure that Rommel left our territory completely, but he was obligated to stay as the head of our security division.

"Don't call me king. We're family. I will not take that title like my father had. You know that my brothers and I are going to share power." I open my arms and offer Jude a hug, which he takes. "I'll handle it too. Why don't you get some rest tonight? You're going to have a lot of shit to do tomorrow as we restructure our pack's responsibilities. I'm going to need you to be our face and voice for a couple weeks, okay?"

Aunt Melina smiles, her face lighting up for the first time tonight. "And he will be excellent. Your father could never see who was truly worthy and the most powerful. He liked to keep those closest to him weak. This is how I know you're going to make a great king."

I hug Aunt Melina next. "Thank you, Auntie. Enjoy your new home. Change anything you want. Donate everything you hate. You're fully in charge here now. I trust that you will care for our family and pack."

She kisses each of my cheeks. "Always, Nephew." She opens her arms and hugs Desmond and Arsenio next. "Your mother would be so proud of you. She is here, watching over you. I hope you know that."

I only smile, not sure if I believe her. I'd hope she was enjoying her eternity in an afterlife better than the life she was denied here.

My brothers and I watch as Aunt Melina and Jude disappear through the entrance and back into the fortress. I scrub my cheeks, wiping away the subtle scent she left behind, wanting nothing more than to just go home, grab Kinsey from Enzo, and cuddle her for the rest of the night even if she's pissed off at me.

Unfortunately, I have shit to do. There's always something.

It's as if we can never catch a break. The moment we find peace, something always comes in to blow shit up. Maybe this is karma for my past actions and how I managed to shift power with brutality, but it was worth it to me. It's still worth it to me. I'd kill dozens of men and ensure that we got what we needed to really protect ourselves. They weren't good. But neither am I. Not now, at least. Maybe one day.

"Arsenio, why don't you escort Holly back to the palace while Desmond and I meet up with the security team?" I flick my attention to Holly, smiling as if this is an extravagant ball and not our father's funeral.

At least she can finally sleep in peace. This was the best gift we could give her.

"Actually, King Wilder. I was hoping that you would let us escort Holly. You have my word that she will be safe. She's not ready to turn in for the night, and I have some movies with her name on them. If that's okay." Beckett stands a couple of feet away, holding his arms over his chest, preparing to be denied.

I force my head to nod, despite not wanting to agree. It takes a lot from me to entrust Holly with his pack. I know he is worthy, but I've spent all my life protecting her. I'm afraid to give that honor to someone else.

"Check in with me when you get home. I prefer you didn't keep her out all night, but she is an adult, so I will leave it up to her." I shift my jaw back and forth, forcing my mouth to stay shut instead of threatening him like I want to.

"You can trust me. I'll take care of her. I promise." Beckett offers his hand to me, and I shake it.

"Only for as long as she allows it. If she changes her mind, you'll respect that. Do you understand?" I know I don't need to say it to him, but I have to say it for myself. I just want to declare out loud that she is not someone I'll trade for loyalty or power. We'll grow it together.

"Absolutely. I respect your plans for our territory and look forward to serving under your reign." Beckett bows formally, showing his gratitude. He returns to Holly, only for her to squeal and jump up into his arms. She grabs Jordan by the hair and ruffles her fingers through it, and the others laugh, breaking their usual composed selves in front of me. That's what Holly does to people. She fills them with light and love and laughter. All the things that my father hated. All the things that my mother cherished.

Who knew it would be so hard letting her grow up and be the adult she has been for a while?

"You did good, brother. Kinsey will reward you when Holly tells her how you didn't put up any resistance toward Beckett's request. I know it's hard to see her being taken care of by another pack, but this is how it should be. We're so lucky that we've managed to give her a choice in her life." Arsenio pats me on the back. "Now, let's get out of here. I don't want to stay away from the palace for long. I don't trust anyone outside of us these days, and Enzo likes to react before thinking. If something goes down, we'll have a lot of blood to clean up."

Enzo has always carried a lighthearted persona as the youngest member of our family. It's what makes him lethal. People underestimate him. It's how I know he's a magnificent protector for our girl.

He does stuff that we can't. He also does certain things, so we don't have to.

"All right. You drive. Desmond, I want you to navigate. I need to put in the request for a meeting with the Pack Regimes." I straighten my suit jacket. "This must be taken care of as soon as possible. Rommel needs to be put in his place. The asshole will see who he's truly dealing with when he stares down the barrel of my gun."

His death is the only option.

It's the only way Kinsey will ever be able to heal.

I will not put her through another tragedy ever again.

"You have to be shitting me. Is he really staying with the Smith-son Pack?" I lean between the two front seats, wishing I were behind the wheel. It's unlike me to let my brother drive, but I just needed to take care of shit.

"He was supposed to be at a hotel." Desmond swivels in the front seat. "Why is he here?"

"Probably trying to bribe his way into an alliance with the Pack Regimes. You know how valuable it is to have alliances from other regions. I want to kill him. I'm going to kill them both. The Smithsons know better than to try and pull shit on us." I fling my door open, not even waiting for Arsenio to put the car in park.

My fury controls me, and I stride away from my brothers, not even caring if it's well past midnight. A light shines from the front windows of the mansion, and I head straight toward the wrought iron gates. Jumping onto the small brick wall, I hoist myself up and over the fence, refusing to use the call box. They'll know I'm coming. I'm not going to wait for them to prepare.

"Wilder, wait up. You can't just go in there with your guns blazing. Please, they'll have the right to shoot you for trespassing." Desmond runs behind me, the thuds of his footsteps twice as fast as Arsenio's.

"They can try. They're breaking our alliance for even hosting this fucker, and I'll let them know it. We don't tolerate backstabbing bastards. I know that they were in negotiations to bring one of our pack's omegas into their household, and I'll deny them now." I stride forward, keeping my hands at my side, not reaching for my weapons even though I want to.

"Wilder," Desmond says, calling for me.

I ignore him and step onto the stone porch of the arched entrance. "Smithsons, open your fucking door. Greet me with the respect I deserve. I know you've invited Mr. Rommel into your household. I'll give you the benefit of the doubt and assume you didn't know he was one of our enemies. Give him up now." I bang my fist on the door, preparing to punch the window to break it open.

I don't have to. The door swings inward, and Bobby Smithson stands in the foyer with his arms crossed over his chest, a robe wrapped around his body. He obviously had been woken up, but I don't think it was by me.

"What is the meaning of this? What are you ranting about? I have no enemies of yours within my house." He shifts on his feet and looks down, lying through his crooked teeth.

I charge forward and lace my fingers around his neck, spinning him toward the wall to hoist him off his feet. "I know Rommel is here. I've been tailing him. He's trying to get my omega."

Bobby grinds his teeth, scowling at me. A couple of clicks sound through the air as his pack mates turn off the safeties of their guns, aiming them at me. I can see the reflection in the mirror next to Bobby. I don't stop, though. They won't shoot me. It's an empty threat.

"We don't have time for niceties. His insolence gives us reason enough." Arsenio surprises the hell out of me and fires his gun, shooting it inches away from Bobby. He damn well could've made a kill shot from over my shoulder, but this is only a warning.

"Now, everyone! Stand down. All we want is Rommel. Give him to us, and we'll leave here like none of this ever happened." Desmond growls with his words, sounding more like an alpha than any of these other bastards standing around. He could take them all down quicker as well. "No one has to get hurt. We just want him out."

"Easy now, boys. I have the approval to be here. Just until the morning. I didn't trust that you would leave me alone, and I was right." Rommel's voice echoes through the arched entryway.

I drop Bobby to the ground, reach for my gun, and aim it at the grand staircase. I pull the trigger without hesitating, hitting and shattering the decorative vase beside him. Rommel ducks and swears, keeping out of view. I shove past one of the Smithson betas and charge toward the stairs. My mind focuses on one thing—killing Rommel. This is what Kinsey wants and needs. Fuck the repercussions. We'll deal with them when we face them.

"Show yourself and be the fucking alpha you think you are, Rommel," I snap, snarling with my words, sounding as feral and dangerous as I truly am with my omega at risk. "I know what you did. You're guilty of crimes against your own damn pack, and it's my duty as Kinsey's alpha and pack leader to see to it that you pay the consequences so she can receive the justice she deserves."

"If you kill me, others will come. You don't want to deal with the most notorious pack in Fall Harbor. Kinsey was supposed to be theirs. As the leader of her pack, it was my right to ensure she found an alpha better than her previously chosen one." Rommel clutches onto the leg of the decorative table, cowering down. "Saint Vista won't appreciate a regional war. But I can prevent it. You just need to hear me out. I don't care who Kinsey goes to. All I fucking care about is getting what I deserve from such an arrangement."

Of-fucking-course. We called it, suspecting that he was after wealth and power, especially knowing what we have as the leading pack of Gilded Sands.

"You think you deserve what exactly? Money? Territory? Kinsey was not yours to use in bartering." I climb the rest of the stairs, training my gun on Rommel.

He grinds his teeth, scrambling to pull a knife from his belt like the idiot he is. I'll blast his brains out before he can sink the point anywhere on my body. "Stand down, Wilder. You don't want to do this. You think you know everything, but the Pack Regimes of Saint Vista suspect you're up to something. They would love you to give them a reason for a hostile takeover. The fact that you gave a new and thriving territory to a beta—"

I shoot at the marble tile next to him, cracking it. "I gave it to a highly trained, respected prince. If they have a fucking problem—"

"I know! I know you did. But they don't think so. Ask Bobby." Rommel scrambles back, taking cover around the corner in a hall leading to the bedrooms. He peeks out. "I'll prove it. They had me come here to help establish another omega club. They want one run by a male alpha on their side, not one of the fucking bitches trying to control us by our cocks. The Smithsons have the first shipment in their basement. Five omegas that were given to Pack Regimes after being picked up."

What the actual fuck? He's fucking lying. He has to be lying. It's in our agreement as the leaders of the Pack Regimes to give omegas the pack they need. It's fucked up, auctioning them, but it was agreed to be better than imprisoning them in sex clubs as perfect omegas to knot with and use without caring for them as they should be. Changing the auctions was one thing. It would be easy enough to persuade the powerholders to give more rights and the choice of alphas to the omegas our region needs to thrive. But establishments like the Knotty Girls Club and Vixen Lounge? I want to burn the region down at the thought.

"He's lying, King Wilder. The omegas I have here are only being housed until the auctions." Bobby's voice rings from below, the alpha standing against the wall with Arsenio cornering him.

"Which auction? I was under the impression there wouldn't be another one until after the breeding season ends." Because part of the auctions is giving omegas and alphas time to adjust. It's to give alphas a chance to bond and get to know their mates, keeping things as civilized as possible, despite the gross circumstances my father helped create decades ago.

Bobby squeezes his eyes shut. "The—the—"

I never expected to believe Rommel, but he's a strategic man. He'd do whatever to save his own skin, no matter who pays the cost of his betrayal.

"He can't tell you because he's full of shit." Rommel remains hidden like a coward.

Bobby growls and charges Arsenio, trying to dodge past him. "You son of a—"

I spin and aim my gun at Bobby from the landing, pulling the trigger. Blood pours from the wound on his chest, soaking into his robe. The alpha drops to his knees, howling in pain. I heave a few deep breaths, wanting nothing more than to finish him off.

"Make me a deal, King Wilder. I'll tell the leaders whatever you need. Make me a deal, and I'll sign the paperwork that guarantees Kinsey is yours." Rommel cautiously steps from the hallway, raising his hands in surrender.

"You traitor! We had a deal!" Bobby hollers, clutching his chest.

"Give me Platinum Shores and show what a reasonable man you are. Show them you can be complacent and smart. Let them believe they can control you. It's what you need to succeed with whatever the fuck you plan to do." Rommel steps closer, keeping his eyes locked to mine.

I clench my teeth, my mind whirling. He shouldn't make so much sense. Guys like him destroy everything in their wake, but they also put self-preservation first. It's the only reason I believe his word about the other leaders.

Breaking his gaze, I peer over the balcony at Arsenio and Desmond, looking to them for answers. This shouldn't be my sole decision. This concerns Kinsey and our pack. It concerns our future.

"Wilder! Wilder, he's manipulating you!" Bobby yells, groaning.

Except he's not. He believes he is, but I'm not stupid.

I can use this to my advantage. Under the Saint Vista Pack Regimes' law of the region, I have the right to punish traitors as I see fit. All I need is to get him to go through with signing the appropriate documents to guarantee us Kinsey, and then I'll kill him myself.

I just hope my brothers trust me.

Kinsey too.

I holster my gun and raise my hand. "I'll tentatively accept, but you have to prove your word now. Tell your ally that the Smithsons sold the omegas out from under them, and they tried to kill you to hide it. Accept the blame for their deaths. Do that, and we'll make a proper deal."

Rommel whips his head up and down, smirking at what he thinks is his success. I remain expressionless, listening to him call in a report to the Lunar Mountain Pack.

"You fuck—" Gunfire silences Bobby as Arsenio ends his life. The Smithsons don't have a chance to retaliate before the three of us open fire, taking down those present to ensure word doesn't get out.

Silence fills the air, and I puff out a breath through my mouth, the bitter scent of the fallen alphas and betas permeating the air. I turn to Rommel expectantly, waving my hand for him to lead the way. I'll never turn my back on him. He's confident enough in our verbal agreement to obey, taking the stairs two at a time.

I join my brothers, their faces expressionless. I can't tell whether or not I'm about to get my ass kicked, but it doesn't matter. Several soft cries and whimpers cut through the silence. I freeze at the dark entrance to a cement corridor, not unlike the security tunnels we have winding through the palace.

"It's okay, knotty girls. I'm not gonna hurt you. I'm saving you." Rommel's voice rises in tone, and he sounds like he is speaking to frightened animals. "Come on. Let's get you girls out of here."

My heart raps hard against my ribs, threatening to break free. A pale-haired blonde steps from the corridor first, her slender, tall form reminding me of Holly.

Disgust twists my stomach. This could've been both Kinsey and Holly's fates.

This could be the downfall of our region if I don't change things.

Desmond steps forward, knowing he's less likely to scare the seven omegas that emerge from the basement—six females and a male. "Don't look around, okay? We're the leaders of Gilded Sands. We have a safe house to take you to. Is that okay?"

None of them argue, not that they would.

I shoot a text to Enzo.


*Me: Make sure you and Kinsey are dressed and available when we get home. Plans have changed. We found a nest of enslaved omegas."*

*Baby Brother: What? Seriously? Was it Rommel?*

*Me: It's too much to explain. I don't want to leave a digital trail. Just be ready.*


"Shall we?" Rommel asks, drawing my attention away from the phone.

I flare my nostrils and glower at him. "Shall we what? You're fucking staying here and taking care of this mess. I'm not getting involved in this shitshow or the paperwork." Reaching for Bobby's corpse, I tug his cellphone from his robe. "I have Bobby's number. I'll call you in the morning. Don't ignore my call."

Rommel presses his lips together, his eyes slits with his annoyance. He looks ready to argue but says, "Fine. I'll stand by, but don't even think of trying to cross me."

Ignoring his comment, I turn to Desmond. "I'll need you to draft up the transfer of power. I'm sorry, brother. This isn't how I wanted things to go."

"We do what we have to," he responds.

He's right. I'll do whatever it takes to ensure our formal bond with Kinsey, even if it means making a deal with the devil. Luckily, Rommel isn't the only monster. I'm worse. He'll regret ever coming here.

I'll show no mercy.

# Chapter Fifteen

## *Desmond*

## Omega Sanctuary

The scent of the frightened omegas nearly overwhelms me on the drive home. I pull through the looming gate to the palace and glance in my rearview mirror. The sun breaks on the horizon as dawn lights the grounds, shadowing everything in a sleepy haze. I don't know what we're going to do from here, but we couldn't just leave these omegas at the Smithsons. Who knows what Rommel would've done?

I don't trust him. I never will. It kills me to think that I'll have to sign away my territory to such a despicable man, even temporary. Because I know Wilder would've never made that deal if he didn't have a plan. We've always tried our best to do things mostly according to the law or with reasons that we could explain to the Pack Regimes. If Rommel was telling the truth, though, they might be coming for us. Most of the leaders are as old or older than our father was, and they're not ready to give up their power despite their ideologies being outdated and cruel. Unfair. I don't give a fuck about their supposed excuse of protecting the most vulnerable in our society by having packs arrange unions or auctioning them to packs of power for a supposed better life. What I care about is giving omegas the freedom they need to truly be taken care of the way they deserve. Like with Kinsey. I never imagined I could fall in love so deeply and irrevocably with anyone. Also, like the love I see budding between Holly and the Silversteins. The world would be a better place if there weren't assholes trying to build walls to keep those they see beneath them contained. I'll do everything I can to tear down the obstacles they claim are for everyone's safety, but we all know that isn't true. It's time we get rid of those stuck in the past. We need to plan for those who will live in the future.

"Welcome to the Gilded Sands Pack palace. This is a private sanctuary, and our security will ensure your safety. We'll be relocating you shortly to the fortress, where we'll get things figured out. Is that okay?" I turn in my seat and glance at the seven silent omegas huddled together in the back cargo space. I didn't want to separate them, and I definitely didn't want my brothers handling them. They're too close to going into rut that they could accidentally frighten them because Kinsey will be the only omega they want around. It's instinctual. Deep-seated but manageable. I just didn't want to test it.

None of them respond, so I assume they won't fight it. They've been traumatized and broken into obedient beings, and it's going to take more than a couple of kind words to get them to open up. But hopefully soon.

I pull out my phone and click on my number one favored contact.

*Me: Can you meet me on the driveway? Tell Enzo to stay inside. I don't want to frighten these omegas, but I need help. You'll be able to show them they're safe. They'll trust you more than anyone.*

*Pretty Girl: Of course. I texted Holly, and she'll be on her way in a bit. She'll meet us at the fortress.*

*Me: Good. It'll be more comforting with both of you.*

*Pretty Girl: With you too. You have no idea the effect you have on others. I'm sure they're already a lot better than they were.*

*Me: I hope so. Brace yourself. This is a bit rough. I'm afraid it might trigger you.*

*Pretty Girl: I'm good. I feel grounded and better than I had. I'm coming down the stairs now.*

I glance up at the front door, waiting for Kinsey to material-ize before exiting the vehicle. She rushes to me with wide eyes, her dark brown hair flowing behind her. She wears a simple blue dress with bare feet. All I want to do is scoop her up and kiss her. Hug her and whisper how much I love her. I hated the way things ended at the funeral, and it nearly broke me watching Enzo drag her away, not allowing her to destroy the man that ruined her life.

It bothers me that I hadn't done it myself, and I'm afraid to tell her that he gets to live another day because he succeeded in manipulating us with his blackmail.

"None of them have said a word. I tried to talk to them on the way back, but they were just far too terrified. Maybe you can get their names or the packs they came from. We're hoping that maybe they're not all considered unwanted, and we can help them find their way home if they want to go." I stroke my fingers on Kinsey's arm, playing with the soft fabric of her short sleeve.

She bobs her head, turning her green gaze to the cargo van. She can't see them from here because of the lack of windows, but I know she wishes she could. They'll probably startle the second we open the back door.

I peek in from the driver's seat. "I'm opening the back up to let my mate in. I don't want to scare you. She's an omega too."

For the first time, I get a reaction, and one of them whispers something to the male omega under her breath.

I smirk at Kinsey and nod, motioning for her to open the doors to the cargo space. She slowly swings them open, keeping her movements slow as if the omegas are frightened animals. I love her so much, watching how cautious and careful she is, handling herself with confidence despite how horrible the situation is.

"Hi there. I'm Kinsey. Is it okay if I ride in back with you? We're going to take you up the road to the fortress. You'll like it there. You'll get your own rooms if you want, or you can share. Ms. Melina is waiting for you. She is the nicest woman. And I promise we'll keep all the alphas away from you. I know you must be so scared right now. I want you to know that you're safe. We will not allow the Pack Regimes to take you back." Kinsey uses my shoulder to step up into the van, and she perches on the wheel well, the small seat just big enough for her. She nods at me to close the door, and I do as she wishes and meet Enzo's gaze from across the yard. He remains in the doorway to the foyer, keeping his distance just as I requested.

He waves his phone at me, and I pull mine out of my pocket to see a text message.

*Little Shit: Is there anything I can do? I feel useless.*

I rack my brain, knowing that he won't be satisfied if I tell him just to wait.

*Me: Can you look over the paperwork for Platinum Shores? Wilder will explain everything, but we're signing over the territory to Rommel for now. This will give us the chance to get him.*

Enzo throws his hand, looking as if he's going to rush me. I quickly jog to the driver's seat and slide in, closing the door and locking it.

My phone chimes.

*Little Shit: You can't just tell me that shit and leave.*

I ignore his text message and put the van in reverse, backing up to turn around, going the way I came because it's shorter than going through the property.

Enzo chases the van for a couple of feet before giving up. He'll reach out to Wilder next, which is better. Because I still have no idea what the fuck he's really thinking and planning. But that's none of my concern right now. I have one job—help these omegas feel safe and comfortable.

I turn on the music to fill the silence, trying my best to give Kinsey some privacy as she murmurs to the omegas, finally getting one of them to talk to her. She's from another region completely, brought in from over the border.

I frown, imagining just how fucking awful it must've been. Shit like that makes me want to stab fuckers in their balls.

How people can be so callous and disgusting is beyond me. I can't grasp treating an innocent person that way. My violence and anger only flares toward those deserving. Those who don't deserve such power.

It only takes twenty minutes or so to get to the fortress, and Jude opens the wrought iron gate for me. I bump his fist as I drive past and head straight toward the back entrance. There are alphas from our pack roaming about, and I don't want to risk them running into us just yet. They need to be debriefed on how they're going to handle the situation under our rule.

I spot Aunt Melina at the staff entrance, and I slow the van and park close enough to the door that no one outside will be able to see us. She was supposed to ensure members of our pack were put to work and out of the way. We still don't know exactly who to trust here, considering this was our father's place.

"I've arranged one of the suites in the royal wing. No one has been there in years. I brought in a couple of cots, because I'm sure these precious babies want to stay together for now." Aunt Melina softens her voice, referring to the omegas as if they are children despite most of them being adults. But that's like her. Apparently, I could be forty and still be her sweet baby nephew.

I smile and give her a hug. "I appreciate it, Auntie. I know this whole thing is a huge adjustment for you. I'm sorry we've had to involve you, but I need help that my brothers can't provide."

"Anything for you, Des. I'm so proud of you. Your mom wouldn't have this any other way. She'd be so impressed by your empathy and kindness. She used to always say that you were meant to lead and not fall in line like the beta you manifested into. She always saw your potential." Aunt Melina squeezes my shoulder one more time before going to the back of the van and opening it up, greeting the omegas with a welcoming smile.

"Come on, my dears. Let's get you out of here and cleaned up. I bet you all are hungry, aren't you? Let me help you get settled. You can call me Auntie. We don't do formal titles in my household." Aunt Melina holds her hand out to a tall, slender redhead wearing just a sheath dress. Dirt covers her calves and feet, and by the way she smells, it's been a while since she's bathed. But that's not uncommon for alphas to do to omegas this time of year. They want the potent scent of their pheromones to get off on. Unlucky me has a strong sense of smell, so I get the brunt of it.

Kinsey steps out after her, wiggling her fingers to encourage the other six to join the redhead outside. They squint in the morning sun, and I'm sure it's been a while since they've gotten some fresh air.

My heart hurts for them. It enrages me that the Smithsons treated them so poorly. They don't deserve omegas. At least Bobby got what he deserved. Hopefully, the rest of his pack will get what's coming to them as well.

I push the thought away, focusing on the male omega as he straightens his back. It's been a while since I've been around one, and he's more closed off and scared than the rest of them.

"Here, take my jacket. You look cold." I shrug out of my suit jacket and hand it to the bare-chested male, allowing him to cover up the fact that he's only in a pair of thin boxers.

He whispers his thanks, keeping his gaze trained on the ground. I wish there was some way I could assure all of them that I wasn't lying about them being safe, but only time can do such a thing along with our actions. But this is a start.

"Come along now, babies." Aunt Melina pats my shoulder. "I'll see you inside. Let me get them settled first, and then both of you can join me."

I nod my head and turn to Kinsey, holding my hand out, silently begging her to take it so I can tug her into my arms.

It's been such a long fucking night that all I want to do is curl up with her in my bed and watch a movie until we both fall asleep.

I catch the subtle fragrance of Enzo in her hair, and I brush it out of the way to see a bite mark on her. He's going into rut any day now. He might even do so before she goes into heat just to be ready. If that happens, I'll be doing a whole lot of shit on my own. The more they knot, the quicker things can happen. Their pheromones and hormones trigger each other. When an omega is absolutely comfortable and ready, her body will do everything else.

"How are you holding up? I feel like I haven't had a moment to catch my breath. I just want to snuggle with you and help you gather whatever you need for the coming weeks. That's the only thing we should be doing. Besides each other." I hum in her ear, sucking on her lobe.

She shivers and groans, tightening her arms around me to bury her face in my chest. "That sounds like heaven. I'm just not sure now is a good time if you know what I mean. When I'm in the moment, I want it so badly it hurts. But the second things cool off...I get nervous. And having my uncle around doesn't help. Whatever happened with him? If he were dead, you guys would've told me immediately."

I frown, not wanting to get into the details. I know how important this is to her and how something simple could send her spiraling. And if she spirals and tries to go to the omegas, they will react.

"We'll go over our strategy when we get back home with my brothers. It's a bit more complicated, but you will be satisfied with the results. He won't be around to bother us much longer. He used these omegas and betrayed the leader of the Smithson Pack to keep his life a bit longer." I run my fingers through her hair, playing with the soft strands. I'm not ready to ease away from her. I'm afraid if our eyes meet, I might spill my soul instead of treading carefully.

"He's the one who told you about the omegas?" Kinsey's curiosity gets the best of her. She's in as much disbelief as we were when he told us. I don't really want to get into the details of Rommel's threat, because if she knew about the black market happening within the Pack Regimes and not just with some of the corrupt fuckers...what am I even saying? They're all fucking corrupt. Even so, she might panic. She might question everything. And the last thing I need is for her to have doubt for even a second.

I know she wants to know everything, and I do want to be honest, but there are some things that are just best left unsaid. Things that she shouldn't have to carry or stress over. She already has enough weight on her shoulders. This is why she has us. We can hold the concrete slabs above her without her knowing, stretching our muscles and living with the burning pain of nearly being crushed as long as she's safe. And when we're ready, she can move forward and out of the shadow of the burden so we can drop it behind us and never have to worry about such treacherous, unnerving worries again.

"Yes," I finally confirm. "He told us about the omegas being trafficked. He was saving his own skin, doing everything he could to keep Wilder from pulling the trigger, which he would've otherwise." I brush my lips to her forehead, doing my best to exude calmness. I'll always be the scent of tranquility and safety for her. She gets enough wild emotions from my brothers already.

"This is fucked up. I'm so glad that you guys got them, though. They're all young and around Holly's age. For at least two of them, it'll be their first heat as well. I think we should offer them suppressant pills if they want them. And if they don't, we should give them a safe space where they don't have to worry. Maybe even introduce them to people you trust. I know that betas can't knot, but you have proved that they can help out just as much. Who knows, maybe they'll find a connection that was never given to them." Kinsey's voice softens as she thinks over her words. "Wouldn't that be something? If we could have a place for unwanted omegas? Or a place for omegas trying to find sanctuary? I would've given anything to have somewhere to go that wasn't the Vixen Lounge. Somewhere that I could just live and let live and also be courted and familiarized with anyone I was interested in, whether it's an alpha or a beta. Even another omega. That's the kind of place we need."

I ease away from her, finally meeting her sparkling green eyes. I never thought of it like that. When I think of omega clubs, I think about those too scared to do anything except submit to the horny alphas who don't want the commitment of taking care of an omega and those who just want to get their dicks rubbed. But this imaginary place, and omega sanctuary, sounds perfect. And now I want to make it happen. I want to do this for Kinsey, so she can feel better about the state of the world, knowing that there are good alphas out there. There are good packs that deserve these precious beings even if they don't have the power to barter for such things.

"We could have two establishments. One where alphas can apply and be vetted out before they even get a chance to meet any omegas. Maybe the omegas can look over their applications and histories and decide whether or not they even want to meet them in the first place." Kinsey's features soften as she loses herself in my gaze, daydreaming about what she would consider the perfect place for people like her. For omegas that found themselves in terrible circumstances they just wanted to leave. To live and to get a choice.

"That sounds incredible. We can make it happen. I know we could. We could even start now. If these omegas have nowhere to go, we can create a place for them. They'll have the option to take suppressants or not. If they want birth control, we'll figure out how to provide it. If they just want to find a pack to create a life with, we'll offer that too. Through a matching club that'll replace any sort of omega sex club. And it won't be influenced by money. It'll be influenced by standup alphas who understand what omegas need instead of thinking of only themselves." I tuck her hair behind her ear. "How does that sound? We can make it work. We can even use Platinum Shores if we want." I try not to frown, because to use the territory, I need to ensure I get it back. I don't say as much, though. I don't want to ruin this moment. Because I know I will fight for it. Wilder unintentionally had given me the best gift. A gift that will benefit all of Saint Vista and even the rest of the regions in California and beyond.

Kinsey bounces on her feet. "I can't wait. I have so many ideas."

"Then let's go inside and get everything situated. This will be a new beginning for many, and you'll be the one to lead the way." I laced my fingers with her.

"Who needs to be alpha anyway? We can lead just as well." She smiles at me, reminding me of the absolute truth. Because she's right. I don't need to be an alpha.

I just need to be me.

# Chapter Sixteen

## *Kinsey*

## The Knotty Princes Club

The scent of fear, grief, and pain wafts through the air. I grab the doorframe, wobbling on my feet. When Enzo warned me that Wilder and his brothers found a nest of omegas, this wasn't what I had imagined. I expected them to be like the Gorgeous Girls of the Vixen Lounge or even the omegas from the Knotty Girls Club. But these omegas look as if they've suffered a far worse fate.

My heart breaks for them, their scents triggering my empathy. It reminds me of how I looked after my uncle had chained me down during my first heat. How bruised and bloody my wrists and ankles were. How tangled my hair was from my sweat and tears.

They need some serious care, and I'm afraid I don't know how to offer it to them.

"Kinsey, dear. Let me through." Melina slides past me, carrying a tray of food. "Why don't you help grab the cart from the hallway? Desmond will be here shortly to help us."

I do as Melina asks, prying my hand from the doorframe to step back into the hall. I spot the rolling cart with pitchers of water and stacked glasses. Beneath those, on the second shelf, lines a stack of clean towels and fresh linens. Garments finish the collection of goods, filling the bottom shelf.

I try my best not to touch anything, knowing that my alphas' scents might linger on me. They grow more possessive, and the second Wilder and Arsenio got home, they smothered me between their muscular bodies, ensuring that their pheromones push away the fear my uncle caused.

I shiver at the thought.

I roll the cart into the suite, closing the door behind me to give the omegas the privacy they need to feel safe in this strange new environment. Melina sets the tray at a table and arranges the plates filled with meats and cheeses, fruit and veggies, nuts and different dips for them to enjoy. She's making it easier on them by not assuming they'll eat whatever is served and giving them a chance to choose.

"Eat whatever you want and leave what you don't. If you want more, all you have to do is say so. There is no limit to providing what you need." Melina motions to the plates and serving spoons. "And when you're ready, I'll bring in some dessert. How does that sound?"

Only three react, nodding their heads, their eyes trained on the platters before them.

I ache at the sight of how uncertain and scared they are. I was lucky enough to be able to escape the sort of life they found themselves in before it even happened to me, really. My experience is nothing compared to this, but it does help me see a bit more clearly. They won't open up until they're ready, and I can't force them. I won't force them to.

"Melina, I'll handle this from here for now. I know Holly will be here soon. Why don't you check on my alphas and ensure everything is okay?" I squeeze Melina's shoulders until she steps closer and kisses each of my cheeks. "You're going to be a marvelous queen, Kinsey. I'm so happy you're a part of our pack and family."

Warmth blooms through my chest, and I stand and watch her exit the suite, waiting only a minute to turn to the omegas.

"Would you like me to get you all plates? I'm sure you're exhausted." I grab the first plate and start dishing a little bit of everything onto it.

The pale blonde stands up from her spot and takes a plate from me, but she hands it to a petite black-haired omega who still hasn't turned her head away from the floor.

"I'll help you," the blonde says, standing a couple of inches taller than me. "My name is Ashley, by the way. I'm from the Koederitz Pack within the Gutter District. My pack fell on hard times, and this was the only way for them to keep going."

I try not to react to her words. Situations like that aren't uncommon. Because omegas are used to barter wealth and power. If a pack that has neither of those things births an omega in their territory, they'll absolutely get whatever they can for it. And Ashley just happened to be put into the situation out of desperation and cruelty. Because her pack took the easy way out instead of trying to find a worthy alpha who would pay for her. It would've been more challenging. Many would think breeding with her bloodline would result in a weaker pack.

"I'm so sorry you found yourself in that position." I offer her another plate to pass out. "But it's so nice to meet you, Ashley." I make sure to say her name, showing her that I'm listening. I don't want her to think that I'm just doing things to be nice because I was told to. "What about the rest of you? Do any of you want to tell me your names? It's okay if you don't. I just thought we could get to know each other better. I know it helps me when I'm scared to be able to find familiarity, and I want to create that for you."

The male omega clears his throat. "I'm Devin."

I offer him a smile and hand over another plate of food. "That's a lovely name. Where are you from?"

"I'm also from the Gutter District. I was picked up with Arielle after we ran away together. She was my neighbor." Devin glances at the redhead beside him, curled in with her knees against her chest.

"That must've been so scary for you. So, you ran away? Was your pack going to give you two to an alpha you didn't like?" I try my best not to pry and instead give them a couple of different questions they can choose or not choose the answer, including one that would just repeat what they already told me. It'll help me know exactly where their comfort level is in this moment.

"We're in love," Devin says, wrapping his arm around Arielle. Her pack wanted to sell her to the Vixen Lounge. Have you heard of that place? They're a bunch of brainwashed omegas that are abused and...I can't even say it. They don't allow male omegas there. We're not as wanted."

I try not to react, keeping my face expressionless. "I know of it. I want to take it down along with any of the other clubs like that. We don't deserve such a life."

A brunette with short brown hair fists her hands and slams them on the coffee table. "We? *We?* You're a fucking privileged omega of the most prominent pack in this area. You have no idea what the fuck we've been through. Don't you dare try to relate with us. You aren't any better. I'm sure you've just stood by and watched omegas fall by packs and power just like yours."

"Stella, shut up. Don't talk to her like that. You know that some of the royals are worse off." This comes from another brunette, one that looks very similar to Stella. They might be sisters.

"Whatever, Elizabeth. I've had to keep my mouth shut for months. I will not just sit here and let this omega try to tell me what I do and don't deserve. She should not include herself in it." Stella turns her attention to me, glaring.

I take an automatic step back at the heat of her gaze. A part of me wants to be angry. Another part of me wants to tell her my life story to get her to realize that I'm no different. But a greater part of me demands I stay silent. This isn't a competition. I don't have to explain anything. And they don't have to see me as one of them. We are different. I was one of the lucky ones, and I really see the truth of it in this moment. I could've ended up like them. I could've died by Madame Tamsin's hands or even my uncle's. I could've been beaten and hurt until I was nothing but an empty shell. But I wasn't.

I'm powerful. I have a choice now, despite what the Pack Regimes think.

"Give her a break. You don't know anything about her." The last omega speaks up, resting her chin on her knees. "I heard the rumors. She got caught passing as a beta after coming into this region without ties."

"Yeah, whatever, Amelia. Still doesn't change my opinion. Look at this place. Look at how the beta treated her. She has a good life. Look at us. We don't even know what's going to happen. They could be nice just to keep us complacent before they sell us again. Maybe they have their own damn omega club where they invite others from the Pack Regimes to beat and brutalize us for fun." Stella heaves a couple of deep breaths, her body shaking with her words.

My anger gets the best of me, and I drop a plate, clattering it on the floor. Food flies everywhere, and the omegas fall silent, staring at me as I lose my composure.

"We would never. And I mean *never* do that. I know I have nothing to offer that will make you believe me, but I was once in your place. My pack was murdered by my uncle, and he..." I swallow, my eyes welling with tears as I relive the moment over again. "He chained me down during my heat in front of the alphas who were supposed to bond with me. He tortured them and beat them anytime they tried to break free while I suffered. And then he murdered them. Right in front of me. Their blood was on me. I barely escaped, and I ran. I ran and didn't look back. I didn't fall in line and instead, I did what I had to and bought my way into a somewhat normal life until I was caught."

My head pounds with my words, and I grip the table, shaking.

"Oh, God. I'm so sorry," Devin says, taking a step closer.

I shake my head, whipping my hair back and forth. "Don't be sorry for me. I made it out okay. For the most part, at least. Because my uncle decided to show up last night. He's the one who told my alphas about you guys. I don't know why, but he had his manipulative reasons. And because of that, we're going to be extra cautious. We're not handing you to the leaders of the Pack Regimes. We're going to do whatever it takes to keep you as part of our pack to give you whatever life you want. If you want to just stay hidden, fine. We'll make it happen. If you want to find an alpha, we'll get you the best ones. We'll ensure your safety. But if you want to just go. You can go. But do not try to tell me what I can and can't relate with. I'm doing my best with what I have. I want to change the world for us. Because we're together in this. You might not think that now because I'm in a different position than you, but in the end, we're omegas, and the Pack Regimes have ensured that we have no rights. I'm going to get them for us."

Again, no one responds.

I close my eyes, squeezing the tears away before they can fall and turn toward the door. "You'll find everything you need on the cart. Melina will be back to check on you."

"Wait," Ashley says, extending her hand to me.

I swipe my hand over my face, smoothing out my features. "No. I need to get out of here. I'm sorry."

Without another word, I stride to the exit, yanking the door open. I shouldn't be mad. I should empathize with them, but I'm tired. I don't even know what to do or how to feel. I just want to go home.

There are a lot of things I should do, but instead, I rest my back to the door. I don't move until Desmond returns and carries me away.

"Kinsey, relax. They're going to be fine. They're not our responsibility. Let our pack handle it. Aunt Melina knows how to take care of omegas. My brothers will ensure they're safe. You need to focus on picking out a dress." Holly stares at the rack of dresses personally selected for me by my guys with the help of the royal seamstress and the team of betas in charge of styling me appropriately for my union.

I don't know how Wilder managed to get everything in order so quickly, but our staff now rushes through the palace, preparing for what is sure to be the event of the season. Not only will I bow and vow my life to Wilder as king, but it's also where he'll declare equal ruling with his brothers over Gilded Sands. Soon after, they'll declare the progressive laws that will stir animosity from the Pack Regimes...after my heat.

"What about this one? It'll show off just enough skin to drive them wild but also give them a reason to tear the thing off." Holly pulls a strapless dress out, the emerald-green tulle and satin material matching my eyes. "Not that I want to think about that. You guys sound freaky as fuck."

Warmth crawls across my chest and travels to my cheeks. "Sorry, they—"

"The less I know, the better. I'm just so excited for you...and for me. Wilder is thawing out to the idea of me getting my own place. I'm going to push him hard after this. He'll want me out of here before you guys start making babies. I'll ensure it." Holly laughs and grabs another dress, the second one a mermaid cut with a sweetheart neckline. The ivory color glitters with crystals in the light.

I shake my head and motion to an amethyst ball gown with a full, bouffant-styled skirt, deep V-cut decolletage, with off-the-shoulder straps and a bejeweled bodice. It's absolutely gorgeous. "Do I even want to know?"

"Let's just say that I'm going to stop ignoring you guys and start interrupting. What do you think? Wilder will help me pack my bags with that plan, right?" Holly picks out two other dresses she wants me to try on first, and the quiet attendant helping us takes them to ready the room.

I haven't been into the downtown area of Gilded Sands except for in passing, and excitement buzzes through me every time I look out the wall of windows, giving me a view of the jacaranda tree-lined streets. I spot Enzo and Arsenio standing near the door with their backs toward us. No bodyguard apart from themselves will do, and while they could've had all the dresses brought to the palace, Desmond insisted we go out and not unintentionally imprison ourselves. He thought it would help settle my emotions after the confrontation with the omegas, and he was absolutely right.

"Don't worry, Kins. They won't peek. The final dress will be a surprise." Holly rubs her hand between my shoulder blades. "Now, let's see how dazzling you look, my gorgeous soon-to-be sister. I can't wait." Holly guides me toward the grand changing area with a long curtain the attendant pulls across, blocking the street view.

"Would either of you like a glass of champagne?" the beta woman asks, motioning to a bottle chilled over ice. "Coffee or water? The princes insisted on catering dessert as well if you're hungry. We're closed to the public for the rest of the day, so please, enjoy yourselves."

"Coffee sounds amazing." Holly skips past me to a lace-clothed table with an assortment of cake slices, brownies, and pie. She fills a plate with more sweets than either of us can eat and brings it to the sleek couch with a coffee table in front of it.

I nod at the woman. "Same for me. I could use a dose of liquid energy after this week."

"You poor dear. I heard about what happened at King Winston's funeral. What an inappropriate time for your pack to interrupt and demand what was owed. Platinum Shores was supposed to be a new haven for betas, according to those who support your brothers. Now..." The woman snaps her mouth shut. "My apologies. How improper of me to bring such negativity into what's supposed to be a joyous occasion."

I sigh and busy my mouth with a bite of frosted lemon cake. I should've known that the people of Gilded Sands would talk. This affects more than just my guys and our immediate pack. Those who reside in the territory live by the laws in place, even if they don't carry the Gilded Sands name, which many don't. Betas outnumber alphas by a lot.

"It's fine, Ms. Lissa. You don't have to worry about anything. My brothers won't let the new part of our territory fail in vain. Desmond will still get it, I'm sure." She lowers her voice. "As long as we get the support we need. That's what the Silversteins told me."

I bump Holly's shoulder, subtly shaking my head. I don't know how close she is to this woman, but the last thing we need is for her to go announcing things we can't be certain of.

"Rumor also says that your brothers have picked out a proper pack for you—one of great power. The Silversteins will be disappointed when they find out. I also heard they're quite smitten for you." The attendant pouts out her bottom lip. "I'm sure they know what they're doing, though. A princess should only bond with a leader from the Pack Regimes."

Holly bristles, sitting up straighter. She opens and closes her mouth, trying to come up with something to say. Swiveling on the seat, she glances at the curtain and back to the woman. "Where did you hear such preposterous things?"

"Your name was available in the registry." Ms. Lissa rubs her hands together. "I'm sorry. I thought you knew."

Holly hops to her feet. "Excuse me a moment."

I get to my feet to follow her. "Holly, wait. I'm sure it's a misunderstanding."

"Which I need to immediately clear up. I'll be right back. Why don't you try on the first dress?" Holly doesn't give me a chance to respond as she bolts out the front door to confront her brothers.

I scrub my hands over my cheeks, listening to her voice sound out even through the glass door. It takes everything in me not to follow her, but I suddenly just want to hurry and pick out a dress. My fear instincts prickle, now being alone with this beta. Why would she bring up such things? It was like she was purposefully trying to get under our skin, and it worked.

"This way, Ms. Kinsey. I have the changing room all ready for you." Ms. Lissa opens the wooden door to a large changing area with wall-to-wall mirrors. The dresses hang neatly on hooks, and she has several pairs of shoes and veils ready for me as well.

I turn my attention back to the curtain, hoping to spot Holly to wave her in, but she's just out of view. All I can see is Enzo's tall frame outlined in sunlight.

"Don't be shy, dear. If you would like me to step out, I will, but it would be much easier if you let me help you. There isn't anything I haven't seen." Ms. Lissa crosses her arms and takes a step back, giving me a once-over.

I stiffen at her words, the sudden nerves bunching my muscles. I don't know what it is, but I need to get out of here.

"Let's try on the amethyst one first. I saw how your eyes lit up with it." She touches the flouncy fabric that will twirl out with my movements.

I suck in a long, deep breath, slowly unbuttoning my blouse, taking my time, praying that Holly returns soon. I want her to be the one to help me. She should be the one to see me before the attendant does. All she was to do was be ready to make adjustments, giving us time to do things as we please.

"Here, let me help you. Your fingers are shaking. You must be so excited to be bonding with royalty." Ms. Lissa grabs the hem of my shirt and starts unfastening my buttons.

I recoil at her touch, bringing my hands up to my face protectively. And then I catch a strange scent. It's different from when we first arrived. I can't put my finger on it because it's so subtle, but I'm starting to believe this woman isn't truly who she says she is.

My eyes widen, and I yank away from her, looking for my purse that I left on the couch. I didn't think it would be necessary to hide a weapon on my person, considering I'd be changing in and out of dresses with my guys outside.

I spin again, trying to dodge around her, but she charges me and pushes me against the wall. Covering my mouth with her hand, she silences any sort of scream that can escape my lips.

"Calm down, Kinsey. I'm not going to hurt you. All I have for you is a message that you need to pass along to your alphas. Now listen carefully. Your pack took some things that don't belong to you. You need to return them to the Gutter District, where they belong. They were already claimed by a handler that was preparing them for the Devil Lands. She wants them back. If you don't comply, she'll ensure that the Pack Regimes know about the illegal activities your alphas have been up to.

They'll be stripped of power and outcast from Saint Vista." Ms. Lissa flares her nostrils as she takes a step back.

I realize that she's not a beta. There's no way. I think she might be an omega. Her suppressant pills are wearing off, and her high emotions are triggering her pheromones.

Or maybe it's me. Maybe it's my alphas outside. I don't really know, and I don't really care. All I care about is the threat she wants to be passed along for…it has to be fucking Madame Tamsin. She's the only one who ever used the Devil Lands as a threat. She's the only handler in the Gutter District. And now, she has it out for us. She's embarrassed that she was put in her place and made to beg for forgiveness from me.

The chime on the door rings, and Ms. Lissa hurries away, heading down the hallway that leads out back. I stand in shock, staring at the dresses and then at Holly, who peeks her head in, her smile melting off her face the moment she sees me.

"Get your brothers. Now!" I say, dodging past Holly to head toward the back hallway. I only peek my head in, seeing a couple of closed doors and what looks to be a back exit.

"Kinsey, what's the matter? What happened?" Arsenio grabs my wrist, easing me away from the hallway, taking the spot I filled. "Are you hurt? What's going on?"

I shiver, my heart racing. "I was threatened by that attendant. She gave me a message to pass on to you."

Arsenio growls and charges into the hallway, kicking open the first door to check inside. I stare behind him, not wanting to take my eyes off the situation. I worry about Arsenio and any sort of confrontation.

Warm hands slide around my waist as Enzo tugs me back. "Tell me—"

"Brother, get in here." Arsenio's voice bellows through the air. "Kinsey call for medical. There's a beta tied up and unconscious."

My legs wobble as I yank from Enzo and head back toward the couch for my phone. Holly already presses her cell to her ear, calling for a medic. My head spins with a dozen emotions. Why is the world out to get us? It's as if the only way to make it in this world is to be worse than our enemies. Because those who try to do good only get hurt in the process.

"What was the message, sugar? What did the attendant say?" Arsenio returns to me, leaving Enzo to tend to the worker, who must've been attacked so that the passing omega could get close to me.

I want to think that we should've been better prepared, but there was no way of knowing. We thought she was handled. Madame Tamsin wasn't supposed to bother us again. But there's nothing like an eternal grudge that an alpha will carry.

"She wants the omegas you guys picked up. An alpha claims they belong to her. I think it was Madame Tamsin." I rub my hands together, shifting on my feet. "She's insane. We can't do that to these omegas."

"We won't. Tamsin thinks she can manipulate us like everyone else, but they don't know what we are capable of. She won't be a problem for long. I'll ensure it myself tonight. You have my word." Arsenio touches my chin.

"I want to go with you to the Vixen Lounge. I need to see it for myself. I need to be there for her Gorgeous Girls." I expect him to deny me. I expect him to want to lock me away until he and his brothers murder all of our enemies.

But he doesn't.

He slowly nods his head. "If that's what you want, then I'll stand by your side. That club is ours. Tamsin will regret ever thinking she was strong enough to control anything in a territory. We'll make her pay."

# Chapter Seventeen

## *Kinsey*

## Revenge

When Wilder commanded Jude to gather their army, I didn't expect it to be so many people. Where I grew up, things were run by gangs, and gang wars usually consisted of one or two vehicles with a couple of alphas and weapons.

Our sedan rides in the middle of a caravan of ten SUVs, with at least sixty members of the Gilded Sands Pack. Many are betas, but they're well prepared and heavily armed. My guys are no longer playing around. There's too much at stake. They'll make a name for themselves.

No one fucks with the new kings of Gilded Sands.

"I need you to pay close attention, Kinsey. You're coming with us because I'm not letting my brothers or myself handle this alone, and I'm not leaving you alone at the palace. You're not a soldier. You're our queen, and we will make you the face of our fight for power. You will not leave my side. Do you understand? We're not going easy on anyone." Wilder touches my chin, turning my face, forcing me to meet his icy blue eyes. "Blood will be shed. We have been trying not to be the monsters others are, but I don't see a choice. I'm not giving in to Madame Tamsin's demands. It was bad enough that I had to do so temporarily with Rommel. If you don't think you can stomach it, tell me now."

A part of me wants to tell him that I can't. I can't watch as our pack storms into the Gutter District, taking out anyone who stands against us. Because this is a hostile takeover. This will get us recognized as the brutal monarchy of Gilded Sands, and it might even cause problems with the Saint Vista Pack Regimes. But again, we don't have a choice. I recognize that now. Sometimes you have to be a villain to save the day.

Especially when everyone else are monsters.

Does it make it right? I don't know. After what I've been through, all I can think about is destroying everything to rebuild as I was destroyed and made stronger. Of steel and bulletproof glass instead of the porcelain my parents raised me to be as an omega.

"Give me a weapon, and I'll stand beside you." I hold my hand out to Wilder.

Enzo sets a sheathed blade on my palm. "No, baby. You're going to stand behind him and in front of me. It's Desmond and Arsenio you'll be beside."

I try not to smirk at his words and fail.

"Now is not the time, brother. We're almost there. Word might have already spread, so we need to be on guard. We may not have the element of surprise we need." Wilder squeezes my hand. "But he's right. You'll be behind me."

The glowing city of the Gutter District looms ahead of us like a deceptive mirage. From here, it looks like it's blooming with life, the lights blinding the fact that within the concrete and steel city lies those built with knives and hate. Those desperate and without. It's a city built on the backs of others as the leaders walk on them as if the streets are made of the flesh and bones of the weak.

It's the only territory that switches its leader seemingly weekly because several packs won't think twice before cutting your throat if you stand in their way.

That's why I always kept my head bowed protectively. Why I never stood up or questioned anything. It's why I successfully hid, because no one paid attention to an unwanted packless beta.

"Wilder, do you copy?" Static buzzes through the speaker as his radio goes off, drawing our attention away from each other. "Our eyes spotted Tamsin. She just showed up at the Vixen Lounge."

My chest clenches at the sound of Jude's voice. He leads the caravan, riding shotgun in the front SUV.

"Copy that. We need to split up and surround the block. Separate and park. It's best to go on foot. We'll drive directly to the club. Don't hurt those who surrender. Take anything of value." Wilder adjusts the radio on his belt and pulls out his gun, double-checking the mechanics.

"Father would be so proud," Enzo mutters, doing the same as Wilder as he prepares.

"It's the only way. We must leave them with nothing. We need to make an example out of this area. We already have the destruction of the leading pack of Platinum Shores to our name. Now we'll have the Gutter District. Soon we'll garner enough attention and notoriety to instill fear in the heads of the Pack Regimes where they'll want to create better alliances. And then we will reframe the infrastructure and rewrite its laws. We will not give them a choice. Their time is over. Ours is just beginning." Arsenio twists in the front seat and looks at me. "This is for Kinsey and all of the other omegas and betas that have been wronged."

"Damn straight." Desmond taps his fingers on the steering wheel, following the SUV in front of us as it breaks away from the caravan. It rolls to the curb three blocks over from the Vixen Lounge and parks. I bounce in my seat, fidgeting with my long sleeves and the bulletproof vest Wilder equipped me with for my protection. They all wear them. It'll be what gives us an advantage. Madame Tamsin's too cocky to really think about what she has started. She's trying to take us down with blackmail. Sometimes words aren't enough. It's the actions that will prove a point.

My heart pounds, thoughts echoing in my head. I concentrate on keeping my breathing even, matching it with Wilder's. If he's nervous, he doesn't show it. Neither do the others. Only Enzo shifts in his seat, bouncing his knee, but it's not fear. It's excitement. Nothing gets his adrenaline going like running in to be the brutal knight someone needs.

"Security up ahead. To the right. Sniper watching the entrance. She's expecting us." Wilder motions toward the second story of the building across the street.

Desmond slows, and I realize that Wilder wasn't talking to us. He was communicating it to the Gilded Sands' soldiers.

I squint my eyes, staring out the window, and then I see a small flicker of light. I don't hear gunfire, their weapons now equipped with silencers. At least some of them. It would be better if they don't know we're coming.

"All clear," Jude says, his voice echoing through the sedan.

"Copy. We're going in. Standby." Wilder shifts in the seat, bumping his knees to mine. "Is there anything else you can think of that you haven't already told us? We already know the layout and where her secret access door is to the tunnel beneath. The last time you knew, there were at least twenty omegas?"

I nod my head. "Twenty Gorgeous Girls. I'm not so sure about the traveling girls. I never met them."

"Betas?" Enzo asks, holding his hand on the doorframe, getting ready to fling it open. "Bartender, cook, janitor, and servers, right? The bouncers will be alphas?"

"Unless she changed things. But she was always very particular about how she ran things. It's early enough that there shouldn't be many clients either." Because most don't show up until past the unofficial curfew meant to keep betas in their places as if they're omegas. Only those who work the night shifts are left alone on the streets.

"We're going to capture the clients. Do not kill any of them until we can properly identify which packs they belong to. We can use them as leverage." Arsenio rests his hand on the dashboard. "I need your confirmation, Enzo." He says it because Enzo's more unpredictable. He always acts first without hesitation.

"Fucking fine. Unless they do something stupid. I'm only giving them two chances. I'll give the first warning and then a second as I stab them somewhere unimportant. But if they fight after that, they're dead." Enzo growls with his words, his scent turning spicy at the thought.

"Make it three chances. If you don't agree, then you're going to guard the door." Wilder narrows his eyes. "That's an order as your older brother."

"Three chances. He can handle that." I reach out and rub his arm. "I know he can."

He fake glares at me. "Damn it, baby. You know it'll be more fun my way."

"It'll also be more dangerous. Take them captive. The only one who needs to face punishment is Tamsin. We need to make a point that we'll no longer stand for these underground clubs." Desmond glances at me in the rearview mirror. "Kinsey's sanctuary idea will change everything."

Slowing down, Desmond pulls to the curb outside of the Vixen Lounge. I don't even have a chance to prepare myself as Wilder flings the door open and drags me out with him, keeping me at his back as Enzo looms behind me. Arsenio and Desmond fall in line beside me, and Wilder doesn't even give the bouncer a chance to unholster his gun before he shoots him without mercy.

Several of our pack mates come in from the back, blocking that exit. Enzo raises his gun and pulls the trigger, shooting one of the lights to send sparks over the dancefloor.

"Everyone down and don't move. If you try to fight, we'll kill you. This is a hostile takeover. Tamsin, show your fucking self." Wilder straightens his back, standing even taller.

People scream and yell. Some scramble toward the back exit only to have our betas block their way, giving warning shots at the floor.

"Tamsin!" Wilder steps a foot forward, and I shadow his every move. "Show yourself, or I will shoot every last one of your clients. You will not have another soul come into this club. I don't know what you thought you'd accomplished by threatening my omega, but we don't tolerate such things in our kingdom."

Making a point, Wilder looks toward one of the security personnel hunched on the floor. I recall his name being Steve. He's one of Tamsin's loyal betas. The man cowers under Wilder's gaze, but he doesn't submit. He reaches for his jacket, trying to pull out a weapon like he even stands a chance.

I startle at the pop of Wilder's gun, the shot ringing in my ears.

"You better beg Tamsin to face me, or I'll go through each and every one of you." Wilder looks toward another man I recognize. It's Mr. Holt, the beta that escorted me to clean out my apartment when I was caught.

He meets my gaze, his mouth quivering. "Tamsin, do as he says. You're our leader and alpha. This is your duty."

Again, Tamsin doesn't respond.

Mr. Holt widens his eyes in fear and raises his hands in surrender. "Please, she's behind the bar."

Wilder spares Mr. Holt's life, and he falls back and takes a breath, still trembling. Striding forward, Wilder heads toward the bar. Arsenio takes the spot in front of me, keeping me safely within the circle of his brothers.

I see a strange orange glow bouncing off one of the decorative mirrors behind the bar. My heart seizes, and I scream out, "Wilder, stop!"

Madame Tamsin pops up from her place behind the bar, holding a flaming bottle. Wilder swears and jumps out of the way a second before it hits the floor where he was standing, setting it ablaze. The fire alarms ring, piercing my ears, and water shoots from the sprayers above. Arsenio grabs me and lifts me into his arms, holding me with one hand as he fires his weapon in the direction Madame Tamsin tries to run.

She doesn't make it far. One of the cowering betas sticks out his leg and trips her, sending her sprawling across the floor. She spins and shoots him in the chest, aiming her weapon toward us next.

Several gunshots ring through the air, and I startle, squeezing my eyes shut, afraid to see the outcome. It takes everything in me not to whimper. I bite my bottom lip and squeeze onto Arsenio.

Tamsin growls in pain, and the room falls silent. Arsenio strokes his hand on my back, loosening my muscles. I summon my bravery to straighten up and swivel my torso to look at where I last saw Wilder.

He stands tall, pointing his gun at Tamsin as she clutches a bleeding wound on her shoulder. Her gun lies on the floor a couple of feet away, dropped because she couldn't hold onto it. I release a gasping breath, my nerves settling down. No one stands up for her. No one tries to fight for her.

This proves exactly what kind of alpha and leader she is, one born of power and violence but without loyalty. She is alone. She has always been alone, and this proves it. You can only take so much from your pack before they have nothing left to give or want to give.

"Under the authority of the Gilded Sands' position in the Pack Regimes, I declare you guilty of coercion, blackmail, trafficking illegal omegas, corruption, money laundering, and many other crimes I do not have to list, but mostly you are guilty of abuse toward my mate and queen. You seem to think that you still have some sort of control over her and can threaten her, but it's over. Your life ends here. You will not have a respectable death. I'll not act as your adversary and give you a distinguished end as an alpha. You'll die by the woman you have wronged. She'll be serving justice today. You'll bow at the feet of someone you consider beneath you and learn that she is above you. You're nothing more than a worthless piece of shit who can't stand in her way." Turning slightly, Wilder motions to us, having Arsenio bring me closer.

My chest heaves with my breaths, and I look at Tamsin for the first time. Her eyes lock onto mine as she tries to intimidate me, even now, injured and broken on the floor.

It gives me the courage to do what is necessary. It's what pushes me forward. I never thought she would die by my hands, but I realize it can't be any other way. This is how I'll move past this. This is how I'll protect the omegas that found themselves in a bad position like I had. This is how I'll help the Gilded Sands Pack change the laws within the Pack Regimes. Because I'm not weak like the alphas think. I'm not useless and only good for breeding. I'm better than that. I'm as powerful as my alphas and not because they protect me. It's because they have lifted me up and showed me that I can protect myself. I'm strong. I'm more than just my order.

Wilder takes me from Arsenio and sets me in front of him, adjusting the gun in my hands. He stands beside me, holding his hands over mine as he helps me aim.

"Wait," Tamsin says, her face breaking as she realizes that this isn't a threat. It's a promise. "I'll give you whatever you want. If you want the omegas, you can keep them. Name your price."

A smile crosses my face. I never expected that someone else's fear could smell so incredible. It's the first time I've ever had the luxury of breathing in the fragrance. I savor it for a moment longer, staring at her, continuing to plead for her life.

"There's only one thing I want, Tamsin," I say, finding my voice.

She bobs her head, chewing her bottom lip. "Just name it, Kinsey."

"Your life." I don't give her another second to plead with me and pull the trigger.

Wilder keeps the gun from whipping back at me from the force. Madame Tamsin slumps on the floor, and silence fills the air. No one moves. No one speaks. I'm not even sure anyone is breathing.

Revenge smells so sweet.

It feels even better.

With Tamsin's death, a part of me revives. It's the part of me she stole and tried to destroy.

She can't hurt me or anyone else ever again.

Her reign over the Vixen Lounge and the Gutter District is over.

Her prisoners are finally free.

"Kinsey, you know you're famous among the Gorgeous Girls. We still can't believe your luck. No one has ever escaped getting transferred as a traveling girl." Anita sits beside me in the backseat of the car.

I rest on Wilder's lap as he hugs me, acting as a seatbelt. "I did what I had to. And it wasn't luck. It was fate that the princes of Gilded Sands found me. They technically kidnapped me."

"That's what my dreams are made of. Getting kidnapped by delectable alpha princes and having them take care of me the way I truly want." Anita keeps her hands on her lap, ensuring that she doesn't touch Wilder by accident. It's a show of respect, making sure the boundary is clear to me that she's not going to try anything. Because that was kind of a thing at the Vixen Lounge. The Gorgeous Girls sometimes fought over which alpha they got to be with. It was a competition. Whoever was the favorite always got the best of everything, including the sweet side of Madame Tamsin.

"Well, hopefully your dreams will be a bit different now. No kidnapping. We're going to create our own club and sanctuary. When we take out who is necessary, we're going to create a place where omegas get to judge and look over alphas instead. They'll have to apply to even be considered." I grin, meeting Desmond's gaze in the rearview mirror. I have it all planned out in my head, and I can't wait to sit down to truly work out all the details. After taking the Vixen Lounge, we have at least two dozen omegas that now get to decide their fate. And there will be more. I know it.

"Sounds like a Knotty Alpha Club. Sounds amazing, Kinsey." Bouncing in her seat, she shows she's far less afraid than the nest of omegas that the guys brought to the fortress. It really demonstrates the extreme difference between packs and their plans. The female alphas are always nicer—but even more brutal when things don't go their way.

"More like a Knotty Princes Club. Every omega can find their prince, regardless of status and order." I lean forward and touch Desmond's arm. "What do you think? Sounds like a great name, right?"

Enzo chuckles. "An excellent name. I can't wait to be your knotty fucking prince. Your knotty king."

"As soon as we finish the job. We have a lot of work to do, brothers." Arsenio brings us back to reality, sitting beside Desmond in the front seat. "Are you sure the current leaders are the Demon Knights, Anita?"

She bobs her head. "Absolutely. I was just with Makario yesterday. He's been around more and more, waiting for a couple of us to go into heat. Madame Tamsin agreed to breed us in exchange to ally our packs so she can kick Mr. Donahue out and take over his drug ring."

Wilder groans. "Well, that man will have to thank us. We took care of all of his problems. And now we're going to seize the Gutter District completely."

Arsenio hits the button on his radio. "Jude, do you copy? Head right at the end of the block. I need you to set off the explosives in two minutes. We need the pack to come outside."

"Copy that, king. We're all set. The entire place is surrounded. We have snipers everywhere. We will pick them off as they come out, and then you can head in." Jude's voice sounds on the radio.

"Good. Let's finish this." Arsenio twists in his seat. "Sugar, you're going to stay here with Anita and Desmond. We're going to be in and out."

I lick my lips and reach out, squeezing his hand. "Be safe and quick so we can hurry up and get home."

An explosion booms through the air, lighting up the night sky a block away. Desmond pulls to the curb and parks the car, hitting the unlock button. His brothers rush out without waiting, and another explosion rings out, shaking the vehicle. I cover my ears protectively and stare out the windshield.

Wilder, Enzo, and Arsenio rush forward, their silhouettes haloed in fire and smoke as they head in to finish the battle.

My soul soars. I can't believe this is truly happening. We have taken everything into our own hands, and the world really is burning around us.

And from the ashes, we will rebuild.

The Pack Regimes will fall.

Saint Vista is ours.

# Chapter Eighteen

## *Arsenio*

## No Mercy

"**I**'ll never—"

Pulling the trigger, I silence Makario with a bullet to the head. No mercy. That is our rule when it comes to our enemies. They wouldn't grant it to us either.

My chest clenches as his body falls, joining the rest of his dead pack. Tamsin must've not told the alpha leader that she was starting a war that would end with them on the ground before us. If we had given them a chance, they would've re-gretted every damn decision they made.

If only I got the satisfaction of hearing them beg and plea and offer whatever they had to try to convince us to leave them alone.

Wilder pats me on my back. "We're done here. Set up a video call. We need to act fast and send a warning to the Pack Regimes. Jude verified that the warning explosives were ready. This will be our formal announcement that things are changing, and we will not tolerate the old ways. This will give us a chance to see who our allies really are."

I dip my chin in confirmation and pull out my phone, calling the emergency line that will ring the entire leadership at once. It's a call that they would never decline.

It's a call for war.

We have been planning for this day since the moment we decided we were going to take control and steal the reign of Gilded Sands from our father. We've been stealing arsenals for months and working with those who are against the Pack Regimes. We're not the only ones who want change. Some just want power, but as long as we can control them, things will go in our favor.

"Ten seconds until the last leader answers." Enzo stares at Makario's cellphone, using it to fuck with the leaders of the Pack Regimes. As soon as he answers, the call will begin. "Make sure to give them your bloody side. You know those bastards hide behind those beneath them. When those people realize there is another way, they'll move aside."

Wilder smirks before composing himself, tightening his jaw and glowering in front of me. Blood splatters the front of his shirt, and he looks a bit wild and unhinged. It's perfect for this sort of confrontation. We want the leaders shaking. We want them negotiating to bring peace before war.

That's what the warning explosives are for. They won't take us seriously until we cause a little bit of damage. Lucky for us, we have allies behind enemy lines. We have worked with a lot of shady people and allowing some of the gang lords to access other territories through us has helped immensely.

Was it immoral? Depends on who you ask. Might as well get something out of it, considering they would do it anyway.

"Go ahead and answer, brother," Wilder says, crossing his arms over his chest and straightening his back. I bend my knees slightly, angling the camera so it feels as if he's looking down on us. Sometimes all it takes are some mind games to make a point. They might not be omegas, but we can trigger them just the same. Knowing how easy my father relented to the outside threat of Platinum Shores proves as much. They will always pick self-preservation over anything—even their packs.

Holding Wilder's phone, I reverse the camera to face him while staring at the small cluster of videos popping up. Half the leaders scowl in anger, and the other half look bored. That is until Enzo clears his throat, drawing attention to the fact that he accepted the call from Makario's private line.

Then he shows his body.

"What is going on? What the fuck happened?" Jarvis, the supposed head of our region and the leader of Starlight Horizon, the territory farthest south, raises his voice as he realizes what he looks at. "Did the Demon Knights attack your territory in a power grab? I knew he would fail in controlling that blasphemous territory."

That wasn't the response I was expecting, and I tilt my head, studying Wilder to gauge his reaction.

"Shut up and listen," Wilder snaps, commanding attention from the leaders. "This is a hostile takeover of the Gutter District. They have been found guilty of blackmail, coercion, trafficking omegas, and drug distribution. We have taken it upon ourselves to clean up the mess. If you have any objections, speak now."

Laughter bubbles from the greasy mouth of Herbert, the leader of the Dark Orchards Pack. "You felt this warranted an emergency meeting that couldn't wait until morning?"

"Perhaps they need one of us to take those precious Gorgeous Girls off their hands to find good homes for," Chavez of the Ginger Rain Pack comments, interrupting before they can all deem this conversation worthless.

That's how cocky they are. As long as it doesn't concern them, they don't care.

"You can deliver them to my territory, and I'll handle it from there." Jarvis leans closer to the camera, his wrinkled face cracking with dry skin. "We haven't had a chance to fully work out the details, but as your father's dear ally, we're working on creating our own club, run by the best of us. It is tiresome having unworthy alphas use our breeders for power. We should have free rein. Don't you think?"

I clutch the phone with my anger. "Like the nest of omegas we found starved, tortured, and beaten at Smithsons?"

"What are you talking about? I haven't agreed to authorize any of that. Why haven't I heard of these plans before now?" Armand of the Midnight Meadows Pack speaks up. "That sounds absolutely volatile. Omegas aren't to be misused and mistreated. They're—"

"Get off your fucking high horse. You damn well know you'd bend over an omega to screw if one of those sexy things was offered to you." Jarvis's features darken. "But clearly, your mindset shows how weak you are. Your ideals do not align with our strongest territories, so—"

"Detonate the explosive. Now!" Wilder shouts, his voice cutting over the argument.

Jarvis's eyes widen as dust swirls in front of his camera, the sound of the explosive booming through the line.

"I've had enough. This isn't a meeting but a fucking warning. Now that you have confirmed the rumors, I'm stepping up as head of Saint Vista alongside my brothers. Things are changing around here, and if you choose to stand against us, you might as well dig your graves. You have ruined enough lives and territories." Wilder cracks his knuckles. "You will hand over all unclaimed omegas immediately."

"You've got to be fucking kidding!" Chavez hollers, spitting at the camera.

"Detonate the explosive in Ginger Rain." Wilder nods to Enzo.

Chavez's video feed turns to static, the volume cutting in and out as he yells. It turns off a moment later. Silence falls over the video meeting, and I shift my weight anxiously.

"Let's take a proper vote. If you agree to promote the Gilded Sands Pack as the leader of our region, say ay." Armand tightens his jaw, not giving away his thoughts. He was never an ally of our pack, and now that I know my father was working with Jarvis to establish a new distribution for omegas as if they're objects proves why.

"Ay," Cameron from Shadow Palms says.

"Ay," Armand agrees.

"This is war, you son of a bitch! Do you hear me? I'll destroy you." Edwin from the Rosewood Pass Pack leers at his camera. "I stand beside Jarvis."

Emmanuel growls, the pack leader of the Bronze Desert Pack, reacting for the first time. "As does my pack."

A wicked grin crosses Wilder's face, his blue eyes catching the orange light glowing through the window from the house fire across the street. "Detonate the explosives and send in our soldiers. This war will end before it can begin. Your tyrannous reign is over. You can burn in hell with my father."

Several explosions boom through the line and static takes out the three alphas' cameras, leaving only Cameron, Armand, and Spencer, the final leader and an alpha from Fire Valley on the line. He neither agrees nor disagrees, his lack of support announcing his neutrality.

Wilder wipes his sweaty forehead on his sleeve. "Call your soldiers to duty and be ready. Standby until my call. It's time for change and new power."

"Here, here," Cameron says. "I've been waiting to finally put those old bastards to rest."

Enzo cracks his neck, kicking one of the Demon Knights' pack mates out of the way. "Here-fucking-here."

"The territory is on temporary lockdown. No one comes in or out. All packs have an hour to return, or they won't be able to cross our border until after our official meeting and declaration to the regional leaders of the power switch." Wilder sits at the head of the dining table with the leaders of the packs within our territory.

"I'll verify with the logs and send out the proper alerts," I say, standing at the table, my body too anxious to sit still, especially knowing Kinsey is only down the hall, dealing with stuff that should be our business, but ensuring our territory is safe is what's important.

Beckett shifts in his seat on Wilder's right side. "I can handle the task."

"Why don't you go check on Desmond and see if he needs any help?" Wilder leans his elbows on the table. "We'll text you with anything we need."

Enzo groans and leans back in his chair, clearly wanting to be excused. It's what our father would have done. In these circumstances, I'm thankful for my years of practiced self-control in every aspect of my life. With the arrivals of all the omegas and Kinsey being within their reach, it messes with our minds. I can hide the fact that I'd prefer no other scent mingles with hers. Enzo, on the other hand? He'd make his displeasure clear by scenting every inch of her body, declaring her as his.

I hide my smirk until I turn my back on the emergency territory meeting and stride down the familiar wing leading to the guest suites of the Gilded Sands' fortress.

Stopping at the small table of supplies outside of what we've deemed the omega suite, I wipe down my hands and spray cologne on my neck, wrists, and pelvis for good measure. It won't disguise my pheromones completely, but it will dull it enough that I shouldn't fuck with the omegas senses as long as I keep my distance.

I knock on the door before cracking it open when Kinsey shouts to come in. A collection of different fragrances assaults me, clouding the room, and I meet Kinsey's gaze for a second.

This shit isn't happening.

So much for my control.

Not being able to smell Kinsey immediately annoys the shit out of me, and there's no fucking way I'm letting anyone see as much. I quickly grab the door and slam it shut, striding away like a fucking alpha who just got his balls electrocuted. How have I managed before? I've been to omega clubs like the Vixen Lounge. That never bothered me like it does now.

"Arsenio, wait up," Kinsey calls from behind me, her bare feet thudding on the plush blue and gold floor runner lining the long, vaulted corridor. "My legs aren't as long as yours."

I slow down but don't stop until I reach the open landing with a sitting area looking over the grand salon. "Sorry, sugar. That was...overwhelming."

Kinsey slides in front of me, not letting me keep my back turned on her. She tilts her head to the side and scrunches her nose, staring at me as if she can read my mind. "You're annoyed," she says, doing one better than reading my mind and reading my emotions by my pheromones. No cologne will prevent her from doing so because of our physical bond. It's even stronger now with her heat coming.

I consider lying and telling her I'm not, but I know better. She'd call my ass out. "I just didn't like not being able to smell you immediately. It was...never mind. I realize why Wilder didn't want Enzo offering help, though I'm not sure I could do anything either."

Kinsey smirks before her smile widens and she cups my face. "You can't stand the scent of other omegas."

My sugar has a bit of spice. It turns her on knowing as much. I lick my lips and cover her hand with mine, pushing her fingers deeper into my skin, wanting the weight of her to linger.

"I can't. Not one bit. I hate it." I groan as she runs her fingers under my shirt.

"I don't want you close enough to smell them, either. It makes me...want to prove you're mine." She stretches up and sucks the nape of my neck, pulling my skin between her teeth until she bites me. I grunt at the sensation, my balls aching at the pleasure she arouses even from pain. Because her mark will linger. It'll be here for days. She can taste me on her tongue and indulge it as if I never leave her side.

"I want that. So badly. You are mine." I comb my fingers through her hair, easing her neck to the side, kissing my own trail down her heated skin, now fragrant with the sweetness I desire. The reason sugar will always be her namesake.

Something crashes from behind us, and I jerk away, spotting two omegas running from one of the suites—the one where the nest we found at the Smithsons stays. We hadn't wanted to overwhelm them by putting those from the Vixen Lounge with them.

"Help!" a red-haired woman screams, tripping over her own feet. She hits the floor with a thud, her eyes wide and wild.

Reaching into my jacket, I pull out my knife and rush toward the redhead, my lust petering out with another scream. Kinsey grabs my arm, struggling to keep my pace. I slow down and spin her toward the wall, motioning for her to stay back.

"Text my brothers," I command, unsure what I'm getting myself into.

Kinsey nods, pulling her phone from her pocket as she jogs toward the second suite. Desmond catches sight of us, looking at me. I don't stop to try to assess things. Instead, I charge forward, holding my breath as I hop over one of the omegas crying on the floor.

"You said this place was safe!" a short-haired brunette screams, tears pouring down her face. "He came back. He took my sister!"

He came back? Fuck me. I know who it is immediately. If Rommel was in our territory before the lockdown, he could've been hiding out. He probably took advantage of the fact that we took our best soldiers and headed out, more concerned about our palace.

This room doesn't have any secret passageways, so he had to have come from the balcony. I race forward to the open door and peer into the night. That's when I see the omega crawling on her hands and knees in the grass below. She must've put up a fight because blood covers the tips of her fingers as if she scratched him.

I swing my leg over the balcony and ease my way to the ledge, lowering myself enough until I can jump without hurting myself.

I land in a crouch and hop up, spinning around to check my surroundings. The last thing I need is for Rommel to come charging at me with a weapon.

"He ran that way." The Omega points toward the garden leading to a path that winds through the property. Looming walls surround the place, and it would be nearly impossible for anyone to climb. He might head toward the garage to try and steal one of the vehicles.

I pull out my phone and quickly tap my fingers across the screen.

*Me: Rommel's heading toward the garage. He abandoned the omega.*

*Baby Brother: Heading there now.*
*Boss Brother: Check surveillance. We need to see how he got in.*
*Desmeister: On it.*

A branch cracks from the wisteria trees framing a lattice tunnel, and the brunette omega screams out again.

Rommel comes from the shadows, raising his hands in the air in surrender. He gets to his knees before me, bowing his head.

"Don't kill me. You need me. There's a flaw in your security, and I can help you. That's why I came. I wanted to demonstrate it for myself." Rommel peeks up at me, remaining expressionless. "If I had really wanted the omega, I would have stolen her."

It takes everything in me not to pull out my gun and shoot him right now. I'd have every right to do so. The only reason I hesitate is because his words get to me. He's right. If he managed to get within the walls of a fortress, there is a flaw in our security.

I aim my knife at his neck, tapping it to his chin. "How did you get in?"

"It was pretty simple, actually." He smirks with his words.

I tap the knife harder on him. "Tell me how the fuck you got in here, or I will kill you!" I lose my cool and yell at him. Lifting my boot, I kick him in the chest and knock him flat on his back. I tower over him and stomp my boot into his stomach, winding him. I won't play these games. Not with the safety of my pack at stake.

"Your father entrusted special access to his allies. I overheard Jarvis talking with his pack, planning an invasion." Rommel remains frozen on the ground, his words spinning through my head. "Apparently, he expected you to betray him. Jarvis knew it was coming, and he was planning to take advantage of it, betraying your father just as you had."

Fury ignites inside me, and I reach down and grab Rommel by the front of his shirt, hoisting him off the ground. I spin him and restrain him to my chest, sliding my arm around his neck to put him into a chokehold.

"What do you want? You came here to prove a point for a reason. Tell me what it is you want and what we get for it." I growl with my anger, squeezing his neck tighter, feeling his body start to struggle.

"Power. A seat on the leadership. I want what every alpha wants. His own little omega." Rommel tries to smash his head against my chin, but I move out of the way.

Wilder shouts from the back entrance of the fortress, shining a flashlight over the grounds to find me.

"Give me those things, and I will give you Jarvis's plan. You'll fail otherwise," Rommel continues.

I scowl and ignore him, tightening my arm until I cut off his airway completely. He silently struggles, unable to resist the oncoming slumber with my chokehold. His body slumps, and I drop his deadweight to the ground.

Wilder runs up to me, keeping a foot of distance with one look at my furious expression. He glances at Rommel and shines his light over him. "You didn't kill him."

"He has answers we need. Our bastard father betrayed our pack, giving access to Jarvis. We need him to prepare." I inhale through my nose, breathing in deep breaths, catching a hint of the wisteria flowers.

"What does he want for it?" Wilder asks.

"Nothing he'll get." I kick Rommel again, flipping him onto his back. I don't respond to Wilder and grab Rommel's unconscious body, sliding my hand to the back of the neck, holding his head up to see his face. "You hear that, fucker?" I ask, knowing he can't in this state, but I can't help threatening him. "You'll never get fucking anything from us. We'll get what we need from you, and then I'm taking your fucking head. Do you understand, asshole? No one messes with Gilded Sands."

The only way this will end is with him going down. Our mercy is over. We'll take no prisoners.

Wilder helps me restrain Rommel, and the two of us lift him up and carry him toward the fortress. Kinsey stands between

Desmond and Enzo, waiting for answers. I hand Rommel to Enzo, so I can have a moment with Kinsey.

"Desmond, can you take the omega back upstairs? I want security all around our palace until we get the information we need." I motion to the brunette, still sitting in the grass like she's afraid to even move.

Kinsey slides into my arms. "I was so scared. How the fuck? What the fuck was he even thinking? What are you doing with him?"

I touch her chin. "We're going to ensure that karma pays him back in the form of being our prisoner. And once we get the information we need, you'll have the honor to end his life. He'll never get out of here."

Releasing a shuddering breath, Kinsey snuggles against me. "No, he won't. He will never have freedom again. He will regret all his life choices. I'll ensure it."

I kiss her on her temple. "Damn straight. Now let me get you home. We're going to have to reassess the situation. The fortress might not be the best place for the omegas."

"I agree. I almost think we should just burn this place down and start over." Kinsey rubs her face against my chest.

If only it were that easy. If only we didn't have to destroy everything.

# Chapter Nineteen

## *Kinsey*

### Tease

I sit on the floor in the corner of my room. I've been so anxious while my guys have been getting everything situated with our ally pack leaders and the omegas we now protect. I can't help them much, so I've been rearranging everything over and over.

After dragging my short bookcase next to my dresser, I draped my comforter over the top of them, creating a cozy space for me to relax. Leaning on two of Wilder's pillows, I rest as I hug Arsenio's towel. I cover my feet with Enzo's shirt and hide under Desmond's sheet that I stole from his bed. Having all their scents around me helps calm my heart. I can close my eyes without thinking about gunfire or bodies dropping. I can drown myself in their love, knowing that these men have done bad things to protect me. They've proven that they will do whatever it takes to ensure I'm safe.

"Baby, where are you hiding?" Enzo knocks his knuckles on the doorframe, and I remain in my spot, waiting for him to find me.

"Looks like she's created a new nest. It's going to be any time now." Desmond stops outside of my blanket fort and squats, lifting the edge of my comforter to peek inside. "Come here, brothers. See how cozy and comfortable she looks. You lost another pillow, Wilder."

Wilder play-growls as his bare feet come into view. He must've left his shoes at the door, making sure he doesn't track anything into my room. "You don't think twelve of my pillows is enough? I'm going to have to buy stock in my favorite brand if you keep this up."

Arsenio chuckles and nudges him with his body, getting him to scoot over so he can peek inside as well. "I don't know what you're talking about, asshole. You don't get pillows now. They all belong to Kinsey, and she's being nice enough to let you have one for a day before she snatches it. At least you don't step out of the shower to realize she's taken your towels."

Blush heats my cheeks. "Yours are the softest. I can't help it."

Arsenio reaches in and rubs the top of my foot. "Mind if I borrow one? I need to get cleaned up. I just want to wash the night away."

"You can have one if you let me help you." I gnaw my lip in expectation, knowing he would never deny me.

"I'd fucking love some of your help too, baby. My shoulders are sore, and I could really use someone to wash my back." Enzo's voice deepens with the scent of his lust.

Warmth builds between my legs, and I squirm in my spot, imagining everything I can do to help rid their thoughts of the night.

"I'd love to take care of all of you if you let me. It's all I want right now." I scoot forward until Arsenio locks his fingers around my ankles and drags me out, making me squeal. He's careful not to mess up my nest and doesn't bother taking the towel he requested to have back.

Scooping me up, he cradles me in his arms, pressing his nose to the crook of my neck. "Damn, she smells so sweet. I can't wait to devour her."

I wiggle in his arms and press my palm to his cheek. "No. You're going to let me take care of you."

Wilder grumbles under his breath. "Don't be a brat."

I swivel in Arsenio's arms and grab Wilder by the front of his shirt, yanking him to me. "Don't resist. Like I said, I'm going to take care of all of you right now."

I wiggle until Arsenio sets me on my feet and take a moment to give each of my guys a once-over. They're each a bit roughed up from fighting, but luckily, they have no terrible injuries. They're mostly just dirty, and I want nothing more than to strip them down and wash away the evidence of the war we started.

I turn to Arsenio first. "I want you to stand still while I undress you."

"Whatever you say, sugar," he murmurs, shifting on his feet.

"You guys don't move either. You get to wait your turn." I smile at Wilder, planning to make him wait until last. I can't help wanting to be bratty. He occasionally needs a reminder that just because he's oldest doesn't mean he always gets to go first.

"Damn, baby. You said you were going to take care of us, not torture us." Enzo wags his eyebrows at me, teasing me. His lips curl with his smile, his gaze traveling over me in anticipation.

I reach out and cup his cock through his pants, squeezing him. "A little teasing only makes things that much better."

"Tease too much, and I won't be able to resist you." Enzo wiggles his fingers, popping his hips out a bit to press his cock harder to my hand.

I give him a little flick, getting him to take a step back. He growls again, but his smile never falters. I return to Arsenio and stand in front of him, slowly unbuttoning his shirt to take it off. I draw my fingers over the curves of his abs and up to his pecs, stopping to caress my tongue over each of his nipples, feeling his body pulse under my attention. He reaches to touch me, and I steal his hand, locking our fingers together. I sway my hips and kiss my way back down his torso until I rest on my knees before him. I unfasten his belt and slide it off, snapping it playfully before tossing it aside. He groans as I unzip his pants ever so slowly, taking my time to undress him. He stands naked before me, not caring about being exposed alone in front of us. I kiss the tip of his cock and smile up at him, tasting the excitement already dripping.

"I want to watch you stroke yourself while I undress Desmond next." I spin on my knees and wiggle my fingers at Desmond, getting him to step in front of me. He keeps his hands to himself, drinking me in as I trace the outline of his bulging erection. I unhook his pants and slide my hand in, feeling the hard length on my palm.

"God, I'm so fucking horny. You know you're going to be in a bit of trouble when you're done, brat-girl. You're moving too slow. My body aches for you." Wilder steps into my space and combs his fingers through my hair, tightening his hand to my scalp to tip my head to look at him. "I just want you to know that."

I smile and wag my finger at him. "You may rub yourself through your pants but don't you dare do anything more."

He narrows his eyes at me and gives me a little yank on my hair again, bowing down to caress his lips to mine. "I'll remember this for next time. You're going to whine in desperation, begging to touch me."

I shiver and puff out a breath of air at his threat. "That better be a promise."

I turn back to Desmond and finish undressing him, rubbing my hand over his cock before I part my lips and suck him into my mouth. At the same time, I reach between my legs and wet my hand with my desire, bringing it back up to slide into his ass.

He moans and wobbles, clutching onto my shoulders as I give him more than a tease.

"Damn. She's so hot. I can't fucking wait for my turn." Enzo murmurs the words to Desmond, touching himself as he watches me slide Desmond out of my mouth.

"Come here, Arsenio. Let me give you a bit more." I grab him by the hips and bring him to my mouth, sucking in and out before doing the same to Desmond, working back and forth while Enzo and Wilder watch in anxious anticipation.

Easing away, I smile up at Desmond and Arsenio, licking my lips, treasuring their heavy-lidded expressions. I feel so hot and wanted under their intensity. They want me so badly I can taste the scent of their lust on my tongue. It turns me on even more, and I can't help wanting to rush just a bit. Teasing them backfires on me, and I squeeze my legs together, the sensation igniting an ache at my clit.

"Look at her squirm. You want us, don't you, baby?" Enzo mumbles, messing with his pants.

"I'll get my fill soon enough." I lick my lips, squeezing Desmond's ass. "Isn't that right?"

"Mmmhmm." Desmond arches, silently begging for me to taste him again.

I kiss his tip with a smile. "Arsenio?" I question, stroking him. "You guys will take care of me, won't you?"

He tucks my hair behind my ear. "All night long if you allow it."

"As soon as I'm done. Now, I want you to both prepare the shower. It's going to be a tight squeeze, but with enough soap, we can manage," I say to Arsenio and Desmond, my voice breathy with the thought of taking a hot shower with all four of them. They never complain about how close they have to be when I ask for them to ravish me as a pack, and it just makes me feel incredibly loved. They know exactly what I need and are willing to push through any awkward moments, considering they are brothers.

"Hustle your asses or I'll kick them." Enzo swats at Desmond, but he dodges out of the way and makes it to the bathroom before Arsenio.

I narrow my eyes at Enzo. "Just for that, you're now going to be last. Wilder has been such a good boy that he gets to cut in line."

If the roles were reversed, Enzo would rub it in. Wilder doesn't though. He knows better. If he were to gloat about it, he knows he'd risk me swapping their places again. In this moment, he's giving me a bit of control, and I appreciate it. I really do just want to take care of them.

Enzo turns me toward Wilder and squeezes my ass, rubbing his fingers over my body through my clothes. "Then you better hurry. I'm not going to stop playing with you until you're done. I'm going crazy. Your scent makes me want to bend you over and claim you right here and now. I'm getting anxious just thinking about it. My balls will explode if I can't give you pleasure. That's the only way I'll get relief."

"Maybe that's what I want. For you to explode and have your pleasure all over me. That way, I can remember this moment. It will imprint on my senses, turning me on every time I scent you." I reach behind me and stroke my fingers over the length of his cock through his pants. I do the same to Wilder, sliding down his zipper one-handed until I can pull his raging dick free.

I pull away from Enzo and finish taking off Wilder's pants. He beats me in taking off his shirt, his silent dominance in stealing control back so sexy. I lower myself to my knees once more and kiss his tip, working my tongue over his head and down his shaft until I can gently suck on his balls. Something hard and smooth thumps on my shoulder, and I laugh with Wilder still in my mouth, the vibration of my voice making him grunt. Enzo just couldn't take it and now stands naked behind me, his cock touching the crook of my neck, his excitement dripping onto my shoulder.

I grab him and squeeze, holding him in place, not letting him go. He flexes his cock in my hand, and I crane my neck and lick his tip, teasing him enough that he tugs my hair.

Wilder takes advantage of my distraction and snatches me by the waist, tossing me into the air and onto his shoulder. He rips down my pants and panties together, and Enzo drags them off me, leaving my body exposed to him. I squeal and squirm as Enzo kisses my ass, gliding his tongue over the seam of my body and moans in pleasure at the fact that I can't move. I wouldn't resist anyway, the sensation stealing my breath. A heavy hand smacks my ass next, the warmth zinging through me as Wilder punishes me in a good way. He flips me off his shoulder only to stretch me up until my legs squeeze his neck, and I have to grab Enzo from over his head to support me. My heart beats like crazy, the thrill of feeling as if I'm going to fall heightening everything. Wilder sucks me until I reach my peak, my orgasm so incredibly intense. My eyes roll back with my scream, and I smother Wilder between my legs, not letting him pull away.

Enzo bends me down, helping Wilder carry me through the door so I don't hit my head, and his brothers join them, each grabbing one of my arms until I fall back to have them catch me.

I laugh and struggle in Arsenio's arms. "I'm supposed to take care of—"

Desmond leans down and cuts off my words with a kiss. "You know the rule. You come first, especially when we're all together. This is you taking care of us. Let us love up on you how we need."

The steam of the shower engulfs us as Arsenio holds me with his chest against my back, his hands locked firmly to my legs, supporting my body. Desmond steps between my legs and rubs his fingers over my clit, making me twist and writhe at the pressure. Wilder and Enzo join us in the small shower, our bodies wet and slippery but completely hot and so perfect together. No one fumbles or gets left out, and Arsenio hoists me up higher until he can align his cock to my ass while Desmond slides into me from the front, my slick ensuring pleasure over pain no matter how they penetrate me.

Enzo and Wilder take turns licking my nipples and kissing me, stroking themselves as I lose myself to the ecstasy of being within the circle of their muscular bodies, the water cleansing us and washing away the remnants of the war we had faced.

I gasp as Desmond and Arsenio take turns swinging into me, the rhythm in perfect sync, working me up. I pant and moan, clutching Desmond's taut shoulders. Enzo plays with my clit, taking one of my legs from Arsenio. Wilder takes the other, spreading me open into near splits for them to do as they please. They suspend me lower, and I scratch my nails over Desmond's abs.

Wilder stands taller, stretching his body closer to my face. I reach out and grab his cock, guiding him to my mouth, letting him rest between my lips as I lick the bottom side of his shaft. He thrusts a few times, testing my gag reflex. All I do is moan and breathe deeply with each of his thrusts, taking pleasure from where he can. I blindly rub my hand over Enzo, my mind pulled in four different directions but never apart. It's as if I bind these men together as one, our souls and futures tangled and meant to be together always.

Arsenio calls out with his orgasm, splashing his seed over my back, letting me feel the heat of his desire. Desmond continues on, letting himself enjoy me in this moment for as long as his body will allow. Enzo takes Arsenio's place, sliding his cock into my ass, the slick of my desire intensifying the pleasure, making it easier to fuck me at the pace he enjoys most. Enzo's scent permeates the air, the fragrance of our lust as intoxicating as any alcohol I've ever tasted.

All I can think about is how good I feel. How loved and appreciated I am. How strong I've become, forged from my pain into something invincible. I am invincible.

"She's so beautiful, isn't she?" Desmond grunts as he finishes, still stroking my clit as Wilder fills his place, getting ready to fuck me until I take his knot like I need. I'm so fucking horny. I know that sort of pleasure is what will satisfy me the most.

Desmond's perfect strokes over my body sends me over the edge, and I clench and grab Arsenio's hip, digging my nails into his side. I moan and whimper, squirming with the pleasure, craving for it to never end. I could drown and still be able to breathe.

My guys are my everything, and I need more. We fought for this, and I will relish every second of our time.

Enzo squeezes me from behind, lifting me up higher, locking me in place, his body pulsing with his orgasm. The scent of cinnamon overpowers the vetiver radiating from him and Wilder, and it sets Wilder off as his deep-seated nature locks me in place, his cock engorging as he knots with me, setting me off in wave after wave of orgasmic bliss. His brothers bathe and soap me up while I cling onto Wilder, kissing him and panting, moaning, and just enjoying all of their hands on my body, memorizing every inch of me.

Each of them kisses me and whispers their love until Wilder's cock releases, and I lean back and rest against Enzo, not wanting to be set on my feet. I just want to cuddle and be loved up on until my heart stops racing. I want their closeness and to just feel them here. To smell them. To know that what we have can't be broken. No one will get in our way.

Wilder helps rinse my hair, and Arsenio wraps his towel around me, and the four of them return back to my room and help me get situated in my blanket fort. The four of them reposition my dresser and bookcase enough to fit all four of us, so we can just lie together. I relax as I come down from the high of our passion, the cuddle pile exactly what I need. I stretch out on top of Wilder and Desmond with Arsenio and Enzo on the outside, resting their hands on my body.

This moment feels so perfect. So absolutely incredible.

I have never felt so blessed.

For the first time in a long time, the world doesn't feel like it's out to get me.

It's given me a gift with my pack, and I will never take it for granted.

# Chapter Twenty

## *Enzo*

## Civil War

"**A**re you sure about this, Anita? There can be another way. You don't have to face him." Kinsey bounces on the balls of her feet, unable to quit moving.

She's been up and down all day, moving things around her bedroom while also eating what seems like one meal after another. And I can't control my fucking boner. The second I catch her scent, my dick perks up, ready and waiting.

"I know my way around alphas. Of course, I'm up to this. I'll do whatever I can to help. I just want you guys to be safe and not face retaliation for getting me out of that hellhole club. If this is what it takes to get a life, then I'll do it." Anita offers

Kinsey a warm smile. "All I need is a minute with him, and he'll start blabbing. I've always done this for Madam Tamsin. At least with this, it benefits me too. All the omegas, really."

Because Rommel is a lot tougher than I had anticipated. Usually, guys scream and give in immediately at the thought of pain, but this bastard seems to have a kink for it. He only gives us bits and pieces of information we need. And we need everything right now.

"You'll be heavily rewarded for your help." I keep my distance, holding my breath, so I don't accidentally ruin Kinsey's scent still lingering on my lips. I just want to hold her to my face and breathe her in. It's all I can think about. It doesn't help the situation.

"Your kindness is enough. I can't wait to see how things work out. I had never imagined anything like this would come during my lifetime. You're one of the first alphas I've been able to speak to openly, and I appreciate it." Anita curtsies out of respect, still keeping her gaze trained on the floor. "It's an honor to have you and your brothers as my kings. I'm so thankful for you too, Kinsey. I never stopped thinking about you after Tamsin sent you off. You were always so kind to me at the club."

Kinsey's scent intensifies with the recognition from Anita. I reach out and clutch her hand, pulling her closer to me. It helps keep me in control as long as I'm touching her. She's so ready for her heat. My body is going wild because of it. That's why we need to do this shit now. We need to get everything in order so we can all take care of our girl and not have to be away from her.

Wilder swings open the door to the dungeon, the cement and steel basement stale and cold despite the warmth of the rest of the palace.

"We're ready." Wilder holds out a pair of handcuffs. "Put these on. We have to make it look real."

Anita holds her hands behind her back, allowing Wilder to loosely click the cuffs on. She can still pull her hands out of them, but the way she stretches her fingers, they look as if they're not going anywhere.

"No! Please! I hurt so badly! I can barely handle it. You have to help me." Anita shocks the hell out of me, her voice ringing through the air, echoing through the stairwell. She never gave us the warning, jumping right into her performance as imprisoned omega.

I open and close my mouth, unsure if I should say anything. This kind of roleplay is freaky as fuck, and I kind of don't want to have anything to do with it. I hadn't realized how awful even pretending to lock up an omega would feel. I don't know if it's because of Kinsey or just my nature, but it takes everything in me to remain composed.

"Just keep moving," Wilder growls, his assholeness finally coming into use. "We can't have you roaming around the fucking palace, begging for someone to get you off. If you don't like the toys, then I don't know what to tell you. So go down now. Don't argue. If you make me carry you…" Wilder leaves his fake threat open-ended, tightening his jaw as he glances at Kinsey and Anita. I'm glad he controls the situation. I can't even think straight right now. He's a better actor than me—or more in control. Fuck me.

Kinsey exhales a soft whimpering breath, squeezing me tightly. She doesn't like the way he sounds right now. Her emotions waft around me in a hot wave with her scent. Now I realize that this might trigger her. I was stupid to even agree to let her come with us to make Anita comfortable. Because she went through this exact scenario, except it was far worse. It was real. Anita is only here to bait information from Rommel.

"Come on, baby. Let Wilder handle this. Anita is fine." I stroke my fingers along Kinsey's arm, pulling her in even closer.

Whipping her head back and forth, she denies me. She sucks in her bottom lip and straightens her shoulders. I rub my fingers over hers, hoping she relents. I hate seeing her so conflicted, but I know she won't let me take her away. Her tight mouth proves it. She managed to compose herself with a couple of breaths and blinking her eyes, getting her emotions under control.

"I need to be here. I don't want to just hear what happened from Wilder." Kinsey swallows and shakes out her fingers. "It's not real. It's all just a mind game." She says the words quietly for herself as if she needs convincing.

"I said move!" Wilder shouts, motioning for Anita to head into the stairwell.

Anita whimpers, her voice echoing off the concrete. She struts down the steps with confidence until she reaches the last couple that will bring her into Rommel's view. Rommel now sits on the cold ground, chained to the floor by his wrists and feet.

"Please, help me. You're such a strong alpha. You can take care of me." Anita turns and looks up at Wilder, her eyes wide and her gaze glassy. "You don't have to do this. Just take me back up. I'll do anything."

Shit. I bristle at her fake suggestion. Kinsey clutches me tighter, sensing my agitation.

"Shut up and get away. I can't stand your scent, and since you won't stop trying to seduce every damn alpha, you'll be going into the cell over there." Wilder waves his arm instead of pushing her, but the gesture sends Anita scrambling away.

She cries out, tripping over her feet to land on the ground. Her handcuffed wrists make it impossible for her to get back up. Writhing on the cold floor, she cries, the sound convincing enough to nearly trick me. If I didn't know she was acting, I'd believe her performance.

I expect Kinsey to rush forward and end this before we can get a chance to do anything, but she remains frozen by my side and out of view from Rommel. I'm glad she does because I wouldn't remain here otherwise.

"Hey, honey. Come over here. I'll help you." Rommel clicks his tongue, his disgusting nature coming through as he tries to offer his services to Anita. They're not close enough for him to know that she's not in heat, but she knows how to play the part. I bet she's done it a dozen times with the men who frequented Tamsin's club. There are a lot of bastards into roleplay.

"Thank God. Finally, someone who is strong enough to help me." Anita stretches her neck up, looking at Rommel. She turns to Wilder. "Please, let me go to him. He'll help me. You can let him help me."

Wilder growls and lifts Anita up on her feet, stopping her from moving forward. "No. He's an asshole who isn't cooperating. He wants to see us fall. You're going to have to suffer through this. I'm sorry."

Whimpering, Anita pouts her mouth, jerking her attention back to Rommel. "You have to do something. You said you would help me. If you help them, then you could help me. Please. I'm in so much pain. My body aches. I have a need that only you can take care of. You're so strong and handsome. Please do this for me. I'm begging you."

The omega sure can act. If I didn't know any better, I'd believe her. It's even fucking with my head a little bit, thinking that if she acts like she's in heat long enough, she might actually go into it.

Or maybe it's because Kinsey squeezes my hand and rubs against me, squeezing her legs and shifting as if she's uncomfortable.

"He will not keep his word. The only reason I'm alive right now is because he needs me. I'm sorry, honey. He's not going to do anything for either of us." Rommel grumbles with his words, yanking against his chains as if he can break free.

Wilder stands in silence, looming over Anita and glaring at Rommel. "If you don't give us the answers, I will kill you anyway. But if you do, I'll let you live a bit longer. You can take care of this omega. The only way you're going to stay alive is if you work with us. Do you understand?"

"Please," Anita says, her voice mewing almost in a feline manner. "I'm begging you. Just tell him. I'll make sure he doesn't hurt you. You're going to be my alpha. You're going to be the one to protect me, and he won't hurt the man I choose."

Ah hell. That's what I'm talking about. I don't even have to see Rommel to know that he's already lost his good sense and has fallen to his nature. It's hard to resist an unclaimed omega when you have none yourself.

"Fine. Fine. Jarvis has a skeleton key for the fortress. Your father has a secret passageway that you can access from the very edge of your territory. It is within Mount Gold. It was built before he became king, and it would've been passed down to you had you just waited your turn to take reign." Rommel sneers with his words, his face twisting.

I can't stop myself from stepping into view, and I unsheathe my dagger, handing it to Kinsey. "So, what if they plan to infiltrate the fortress from there. That won't give them access to us here."

"You're wrong. You don't really think that King Winston would've just allowed you to be disconnected from his ruler-ship, do you? There is a connecting tunnel that leads here. Ten miles long. All it will take is an army...one already closing in. Maybe even already here." Rommel purses his lips, his eyes turning toward Kinsey. "You better pray those alphas are as powerful as you think. If not—well, don't you worry. Uncle Rommel has a nice new pack for you."

"You monster!" Kinsey loses her shit, launching away from me and toward Rommel.

Wilder intercepts, scooping her off her feet. I open my arms, readying to catch her as he tosses her back to me, not letting her within a foot of Rommel. My mind races with his comments.

The fucker wasn't only just sent to prove our securities weakness. He was sent as a decoy to the fortress, leaving our palace vulnerable. They could be fucking anywhere. They could've planted explosives.

"We have to move! Evacuate everyone," Wilder says, his voice remaining cold. "The fucker isn't brave enough to face us. If his army lies in wait, it'll be to pick us all off after he destroys our palace. He's not stupid."

"Ding, ding, ding," Rommel says, cackling from his spot. "Don't worry your empty little heads, though. We're safe here. Jarvis wants you alive."

"No!" Kinsey screams, thrashing in my arms, trying to throw herself toward her uncle again.

I grip her tighter. "We have to go, baby. I know you want to hurt him, but we have to go."

"I can't leave him alive. I can't. I can't," Kinsey gives me no choice but to set her down. Arguing will just waste time.

Anita balls her hands, standing near Rommel. "She's right. Alphas like him think they're invincible. Isn't that right?" Slamming her fist down, Anita punches Rommel in the cock, sending him howling and bucking. "You think you have more power than us. Look at you now."

This might be the first time I've ever questioned my power coming from my order. The way Kinsey bounces, looking cold and fierce, unwavering as she prepares to disobey my pleas to let Wilder handle it gets to me in a surprisingly good way. This side of her proves that omegas don't have to be docile and obedient. They can rise up and demand control and authority as much as anyone.

Rommel tries to break free, but the chains hold him tightly. "You fucking bitch! I'll kill you! You'll regret it when you're caught, and I get to put you in your damn place."

Anita grabs him by the top of his hair and slams his head back. "You're all talk. You're worthless. Come on, Kinsey, get your revenge. Get it for all of us who have ever been wronged by disgusting pricks who don't deserve the order they mani-fested into." Anita jerks Rommel's face toward her. "Do you hear that? You're unworthy of any omega. This is how you'll end."

Her words of encouragement trigger Kinsey to step closer, and her scent heats up, her body swelling with rage. Wilder holds his hand up, stopping me from trying to shadow her. He doesn't hold out his knife, but he also doesn't resist as she snatches it out of his hand and strides up to Rommel.

"You aren't gonna fucking do it, Kinsey. You don't have it in you. You're weak. You're as worthless as your bitch of a mother. These fuckers will see just how much you are when you cause their kingdom to fall. They're going to get you, Kinsey. None of these bastards can conquer the true leaders of the region." Rommel snaps his teeth, trying to bite Kinsey as she moves closer.

Kinsey stomps his balls, silencing his threat. "Fuck you! You're the worthless piece of shit. You weren't worthy of leading our pack. You weren't worthy of even being a part of our family. Now you will die by my hands—my supposed weak hands." Kinsey jerks her arm, stabbing Rommel in his gut, making him howl. "How does it feel? Is your regret as bitter as the rest of your life? I am better than you. More powerful than you. I might have been damaged and broken, but I forged my fucking self with fire and steel and determination to never be what you tried to beat me into. You are nothing. Absolutely nothing!"

I gawk at the ferocity of my beautiful woman, tearing into the man who hurt her. A part of me knows I should've done it for her. His blood should've never had the luxury of staining her divine hands. The other part of me? The dominant, vicious part plans to worship her like the deity she is to me. My faith and devotion lie in her and only her. She makes me stronger. Makes me fight harder.

"That's enough. We have to go. We're running out of time." It takes Wilder snatching Kinsey to get her to stop stabbing her uncle long after he has already succumbed to the injuries she inflicted on him. "It's over, Kinsey. He's gone." Wilder embraces her tightly, his strength stopping the trembles quaking through her body.

"Then why doesn't it feel like it was enough? He deserved worse! He—" A wail cracks from her lips, shattering my soul. Her pain and anger resonate through me as if I share her body and mind.

"Shh, I know. I know. Nothing we could've done to him would've ever been enough." Wilder strokes her back, motioning for me to join them.

"He's right. Death doesn't repair the damage caused by the living, baby," I whisper, closing the space to smother her to Wilder, hoping our closeness helps ease her wild emotions even if just for a while. "But time can. Each day that passes will mend you more and more. We are here for you. We're not going anywhere."

"And our enemies? What are we going to do? I don't feel so good." Kinsey's breathing turns ragged.

"She's in pre-heat. You have to get her out of here. Take her somewhere safe." Anita rubs her hands up and down her arms.

Fuck me. She's right. We can't deny it now. Pretending it isn't going to happen does no one any good. We can't fight like this. In other times I would stand beside our soldiers, but now I know I can't. I have to entrust it to someone else.

"Take her to the tunnels and out to the garage. I'll prep security and start the evacuation." If Wilder wasn't holding Kinsey, I'd take her myself. He's not letting her go, though. I'm not sure his body will let him. I can smell his fucking rut from here, triggered by Kinsey. I better hustle my ass, or I'll lose my shit. I need to be clearheaded.

"I'll help. I can gather the omegas. Where do we go?" Anita clears her throat, her body stiff. She senses the rut too. Kinsey could lash out at her, so she'll be as cautious as I am until we're all safe.

"I'll text Holly to meet you. She knows the way." I nudge Wilder, pushing him to move. "If I'm not out in ten, leave without us. We'll reconvene at the safe house." I don't say exactly where in case. I half expect Jarvis's army to be waiting upstairs, knowing we know they're going to try to fuck shit up.

"You better be out in nine, brother," Wilder warns.

I unholster my weapon. "Just go."

I wait until Wilder disappears, taking the secret passage to the garage. It's the only safe place I know for certain in our palace. Only our immediate pack can open the doors. It's why I need Holly to meet Anita. She can help with the omegas while I focus on everything else.

"Let me go first. I'll make sure it's all clear." I pull out my cell phone and click on the security feeds first, seeing nothing out of the ordinary. But I don't trust them. If they were able to get inside, they could've hacked our systems. We could never know.

*Me: SOS. Bomb threat. Activate evacuation protocols now.*

*Arsehole: Fuck. On it.*

*Me: I need all security doing a sweep. Dad had an access tunnel from the fortress to here. We need to get out of here. Kinsey is in pre-heat.*

*Favorite Brother: I can stay and make sure everything is taken care of. I'll catch up.*

*Me: No, Kinsey needs you. I'm going to entrust everything into the Silversteins' hands. We will reconvene when Kinsey is safe.*

*Arsehole: Got it. Starting evac now.*

An alarm blares through the air, startling Anita. I motion for her to cover her ears and follow me up the stairs. I click through my phone, checking the security fields one more time before I shoot a text to Holly. She might panic if she doesn't know what's going on, but she's also probably with Beckett.

*Me: Holly, meet Anita at the top of the stairs. I need you to get all the omegas into the panic room. We're going to evacuate. We got information from Rommel that shit's going down. Wilder thinks it could be explosives.*

*Baby Sis: Fuck. Okay.*

I love the bravery of my little sister. It makes me feel like I have done at least some things right in life, teaching her to be empowered and to have confidence. My brothers and I have ensured that she isn't one to easily bow or break.

"When we reach the main floor, stay close. I'm going to lead you to the stairs, and you're going to meet Holly there. She's going to take you guys to the panic room." I reach the top of the stairs and kick open the door, not bothering to take it slow and easy. My adrenaline pumps, my ears pounding. The alarm continues to ring, but apart from that, there's no one around.

It's too quiet. Unsettling. I brace myself for the worst.

Nothing happens.

The grand hallway stays clear all the way to the curved staircase leading up. I motion to Anita to hurry, and I jog forward, heading toward the staff wing. They should already be evacuating, but I won't leave until I know that they're safe. As their alpha, it is my duty to protect them.

Unease flows through me, prodding at my deep-seated nature. My muscles remain tense, my movements precise. I steal myself passing every archway and door, expecting one of our enemies to pop out to try to kill me.

Again, the palace in this location remains still. The alarms continue to ring, but I tune them out. I focus on movement. Any screaming. Something to alert me.

I slow down, passing the grand dining hall, and making my way to the kitchen. There's a servant door through the back, so this would be one of the evacuation locations.

I push open the swinging door, spotting no one.

Fuck. There are people here.

I didn't notice them at first because a couple of bodies lay on the floor. How the fuck did this happen?

I charge forward and flip over our head chef, pressing my fingers to his throat. His pulse thrums steadily, bringing me great relief. He's alive.

Scooping my arms under him, I lift him up and rush toward the back exit, sitting him down outside. I go back for another one of our servants, double-checking to make sure she's still breathing as well. They've all been knocked out.

I blink my eyes, my body starting to feel heavy. It's still in the air. Fuck me. If I don't get out of here, it'll knock me unconscious too.

I pull my shirt up over my nose, holding my breath to relocate the sous chef. There are about five more staff members in here, but I'm not sure I'm going to get to everyone.

The alarms turn off, the residual sound still ringing in my ears. At least Desmond muted them, making it easier to focus.

If any of our awake staff members haven't heard evacuation alarms by now, then something else is up with them.

*Baby Sis: SOS! Help us!*

Holy shit. I don't even have to ask her what's going on to know that the omegas have been affected too. I'm torn between helping the staff here and running upstairs. But Holly will always come first. My family. Does it make me a bad man? Maybe. I never claimed to be good, though.

I shoot a text to Arsenio, telling him the situation.

My phone chimes, but I don't look at it. I need to get upstairs.

I charge from the kitchen, my boots thudding on the floor. All I can think about is a ticking clock, counting down the seconds until something catastrophic happens. It's the not knowing that freaks me out. And there's nothing more that I hate than being scared. Nothing should scare me.

But I know I'm not invincible.

"Holly!" I yell, keeping my shirt over my nose despite it leaving me vulnerable to a physical attack if someone were to pop out from one of the rooms. Staying conscious is a priority, though. I can fight with my hands if I have to.

"Enzo! I can't get into one of the suites. The omegas are all passed out in the other. Something's going on." Holly stands at the top of the stairs, covering her nose and mouth just as I am. She knows how to handle emergency situations just as well. "It's taking too long for me, and I need help carrying them. I have a massive headache. I'm scared."

I bound up the stairs, taking two at a time until I reach Holly. "Get Anita and head to the tunnels. I don't want you going to the panic room in case. Head to the garage. Wilder is already there."

"The Silversteins were helping with security. They haven't come back yet." Holly shifts nervously, her fear palpable with her hearty scent.

"They'll be okay, lil sis. Let's worry about you and the others. We have to get out of here. We think that Jarvis is about to blow this place up." I press my hand to Holly's back, getting her to run to the suite with the open door.

I spot three unconscious omegas from the nest we found at the Smithsons, and Anita hollers for us from the wardrobe with an access door. She struggles to drag the male omega, and I quickly run in and scoop him up, taking him into the concrete corridor.

"I'm going to go check on the others. Since you can't get in, they might've just locked the door in fear because of the alarms." I motion to a pile of blankets. "Roll them onto those. It'll be easier to drag. Save your energy."

Holly and Anita follow my instructions, and I race from the room to the one next door. I don't bother checking the doorknob and instead kick my heavy boot over and over until the wood around the knob fissures and cracks, allowing me to yank the handle off. I flick out the lock and shove the door open, the hazy air engulfing me.

A gunshot pops, and a bullet hits the wall behind me. I jump out of the way, shielding myself from a spray of gunfire. Several soldiers stand with gas masks and protective gear near the balcony, loading all the unconscious omegas.

Jarvis wouldn't risk their lives. He wants them for himself.

But I can't fight the soldiers alone. My head pounds with a throbbing headache.

I make a tough decision, one that Kinsey could possibly hate me over. But what am I going to do? I'm one man. Our palace is under attack because of our fucking idiotic father, setting us up even in death.

My priority is to get Holly and Kinsey to safety. Our territory won't survive this without us. It's hard to abandon our security and soldiers, but I have to trust that I've trained them well. We're one of the only pack leaders that immerse themselves and fight alongside their people.

Rushing back to Holly and Anita, I slam and lock the door, shoving a dresser in front of it. I push the bed over next and block a clear path to the wardrobe. I catch up with Holly in the corridor, scooping up two of the omegas, carrying them on each of my shoulders. I drag two more on the blankets, allowing Holly and Anita to grab the final one.

The floor rumbles, shaking the corridor, but it doesn't feel close enough to worry me. It's a warning explosion—one to send us into a panic.

"Move faster!" I holler, craning to look at Holly and Anita. "Move!"

All I can think about is losing everything.

What if Rommel was right? What if Kinsey learns how weak we might truly be?

From the open balcony, I stare at the smoke wafting from the horizon. The war goes on without us, but my people won't bow to another authority. Our allies send in reinforcements, pushing Jarvis's army out as we speak. My fears were unwarranted, and I shouldn't have doubted our capabilities. We don't have to do everything ourselves. Giving responsibility and power across other packs makes us stronger as a territory. It also allows me to breathe, knowing no one will find us here, in the home of my mom's pack. Kinsey rests, her exhaustion getting the best of her. I'm just so thankful we can take care of her now.

My phone buzzes from my pocket.

*Asshole Bro: All good?*

*Me: Kinsey's asleep. She collected all the pillows, blankets, towels, and our spare clothes. She's getting close.*

*Asshole Bro: She can have whatever she wants. Can you meet me in the hall in five? I don't want to wake her. She needs to rest.*

*Me: Glad we agree. I'd fuck you up if you disturbed her.*

*Asshole Bro: You could try.*

A soft whine sounds from Kinsey's nest, her blanket fort now a mansion with everything she could get her hands on that smelled like us. It fucks with my head that I couldn't give her more, so I've been scavenging the place and wearing everything I can, leaving my scent. My brothers are going to bust a nut when they see how Kinsey literally stole everything of theirs we had packed in our emergency bags in the garage. I don't think it'll ever be enough. I've seen an omega nesting before, but it was nothing like this. I think her taking suppressant pills will guarantee one helluva heat. She's going to want to fuck me for days, and I'll gladly abide even if I lose my cock in the process.

Strolling to the mass of blankets shielding her from the rest of her new room, I squat down and peek inside. Kinsey's damp hair sticks to her glistening cheeks. My balls throb, catching her stroke herself in her sleep, and if my phone didn't buzz again, I'd squeeze my big ass in with her to give her relief.

*Asshole Bro: We're outside. I hope your head is clear enough to double-check my plans.*

I glower at the screen without responding.

Pinching my thigh hard enough to get myself to focus, I stand up and jog across the room. I fling the door open, expecting to see all my brothers, but Beckett stands beside Wilder. The second I'm within their space, I growl and shove Beckett away. If he even gets a hint of Kinsey's scent, I'll punch him. I suddenly want him nowhere near her.

Wilder hooks his arm across my throat, winding me as he yanks me away. "Calm the fuck down. I know it's fucking hard but keep your shit together."

"He's too fucking close to her," I snap, growling again. "She needs rest. If she even catches a breath of him, she'll panic. Her body's preparing. I won't let anything fucking ruin it. She's been through enough."

Beckett raises his hands in surrender, stepping back until he's twenty feet away. Smart man. "My apologies. I wasn't thinking."

"Neither was I," Wilder says, scrubbing the back of his neck, inhaling a deep breath as he recognizes Kinsey's pheromones calling to us, even in her sleep.

"Obviously. I don't want her alone for long. She'll wake up if she realizes I'm not there." I lean back, peeking into her room. At least she didn't hear me nearly attack Beckett for intruding.

Wilder puffs out a breath. I'm nearly certain he's trying his best to hold it. His muscles ripple, his innate need to be with Kinsey trying to steal control. "I just wanted to update you. Our spies sent images of Jarvis calling back his army. Desmond and Arsenio went to Mount Gold to track the tunnel. Our bastard father also wasn't an idiot because it works both ways. We found the skeleton key for Jarvis's castle. Though if my plan works, we won't need it." Again, he releases a sharp breath, shaking his head.

I throw my hands up in annoyance. "Spit it out, brother."

"They tried to beat us by gassing our people. But it also gave us a chance to fight back. We're going to take a lesson from Father. Instead of invading with force, we're going to drug their water supply." Wilder thins his lips, meeting my eyes.

The brilliant bastard.

He had mentioned Dad taught him something. I just hadn't realized it was pulling the shit he did to us on an entire fucking territory. To be able to do something like that, we'll have to make a deal with...I never expected Kinsey's use of suppressants would eventually lead us to this moment.

The fuckers of the Pack Regimes are going down. We can safely dismantle their infrastructure without complete annihilation.

A cocky-ass grin stretches across my face, and I swing my arm around Wilder, scrubbing my knuckles through his hair. He grunts and socks me in the gut. I wheeze with laughter, my mood shifting from annoyance to joy.

"Fuck yeah! What's the price? I know Donahue won't give us the product out of the goodness of his heart." I smack my hands together.

"A lot of fucking money, access through every territory, and an agreement for him to be the sole distributor of all pheromone and hormonal narcotics. He recognizes the fact that business will be booming with the changes." Wilder scratches his cheek, keeping his eyes trained at Kinsey's bedroom. "We're not covering the sole cost. We'll pay the debt with the assets we acquire from our takeovers."

"It's the one thing all of the best packs I have agreed on. We're not going to end up fighting over wealth. Everything that we take will go toward our people." Beckett speaks up from down the hall. "There will also be a vote for who takes the fallen territories with the agreement of rebuilding with alliances in mind. We can't have other regions think ours is growing weak."

Because word probably has already spread. This would've been the first civil war we've had in over a century. That's how long the current bloodlines have been in power, including ours.

"What about Platinum Shores? Is Desmond still taking it?" I can't help asking. A part of me still clings to my jealousy.

"Actually, he has declined to take it. The last week has really gotten to him. He doesn't want to be away from our territory. This is home." Wilder shrugs her shoulders. "What about you? Do you want it?"

"What about Arsenio?" He would be the one expecting to take it since Desmond doesn't want it any longer.

"He doesn't want to either," Wilder says, resting his hand on my shoulder. "You don't have to make the decision now but—"

Kinsey whimpers from the room, her voice crying out. I whip my attention toward her nest, watching as the blanket shifts.

It's in this moment that I realize I don't fucking want Platinum Shores. I don't need Platinum Shores. Everything I could ever want in the world is in that small fort.

"My answer is no. I've changed my mind. There's no fucking way I'll ever be more than down the hall from Kinsey. Hell, you might have to deal with all of us sharing a room." I try to move past him, but he blocks me, slowing me down so I can't get to her as she makes her way out of her nest.

"If you're sure, I'll make it official. We'll give Platinum Shores to Holly, and she can share it with the pack she desires most." Wilder looks down the hallway at Beckett, his face expressionless.

It was already unheard of to declare a beta as a leader. But to give an entire territory to an omega? Holy shit.

"You do that. Good luck. I'm going back into this comfy little nest to cuddle with our girl. You better fucking hurry up. You might only have hours. I'm going to need backup. It's going to be intense as fuck because of how long she's put it off." I leave my brother in the hallway, striding back to Kinsey as she whimpers again. I scoop her into my arms, and she groans and buries her face in my chest, shifting onto me.

The world could be burning outside of these haphazardly hung sheets, and I wouldn't notice now. This is what I've been waiting for my entire life. The girl of my dreams hugs me, seeking comfort from me in a moment that will be one we'll never forget. Because we'll truly bond.

She will bless me as a wife and with the family of my dreams.

I'll stop at nothing to make it happen.

# Chapter Twenty-One

## *Kinsey*

## Platinum Shores

I'm so fucking uncomfortable. I'm freezing one second and sweating the next, and my stomach won't stop growling. Exhaustion clings to me, yet I can't keep still. And every time I fall asleep, I lose myself to my nightmares.

My uncle's wicked face hovers over me, smiling as I cry in agony with my wrists and ankles bound. There's nothing I can do to find relief from my body's need to breed. Growls and hollers ring through the air from across the room, threatening my uncle but unable to follow through.

There's nothing anyone can do.

I must suffer in silence as he shoves a gag in my mouth.

I can't see anything through my tears. And then the gunshots startle me.

"Hey, baby. You're okay. You're safe." Enzo strokes his hand along my side, pulling me from the vivid nightmare, or maybe a memory, my mind too hazy to think of anything right now. "Let me help you. You look like you need some attention."

I squeeze my legs together, feeling my clit throbbing, my body wet as it counts down the seconds until I can't think about anything other than my heat and what it means.

"This is too much. I think I want a suppressant pill." I hang my head, shame clinging to me. I thought I could get through this, but with every passing minute, my fear grows. All I can remember is the pain.

But this is different. I'm not alone. I'm not unwanted or forgotten. I'm so very loved.

Why can't my mind grasp it?

Enzo touches my chin, tilting my head up as he leans over me to look at my face. He keeps his body flush to mine with his other hand firmly planted on my stomach, the weight of his skin helping to ease the mild cramps.

"Let's talk about this. I'll get everything you need if that's what you truly want. But if you have even a little bit of doubt, I think you should wait it out just a bit longer. I'm here for you. Whatever you decide. I've become quite talented with my hand over the years, if you decide that you want to kick me out.

I can rut on my own. But you, Kinsey? You going into heat by yourself isn't happening."

I lick my lips, my pout quivering. I have more than just a bit of doubt. I'm completely torn. I want so badly for this moment, but the dark part of me just can't let go of what happened before.

"You're right. I can wait it out a bit longer. I just..." I let my voice trail off.

Enzo snuggles against my back, spooning me from behind. He nuzzles his face to my throat, sliding his hand across my hip and to my pelvis. "Let me massage you for a bit. You might settle down. That's what I'm here for. Just close your eyes. Listen to my voice and relax."

Enzo kisses the nape of my neck, sliding his hand into my panties and between my legs, rubbing circles over my clit, igniting pleasure inside me. I gasp and squirm, the sensation more intense than usual.

"You are the most beautiful woman I have ever seen," Enzo murmurs, his voice soft and husky, filled with his desire.

I moan and ease my legs apart a bit more, wanting him to caress me more fervently. I just want the ache to go away. I want to be filled with satisfaction instead of feeling like I'm on the brink of being empty.

"You're also kind and compassionate. Your ideals for our future make me so very proud of you. I fall in love with you more each and every day." Enzo dips his finger inside me, rubbing just the right spot to make me moan louder. His hard-on rests between my legs, but he doesn't try to fuck me.

"I love you too," I whisper, my voice breathy and whiny.

"You know what else I love?" Enzo nips my skin.

"Hmm?" My mind whirls in ecstasy, my body screaming with joy. The contentment of being so close to him, drowning in the intensity of his scent, and feeling the pleasure he can awaken in me drags me closer and closer to the edge.

"How fucking wet you are. How tight. How your body calls to me. You don't know how much I just want to fuck you until you're filled with my seed. Until I knock you up, so I can kneel before you and kiss your swollen belly, growing with the life that we have created together. It's all I can think about." Enzo strums his thumb over my clit as he fingers me, using his other hand to caress my nipples.

I sigh and pant, imagining the sort of life we can create. It makes me feel powerful. "I want that so badly."

"Good. It'll be perfect. You'll have everything you ever want and desire. You will rule by our side, ensuring that we always are guided in the right direction. You're our perfect omega. You'll bring such beauty and prosperity to our lands." Enzo rocks against me, grinding his hard-on between my legs, just feeling the heat of my body as I dampen my panties.

"I can't wait. I need you right now." I reach behind me and yank at his pants, pulling the soft fabric down to expose his cock. Adjusting my body, I guide him into me, loving how it feels with his arms around me and him throbbing inside me. I orgasm with the pressure of his finger still exploring my clit, and I scream out in pleasure. He rolls with me, getting on top of me, lying flat on my stomach, and he thrusts deep inside me. The pillows elevate my hips, and I can't stop my mouth from shouting my pleasure over and over again. With every deep thrust, the ache inside me lessens. My need purrs with satisfaction. My body feels so amazing. So alive and loved and complete.

Enzo grabs my hair, tossing it out of the way so he can suck on my shoulder. He growls with each penetrative thrust, going wild with his nature. He slides his hand beneath me and touches me in a way that makes me whimper. I need him to knot with me. I can't stop thinking about it.

And then pressure swells as he engorges with his lust, locking me to him in a wave of pure, explosive bliss.

Hugging me, he puts more weight on my body, his skin against mine sending electricity from my core and into my toes. I stretch my neck and kiss him, tasting the sweetness of his mouth, the softness of his tongue gliding over mine. The passion of this moment spills through me, lighting me like the sun breaking dawn.

His body releases me after a long while, and the moment of pleasure suddenly fades, leaving me breathing heavy and hot.

"You're on the cusp, baby. I can smell it." Enzo slowly slides out of me and rolls off only to grab me and put me on him. "My brothers need to hurry up so we can lock ourselves away."

I rest on top of him, my ear against his chest, his quick heartbeats like music. A melody of his soul. "They don't need you?" I ask, my heart skipping a beat at just a thought.

"They'll have it handled. They're currently making the negotiations right now." Enzo rubs his big hand up and down my spine, his comforting touch enough to make me drowsy. I could fall asleep right in his arms, but a part of me wants to know more. They haven't given me all the details of what is to come. All I know is that they're making a deal with Donahue.

Enzo's phone chimes from the floor, and he groans and shifts, stretching to grab it from the pile of pillows I made. "I have to get it. They're supposed to keep me updated."

I snatch his hand and hold the phone closer, so I can see it too, sliding to rest my leg over his as I cuddle his side.

*Asshole Brother: We're pulling up. Is Kinsey awake?*
*Me: No. She's out. Leave us alone.*

"Enzo!" I say, raising my voice. He's a bit possessive after his knot, and if I let him get away with it, he'll keep it up. It's an innate behavior with his rut.

*Me: Kidding. Did you bring food? That's the only way we're coming down.*
*Asshole Brother: A feast.*

I wiggle beside Enzo until he forces himself to move. Just the thought of food sends my stomach screaming, the sound of it hurrying Enzo to move faster. We clean up in the shower, the heat of the water soothing my aching body. I cringe at the idea of putting pants on, so I steal Enzo's big T-shirt before he can put it on and shrug into it.

"So hot. It's way better on you. Spin around and bend over. I need the full effect." Enzo twirls his finger, rubbing his cock through his pants.

Shaking my head, I deny him, puffing my lip. "If I do, we'll never leave this room, and I'm starving."

"We'll serve you in bed," he comments, smirking.

That sounds luxurious.

"Not with Holly around. You know she's here." I hold my arms out, wanting him to pick me up. "Resist for just a bit. We both need to save our energy. It'll be worth it."

Enzo squeezes my ass, adjusting me low on his body, rubbing his massive hard-on between my legs. "Hell yeah. I'm going to knock you the fuck up. I can't wait."

Warmth sizzles between my legs, his comment igniting something fierce and all-consuming inside me. I nearly grab Enzo's cock to slide between my legs. I can't think about anything else.

"Hey, brat-girl. Is my brother holding you hostage?" Wilder pounds the door, shaking the wood. "I don't want your food getting cold."

I moan and ease my face away from Enzo's chest. "Food sounds so good."

"Sex is better," Enzo mutters, tightening his fingers to my bare ass.

"There's dessert." Wilder taps his finger to the door, not trying to open it. "Lots and lots of it. All your favorite main dishes. We didn't know what you were in the mood for, so we brought everything we could think of."

I pat my palm on Enzo's cheek. "Food will make sex better."

"Goddamn it. I can't deny you." Enzo swings around, shuffling to the door. He groans as he opens it and again when he slides past Wilder, not letting me on my feet.

"Keep hogging her and see what happens, brother," Wilder calls from behind us, rushing to dodge past. "Don't think we won't team up against you. Restrain you and make you watch us pleasure her."

"Sounds kinky." Enzo chuckles, spinning me around, playing keep away with Wilder.

A dozen savory scents hypnotize me, dragging my attention away from Enzo and Wilder's playfulness. Desmond and Arsenio set up dozens of different containers on the counter. I twist and shimmy, forcing Enzo to plop me on my feet. I shriek as Wilder charges, a sexy grin lighting his face as he attempts to scoop me up next. I hunker down, surprising him. As he jumps to avoid tripping over me, I scramble toward Arsenio and Desmond.

"Whoever saves me from their play fight can feed me. I'll sit on your lap." I stay on the floor, raising my arms up.

"Damn it, baby!" Enzo shouts, his laughter ringing out, the lightness of his voice sending my heart fluttering. "Pitting my brothers against me."

"You could always work together," I tease, squealing again, the world blurring.

Arsenio tosses me on his shoulder, whirling me around. Someone smacks my ass, exposed for the four of them to see. I cackle and thrash, my body going wild under their attention. If we didn't hear laughter from the hall, coming from the direction of Holly's downstairs bedroom, I might've begged to be tossed on the table and devoured.

"Maybe not in front of your sister," Holly calls, her voice growing in volume.

"Which is why we need to eat, discuss a few things, and send you away. Not that we don't want you around...but we don't want you around. Even thinking about you hearing anything ...just no." Desmond shudders.

"Complete boner killer." Enzo twitches his fingers at Holly. "Plus, you smell like Beckett. I like the guy and all, yet I'm irritated."

"Which is why the Silversteins are staying in my room until we're ready to go." Holly smiles at me. "We won't be long. They're honored that our pack has entrusted them with not only taking care of me but also our territory."

I know that it bothers all my guys that they were surprised by Jarvis. It also bothers them that they're not fighting on the front line like they prefer. It has been instilled in their minds that they should do everything themselves because that's the only way it would be correct. It's something hypocritical that King Winston used to demand. He hadn't done much apart from bossing everyone around ever since my guys manifested into their orders.

"And I'm honored for their alliance. I still struggle to give you the freedom you desire, Holly, but I'm working on it. I promise you that. I know you're ready to start your own life and pack. We just don't want you to forget that you will always be part of ours." Wilder motions for everyone to sit down at the table, and he puts together two plates of food. One for me and one for Holly.

His brothers wait until we are served to get up and fix themselves something, and I sit on Arsenio's lap, allowing him to busy himself by feeding me.

"You couldn't get rid of me even if you tried, big brother. I have too much fun teasing you and teaming up with Kinsey to mess with your shit." Holly grins and takes a bite of pizza, the cheesy and saucy goodness making my stomach grumble harder.

Arsenio watches me stare at the pizza for only a second before he picks it up and holds it in front of my lips. I hum as I take a bite, an explosion of garlic and tomato sauce coating my tongue. I can't help taking it from Arsenio to feed myself. It's as if my body demands I eat faster than he offers. Everyone studies me with various expressions on their faces. Desmond looks amused as hell, and Enzo narrows his eyes in envy like he wishes he were the pizza I'm so focused on devouring.

I wave my hand and mumble between bites, "Stop staring. I'm starving."

"Just make sure to chew and swallow, baby. We don't want you choking." Enzo shifts his jaw. "Though I know just how much you can fit in that pouty mouth of yours."

Holly throws a roll at him, smacking him right in the fore-head. "If you don't stop, you're going to find out just how much you can fit in your fucking big mouth. Death by bread-stick. Now, I know it's hard for you all to focus, but you called this meeting for a reason, remember? We have to ensure our borders are bulletproof. We also have Platinum Shores to think about. I know it's not a priority, but there are innocent people there. I wouldn't put it past our enemies to attack there first to cause unrest."

Silence falls across the table as my alphas think about her concerns. I always knew she was strategic. She's a bit sponta-neous, yet she knows how to run a pack and a territory because of her brothers. This might be the first time she has ever been invited to a meeting, considering that King Winston always held them before and even excluded Desmond sometimes. But now? She impresses me. All her brothers, too.

Wilder rests his hands on the table, holding Holly's gaze. "You're absolutely right. We've been discussing Platinum Shores and have decided that none of us wants it."

Holly grimaces. "Those people need us. Their former rulers were pieces of shit. I wouldn't put it past some other asshole pack to try to just scoop it up in a power-play."

"We know, which is why we're naming you the leader of Platinum Shores. It's your territory. For you and the pack you choose to rule beside you." Wilder pulls out his phone and touches the screen a couple of times. "If you accept, I need you to sign this. With the final approval, our allies will make it happen."

Holly drops her pizza back on her plate and sits in shock, opening and closing her mouth. "Are you serious? I'm an omega. They're not going to stand for it."

"They've already agreed. This is the right thing to do. You'll be a fantastic leader and queen, lil sis. I know you will." Arsenio reaches out and scrubs his fingers through her hair, messing the strands.

Desmond squeezes her shoulder. "We'll be your advisors until you get the hang of things. You will not just be thrown to the packs."

"So, you better say fucking yes. You wanted to move out on your own, so you might as well have a whole territory." Enzo wags his brows.

Holly bobs her head, her eyes wide. "Okay, yes. Yes." Hopping from her seat, she tackles Wilder from behind, hugging him while not letting him get up. Desmond stands and opens his arms, squeezing her with affection. Enzo offers her a high-five and then grabs her hands, spinning her around, sending her into a laughing fit.

I slide off Arsenio's lap, jumping up and down, the excitement coursing from her contagious. We screech and bounce, smiling and laughing. Arsenio hugs me between him and Holly, and the rest of his brothers engulf us in a group hug I want to last forever. This is what a pack and family is supposed to be like. I'm so lucky that I found myself with them. There is no other life I want.

"You're going to be an amazing ruler, Holly," Wilder says, getting her to sign the digital contract. "You'll lead the way to a new beginning."

"We all will." Holly cups my cheeks, her smile as bright as the sun streaming in through the window. "They will see. I'm not going to bow or break."

I savor her confidence, hoping it passes on to me. I'm ready to prove to the world that omegas are more than what alphas make them.

Because we make alphas too.

They will see.

# Chapter Twenty-Two

## *Kinsey*

### Bright Future

**M**urmurs hum through the air, pulling me from my sleep. I don't know how long it's been, but the sun shines through the window. It must've been a day, at least.

"It'll take at least a couple of days for the water supply to work its way through the enemy territories. Our allies are pulling back to wait it out." Wilder whispers the words, his voice lacing around me.

"Holly made it to Platinum Shores. The announcement won't be made until the power shift. She already has access to their systems, though. It'll give us an advantage. No one will expect it from her." Arsenio lowers his voice, adding something I can't hear.

A shock zings through my body, stealing my breath. Oh fuck. Fuck.

Panic rushes through me. This is it. I can't deny my body any longer.

A wave of cramps pulses through my body, my clit throbbing and my nipples aching. My mind fogs with a need so intense that I cry out, reaching down to touch my soaking wet panties, the slick so bad that it's dripping over my thighs. The touch of my fingers triggers tingles, stealing away the throbbing pain. So, I continue stroking myself, trying to find relief.

Wilder's scent engulfs me before I see him kneeling by my side. He purrs, the rumbling of his desire setting me off. My muscle spasms control my body, and I can't seem to do anything other than stroke myself. It takes him lacing his fingers around my wrist and pulling my hand away to get me to stop.

I arch my back and whimper, the noise pathetic and desperate, but I can't control it.

"I'm here. I'll take care of you." Wilder moans, his fingers exploring between my legs at the same time he yanks my panties down.

The annoying ache melts away into complete pleasure, and I gasp and spread my legs wider, wanting nothing more than for him to give me his knot.

"I want you. I want you so fucking bad. The anticipation hurts." I breathe heavily, shifting and moving, my body exploding at his closeness, his pheromones triggering me into action.

I throw myself at him, landing on top, bending down to kiss him. He bites my lip with a growl, his nature controlling his movements.

"Damn. I want her on top of me." Desmond appears beside us, grabbing at my big T-shirt to pull it over my head. "Come here, pretty girl. Let me hold you."

I can't find my voice, my mouth continuing to disobey my brain, whimpering and mewing like an animal. Rolling me on top of him, Desmond wraps his arms around me, stroking his fingers over my nipples. My back rests against his chest, leaving me exposed for his brother as an offering of pleasure. Wilder fills the space between my legs, gliding his tongue over my clit, making me scream in ecstasy. He only stays there for a minute like he just wanted a taste, and then his weight sandwiches me to his brother as he slides inside, the girth of his cock stretching me, giving me exactly the pleasure I need.

"Arsenio, Enzo?" My voice pleads with their names, my desire wanting them nearby.

"I'm right here, baby." Enzo touches my cheek, taking my hand in his, squeezing it as he kisses me next. "Let my brothers take care of you."

"But I want to taste you," I complain, panting and scratching my nails into Wilder's back, his thrusting growing more intense. Without hesitating, he shifts up, giving enough space for me to arch up, and Desmond presses his hand into my back, supporting the position.

Enzo guides his cock into my mouth, the taste of his pre-cum sweet yet spicy like his desire. Arsenio takes my other hand, encouraging me to stroke him the way he craves as he waits his turn. My body explodes again with relief, lust clouding my thoughts, and all I can think about is the pleasure coursing through me.

Desmond shifts slightly beneath me, his hard cock testing my ass, and I rock my body, my slick so slippery that he glides inside me, adding to the pressure and bliss.

He groans under me, and Wilder helps keep him in rhythm. Electricity sings through me, Wilder's cock engorging as I take his knot. Shadows edge my vision, and I moan, the ecstasy of his seed filling me better than it's ever been before. I hum and wiggle, my voice vibrating over Enzo.

"Fuck, that feels so good," Enzo says, stroking his fingers through my hair, brushing it away to look into my eyes. "You smell incredible. I can't wait to fuck you."

"Me next, brother," Arsenio says, his voice deep and growling but not threatening.

Wilder massages his fingers over my clit, making my body squirt, my orgasm more intense, feeling as if it has doubled, triggered by his seed and the other by his fingers, and I scream, the relief comforting and amazing.

Desmond grunts from beneath me, his warmth flooding my body. I can't get enough. I want more. I need more. I never expected to feel such sensations, their desire and pleasure reacting to me as if it's my own. Wilder hugs me close, waiting for Desmond to ease out of my ass so he can roll over.

"Damn, baby. Look at you drip. I want to knot with you so badly, but I can't wait. I need that sexy ass." Enzo grabs my hips from behind, my knees planted at Wilder's sides, his body filling me with a never-ending orgasm that makes me just moan my agreement.

My guys ravish me in a way that I never want to end. Any fear or panic that had crossed my mind melts away under their attention, their sweet words of adoration and love keeping me connected and with them despite my body feeling as if it rejects my soul to fly above me.

Sliding into my ass, Enzo moans, picking up his pace, using me as of vessel for his contentment and need. He digs his fingers into my hips, his nails biting my skin in a way that shocks me right in the clit. I bow down completely and bite Wilder on the nape of his neck, wanting to mark him as he claims me, his knot loosening enough for him to slide out.

The ache steals my breath again, and I pant and whimper, reaching out to Arsenio, crying his name to help me. He adjusts his body, his muscles rippling as he waits for Enzo to lift me up enough for him to get beneath me.

Desmond reaches between us, strumming my clit with his thumb, playing with my body as if my moans of pleasure are music to his ears.

Wilder lies beside us, stroking his cock, his need already hardening him again.

I reach out and grab his hand, just wanting all of them to touch me. I don't want to feel any space between any of us.

Arsenio releases a guttural noise, his teeth biting into my skin as he thrusts inside me, hard and fast, matching Enzo's pace. I lose myself to their desire, the relief from them like slipping into a warm bath.

I sigh in relief as his knot takes hold of me, locking me to him as an orgasm steals both of our breaths away, his seed exploding through me with a sensation that leaves me quaking. I can't believe I'm so lucky to have such amazing men in my life. My alpha protectors. My beta confidant.

"You're going to be so beautiful pregnant. You'll glow with power. Our children will have lives far better than we had. They will never know the pain we suffered. I vow to you only bliss and comfort." Arsenio kisses me again, gasping his words as he comes, his seed filling me up, his body yearning to breed and impregnate me.

In this moment, I realize how much I want to be a mother. How much I desire to share such a life with them. An unbreakable bond that will bear power and love and a future beyond my wildest dreams.

My body relaxes, my need subsiding as content washes over me. I just want to lay in their arms forever, blanketing myself in their love and affection.

But the contentment doesn't last long. I realize it's because Arsenio and Enzo both pull out, their sudden absence sending my body craving more.

"Hey sugar, drink some water. We're going to get in the shower and clean off. I know you're aching, but this is important." Arsenio scoops me up. Enzo beats everyone to the bathroom, turning on the shower to quickly clean up, his excitement as strong as his fragrance permeating the air.

I sip a glass of water, the coolness quenching my dry mouth. Wilder kisses me as Arsenio strokes my muscles, massaging me all the way down and in between my legs, helping subside my throbbing body.

The three of them keep me surrounded with their scents, their bodies warm and inviting. I rest my head on Arsenio's shoulder, just needing to be cuddled and carried. Enzo comes from the shower, his body glistening and clean, his hard-on ready to claim me next. This is the moment he's been fantasizing about, his need to breed with me all-consuming.

"You're so fucking hot, Kinsey. Tell me how you want it." Enzo grasps my chin, pulling me closer, stretching me in Arsenio's arms.

"I want to be held. I want to be propped up and fucked as hard and as fast as you want. Make me squirt. Make me scream. I ache for you. I want your seed. I'm desperate for your knot. Give me what I want." My voice rises with my demands, goosebumps prickling over my body at the thought.

Wilder grabs me from Arsenio, lifting me up in his arms and holding me by my thighs, spreading my legs open for Enzo as he rests his back on the cool wall of the shower, so I don't have to. Arsenio and Desmond help support my legs, and the three of them watch as Enzo enters me. Desmond strokes my clit with his fingers, adding to the sensation, and Arsenio plays with my pebbling nipples, the steam of the shower hot and battling the cool air, our skin damp and slippery. And it feels so good on my muscles. I will feel this for days. Maybe weeks.

I stretch my arms and stroke Arsenio and Desmond, my hands desperate and fast, matching Enzo's thrusts. His knot swells, locking us in place with an intense orgasm. It freezes my body as my muscles spasm, and I rest my head back on Wilder's shoulder, turning my head to taste his lips, to feel his teeth nip me and his tongue glide into my mouth, muffling the sound of my moan.

"You're so tight, baby. I'm not sure my cock will ever let you go. I could live in your body if you let me." Enzo touches my cheek, rubbing his hand over my skin and down my body. He reaches around and slides his finger into my ass, slowly teasing my body, adding to the pressure.

I arch in Wilder's arms, the sensation driving me wild. I want to be filled up with them. It's the only way I will ever be satisfied. They need to use my body in any way they please. Because their pleasure is mine.

"Fuck me, Wilder. I need more. I want to feel you inside me." I reach up and grip his hair, licking my tongue across his jaw.

Enzo takes a step back, taking my weight and allowing Wilder to adjust himself. My slick soaks him, my need clear as my body draws him closer. He presses the tip of his cock to my body, slowly gliding it in as if he wants to indulge in every second.

I gasp at the increased pressure, my orgasm intensifying with Enzo's seed and Wilder's double penetration. The two of them work together, ensuring that I'll never be able to catch my breath.

The four of them take turns, pleasuring me over and over, not allowing my body even a second to feel empty. Enzo lathers my hair and cleanses my body. They only wash their scents away so I can experience them all over again, ensuring that my body doesn't get used to it. The scent will remain intense. They please me continuously until I can only moan, my muscles begging to rest.

I've never been so taken care of in my life. Arsenio continuously offers me water, ensuring that my voice doesn't go hoarse. Enzo brings out toys, helping to add to the pleasure as they focus on giving me what I need from their knot. Desmond fucks me as they do, nipping and biting and treating me as if he's my alpha despite not being able to knot.

Enzo slides a plug into my ass, stretching me enough to feel the intensity of their pleasure. He adjusts a small vibrator on my clit, using a remote to pulse it every couple of minutes, the shocking sensation intensifying my orgasm, never letting it end.

They fuck me long into the night and into the next day until our exhaustion takes hold, my body aching with good pain. I fall asleep between Wilder and Arsenio, listening to the sounds of their heartbeats.

I lose myself to their love and comfort, knowing that I'm safe. I'm protected, and they will always guarantee that I get what I need. Their scents linger with me, their marks across my body and mine across theirs. I've never been so happy. I've never felt anywhere near as close as I do now, knowing that our future together will last forever. This is everything I could've wanted. A pack of loving men. A life where I don't have to worry about where I stand and who controls me. And being able to raise a family equally with love and power.

Now I want to guarantee it for every omega. Every beta and alpha too. Because we are better together. Standing tall and powerful.

We will breed a bright future.

# Chapter Twenty-Three

## *Kinsey*

## Enemy Lines

"Take another bite. I know you're not hungry yet, but I need to make sure you eat." Arsenio offers me a forkful of eggs. "You need your energy."

"I need you to kneel down and kiss me where it aches," I counter, forcing my mouth to open for him to feed me.

My demand elicits a surprised laugh from him, his handsome face lighting up. He lifts an eyebrow, glides his tongue over his bottom lip, and eases to the floor. Resting his warm palms on my knees, he spreads my legs wider, easing them onto his shoulders.

I grip the table and moan, the sensation of his mouth awakening my body again, igniting my desire. I comb my fingers through his honey blond hair, guiding his head to lick me harder. I squeeze him between my thighs, my muscles pulsing with an orgasm. He's mastered exactly what I like and what gets me off the fastest, so he can give me one after another.

"Need some help, brother?" Desmond strolls into the kitchen, a towel slung low on his hips, showing off the V pointing to his hard-on. Arsenio's phone dings from the spot he left it on the counter, and without Arsenio needing to ask, Desmond scoops it up.

"Fuck," he growls, tightening his jaw.

My heart skips a beat. "What's wrong? Are the others okay?" Because they had to step out for an hour to solidify plans. My heat subsides somewhat, though my desire lingers. I'll feel normal again in a couple of days as my hormones level out.

Desmond doesn't respond right away, pinching his chin in thought. "Jarvis's army is gathering again. The water plant doesn't provide water to his castle or his troops."

Arsenio growls between my legs, the vibration shooting pleasure to my core. "Let me see."

Desmond cautiously strolls closer, keeping his expression even. Arsenio's rut controls him, his aggression unintentional since he's been alone with me for a while. Holding out Arsenio's phone, Desmond lowers himself to the chair beside me so he doesn't tower over either of us.

*Boss Bro: We have a problem. Starlight Horizon predominantly uses well water.*

*Boss Bro: I think we should go in for Jarvis ourselves. I don't want to wait any longer.*

*Me: I'm out. Kinsey's still vulnerable. She needs me.*

*Boss Bro: She is coming with us.*

*Me: Fuck no.*

*Boss Bro: That's an order. It needs to be us to take care of this. He's not only gathering his armies, but he also announced that any packs who stand with him will be guaranteed territory. He's targeting the criminals and causing unrest. They're taking shit to the street. Scaring civilians. If I could do this alone, I would. I don't want Kinsey to go as much as you, but we have to.*

Arsenio squeezes his phone so hard that I think it might break under his strength. His anger swells, heating me up even more. I grow anxious under his emotions and want nothing more than for him to relax.

"We'll have an armored car. She won't be exposed to any danger. I know you struggle to pull yourself from your rut but think about how worse it'll be if we stay. The peak is over, and she's coming down. Right, Kinsey?"

My stomach twists, thinking about leaving this spot, but I know he's right.

I grab Arsenio's face, pulling him up to kiss him, holding his lips to mine until he groans and slides his hand lower down my back, pulling me to the edge of my chair. "I know you want to hide away and just take care of me. I know you don't want me involved in any of this, but we are a pack. If your brother needs you, then you will be by his side. And I will be by yours. You can't ignore this sort of responsibility. We can't jeopardize everything now. The other territories are complacent. This could end up being for nothing if we don't act."

"You should be my only responsibility." Arsenio sucks my bottom lip between his teeth, kissing me again.

I giggle against his mouth. "I am, which is why you have to do this too. Now let's hurry up and get ready. I don't know how much longer I can go before I try to seduce you again."

"All right, fine. Let's fuck shit up, celebrate with a feast, and bang each other for the next year," Arsenio mutters.

I smile against his mouth. "Nothing has sounded better."

Arsenio motions to Desmond. "Get everything in order. I just want this to be done."

"We have eyes on all influential packs. The narc cocktail is being pumped through the systems again. Jude is on-site, drugging the well water of his security. We paid off several of his betas, using his tactic of offering territory since he kept the offer for alphas only. The dumb shit. By tomorrow, we'll have a bunch of docile sleepyheads. The last thing for us to do now is wait for Jarvis to take the bait." Desmond stands outside the armored car, shielding his eyes from the sun. He goes over the maps on his phone, bringing up some satellite images.

"Do you think it's really going to work?" I ask, rolling Enzo's hoodie in my hands. Butterflies seemingly storm my stomach, twisting my nerves. I have to concentrate hard on keeping my mind off the residual ache between my legs. It helps that Arsenio overpacked, allowing me to bring whatever I wanted.

My back rests on a pillow in the corner of the bulletproof vehicle. Despite the metal surrounding me, it's cozy and comforting in my makeshift nest. To my pleasant surprise, Wilder and Enzo added a couple of extra pillows and blankets for me.

Still, I'm antsy as fuck.

"Absolutely. Jarvis frequented the Vixen Lounge and bought access to one of the traveling omega entertainers. He hadn't returned her before Tamsin died. Anita knew how to contact her." Desmond shakes out his fingers, loosening his muscles.

I twist my mouth, sucking on the inside of my cheek. "Oh." I had no idea.

I don't know what else to say. My emotions get the best of me, and I stare at my hands, using my index fingers to rub the glittery nail polish on my thumbs. How many more omegas are lost to the Knotty Girl's life because they no longer have Tamsin to bring them back? My heart aches, feeling like it slides in my stomach.

Wilder climbs into the back from behind the wheel. He crawls to me, sitting in the corner in the small space beside one of the empty safes. There is no room for him to fit in what Enzo deemed my comfy cubby hole, so he latches onto my ankles and slides me out, the pillow slipping with me.

"We'll find every unbonded omega in our region. I promise. As for the ones bonded, we're going to ensure they're happy, safe, and where they want to be. It won't happen overnight, but it will happen." Wilder brushes his lips to mine, kissing me softly. It's as if he can read my mind, and I'm grateful that he knows me enough to reassure me without me having to voice my concerns. It's not always easy. My mouth dries at the thought of even trying to tell him every damn thing threatening to leave me spiraling.

Wilder's phone vibrates, the sound buzzing from his jacket pocket. He ignores it to kiss me longer, and it takes Desmond smacking his hand on the metal door to get him to pull away. My heart flutters at the scent of his vetiver and woody fragrance, his closeness stirring my deep-seated nature.

I snatch him by the neck, locking him in place. I don't want even an inch of space between us. The thought tears through me, and I whimper, my body warming even as I shiver. Widening my eyes, I stare at Wilder, my good senses fighting against my body's reaction to his closeness. He flares his nostrils, purring deep in his throat, the noise quaking through me right to my clit.

Shit. My body demands attention.

"Shit," Wilder murmurs, once again, seemingly to hear my thoughts. "We have to—"

A gunshot startles me, knocking the sense back into me. Desmond aims his gun a second time, pulling the trigger. "It's security!"

"Arsenio, drive!" Wilder commands, pulling away from me, watching Arsenio move from the passenger's seat to behind the wheel. "Enzo, Desmond. Take them out! If they call us in, it'll ruin the element of surprise and endanger our team behind enemy lines."

Arsenio stomps the throttle as Enzo jumps from the back, slamming the door closed in the process. I squeeze my eyes shut, wishing he and Desmond wouldn't have abandoned us to take down the security. They already feel so far away, though I know we'd never leave them.

"Head north and turn right. The underground access to Jarvis's garage shouldn't be far. The guards have been subdued." Wilder squeezes my hands between his, still refusing to move even an inch away. "Enzo and Desmond can draw the focus on them, so we can sneak in as soon as we get the word. The omega is meeting us. She'll be the one slipping Jarvis the tranquilizer."

My heartbeat thuds wildly, bouncing around as much as the armored car driving over a curb and onto rougher terrain. I pull Enzo's hoodie closer to me, bringing it to my nose to inhale a deep breath. It only helps a little.

"Here, Kinsey. Take this." Wilder shrugs off his jacket, draping it over me. I bury my nose in it, scooting back into my cubby nest even more. Having everything snuggled around me makes me feel safer, calmer. Protected. "Good, brat-girl. Just focus on me. We'll be out of here in no time."

It's all I can hope for.

"Maybe we should give her a suppressant pill," Arsenio says, speaking up from over his shoulder. "It could help."

"It's too late. I just need time for my hormones to balance out on their own. We mated. I don't want to risk anything." I lick my lips, squirming in my spot, wishing I were at home in the nest I made for this. It was more comfortable. Full of everything I love and things that smell like all my guys. "But I'm okay. I'm not in any pain or suffering. I'm just...still fucking horny as hell. I'm a bit hungry. Tired."

"I have her bag stashed in the safe across from you. It's open." Arsenio turns the vehicle, and I bump against the wall separating the front. There's only a small walkway from the cabin that can lock at a moment's notice.

"I packed a bag too." Wilder reaches behind him, pulling what looks like a lunchbox from under the seat next to the safe. "Lots of protein for energy. I had a feeling you might just pack all the sweets. I know that was Enzo's plan."

"I have to give my sugar what she likes," Arsenio says, his voice remaining even. He doesn't have to raise his voice for me to know that he might be a little annoyed that Wilder thought he wouldn't properly pack things for me. "But I also made her a cheese and meat platter. Plenty of protein."

My stomach growls, and I flick my gaze to Wilder and back to my stomach. "I want that."

He raises his eyebrow, opening the lunchbox to reveal that he also had the same idea as his brother, pulling out different meats and cheeses along with some fruit instead of the cookies I know are most likely hidden in what Arsenio made me.

I narrow my eyes, pressing my lips together.

"You can have the dessert after. I want you to eat this up now. You need your energy." Wilder takes the initiative and lifts a cube of cheddar cheese before wrapping a circle of salami around it. He brings it to my mouth, watching me with such intensity as I carefully, slowly take a bite. And then I bite again, grabbing his fingers between my teeth, playfully giving him a bit of my wild side.

He grunts and yanks his hand away. "You brat."

Arsenio chuckles. "She doesn't like to be fed. She bit you, didn't she?"

I grin as I chew and grab the container from him, popping a few more cubes of cheese into my mouth. "I would be here forever if I let you feed me. You guys are always fixated on my damn mouth. I just want to eat."

Wilder play-growls and scrubs his fingers through my hair, messing up the strands. "You can feed yourself that. But the dessert—"

"Will be my reward for bringing it," Arsenio says, cutting off his brother. "Now get up here, Wilder. I need your eyes. We just got the alert."

I never imagined I would be sitting in the back of an armored car, stuffing my face with meat and cheese, feeling horny as fuck yet lighthearted, a bit scared too because of the whole situation, but at least it's a bit entertaining. Hearing my guys' banter lifts my spirits, and I can't wait to just get home. They're doing their best to take care of me while also taking care of our territory and region. Some people might think they're villains because of how they are taking over with force, but they're truly my heroes.

"Enzo says it's all clear. They're going in now. We should be able to get in and out without a problem," Wilder says, standing hunched over in the walkway, staring at the windshield instead of taking a seat. I can tell he doesn't want to be far from me.

"Don't fucking say that shit. You're going to jinx us." Arsenio smacks the wheel, the sound loud enough to bounce through the cargo area.

"I don't believe in jinxing anything. Our strategy is solid. Have some faith in us, brother." Wilder twists and looks at me. "Right, Kinsey?"

I dip my chin in affirmation, continuing to stuff my face. Now that I started eating, I can't stop. I hadn't realized how hungry I really was. "Mmmhmm."

"Over there. Stop at the end of the block. There's an orchard on the backside of the property. She's going to meet us there." Wilder shifts on his boots, patting down his holsters and jeans, double-checking his weapons.

The armored car comes to a stop, jolting me into the partition wall. Wilder's scent wafts through the cargo area, its vetiver and woods fragrance like a warm blanket as it drifts over me. I squeeze my legs together, fidgeting and bouncing my feet.

"I want you to behave for Arsenio. Try not to seduce him. We need him ready to drive." Wilder rustles his fingers through my hair again, stroking his palm over my cheek and down to squeeze my shoulder. "I won't be long, okay?"

"You better not be." My stomach twists again, my nerves getting the best of me.

"We can watch them from here, sugar. If you're up to it." Arsenio calls my attention to where he sits in the driver's seat. "Maybe you can eat that dessert."

I push to my feet, hugging Wilder from behind, strolling with him as he heads to the passenger side, choosing to exit through the front instead of the back. He kisses me before opening it, and I have to force myself to stay in place instead of following him. Because I don't want him to go.

It's bad enough that Enzo and Desmond aren't here either.

"Come on, Kinsey. You can sit on my lap." Arsenio wiggles his fingers at me, silently encouraging me to come closer.

I do as he asks and slide onto his lap, feeling his hard desire beneath my ass. I can't stop myself from rolling my hips and wiggling, clutching onto the steering wheel as his pheromones set me off.

I train my gaze out the windshield, my mind and body separate as I struggle to remain in control. Wilder aims his gun at the ground, cautiously treading his way toward the orchard.

Arsenio's phone chirps and he pulls it out.

*Baby Brother: Abort mission. Jarvis is with the omega. We got a visual. She's been compromised.*

"Oh, no." Without thinking, I slam my palm to the horn, sending it blaring through the air.

Wilder jerks his attention in my direction, and I wave my arms at him, hoping he sees me. Spinning around, he turns back toward the orchard, raising his gun.

He fires, but several more pops blast through the air.

Wilder drops to his knees before landing face-first on the ground. Swearing, Arsenio sides me off him and grabs his gun from its holster.

I scream, watching as a man leads an omega through the trees by her hair. He waves his gun, aiming it at our vehicle.

"Arsenio, stop." I grab him before he can rush to Wilder.

The man aims the gun at us and shoots.

He shoots again and again.

I don't move for my spot. I don't duck as the bullets plink off the windshield.

I can't take my eyes off Wilder. He doesn't get up. He doesn't move.

My heart shatters.

It feels as if my world is over.

# Chapter Twenty-Four

## *Kinsey*

## War

I scream, crying and smacking my hands against the windshield. Jarvis glowers, continuing to shoot until he runs out of ammo. I've never felt such pain before in my heart. I feel as if I'm about to die. This can't be happening. This can't be fucking happening.

"Kinsey, we have to get in the back. The windshield will eventually give out. He won't be able to get through to the cargo." Arsenio tries to move me, but I swat him away, my cries ringing in my ears as I lose control.

And then I see it.

Movement.

Wilder pushes on his elbows, aiming his gun at Jarvis, and he shoots him in the back. Jarvis spins around in surprise, not falling to the ground. He scrambles, looking for coverage, but the nearest tree is a couple of dozen feet away. And he hasn't reloaded.

Reaching into his jacket, he tries to grab another weapon. Arsenio flings the car door open, and he and Wilder pull their triggers at the same time, shooting Jarvis with perfect accuracy. I squeeze my eyes shut, watching as the alpha collapses, his head unprotected and vulnerable.

Holy shit. They did it. They still managed to take him out, even though things didn't go as planned. I suck in a couple of deep breaths, sliding across the seat until I drop to the ground. Wilder hops up and runs to me, not letting me get far. I jump into his arms, wrapping my legs around him and hugging him so tightly that he grunts.

"You fucking scared me. You really fucking scared me. I thought you were dead." Tears blur my eyes as I relive the moment over again.

He kisses my temple, shifting my face until he can kiss my tear-stained cheeks, working his way down to my mouth. He brushes his lips to my trembling ones, breathing heavily, his emotions playing on mine.

"I'm so sorry you had to see that, Kinsey. I needed to surprise him. He hit my bulletproof vest." Wilder eases away, showing me the metal fragments buried into his protective gear. "He was too much of a cocky bastard to double-check to make sure he actually got me. He wanted to go after you. Hurt you. That's the worst way to destroy an alpha."

"I still want to spank you. I don't think my heart's going to ever slow down. I feel sick." I inhale a slow breath, shuddering with the nerves.

A soft cry steals my attention, and I peer over Wilder's shoulder at the omega entertainer that Jarvis dragged out here. Arsenio keeps his hands in the air, shuffling closer to her. She's probably wound up from Jarvis's pheromones and the fear he instilled in her.

"You're safe. I'm from Gilded Sands. Take a deep breath. I'm not going to touch you. I'm just trying to get a look at you to make sure you weren't injured." His voice remains even, and he pulls out his cell phone, calling his brothers.

The omega cowers against the tree.

"Desmond, I need you. Jarvis is dead. Alert the soldiers. We'll make the formal announcement on the way home." Arsenio shifts and looks at me. "Kinsey, will you help me? It looks like she's bleeding."

Wilder tightens his hold on me for a second, his deep-seated nature not wanting to let me go. I stroke my fingers over his jaw, kissing him one more time, and then I loosen my legs until I land softly on my feet.

My legs wobble with each of my steps, my whirlwind of emotions leaving me weak. Exhaustion threatens to send me to the ground. It's as if everything just hits me at once.

"Oh, no." The soft voice murmurs to the air. "Let me help you." I don't even get to take another step before two cool hands grab mine. I turn my attention to the omega standing before me. I don't remember seeing her move. I think everything is just too much. It's taking a toll and I'm crashing.

"I'm supposed to help you." I blink my eyes, my whole body going out of whack.

She laughs softly, squeezing my hands. "Was this your first heat? You shouldn't be out here. You need days to rest."

"No, it's just been a while." I waver on my feet again, turning toward Arsenio. "If it's okay, we'd like to take you back to our territory. We've taken all of Madame Tamsin's omegas. You will be safe."

"Will you help me get home to my pack in Pacific Crest? I was kidnapped by an enemy of my alphas. I just want to go home. It's why Madame Tamsin deemed me a Knotty Girl. So, I wasn't allowed to be seen in the club." The omega crinkles her nose at the thought. "I just hope they haven't claimed another."

If their bond was built on more than just breeding and the trading of power, there's no way those alphas would just meet with another. Even if it wasn't something serious, it would still be unlikely.

"We just need your pack name. We'll call it in immediately." Wilder speaks up for the first time since the omega got within my space. Both he and Arsenio keep their distance.

"Lavender Hills," the omega says, her face softening as if she daydreams about home. "My name is Cecilia."

I give her hands a little shake. "We'll get you home, Cecelia. We promise."

She finally releases me, taking a step back to put space between us. Wilder fills the spot she left behind, lifting me back into his arms so I can hug him with my whole body. Arsenio motions to Cecilia to follow him to the armored vehicle. She gets in back, staying in the far corner, ensuring that she doesn't intrude on our space. It only takes thirty minutes for Enzo and Desmond to appear with a dozen men.

"Everything is in order. We're going to guard the perimeters, ensuring no one leaves. We've captured as many of their soldiers as we could as long as they surrendered. News will spread fast. They had expected a war. Jarvis was trying to draft every pack to join him, but there was resistance." Desmond stands next to Arsenio, showing him some images that he doesn't let me see.

"What about news from the others?" Wilder asks, still holding me in his arms. "Do they need assistance?"

Enzo shakes his head. "They're treating Jarvis as an example. They don't want to lose their lives over this. Not everyone is so bullheaded. We can make a difference peacefully from here."

"I can't believe it's over." I rest my chin on Wilder's shoulder. It's hard for me to truly embrace the thought. Because every time something good in my life happens, something shitty always follows.

"Believe it, Kinsey. This is real. We're safe." Wilder snuggles me as his brothers surround us, enveloping me in their arms.

"Then let's go home," I say. "I'm so fucking ready to just go home."

Arsenio plays with my hair. "Soon, sugar. There are just a few more things we have to take care of first."

"Drugging the well water did the trick." Jude stands in the grand foyer of an enormous stone castle overlooking an expansive valley.

This is my first time getting to see such a large territory, the border wall a faint line in the distance. A place so breathtaking shouldn't carry such a heinous reputation. It's why my guys are handling it personally, going after any threat that could try to fill Jarvis's place.

"They're all bound and ready for transportation." Motioning toward a dark room, he points out Jarvis's closest pack mates. The staff sits on the floor together across the room, being treated as victims of their circumstances and not prisoners.

"Did you find the omegas from the Vixen Lounge?" Wilder asks the question on my mind. We couldn't get to them when our palace was ambushed. Only the ones saved from the nest my uncle told us about made it to safety.

"Not only from there. You're going to want to see this." Jude tilts his head in the direction of what looks like a long hallway with a wooden door at the end. My guess is it's the dungeon and something similar to ours. "It might be best if Kinsey stays here. It could upset her. You guys are going to want to cover your noses. The pheromones are intense. He had hormone shots administered to them, trying to get them to go into heat. Some fucked up shit."

I shudder a gasp, a small cry escaping my mouth. How horrifying. Those poor omegas. If Jarvis wasn't already dead, I'd kill him again. I'd cut off his balls and dick, shoving it down his throat so he could never mate. I've heard rumors about shit like this happening, but I never really saw it. It's possible that Madame Tamsin had done such things, but the Gorgeous Girls never complained. I never saw anything myself.

"I need to go to them. Me and Desmond only." I look at Wilder, Enzo, and Arsenio. "You handle the fuckers here. You find out everything you can about what he was doing. I don't want you near the omegas. You'll scare them."

I might even scare them but will deal with that when I get there. All I can hope is that the ones who recognize me will know I'm a safe person. I hope they'll recognize my scent through their heat-induced craze. They'll be more wild, especially since they didn't have time to prepare themselves.

God, help me. I hate this.

Desmond drapes his arm over my shoulders, pulling me in close. "We will do everything we can to make sure they're comfortable and unafraid. If they panic with us, we'll leave whatever they need to help out and then return for them when it's over. I'll have Aunt Melina come to ensure they're getting through everything okay."

My throat burns with unshed tears, and I bite my cheek to keep my mouth from quivering. "That's a good plan."

He digs his fingers into my shoulder. "Remember, it's over. We've won the war."

"I just hadn't realized that the aftermath would be so bad." I close my eyes, inhaling a deep breath. I can't go facing the omegas if I'm not in complete control. And it's hard. My body is still out of whack. I can feel the agitation boiling just below the surface. Anything unpleasant could make me snap.

"The worst is over. Everything will get better from here. Promise." Desmond guides me forward, keeping his pace slow and even, ensuring that he doesn't work up even an ounce of sweat.

The door at the end of the dimly lit hallway is open a crack as if whoever looked in here left in a hurry. My heart thrashes, the quick beats pounding in my ears. I can smell the scent of the omegas already. I crinkle my nose at the potent, unpleasant scent. While an unclaimed alpha might find them irresistible, heats tend to repulse other omegas and their bonded alphas. It's our bodies trying to isolate ourselves with those we want to mate with without being bothered by others.

"Jude wasn't lying. I don't think I've ever smelled something so..." Desmond shakes his head, not finishing his thought out loud.

"I can go in alone if you want. I know it's a bit gross." I bring my shirt up to my nose, breathing in the woody, spicy scent of my guys still lingering on me. "I just want to see how far into it they are. If they are from the Vixen Lounge or another club, they would never have been suppressed and will most likely end pretty quickly. A day or two for the peak of it."

I never thought mine was going to end, the third day the most intense, and I still feel like I'm coming off a lust-filled high even five days after it initially began. Fuck. I can't believe it's been that long. I can hardly remember anything besides the pleasure. It felt so hazy and surreal. Despite that, it was perfect.

Not like we're about to discover right now.

"I'm good, Kinsey. I need to stay with you in case. I don't know if they're out of it or what. I don't want you to get hurt."

Desmond pushes the door open completely, his chest heaving. He tries not to cough as the fragrance overwhelms him. He grabs his shirt and pulls it up, mimicking me.

"After you," I say, waving my fingers toward the dark stairwell. Knowing that he won't let me go alone means that I also don't have to see things first. If it's too much, Desmond will stop me.

I hope he doesn't. Because if that's the case, then it means he knows I can handle it.

"Stay close. I don't want to startle them too badly by turning on all the lights. I know you prefer things dim, not overwhelming." He pulls out his cell phone from his pocket and turns the flashlight on, lighting the stairs without setting the place aglow.

"Hello? We're from the Gilded Sands Pack. Do you know who we are? Are you able to speak?" I ask, projecting my voice. If they're suffering and uncomfortable from not getting what they need during this drug-induced heat cycle, then they most likely won't be coherent. An alpha helps keep an omega grounded through it all.

"Kinsey?" A soft feminine voice swirls in my ears, bouncing off the concrete walls. "It's Missy. Do you remember me?"

I open and close my mouth, sliding past Desmond to take the lead. It's as if my feet disconnect from my brain, my instincts dragging me forward to one of Madame Samara's omegas from the Knotty Girls Club. I never thought I would see her again. If she's here, that means the place might be gone.

"Who else is there?" I ask, stopping at the bottom of the stairs, the dark room full of shadows and figures that I can only partially see from above.

Several whimpers and cries snatch my attention, igniting a wave of empathy inside me, watering my eyes. I know what this is like. I've been in this position, forced to experience a heat without being able to either take care of myself or have my alphas take care of me.

"I don't know. We're all separated. Caged. I haven't seen the omegas from Madame Samara's in weeks. He separated us." Missy's voice grows louder, her ability to remain in control admirably. "I'm the only one who wasn't injected with a hormone shot. I bribed the guard. I know my way around assholes. I couldn't do the same for the others. A whole group was just brought in a couple of days ago."

"Is it okay if I turn on my light? I need to see. I don't want to startle anyone." I remain in my spot with Desmond lingering behind me, staying utterly silent and letting me control the situation.

"Yeah, we've been kept in the dark. It might help them bring back their senses enough to get them to listen." Missy sniffles, her sadness over being mistreated prevalent. "No one has said a word. Just crying and complaining."

I nearly lose the contents of my stomach, just the thought sickening me. Disgusting alphas. This vile pack.

"I'll find the light switch." Desmond shifts past me, meandering along the wall, using the glow of his phone to light the way.

I timidly stepped forward, my legs heavy with my trepidation over what I'll discover. I know it's bad. But how bad? I guess I'm going to find out. Balling my hands into fists, I steal myself, expecting the worst thing imaginable.

I shuffle my way to Missy, getting a better view in the dim light nearby. She sits in the corner of the cage, wearing what looks like a costume from the Knotty Girls Club.

When our eyes meet, I rush forward and kneel on the cold concrete floor. I rattle the lock on her cage, my emotions getting the best of me. Tears leak from my eyes, the flood of warmth streaking my cheeks.

"We need a key," I call, trying to break the lock as if I could ever be strong enough. I don't care, though. I still have to try.

Light floods the room, shadowing my vision. The soft cries turn silent as the omegas gain awareness that something is different through the desperation currently consuming them.

"I have them." Desmond shows off a key ring he must've found while looking for the lights. There would be one down here for whoever was taking care of these omegas.

Messing with the lock, Desmond finds the right key and pulls the cage open, shifting back. He looks around and finds some cabinets with supplies, including a stack of towels. He jogs back to us and hands me the towel, letting me help Missy from the cage. I adjust the towel over her shoulders, giving her a once-over to make sure she isn't injured.

"Will you get Jude to help us? We need to get them out of here. I think it's the only way it's going to help." I keep a foot of space between Missy and me, not touching her just in case she doesn't feel comfortable. I know I wouldn't want anyone to either until I was somewhere I felt safe. I'm sure it could be like that for a lot of the omegas. "Why don't you go up with Desmond? They're arranging transportation upstairs."

Missy shakes her head. "I'll stay and help. I'm only hungry and tired. I need to stay distracted. I'm just so happy you came. I thought my life was over."

"I understand that. I have felt that many times in my life. It's why we're changing things. We're going to stop shit like this from happening to omegas. It's time the cruelty ends." I listen as Desmond and Jude tread down the stairs, heading in our direction.

Surprising me, Missy throws her arms around me, hugging me close. I give in to her need for affection and hug her back, only pulling away when she does.

Neither of us talks as we make our way to the wall of cages filled with omegas. I straighten my shoulders, trying my best to stay calm for their sake.

"I'm here to get you out and somewhere safe. I know you're scared, but we'll get through this." I shift on my feet and meet Desmond's gaze. "Together."

From the rubble, we'll rebuild. We'll unlearn things that others tried to instill in us. We will finally find the peace we need to thrive.

I can't wait.

# Chapter Twenty-Five

## *Wilder*

## New Order

I sit at the head of a long table, the camera pointing in my direction. To my right, Holly sits with her back straight and her chin high. She doesn't glance down at all as the alphas from other territories look in her direction. Beckett stands behind her, holding onto her chair. Against the wall is the rest of his immediate pack, acting as a support system. I still can't get over it. She looks far too much like an adult. I don't want to believe it. I know she is one, but it still doesn't get easier passing on such a great responsibility of caring for her to someone else. They haven't made it official because Holly wants to know what it's like to be alone and in charge of making her own decisions, but I know it won't be long until they agree to an official bond.

Arsenio, Desmond, and Enzo stand behind me, taking their positions as equal leaders of the Gilded Sands territory. Kinsey perches on the floor beside me, resting her head on my thigh, her closeness really testing my ability to focus. She's coming down from her heat, and there's no way we were going to let her even a foot away from us. She didn't want me to handle this alone, though. She wanted my brothers to be beside me, and I'm glad for it. I feel more powerful with them. Even more so with Kinsey, stroking her hand up and down my shin, the sensation tightening my balls. She's going to be in so much trouble when this announcement is over.

"We are connected to all territories in Saint Vista. We'll start rolling in two minutes." A beta in a suit stands behind the camera, remaining expressionless, but I can tell he's just as anxious to know what's going on as I'm sure all the people of Saint Vista are. The whole region is on lockdown and waiting in anticipation to hear why there was a war and what happens to them now.

Armand, Cameron, and Spencer from our allying territories finish off our group. We are officially the leaders of the Pack Regimes until the proper authority is put into place in the territories that have fallen.

"Sixty seconds." The cameraman looks through the lens and then adjusts his video monitor. This moment will put me and my pack in history. Those before us will be forgotten as we pave the way for a more equal future. We are taking Kinsey's idea about a club for alphas and turning it regional. And maybe as others see our region thrive, they'll begin to change, and the ripple effect will spread far and wide across the world.

"Ten seconds." The beta counts down on his fingers, pointing to me when the red light on the camera lights up, ensuring that our faces appear across every phone, TV, and our voices hum through all radios and the loudspeakers used to send direct messages to the territories.

"This message has been long awaited, and it's with great seriousness that we announce the reformation of the Saint Vista region." I rest my hands on the table, summoning the power of my pack behind me. "We understand that many of you have experienced unthinkable tragedy over the last few weeks as the war between territories ignited and surprised everyone. But from the devastation of our actions, we will rebuild and be stronger than ever. I'm formally announcing that the following leaders and their packs have been thrown from power. Herbert of the Dark Orchards Pack. Chavez of the Ginger Rains Pack. Emmanuel of the Bronze Deserts Pack. Edwin of the Rosewood Pack, and the head of the Saint Vista Pack Regimes, Jarvis of the Starlight Horizon Pack. Until new leaders have been selected, you'll be in the care of Gilded Sands along with those remaining allies. We will mourn for the week, but then we will pick back up. I also wanted to announce for the first time in our history, we have elected an omega to lead a territory. Holly from the new Platinum Shores Pack. She will create great change alongside us as her advisors."

In this moment, I wish I could see the reactions of every alpha across the region. I'm sure there will be some who need to be put in their places, but I'm also sure that omegas and betas will celebrate such a monumental occasion.

"Please know that anyone who speaks out against our decision will be handled accordingly. We will rule with an iron fist until the adjustment phase is over. It will be hard. It will be new and unfamiliar. But in the end, it'll be worth it. We will not tolerate the division of orders any longer. We will not tolerate the mistreatment and use of omegas as a power-play or property. We will not tolerate the inhumane treatment of omegas and betas alike. Our strict rule will affect those who think they are better and deserve more because of their alpha order. That is no longer the case. Alphas are nothing without betas and omegas. We will be stronger together. We will offer a choice. We will also need to learn and grow and accept a new regional order. Thank you, people of Saint Vista. It is an honor to lead you to this new change."

I nod my head, motioning to the cameramen to cut off the live stream. The people will not be left floundering with this news as we have all selected worthy packs to help with the transition.

Enzo squeezes my shoulders, leaning over and grinning in my face. "Dad would be so fucking pissed off right now. He'd be kicking and screaming, throwing one hell of a tantrum."

"I'm sure a lot of hotheaded alphas are doing the same." Armand offers me a nod in respect. "It is an honor to finally be able to reform our laws. We will thrive."

He's right. It's all I could've asked for. The pain, the anger, the bloodshed were all worth it. I will never take this power for granted.

Kinsey shrieks, ducking down, forcing me to jump over her. I flail my arms, almost tripping over my own damn feet. I spin around as she hops up, her smile as bright as her emerald-green eyes.

"You can't run from me forever, brat-girl." I growl with a playful smile, faking her out by lunging but not moving from my spot.

She jumps and dodges only to stumble across the workout mat. I charge her, scooping her up and tossing her on my shoulder. She laughs, hanging without resistance. So, I tickle her. I want her to fight me.

"Take me down, brat-girl," I say, poking her in her sides, scrubbing my fingers up to her ribs. "You can't just give up."

Kinsey thrashes, laughing as I move my hand, tickling the back of her knee next. Smacking her hands to my shoulder, she shrieks again, using her weight to throw me off balance. I wobble, repositioning my legs. Kinsey stops fighting again, accepting defeat.

"You're too strong. I can't do it." Kinsey yanks at the hem of my shirt, trying to tickle me back, but it doesn't work...not in the way she wants, at least.

"Come on, brat-girl. I know you have it in you. I want you to try harder. Figure out how you can throw me off balance." I stroll a couple of feet, picking up my pace. "If you were being taken, you wouldn't think about the possibility of getting hurt. You'd do anything you could."

Kinsey groans and remains placid for another minute, but I don't stop. The only way I will ever put her down at this point is if she forces me to. I can run for a long time and not get tired. She's got to be uncomfortable, though. My shoulder is not exactly soft.

Kinsey finally wiggles again, but she doesn't hit me. Instead, she manages to snatch the back of my shirt and twists my collar, pulling the fabric so tight that she chokes me. I expected her to try to punch me just right. I never expected this. I grab the shirt, trying to rip it free. She takes advantage of my slowing stride, managing to kick her leg up and knee me in the side of the head only to reposition herself, squeezing my neck with her legs. And then she locks her arms around my waist and throws all of her weight backward, bending her body with enough force that I have to either drop her or land on top of her.

I let her go, and she flips, managing to plant her feet on the mat. She charges me before I have a chance to spin, jamming her shoulder right into my lower back and sending me sprawling.

I lie face down in total shock. I didn't teach her this move. She managed to overpower me and take me down. Holy shit. My cock throbs at how sexy she is in this moment. I'm not usually one to be dominated, but I love how she figured out how to defend herself.

"Wilder? Are you okay?" Her soft voice draws my attention as her shadow falls next to me.

I clear my throat, keeping my voice deep. "Yeah, brat-girl. I'm just a little—"

She lands on my back, sliding her arm around my neck, yanking my hair, stretching me up to look at her. I gasp as pain steals my breath, her knees digging into my spine.

"How about now?" Her lips curve in a smile, her eyes flashing with a new wickedness I want to devour. "Are you ready to call mercy?"

I break my hand free and jerk it up, trying to snatch her wrist, but she throws herself forward, smashing my face into the mat. Her knees shift then she pins me with her thighs, her scent engulfing me.

"You can't escape me now. Now beg for mercy. Who's your alpha now?" She laughs with her words, her comment goading me on.

"You're in so much trouble, brat-girl." I try to break my hand free again, but she snatches my arm and twists, sending a shocking pain up to my shoulder.

"Beg for mercy, and I'll reward you. You can thank Arsenio for teaching me this move." Kinsey flexes her thighs again, getting right to my cock. She likes when I struggle beneath her, my head rubbing her in just the right spot.

"Never. I'm going to give you five seconds before I get you and do as I please." I shift my shoulder, planting my hand on the floor. All it will take is pushing up to be able to knock her off me. But I have another idea.

"Five. Four. Three. Two. One. Beg me, Wilder," Kinsey says, her voice cracking with her laughter.

That's it. She just poked the beast.

I shove my palm to the ground, using my knees to propel me up until she's riding on my back as if I'm a bull. She screeches and tries to scramble off me, but I manage to push up to kneel, flip her around, and bring her back down right on my face. I shift her shorts out of the way and glide my tongue against the seam of her body, loving that she doesn't wear any panties. She moans loudly, her voice echoing through the gym. She doesn't fight me and gives in to our nature, rocking on her knees, fucking my face the way she desires. I can't get enough.

I suck and kiss her clit, her pussy dripping with her slick, her sweet scent like paradise. She pants and fidgets, her orgasm building. I grip onto her ass cheeks and hold her in place as she screams out with her orgasm.

Sliding her down my body, I flip her off and rip down her shorts, exposing her body to me completely. I yank her shirt off next, bowing down to drag my tongue over her hard nipples as I yank my pants down with one hand, freeing my cock.

I stretch her leg over her head, pinning her other one as I adjust my body. She snatches me by the shoulders, yanking me down until I meet her lips. I kiss her as I align our bodies, thrusting deep into her, her pussy clutching me, increasing my pleasure. We moan in sync, the pleasure, and ecstasy mind-blowing. There's just something about this moment, the raw need coursing through us, that sends me over the edge. My cock swells as she takes my knot, and I growl as I come, filling her with my seed. She squirms, locked to me how she desires. Her muscles spasm, the intensity of her orgasm hard enough to feel along with mine, and I lose myself to her everything. She bites my neck, burying her nose in my throat. I purr at the sensation of her mark marring my skin, the pleasure aroused in me something I never want to end.

Because Kinsey is my mate. My everything. And seeing her power today proves just how amazing she is. I have dreamt of such a bond my whole life, never expecting that it would lead to changing my world completely.

And not even solely my world. Everyone's world.

An alpha is only as powerful as their omega, and mine is the strongest in the universe. The world is a better place because of our love and loyalty.

With Kinsey, I have never felt so complete. So loved. She is my perfect woman. I am stronger because of her. We are stronger together.

Forever.

# Chapter Twenty-Six

## *Desmond*

### Bonding Moments

I look over the application for the hundredth time, making sure we haven't left any important questions off it. This is the twentieth draft over the month, and I think it's finally perfect.

"What do you think, Kinsey? I'm pretty sure it includes everything you've asked for, along with what some of the others suggested. There will be a background check, pictures, even something with their scent." I tip my head up and look at my beautiful omega, her dark hair cascading over her shoulders as she smiles at her phone.

Kinsey perches on the arm of my chair, setting her phone on her knee to meet my gaze, her emerald eyes the perfect shade of green. "The best way to test it is to put it out there. The omegas are so excited. They haven't stopped texting me since I told them we would finalize it today."

I reach up, caressing my fingers over her cheek. "I'll put out the announcement now. We've converted the ballroom of the fortress to the club they can mingle at in our territory. Once all the territory leaders agree, we'll start rolling this out across the region."

"I still like the idea of calling it the Knotty Princes Club. The omegas agree. They want to be the ones to frequent the place, checking out all the alphas the way they have been checked out before." Her smile widens, and she shows off her straight teeth. "Do you think the alphas would go for it?"

"If they want to find an omega to bond with, they fucking better. They're going to learn real quick that omegas don't absolutely need them anymore. There are plenty of betas out there ready for the job." I laugh with my comment, wagging my eyebrows at Kinsey.

"And you're absolute proof." She slides off the arm of the chair and into my lap, snuggling her nose to mine, kissing me softly. "Maybe that'll help. Omegas could use a beta like you to be their confidant. To be able to talk them down when they feel out of control. To back their alphas up when needed."

"Back them up too." I kiss her softly, molding my lips to hers, just relishing the sensation of our skin touching.

We sit in silence, just being together and playing on each other's tranquility. It's been so long since I felt so relaxed. We're not heated with desire and just loving up on each other in the way we both need. It's moments like these I will never forget. I'll cherish every second of every day that I could just share a breath with Kinsey, listening to her heart beating, feeling the weight of her body close to mine, imprinting the sweet perfume of her skin in my mind.

She swivels on my lap, keeping close while looking over the application again. I hug her, resting my hands on her stomach. She fiddles around for another moment before shifting back to me.

"Let's go ahead and send it. If I continue to look at it, we might keep changing it. The only way to know if it's suitable is to test it. Anita wants to look at the applicants first." Kinsey rests her head on me.

I dig out my phone, spotting a message flashing on the screen. I quickly send the application draft to Holly to go over it with the current omegas under our care for one last read-through.

I click on the text message next.

*Baby Bro: Have you done it yet? I don't know how much longer I can wait.*

*Arsehole: Has she asked?*

*Big Brother: She hasn't brought it up with me, but I'm not sure she will. She's nervous but doesn't want to mention it because of everything else.*

*Baby Bro: I'm going to die if I don't find out soon.*

*Holls: Do you need me to bring it up again? She thought it was too early last time. I don't mind.*

*Arsehole: Maybe we should meet as a pack. Give it to her as a present.*

*Holls: Pregnancy tests are not gifts. But you guys better fucking have something planned either way.*

*Baby Bro: Des? Are you reading this? You're ignoring us. What gives? Is she trying to grab your phone?*

*Big Bro: Careful what you say. You know she'll be a brat if you call her out.*

As if Kinsey knows we have a private group chat going on without her, she narrows her eyes at me, stretching to try to look at my phone. "Your phone's blowing up. What are you guys talking about? You know I don't like surprises. Show me."

I smirk and hand over the phone, amused by my siblings. It's driving them crazy that they don't know whether or not

Kinsey is pregnant. Kinsey and I have talked about it, and she just wanted to get everything else done before focusing on herself. She thought it was important to remain clearheaded as we adjusted during the transition of power. I agreed with her. I've been ignoring my brothers' complaints and anxiousness.

Kinsey releases a breathless laugh. "I feel like they're going to team up and tickle me until I pee myself to test."

I bellow a laugh, her comment playful yet serious. It's one of the things I could see one of them fucking doing. They're just that crazily excited.

But I also think it stresses Kinsey out.

"I'd never let them. They need to learn patience." I brush my fingers through her hair, moving the strands.

"I'm just nervous, is all. What if...?" She lets her voice trail off, her expression darkening. She doesn't say anything as her eyes gloss over with her thoughts.

"We'll get through anything regardless. I know that this is a huge, life-changing situation, Kinsey. I know that you want nothing more than for everything to go as you hope. But don't put too much stress on yourself. We've been through so much already. Why don't we take it one step at a time?" I offer her a soft smile, grasping her chin to kiss me again.

"Will you help me? I don't want everyone to wait with us. I'm afraid to see their reactions if it doesn't go how they expect." Kinsey chews her bottom lip, dragging it across her teeth. "Is that selfish of me to want? Just me and you?"

"Nothing you choose is selfish because it is your decision. They will be there to support you no matter what. And if anything, they'll be more determined than ever. You'll never leave the bed. Maybe the shower. The kitchen when you get hungry. But maybe you can sneak away with me, and we can have a little extra fun. Let you burn off some steam by taking control. Putting my ass in place like you like. Like I crave." I hum under my breath, imagining all the passion in store for us. The intimate moment of me bowing before Kinsey as she claims me sends my muscles rippling as my cock hardens, my ass clenching at the thought.

Her grimace melts away, and she nuzzles her nose to mine. "I love that your ass is mine. It's so hot seeing how much you enjoy me pinning you down and having my way. Taking my cock." Her cheeks flush with her words, her desire emanating in the air between us.

"Keep talking to me like that, and my brothers will have to wait another couple of weeks. Because I'm about to lock us away. Just you and me." I growl and squeeze her thigh, dragging her a bit closer to feel how hard I am. "Or maybe...that can be a reward. Be my brave girl, and let's find out what's in store for us, and you can fuck me how you desire. I might even have a new toy for you."

Kinsey's eyes widen as she squirms on me, turned on by the idea. Dipping her chin, she bobs her head, my bribery working.

"I want you so badly." Her voice turns husky. "You make me feel the most powerful. So in control. I can face anything. I think I'm ready now."

"Of course, you are. We're ready for anything." I kiss her and scoop her up in my arms. "Now come on. You're going to make me the happiest beta in the world."

Kinsey sits on the counter, closing her eyes, refusing to look as the seconds pass after she has taken the pregnancy test. I don't look at it either, watching her and waiting for the timer to go off.

"Take a breath, Kinsey." I squeeze her knee, getting her to peek at me through her lashes.

She inhales and exhales. "The anticipation is killing me. I had no idea how badly I really wanted to be a mom until this moment. I want to give our children a better life."

I rest my hand on top of hers. "And we will."

I sneak a peek at the pregnancy test before the timer goes off, my curiosity getting the best of me. The digital screen flashes with the word *pregnant*, and I feel as if my soul abandons my body for a split second, screaming a prayer of thanks to the universe.

"We definitely will. Look." I hold the pregnancy test up in front of her, giving her a little shake. "Open your eyes."

Kinsey squeezes her eyes, not opening them just yet. I run my finger over her tight eyelids, getting her to relax. She flutters her eyes open, her gaze darting back and forth until she realizes that I hold the pregnancy test in front of her.

"You're going to be an incredible mom. The best. I'm so happy we're growing a family." I grin, studying her face, her shock leaving her frozen. Again, I give her a little shake. "I love you. I love you so damn much."

Without a word, Kinsey launches herself from the counter and into my arms, her voice squealing as she hiccups, torn between crying and laughing from her excitement. I spin her around, kissing her with enough passion to leave her breathless.

"I can't believe it. I can't believe this is happening. I'm so happy." She murmurs the words, her voice shaking.

"I'm over the moon. I'm already so in love." I lift her higher until I can kiss her stomach, nuzzling my nose to her skin.

"I can't wait to tell the others." She hiccups again, her face beaming despite the tears sheening over her cheeks.

"We can save our celebration for later." I kiss her as I carry her from the bathroom and back into my suite.

I catch a whiff of Enzo's fragrance. I pull away from Kinsey and bark a laugh, seeing him standing completely naked, a rose between his teeth with a collection of toys on the edge of my bed. He's fucking crazy, but he knows exactly how to set Kinsey off in the best way. I can't even be mad at him for not giving us the space we requested, knowing that Kinsey was nervous.

"Before you beat the shit out of me, Desmond, I come bearing gifts. I just couldn't fucking wait. I knew the second you didn't answer that you guys would be in here. Wilder and Arsenio went out to distract themselves, but fuck that. You're my favorite brother, and I knew my dream was coming true. I knocked you the fuck up, baby. I could feel it deep in my bones. You're already glowing." Enzo strides forward, unashamed and clearly excited by the news. I don't look at him, but I can just tell by the scent of his desire.

"We're having a family!" Kinsey screeches. "I'm going to be a mom!"

Enzo kisses her in my arms, his joy crashing over me. It's contagious, and I chuckle and scrub my knuckles over his hair.

"Let's celebrate." Enzo motions toward the bed. "Just the way you like, baby."

Kinsey wiggles in my arms until I set her on her feet, and she grabs Enzo by his cock and squeezes. "I'm going to tell you now that I have plans with your brother and know that I'm following through. His ass is mine. If he's okay with it, you can join us, but I'm in control. Do you think you can handle it?"

Damn. Her commanding attitude strikes me right in the dick, turning me on even more.

Enzo smacks his hands together and rubs his palms. "We're a fucking pack. Whatever you want, baby. If you want to peg my brother, we're going to ride that fucking train. This is about you. Our girl always gets what she wants."

"What if I want your ass too?" Kinsey bites her lip, clearly teasing.

Enzo howls a laugh. "You created a fucking monster, brother. And for that, Kinsey, your ass is now mine."

Should this be awkward? Maybe. Am I phased by these weird ass bonding experiences? Nope. We already share our girl, and it can only make us stronger.

"If you're a good boy," she teases, yanking her shirt over her head. She strolls to the bed, looks over Enzo's collection, and shakes her finger. Turning to me, she asks, "You said you had a surprise for me. Show me. I want to know exactly how you want to be fucked."

I adjust my hard-on in my pants, my cock twitching in anticipation. I don't know exactly what I'm getting into, but if Kinsey is in control, I know it'll be a great time.

I stroll past her, playing with her tits as I do, and she surprises me by jumping on my back. I laugh as I carry her to my nightstand, pulling out a black box. I gingerly open it, revealing the strap-on with a curved dildo that will fuck her as she fucks me.

The vibration should be incredible for both of us, and I shiver at just the thought.

"Goddamn. That thing is a beast." Enzo looks at the box and then at Kinsey. "So much fun."

Kinsey slides off my back and snatches the box from me, grabbing my wrist and pulling me closer. She glides her fingers across my waistband, stroking me through my pants, before hooking her fingers to the hem of my shirt, pulling it up. "I want you to get on the bed. Enzo's going to help me put this on."

I refrain from saying, *yes, ma'am,* my certain need to abide by her commands consuming me. Is this what I'd be like as an omega? Easily agreeable yet excited to not have to worry about controlling anything? I never imagined this kind of roleplay, but it gets more exciting by the second. She will do everything to give me pleasure. And I will do everything to get her off on power.

I growl at her and cup her pussy with my fingers, stroking over the damp fabric of her panties, already ready and waiting for a good time. She moans and crashes her mouth to mine, taking down my pants blindly, undressing me as if it's her sole purpose in life.

Kinsey spins me and smacks my ass, nudging me toward the bed. I grab my throbbing cock and stroke, watching in anticipation as Enzo helps Kinsey step into the strap-on. He adjusts it for her, the horny bastard a pro. I've always known he had a fascination for sex toys, but it looks like it's really going to come in handy.

It brings a new meaning to brotherly love.

"Go on, baby. Get comfortable with Desmond. Show him what kind of alpha you would be." Enzo perches on the edge of the bed, wiggling his fingers and getting Kinsey to join us. She laughs and plays with the strap-on, her fingers gliding with the lube Enzo added.

"Are you excited that I'm pretending to be an alpha, Enzo?" she asks him, her voice turning breathy. "Aren't you jealous that I'm going to fuck the cum out of him?"

My ass puckers in anticipation. I never knew this was my thing, but goddamn it. My beautiful woman makes me feel so powerful even when I'm vulnerable.

"When you put it like that..." Enzo reaches out and smacks her ass, pulling her up the bed.

She giggles, the lightheartedness of her voice like music to my ears. Silent anticipation falls between us, and Kinsey moves closer, grabbing my hips and rubbing her fingers into my sides. "I love you so damn much. So, so damn much. You both make me so happy. This is our life now. Unexpected excitement. Incredible news. Laughter. Sex and passion. Everything we could ever want."

"Absolutely everything," I murmur, my breath panting as she aligns the strap-on with my body, just teasing me with the tip, getting me used to the sensation. My eyes roll back in my head as she reaches around and strokes my cock, intensifying the pleasure, turning me so hard that I feel like I already might bust a nut.

"You love it, don't you?" she murmurs, her voice soft yet sexy as hell. "You love when I fuck you like this."

I moan with pleasure, her hand sending me spiraling in a hurricane of ecstasy. "Yes. So much. Fuck me harder. Fuck me until I come."

Enzo shifts on the bed, and I catch sight of his reflection in the shiny backboard of my bed. He mounts Kinsey, and I listen as she gasps a breath and moans, bending forward onto me. She sinks her teeth into my shoulder blade. Our lust fills the air, our heavy breathing and moans the only thing sounding out, the melody of our passion so perfect that my body sings along until my nuts tighten, and I grunt, coming so hard that I bow, the breath escaping me.

"So good," I say, my body trembling as I come down from the high of pleasure.

Kinsey slows, sliding the toy out of me. She locks her finger to my side, getting me to roll over. She kisses me as Enzo fucks her from behind, her body rocking on top of mine, none of us caring about the mess or anything else for that matter.

Because just being together, loving each other, and bonding in unimaginable ways is what's important.

I kiss Kinsey, rubbing her clit, ensuring she comes again and again until Enzo finishes, his breath heaving as he rests on top of her, sandwiching her between us.

"My beautiful soon-to-be wife. I can't wait for our ceremony. You'll be the most magnificent mother, wife, and amazing head of our family. Life will be perfect." I comb her hair out of her face and behind her ear.

Enzo kisses her temple. "Just like you."

# Chapter Twenty-Seven

## *Kinsey*

## Perfect Life

Desmond and Enzo help me set up the balloons in the dining room as the staff sets out the banquet before us. We have invited our closest family and friends to join us in a bit. But first, I want to surprise Wilder and Arsenio, who have been waiting in anticipation but also giving me space. I can't wait to see their faces. This moment will be one we remember forever. Every little moment of my life has added up to create the start of my perfect future. I used to stress about all of the big things, but it's all the little things that truly add up to make something wonderful.

"They just pulled up," Enzo says, looking at his phone.

I nod my head and stroll toward the archway leading out. "You guys finish up here. I want to give them their moment now."

Desmond brushes his lips to my temple as he crosses toward the decorations that still need to be hung. "Absolutely. Take however long you want."

"But remember, we have guests coming." Enzo grabs some streamers and haphazardly hangs them as Desmond follows behind him, straightening them out.

I blow them a kiss and head toward the garage door, knowing that's where they're entering from. I adjust my handmade shirt, the words *KNOCKED UP BY AN ALPHA* scribbled across the front in permanent marker. It's cheesy as fuck, but I love the hell out of it. The thought spins through my mind over and over.

I'm going to be a mom.

We're starting a family and growing our pack.

I listen to the door beep as my guys unlock it, swinging it open. Placing my hands on my hips, I pose, trying to remain expressionless. Neither of them reads my shirt, their faces twisting with concern.

Arsenio steps forward. "Oh, sugar. What's—"

I raise my hand, stopping him. "Get on your knees. Both of you."

They look at each other curiously, and if Arsenio didn't act first, I'm certain Wilder would argue. I need them to be on the same level as the sloppy scrawl on my shirt, so they read it. I'm dying to watch the realization hit them.

"This little command better lead to you resting your legs around my neck while I taste that pussy of yours. Arsenio will take care of that smackable ass." Wilder flicks his tongue at me, purring at the thought.

I squeeze my legs together, his ability to flip on my switch of desire mind-blowing. I don't know if it's because things are finally settling down or what, but if I allowed it, I would just be surviving on orgasms and snacks. Not that it's a bad thing. But I also don't want to isolate ourselves. I want to be an example to the world.

"Maybe a bit later. We have some guests coming over." I take a step back as Arsenio tries to snatch me.

Wilder and Arsenio stare at each other from the corner of their eyes.

"I've decided to throw a last-minute party," I add, playing with the hem of my shirt, yanking it and shifting it, hoping to draw attention.

They're so enamored with me that they don't pay attention to certain things unless it's something completely out of normal like a sexy dress or if I were standing here completely naked. Maybe I should've just written the words on my skin.

"What's the celebration?" Wilder remains expressionless, his curiosity making him wiggle on his knees.

I lift and drop my shoulders. "I thought this would be obvious but—"

"Holy shit! Kinsey! Is this for real?" Arsenio launches to his feet, catching on before Wilder. Once Enzo and Desmond find out how oblivious he was toward my attempt to surprise him, they are never going to let it go.

Scooping me up, Arsenio spins me around with a laugh, his face beaming a smile I want to remember always.

"What the fuck am I missing?" Wilder crosses his arms, his curiosity turning into annoyance.

"Open your damn eyes and look at our beautiful woman. Look at every damn inch of her." Arsenio sets me back down and spins me to face Wilder.

Wilder's eyebrows knit together as he stares at my face and slowly draws his gaze down to my boobs, and then his mouth opens, his jaw slacking. A dozen emotions flicker across his face in a matter of seconds, and he rushes and drops to his knees in front of me again, engulfing me in a hug around the waist as he yanks at my shirt and presses his lips to my torso, kissing me a dozen times as he purrs and whispers his affection and excitement.

"We're having a baby!" Wilder shouts, standing up without letting me go. "We're having a fucking baby!"

"Fuck yeah, we are!" Enzo hollers, standing just down the hall with Desmond. "Now shut your fucking mouth before someone hears you and spreads the word before we can tell our pack. We're having a feast to celebrate. Everyone is on their way now."

Arsenio steals me from Wilder and cradles me in his arms like a blushing bride, snuggling his face between my breasts as he curls me up to him. "You've made me the happiest man alive."

"I don't know about that, brother. You have some major competition," Enzo says, bouncing on his feet. He looks giddy as fuck and cute as hell. He's been dying to shout everything to the world.

"I'll take it. You want to play this game?" Arsenio raises an eyebrow with a smirk. "Don't think I won't post it on every fucking billboard in the entire region."

"I'll fucking figure out how to etch it into the side of a mountain." Enzo traces the air, pretending to write his excitement out.

"I'll do one better. I'll prove it to Kinsey every second of every day for the rest of time." Wilder reaches into his jacket, pulling out a small box. "I've been waiting for the perfect moment, and this one is even more so than I imagined and the first of many to come." Wilder gets down on one knee before me.

"Oh, so we're playing it this way," Desmond teasers, his voice light. He follows Wilder's example and gets on a knee, pulling another box out, the one that he's been holding. "You know we were going to do this together, but considering how our brothers decided to beat us to it."

My heart flutters in anticipation. I knew it was coming because Arsenio and Enzo had already asked me, but it doesn't make it any less special. If anything, it makes this moment even more amazing. Unforgettable.

"It's not usually custom for a beta to propose, but we're unlike any other pack. My vow to you is to always stand by your side and be whoever you need me to be. I love you, Kinsey." Desmond reveals the thin band encrusted with jade and diamond stones. They glitter in the light, the pretty cut of the ring absolutely stunning.

"And I vow to always ensure you come first. In any way you like." Wilder winks. "I also promise to care for you and our pack. Be the guiding force and also the man who can recognize when to let others lead."

"You forgot the part about not being a dick," Enzo says, giving his brother a shake on the shoulder. "And also relinquishing your rights to owning any pillows. They belong to our girl."

"As long as she accepts my proposal. Because I love you, Kinsey. This moment, knowing that we're having a baby, that's all I could ever dream of. I need you as my wife. I need to declare it to the world. Because my brothers are right. You've made us all the happiest men alive."

"And I'm the happiest woman." I let Arsenio set me on my feet to hold my hand out to Wilder and Desmond, allowing them to slide the rings onto my fingers to join the ones I wear from their brothers. "I'll be the happiest wife."

Holly twirls around me, laughing and smiling as we walk together, surrounded by her brothers and the Silverstein Pack. We head toward the newly renovated ballroom at the fortress, the space now deemed the private Knotty Princes Club, the lounge where alphas get to be on display, doing whatever they can to impress a possible omega mate.

"What would an alpha have to do to impress you, baby? I kind of feel as if we need to re-create this later tonight. I want to show off my skills and seduce you." Enzo flexes his biceps, showing off his muscles in his tight T-shirt.

I tap my finger to my chin, amused by his need to continue to keep things interesting. "Well, the things I'd like would be inappropriate for a public club. You'd have to get me into a private room first. Maybe make me laugh and charm me with your witty personality. Then we can discuss showing off your goods."

"Goddamn. You're just afraid that one look at me will have you bent over and waiting for me to ravish you." Enzo grabs my hand and spins me around.

"It might work if you reversed the situation. You know, bend yourself over. Let me be your alpha." I can't stop the burst of laughter chiming from my mouth.

Holly grimaces and crosses her arms, forming an ex. "Okay, you just scarred me for eternity. I did not need that visual, you freaks."

"If only you knew, little sis…" Enzo ruffles her hair.

Groaning, Holly smacks his hand and skips a couple of feet forward. She plugs her ears with her fingers. "Babies are magical. They just appear. It takes an alpha seed to be buried in an omega's love and poof. That is how my niece or nephew came to be. No one tell me otherwise. I'm not going to ever think about how it's done with you guys."

"You hear that, Beckett? That's exactly how it's done. Don't you fucking think otherwise." Wilder punches Beckett in the arm, making him bark a laugh.

"That's enough," I say, sneaking next to Wilder and squeezing him. "If you all keep talking about baby-making, we're going to have to cut this trip short. I don't know about you, but I really want to see how awesome our club is."

"She's right. There's a waitlist and everything. Other territories keep inquiring about when things will be open for them."

Desmond pulls out his cell phone and looks at the screen. "We've already made our region famous. I've had other Pack Regimes reach out to us to see if they can check things out for themselves."

"Just wait until we have a baby boom," Arsenio says, winking at me. "We'll have to shut down every season. Packs are going to grow at an incredible rate. I can't wait to see the next generation."

I touch my hands to my stomach, imagining what it would be like to hold our child in my arms. "Me too."

Music hums from the arched doorway to what was formally the ballroom. The expansive entertainment area now has booths lining the walls and tables and chairs set up everywhere. A dance floor is the central focal point, and it is more casual than luxurious, a place that welcomes anyone who has an interest in finding a mate.

And it's not just exclusive to alphas and omegas. Betas are welcome to mingle too. There are so many betas in the world that get overlooked because alphas have made it so, but things are changing. This is about bringing packs together. No matter what order they manifested into.

I spot the two-way mirrors along the back wall where the bar has been expanded. Behind them are dozens of rooms where omegas can just watch and decide whether or not they will agree to meet with another. Every person that comes into the club submits an application. There are tablets at the bar that allow them to look over things and also put in a request to meet one-on-one. There is also the option to just hang out and see if you mesh without any of the technical stuff. Because what's most important is that everyone gets to choose. People will no longer be used to barter power or to gain anything. Our society will be better for it.

"Kinsey!" Anita's familiar voice rings out, drawing my attention to the omega as she sits at a high-top table, wearing a glittering mini dress, stilettos, and diamonds in her ears. "I'm so happy you came."

Anita hops from her seat across from a couple of other omegas, and she saunters in our direction. She stops a couple of feet away and raises her eyebrows, flaring her nostrils. As someone who has been in an omega club for who knows how long, she would be able to catch the scent of a bond.

"Of course, I wouldn't miss it. What do you think of the renovations? We couldn't have done this without you." I hold out my hands to her, getting her to step closer.

"Yes, you could have, but I'm thrilled to do whatever I can. I'm just glad that I can manage things for you. Especially n ow...is a congratulation in order?" She grins with her words, already assuming the answer.

I bob my head and smile. "It is."

She squeals and jumps up and down, pulling me into a hug. Holly feeds off our excitement and joins us, the three of us surely drawing attention from everyone in the room.

"I'm so happy for you. I mean it. You deserve it." Anita takes a step back. She turns to my guys. "As do you. You continue to prove just what amazing leaders you are. I look forward to knowing that our territory will never be taken down a dark path again."

My heart fills with such joy that I turn and open my arms for my guys to hug me. Anita pulls Holly away to show her everything, and the Silverstein Pack follows behind them. I savor this moment. It feels amazing to finally have peace. To have a place safe from any threats.

My life is a dream come true.

"I'm so proud of you, Kinsey. I can't tell you enough. When we had planned the hostile takeover, we didn't think much about what happened after. You are the reason we have succeeded. You are now the reason we will continue to grow and thrive." Wilder kisses me softly, and I rest my face against his.

"It's not just me. It's all of us. Together and united equally." The four of them hug me, squishing me between their bodies in a protective circle. "This is just the beginning."

And for the first time in a long time, I know that whatever happens next will be even better. This is my perfect life, and I will savor every second of it. Forever.

# Chapter Twenty-Eight

## *Kinsey*

## Unbreakable

I stand in front of the full-length mirror, staring at the emerald-green ball gown with crystals glittering on the sweetheart bodice. I loved it since the moment I saw it, and I wasn't sure I'd ever have the chance to wear it. It felt as if the universe was against this union, but in actuality, it was just the world wanting to set itself right to ensure it would be the wedding of all of our dreams.

"You're absolutely stunning, Kinsey." Holly helps fasten an emerald necklace around my throat. "I can't wait to see my brothers' faces. I've never seen them smile so much in my entire life. You're so perfect for them. I want you to know that. From the moment we met, I knew you'd be my sister."

I turn around and throw my arms around her, hugging her close and kissing each of her cheeks. Tears rim her eyes, and she sniffles, but I know by her scent that she is as excited as I am.

"And I'm so thankful for you. You mean the world to me, Holly. You have no idea how grateful I am that you agreed to walk me down the aisle." Because it's usually the parental omega's job as the one who brought another into the world to do so. Holly is the closest I have. She brought me into her family without hesitation, showing me just how loving and caring she is.

"I wouldn't have it any other way. It's an honor. And maybe you can do the same for me one day." Holly kisses my forehead and pulls away to give me another once-over.

"Could be sooner rather than later." I dance in my spot with my comment, knowing that the Silverstein Pack will do whatever it takes to bond with her. Who knew that a small adventure to a diner would change everything for her? Life is funny like that.

Giggling, Holly reaches for the cascading bouquet with an arrangement of white florals and hearty green leaves to match my dress. The fragrance permeates around us, reminding me of walking in the garden. "Let's focus on you today, Kinsey. I want this to be one of the most magical of your life."

"It already is." I slide my hand through Holly's elbow and give myself another look in the mirror. My guys are going to want to tear this gown off the second they see me, my clothes acting as the wrapping of a present they've been craving.

I straighten my shoulders, remembering that I no longer need to look at the floor when entering a room full of alphas. I will finally see the world as it was intended, with confidence and bravery.

Holly guides me from the room, and I spot the Silverstein Pack waiting outside. They will escort us to the gazebo, where we'll have the small ceremony with only those closest to us. Our reception is another story. We've invited the territory to celebrate. There will be parties in the streets and parades, according to Holly.

I just can't wait for this moment. It feels as if it's the one I've been waiting all my life for.

Bright sunlight streams from overhead, peeking through the sprawling trees, peppering the path with starbursts through the shadows. The scent of white florals grows, the garden thriving around us. It's beautiful with the ribbons lining the walkway and dozens of extra bouquet arrangements and gilded pots adding to the already beautiful gazebo.

A loud whistle sounds through the air, and I catch Enzo's gaze as he wags his eyebrows at me, biting his lip and winking. I feel so incredibly beautiful and sexy in this moment. Arsenio catches my attention next, his smile so big that his eyes squint and Wilder drops his arm over his shoulders and gives him a shake, laughing as he bounces like an excited boy. Desmond tilts his head with a soft smile, his love radiating from him as if it's tangible, and I want to relish every second of it.

Music begins to play, and Holly walks beside me, sauntering down the petal-filled aisle. My jewelry sparkles, sending beautiful green light bouncing across my skin. Rainbow fractals dance across my vision, and I can't stop smiling so much that my cheeks hurt. But it's a good pain. I'd never trade it for anything in the world.

"Please rise for the bride," Melina says, standing in an ornate robe custom for the ceremony she will officiate.

The music changes into a piano symphony, and I never take my gaze away from my guys, giving each of them my attention, the world fading as if the rest of our pack isn't here.

Wilder steps forward, and Holly hands me over to him. I can't help myself, and I kiss him, making Melina laugh. Enzo, Arsenio, and Desmond all take a turn, and the music fades to where all I can concentrate on is the melody of our hearts.

"My beautiful omega," Wilder murmurs, squeezing my hand. "You're truly magical. You know that, right?"

I can't stop smiling at his words.

"Are you ready to be my queen?" he adds.

"Because we are ready to bow to you, baby." Enzo plays with my hair. "We'll worship you forever."

"And I will do the same for you, my kings. This is everything I could've ever wanted and more." I turn toward Melina, and she nods her head.

"Today is a blessed day in our territory of Gilded Sands," she begins. "It is an honor to bring together this beautiful omega with her alphas and beta in perfect matrimony."

Not only perfect matrimony. A perfect bond. A perfect life. And mostly, a perfect future.

I stand beside my guys, my head high and their love keeping me grounded. They will always lift me up and treat me as an equal. I'm not just an omega. I'm their lover and best friend. I will be the mother of their children.

Our lives are just as perfect as our love.

And no one can ever take that away from us again.

We are the Gilded Sands Pack.

We are unbreakable.

"The Bowing Pack would like a moment of your time, brother." Arsenio slides his arms around my waist, hugging me from behind. Taking my hand, he spins me away from Wilder, drawing me into his embrace. "I'm sure our girl could use a break. She barely touched dinner."

"Because I'm waiting for dessert. I saw that tiered cake I know you guys have hidden in the kitchen." I lick my lips teasingly, my smile growing wider.

"There's more than just cake back there. How about we sneak out for a bit, sugar? You should be able to stuff your face to your heart's content without having to worry about everyone watching you. Plus, I don't want anyone else to have that sort of luxury. It's too damn sexy." Arsenio snuggles his nose against mine before kissing me softly.

I moan as his hand travels down my back and rests just above my ass. Wilder excuses himself and heads toward a couple of intimidating-looking men standing in their finest tuxedos by the bar. Desmond and Enzo speak to another few alphas, including a woman as tall as Wilder, and I smile at her when our eyes meet. No female alpha scares me like they used to. Without the constant battle for power, people have changed for the better.

"You're too much. Eating isn't sexy. At least, not me doing it. I do like to watch you eat...me." Flush warms my body as I whisper the comment, loving how it sets Arsenio off, turning him on and enhancing his delectable fragrance. He wants me. He craves me. I don't even have to ask him to know.

"As you wish, my queen." Arsenio lifts me off my feet and spins me around quick enough to make me squeal.

He rushes through the grand ballroom, ignoring everyone as we pass. And I love it. It's so nice not getting stopped every couple of feet. It's our day to do as we please. Packs respect us more than ever before and no longer carry the expectations they used to. It helps that those who were cruel and unwavering in their belief of everyone being beneath them have been imprisoned. We will not tolerate the bullshit any longer. Harsh? Maybe. But until we have a solid ruling foundation, it's what it is. They're getting the treatment they once gave us. Karma is ruthless when she has to be.

Arsenio makes our way to the industrial-sized kitchen with a dozen people flurrying about. He requests everybody to leave, and the servers grab what they need and exit without question. I spot the metal counter with the tiered cake, ready to be cut and passed out to the guests in celebration of our union. Beside it is a doughnut tower and trays of colorful French macarons. My mouth waters just looking at it. Everything smells sweet and delicious, setting off my stomach.

Arsenio tilts his head with a laugh, popping me right onto the prep counter and spinning to grab one of the doughnuts first. "Had I known you were this hungry, I'd have stolen you from my brother sooner." Breaking off a piece of the doughnut, he holds it to my lips.

His body shifts in anticipation. He never knows how I'll take a bite of his offering. Sometimes I'm a bit aggressive on purpose, snapping my teeth through his fingers just like how I did the first time we met.

But not this time. I want to get to him in the best way. Stretching my neck, parting my lips slowly, and gliding my tongue across my bottom lip. Arsenio's breathing quickens, and I nibble a small bite, savoring the burst of sweetness from the glaze. I close my eyes and hum.

"This is so fucking good. I want more." I reach for the doughnut only to have Arsenio shake his finger at me, offering once again another bite. I squirm on the counter, using my legs to pull him closer to me until his body meets mine. I hold a piece of doughnut between my teeth and wait expectantly for him to eat it from my mouth. He sucks my bottom lip with a groan, his hand now trailing down my side. I pluck the doughnut from his fingers and grin as I take another bite, giving him a once-over.

"Are you hungry?" I ask, my voice breathless.

Arsenio takes a step back only to reach down for the hem of my dress. He hikes it up enough to duck under it, and I slap my hand to the table, nearly lying back as he shifts my panties out of the way and kisses me between my legs. My voice echoes through the huge kitchen, and I squeeze Arsenio between my thighs. I can hardly take the ecstasy awakening in me, his tongue swirling over my clit as he slips two fingers into me, adding pressure to my body.

I rock my body, riding Arsenio's face until my orgasm blast through me, sending me falling backward on the counter. Arsenio slows but doesn't stop, continuing to finger me as he peeks out from beneath my gown.

"I need more. Give me your knot. I don't care if there's a party going on outside." I reach for him, getting him to stand up straighter.

He doesn't argue or resist me, caressing my cheek as I unfasten his belt and pull his cock free. I'm so fucking horny. I can barely think about anything else. I don't want to think about anything else. All I want to do is satisfy my alpha and give him the pleasure he deserves.

Aligning his body to mine, Arsenio watches as he slides his tip inside me. I glance from our bodies connecting and to his face, enjoying how the pleasure furrows his brows with his soft moan. I hook my legs around him, pulling him closer until he thrusts inside me. He braces on the counter with one hand while holding me in place with his other, rocking his body sensually at first until his knot locks us in place. I moan at the pressure, sliding my hand between us to rub my own clit, giving him the show he desires. He moans with me, keeping me close as he thrusts over and over again, setting me off with his orgasm, the bliss hazing my vision.

"I love you. You have no idea how much I fucking love you. I was dying for a moment alone with you. When I'm with you, the world can never be wrong." Arsenio gasps with his words, his need to declare his affection as sweet as he is.

"I'm your omega and wife. I'll do anything and everything for you. I want to be all that you ever need." I reach up and pull him closer until our lips meet for another kiss.

Our tongues glide together, and neither of us speaks through our moans, the orgasm clinging to both of us enough to satisfy us in a way that allows me to forget everything but him.

We don't stop kissing until his body releases mine, and I hug him close, just wanting to hear his heartbeat and feel it against my cheek.

"This is why I prefer to cook in my suite. So, this is where the real party is, huh?" Enzo's voice sounds from the doorway. "I came to bring you dessert and didn't realize you were already getting your fill, baby. Ease away, brother. I want to see her drip. Give me that since I wasn't invited and had to deal with the bullshit politics of forming alliances. But what can I do? People love me." Enzo laughs with his words, his intense scent wafting closer with his movements. "All hail me as king."

I stretch a hand to him, luring him closer. "Don't let Wilder hear you."

Shaking his head, he says, "That was his idea. He tried to bribe me to run things for the rest of the year because all he wants to do is fuck you...which Arsenio seems to have also taken advantage of."

Arsenio groans with a chuckle, slowly easing away from my body. "At least get the perk you want. Look at her drip. So hot."

"Would be better if it was mine." Enzo play-growls and humps the air.

I can't stop the laugh escaping my mouth. Reaching out, I playfully smack Arsenio on the arm. "Ugh, really? That's a bit much."

Enzo's face lights up with his snicker. "I don't even fucking care that it isn't my splooge. I'd fuck you senseless right now if you'd let me. The guests can wait a bit longer for our dance."

"And it's a good fucking thing I knew you'd guys sneak here, so I have a backup cake for the guests." Holly curls and uncurls her fingers. "Who have been waiting long enough. Give the people what they want. They're calling for their queen."

I close my eyes, listening as the music softens and murmurs chant through the air. She's right. They're calling my name.

Wilder and Desmond appear at the door, grinning and the happiest I've ever seen them. The emcee calls for quiet, and I quickly let Arsenio clean me up. I stroll forward, my heart pounding in anticipation. I never knew this day would come.

"Alphas, betas, and omegas, it's a great pleasure to introduce your reigning pack and your queen." The voice booms through the air, followed by cheers that quake the walls.

"Please officially welcome Kinsey of the Gilded Sands Pack and the ruling alphas and beta of the Saint Vista Pack Regimes."

I kiss each of my guys, letting Wilder carry me like the blushing bride I am.

He brushes his lips to my ear. "I love you, my brat."

"We love you so much," Arsenio adds.

Desmond and Enzo keep close, and Desmond strokes his fingers over my cheek. "Here's to our future."

Enzo squares his shoulders, overlooking the room with the cheering crowd. "Long may we reign."

"Long may we reign," I repeat, inhaling the scent of perfection and eternal love. "Long may we love, laugh, and grow."

# Chapter Twenty-Nine

## *Kinsey*

## Epilogue - Gilded Sands Forever

"He's beautiful. I can't believe he's ours. Look at those little fingers and toes." Desmond strokes his fingers over the dark hair of our son, resting on my bare chest as I cuddle him close.

"Look at that pouty mouth like his mom. He's trying to find her nipple like me." Enzo chuckles, guiding his fingers over our baby boy's cheek, carefully helping me latch him on.

"Don't look so jealous of Landon." Wilder rubs his fingers through Enzo's hair. "Maybe she'll let you taste next."

I laugh in exasperation. "Wilder!"

"The only one eating next apart from our handsome boy will be Kinsey. Do you want sweet or savory, sugar? You have to be starving." Arsenio stands in the kitchen of my suite, pulling a bunch of things out of the cupboard. "You need your energy."

"Both. I want you guys to take turns feeding me." I smile with my words, leaning back against the fluffy pillows surrounding me. It's only been a day since I gave birth, but I'm so madly in love with this precious little boy in my arms and the men who care for me.

"You got it." Arsenio smiles at me, his happiness palpable even from here in my nest with everything I love. "Anything for you."

I inhale a breath of the powdery yet citrusy scent of our boy, imagining the amazing life we have paved before him. I never knew that I could already love someone before I met them, but this just proves it. My love is powerful and everlasting. And the love I have for my pack will never end. It will keep growing and growing each passing day.

"He's right. Absolutely anything. You deserve it. I'll take care of everything you need. You'll never change a fucking diaper. You'll always get as much sleep as you need. I'm already a champ at getting him to latch. We got this, baby." Enzo kisses my forehead. "Isn't that right, brothers?"

Desmond chuckles. "Right."

"Whatever gets you to bring at least ten more into our family. I never thought I could love like this. You have changed my life. I'll never take it for granted. I've never been so happy." Wilder rests beside me, kissing my other cheek.

I laugh and shake my head. "Ten?"

"At least for me. I think Enzo wants twelve." Wilder flicks his brother, the two of them laughing.

"Whatever keeps me buried between her legs forever." He laughs again, his melodious voice filling me up.

"I love you and your ridiculousness. How about we enjoy this moment first?" I kiss our son's head. "Because I can't get enough of him. He's so perfect."

"He is, isn't he?" Desmond asks, the warmth of his words like a comforting blanket. "He is his mother's son, after all. He will do great things."

"We all will," I say, letting their scents wash over me in a cloud of joy and adoration. Of unending devotion and loyalty. I snuggle Landon close. "You're going to love our pack as much as we love you, son."

Wilder squeezes my hand. "We promise."

It's a promise we will always keep. A promise for our future, our territory, and mostly, a promise to us. Our pack will thrive.

~The End~

# About Ginna Moran

GINNA MORAN IS the *USA Today* Bestselling author of over seventy novels including the popular The Pack Mates of Lunar Crest and The Seven Sinners of Hell's Kingdom reverse harem novels.

She always carried a fascination for all things paranormal and wrote her first unpublished manuscript at age eighteen. Her love of the supernatural grew stronger through her adult life, and she now spends her days with different creatures of the night. Whether it's vampires, werewolves, dragons, fae, angels, demons, or mermaids, Ginna loves creating and living in worlds from her dreams.

Aside from Ginna's professional life, she enjoys binge-watching TV, crafting and design, playing pretend with her daughter, and cuddling with her dog. Some of her favorite things include chocolate, mermaids, anything that glitters, learning new things, cheesy jokes, and organizing her book-shelf.

Ginna is currently hard at work on her next novel and the one after, and the one after that.